London Borough of Houn... Brentford Library

This item should be ret...

and Katherine

SARA ORWIG

C0000 002 724 804

All rights reserved including the right of reproduction in whole or in part in any form. This edition is published by arrangement with Harlequin Books S.A.

This is a work of fiction. Names, characters, places, locations and incidents are purely fictional and bear no relationship to any real life individuals, living or dead, or to any actual places, business establishments, locations, events or incidents. Any resemblance is entirely coincidental.

This book is sold subject to the condition that it shall not, by way of trade or otherwise, be lent, resold, hired out or otherwise circulated without the prior consent of the publisher in any form of binding or cover other than that in which it is published and without a similar condition including this condition being imposed on the subsequent purchaser.

® and ™ are trademarks owned and used by the trademark owner and/or its licensee. Trademarks marked with ® are registered with the United Kingdom Patent Office and/or the Office for Harmonisation in the Internal Market and in other countries.

Published in Great Britain 2014
by Mills & Boon, an imprint of Harlequin (UK) Limited,
Eton House, 18-24 Paradise Road, Richmond, Surrey, TW9 1SR

THE RANSOMES: MATT, NICK AND KATHERINE
© 2014 Harlequin Books S.A.

Pregnant with the First Heir, *Revenge of the Second Son* and *Scandals from the Third Bride* were first published in Great Britain by Harlequin (UK) Limited.

Pregnant with the First Heir © 2006 Sara Orwig
Revenge of the Second Son © 2006 Sara Orwig
Scandals from the Third Bride © 2006 Sara Orwig

ISBN: 978-0-263-91208-1
eBook ISBN: 978-1-472-04503-4

05-1114

Harlequin (UK) Limited's policy is to use papers that are natural, renewable and recyclable products and made from wood grown in sustainable forests. The logging and manufacturing processes conform to the legal environmental regulations of the country of origin.

Printed and bound in Spain
by CPI, Barcelona

PREGNANT WITH
THE FIRST HEIR

BY
SARA ORWIG

Sara Orwig lives in Oklahoma. She has a patient husband who will take her on research trips anywhere, from big cities to old forts. She is an avid collector of Western history books. With a master's degree in English, Sara has written historical romance, mainstream fiction and contemporary romance. Books are beloved treasures that take Sara to magical worlds, and she loves both reading and writing them.

With many thanks to Melissa Jeglinski
and to Jessica Alvarez.

One

She was born to please a man.

The auburn-haired waitress behind the wooden counter had lush, come-hither looks. Her pouty lips promised sexual gratification. The sensual way of moving her ripe body made a man think of hot sex. Judging by her flat stomach, it was difficult to believe that she was three months pregnant. Her cutoffs revealed long, shapely legs that added to her appeal. At ten o'clock on a July Saturday night, male customers in the smoke-filled Texas honky-tonk constantly watched her move around the room. Matthew Ransome was certain that Olivia Brennan was so accustomed to men staring at her that she wouldn't wonder about his glances.

In the red T-shirt and cutoffs that was her uniform at Two-Steppin' Ribs, she waited on a customer in a nearby booth. Three musicians played country-western music while boot-scooting couples circled the dance floor. Even though he occasionally chatted with passing friends, Matt's attention remained focused on Olivia.

In the time since he had arrived and ordered his rib dinner, slowly eating and sipping one cold beer, Matt had watched half a dozen men hit on her. Some touched her, taking her hand or her wrist, patting her rear. She twisted free, or shaking her head, sidestepped groping hands, and he guessed she was being asked either to go out after work or—judging from the rough crowd—to have sex. He was surprised by her solemnity. She rarely gave more than the most perfunctory smile, not at all what he had imagined about her.

Matt watched locals he knew—Pug Mosley, the manager of the honky-tonk, openly flirted with her and several times during the evening let his hand brush her bottom. Once she spun around, telling him something. He grinned, shrugged and said something in return before he walked away in his usual swagger.

Fighting the urge to step in when Pug talked to Olivia, Matt intended to keep his approach to her low-key.

From what he had learned about her from the Fort Worth private detective he had hired a week ago, she wasn't dating anyone and there hadn't been a man in her life since Matt's brother Jeff. Matt found that difficult to believe except he had great faith in his P.I. With her body and mane of unruly auburn hair, she looked sexy and wild, like a woman with many partners.

Jeff could get mixed up with some shady people and seldom had there been a woman in his life that he had brought home. Including Olivia, who was carrying Jeff's child.

Nearing midnight, another local drifted to Olivia, just as obviously flirting with her as other men had. And received the same reception that was so cold Matt could discern her response without hearing a word of her conversation. Since she had been unreceptive to every man in the place, Matt reassessed his opinion of her as easy. He had never seen a female his younger brother couldn't charm, but Matt was beginning to wonder if Jeff was one of few men with whom she had ever had a relationship. Matt's opinion of her climbed a notch.

A small voice inside Matt insisted that he walk away now and never look back. Logically, he knew he should forget Olivia Brennan, but he couldn't any more than he could stop breathing.

Finally, after midnight, she was alone, standing behind the counter with no one around her. Silently warning himself he was seeking a hell of a lot of trouble, he slid out of the booth and circled the dance floor, crossing the room beneath revolving ceiling fans.

When he stopped in front of her, she looked up at him, turning the full force of big green eyes on him. Even in the dim light of the honky-tonk, he was mesmerized, and for a moment, she seemed as ensnared as he.

Attraction, as hot and tangible as a lightning flash, burst between them. The bar and people around them vanished from Matt's consciousness while he focused totally on her. Desire aroused him, a startling need to explore every inch of her ripe body and her sensual mouth. Once again, he knew why his brother had been attracted to her and why every man in the place seemed aware of her. She exuded a blatant sexuality that was all the more powerful up close.

While seconds passed, she stood as still as he did. Then, inhaling deeply, she turned her head, and the eye contact was broken.

As she started to walk away, Matt regained his wits.

"Wait—" he said. When she paused, he held out his hand. "I'm Jeff's brother Matt."

Her eyes narrowed. "I'm sorry about your brother," she stated coolly without taking Matt's hand. Once again, she moved on.

"Wait a minute. I want to talk to you," Matt said, catching up with her. "When do you get off work?" As silence stretched between them, even in the dim light, he saw the flash of fury in the depths of her eyes.

"Look, Jeff and I parted ways a while back," she said. "I don't know why you found me, but there was no longer anything between Jeff and me. You and I have nothing to talk about." Her words poured out swiftly in a throaty voice that was as sexy as everything else about her.

"There was a baby between you," Matt reminded her. "A baby that you and I will both be related to and need to talk about," Matt continued as his insides coiled in a knot. "I'm the uncle, so you give me a few minutes."

She bit her full underlip with even, white teeth and her mouth tempted him to forget the object of why he intended to talk to her.

"I can't guess what you want. Words won't do you any good," she insisted, shaking her head. "I'm through with your family. I don't want to see any of you." Suddenly she leaned closer, lowering her voice. "If you think I'm giving up my baby, you can forget it!" She turned her back and started to walk away.

Momentarily taken aback, Matt stepped in front of her, blocking her way. "I'm the baby's blood relative. You can't dismiss me like that. I want to talk—when and wherever you agree to. If you don't consent, we'll discuss the baby in a court of law. Take your pick."

Glaring at him, she visibly bristled. As she inhaled deeply, he was aware of the strain of the red shirt across her lush breasts. "I don't get off here until two in the morning when we close," she said.

"I'll wait. I promise you, we're going to have a discussion."

"All right. Two o'clock in the parking lot," she said in a level tone of voice even as her eyes sparked with fury.

"Fine. In the meantime, you can bring me some coffee. I'm in a booth on the other side of the room."

Nodding, she walked away and he couldn't keep from watching the sway of her hips.

She turned and slanted him a look over her shoulder, catching him watching her. He clamped his lips together. She had to be aware of the effect she had on men. At least she hadn't been coming after him for money which had surprised him because as soon as he learned about the pregnancy from Jeff, that's what he had expected.

"Damn, Jeff," Matt said under his breath, anger and pain mingling as he thought about his reckless younger brother whose wild lifestyle had caught up with him when he'd died climbing mountains in the Himalayas.

Matt dallied over the cup of coffee until it was obvious that closing time approached. As he stepped to the cash register, Olivia lingered to take his money.

"You can wait out front," she said, giving him another blast of her mesmerizing green eyes. Her low, seductive voice glided hotly over his every nerve. "Employees park in the back and when I'm finished closing, I'll drive my car around to the front. Our chat has to be brief. It's late, and I've had a long day."

He nodded. When he stepped outside, he heard the lock click in the door behind him as it shut. Yellow light from a tall lamp shed a bright glow over the graveled lot. Beneath a sliver of July moon a south breeze tugged at locks of his black hair.

Wondering how long it would take to close, Matt strolled behind the wooden building. Brown paint peeled in spots and the big blue trash bin overflowed with cartons and bottles. Another light on a tall post shone over the graveled area. Three ancient cars with assorted dents and scrapes were parked in the back. Matt's jaw tightened with disgust when he looked at the empty lot. Beyond the circle of light was a field with a grove of scrub oaks. Without security of any sort, the lot was no place for a woman alone at two in the morning.

Matt waited while the employees locked up, dimmed the lights and left, two women and a man coming out at the same time. As the burly man started toward Matt, Olivia caught his arm and said something to him. Giving Matt a long look, the man walked to his car. While the man and woman climbed into separate cars and drove out of the lot, Matt strolled over to Olivia. She stood with her hands on her hips.

"Jeff and I split. I don't think you and I have much to talk about."

"You're carrying his child. He told me and he was certain the baby was his."

"This is his baby, all right," she said. Her face was bathed in light, and Matt could see the fire dancing in her eyes and hear the anger in her tone which heightened his own irritation over her uncooperative attitude.

"Look, I'm related to your baby. Jeff told me you don't have any family and you're on your own. I want to help you."

"Thanks, but no thanks. You don't owe me anything, and I'll take care of my baby," she declared stiffly with a toss of her head that sent her thick mane swirling across her shoulders.

"Why make it more difficult for yourself and for the baby?"

"Jeff didn't want any responsibility for his child. Far from it. His exact words were: 'I don't want to ever know or even see your kid,'" she flung at Matt, and pain stabbed him. "He told me I should have been more careful. He was right there. I don't want any part of anything or anyone connected to Jeff!" she exclaimed firmly and turned to walk to her car.

Matt bit back angry words. It hurt badly to hear that Jeff had denied his child. Jeff hadn't told him that, but then, his kid brother would have known how Matt would react to such news.

Matt hurried ahead of her and blocked her from getting into her car.

"Get out of my way," she said.

"I want to talk. Surely you can give me a few minutes."

She inhaled deeply, and he resisted letting his gaze lower to her full breasts, but it was an effort.

"All right, for only a few more minutes." She crossed her arms over her middle and raised her chin and he knew he was in for a fight.

"This baby will be the only one of the next generation in my family."

"You can't have children?" she asked.

"I'm not a marrying man. I'll never marry anyone."

"That didn't slow your brother down. And he didn't care if this baby was the last of your family. Blood relations didn't seem important to him," she said, and Matt could easily hear the bitterness in her voice. Her fists were clenched, and he realized instead of a rift between Jeff and Olivia, Jeff had created a bottomless chasm. She was all but shaking with fury.

Matt fought to bank his own anger that she was being so almighty unreasonable when he offered help that she seemed to desperately need.

"As I recall, there were several of you—a brother, Nick, a sister, Katherine. Can't they produce grandchildren?"

Matt shrugged. "Perhaps someday, but who knows? Nick and Katherine are on the wild side and not likely to settle down soon."

"Like Jeff," Olivia said with bitterness in her voice again.

"None of us is as wild as Jeff was," Matt snapped. "Jeff took whatever he wanted and indulged himself. He thought he was invincible, but it turned out that he wasn't."

"Look, I'm trying to help—"

She shook her head. "No, you're not. You want something. If it's my baby, forget it. And don't think you can go to court and get my precious baby. I'll fight you every inch of the way."

"Will you listen to me?" he said patiently, and she arched her eyebrows.

"I'll listen, but you're on limited time that's growing shorter."

Matt wanted to shake her. Instead, he nodded. "I'm sure you don't make much money as a waitress here. I want to take care of you and the baby financially."

"I don't need your help. End of conversation. You have no claim on me. If you want to go to court over it—go. Since you're not the father, you won't have a strong case. They would give a father rights, but an uncle? I'm willing to take that chance. You stay out of my life. Your brother was a jerk! Now get out of my way."

She slid into her car, slammed and locked the door. The engine rumbled to life with a persistent knock. She backed up, swung in a circle and drove away, crunching gravel beneath the tires.

"Dammit!" Matt swore and clenched his fists. He strode angrily to his pickup, climbed in and headed toward Rincon, Texas where he knew she lived on the fringe of town.

He would try to talk to her one more time before he called his attorney. Little stubborn witch!

Jeff disowned the baby. Matt gritted his teeth as he reflected that most of his life he hadn't understood his kid brother. Without a doubt, the feelings had been mutual. Matt knew his single parent father had done the best he could, but he had been too indulgent with all of them. Jeff, the youngest, he had spoiled rotten.

Matt drove through the neighborhood of small frame houses with dented, ancient cars parked in front yards and lawns high with weeds. When he reached her darkened house, he discovered that Olivia had not come straight home. She might not be coming home tonight at all.

In disgust, he wondered if she had taken up with a man. He shrugged away the unwanted notion, reminding himself that there hadn't been any mention from the P.I. of a boyfriend. Tonight she had given the cold shoulder to every man in the honky-tonk.

He slowed and parked in front of the house. In the next block he saw a man stumbling along the sidewalk until he turned and disappeared inside a house.

Olivia's car approached and turned into her drive that was no more than a gravel path. When she stepped out of the car, she picked up a grocery sack and walked toward her house, merely glancing at him when he emerged from his car.

"We've talked," she said when he caught up with her. She brushed past him and climbed rickety steps, crossing the porch to unlock her door. Matt followed and held the screen door. He stood close enough to get a strong whiff of the odor of cigarette smoke trapped in her hair.

She looked up at him. "You're not welcome here. I've said all I need to say to you."

"Listen. You're carrying a Ransome. I want to help you and you damned well need support. Stop being so stubborn and listen to what I have to offer. For all you know, you could be turning down a million bucks."

Her eyebrows arched. "Am I?" she asked, startling him at her change in temperament because he thought he heard amusement in her voice.

"Let's go inside and talk," he answered. She gave him a level look and he wondered if she was going to send him on his way, but she shrugged and entered her house, leaving the door open behind her.

He followed her into a small, frame house that had to be nearly a hundred years old. White paint had peeled from the cracked walls, revealing a coat of dark blue paint. The furniture was threadbare and looked older than he was, yet there were some green plants and a few touches that contrasted with the dilapidation.

She tossed her purse on the sofa, set down the sack of groceries and motioned to him. "Have a seat."

"How long have you lived here?" he asked, looking around and sitting on an overstuffed chair covered in a faded, flowered slipcover. A blanket was thrown over the sofa and he suspected it hid holes.

"Almost a year now."

Leaning forward, he rested his elbows on his knees while he watched her kick off her shoes and rub her foot.

"I know you're going to school. You don't have any family. You work in a dive and you reek of cigarette smoke. The bar can't be healthy for your baby or you."

"I'm trying to get another job that pays at least as much as the one I have. I don't have the skills or the wardrobe for an office job," she said, thrusting out her chin defiantly. "Pay is higher at Two-Steppin' Ribs because the bar is out in nowhere."

"How many hours are you taking this semester?"

"Two classes—six hours. I'm in pre-law."

"You're a sophomore, aren't you?"

"I think you already know the answer. And you're thinking that a sophomore is not much for someone who is twenty-two, but it's the best I could do," she replied, curling her long legs beneath her and settling in the corner of the sofa. His gaze slid along her legs. He tried to keep his thoughts on his mission, but he was responding to her physically in a manner that shocked him.

"All right. Here's the deal," he said. "I'll send you to school. You quit that job and move out to the ranch with me—"

"No way! I'm sure you think I'm easy, but I'm not climbing into bed with you to get my tuition," she said, flinging the words at him and standing.

"Sit down," he said with such ice and authority that she did. "I don't want your body." Even as he said the words, a devilish urge made him too aware that he was lying to her as far as what his body desired. Yet he could control himself and good sense kept telling him that he shouldn't want her physically. She would be pure poison. He didn't want to get involved emotionally with any woman.

"I'll pay for your school, let you quit that damn job," he repeated, "take care of you and the baby. I'll pay your medical bills—"

"No one is that filled with benevolence. What do you want out of this generous offer?" she asked in a cynical voice.

"Stop fighting me," he said, gazing steadily into her green eyes and thinking that every inch of her made a man think of sex. "I want to know my niece or nephew. I want to make sure this baby is taken care of in the manner he or she should be. I don't want your body," he reaffirmed, trying to avoid looking at her lush body and failing annoyingly to stop thinking about it. "I want to know your baby. I want to see you able to take care of yourself and the baby. I can pay for your education. In turn, this Ransome will become part of our family. Dad has had one heart attack already. I want him to know his only grandchild."

"If you want your father to have a grandchild so badly, you should rethink your stance against marriage."

"I married once and never again for me," Matt replied grimly, refusing to discuss the matter further.

"What happened? She didn't like your bossy arrogance?"

He banked his irritation and ignored her question. "Your baby will be the only Ransome in the next generation. My dad isn't getting any younger and he desperately wants a grandchild. I think he's given up on all of us, but now, with your baby, his hopes are rekindled."

As Olivia bit her lip, Matt couldn't resist looking at her mouth.

"Look, dammit. What are you holding onto here besides your independence?" he asked. "This isn't a castle. Your job is tough and tiring and pays little. You work in an unhealthy atmosphere. Men hit on you, and I can imagine what they're saying to you—"

"And you won't hit on me?" she asked in a sarcastic tone.

"No, I won't," he said flatly, trying in vain to shove erotic images of her out of his mind. "You know you're an attractive woman, but you're like a relative," he said, while an inner voice laughed and he wiped his perspiring brow. When had the temperature in the small room climbed so high?

"What do you want?" she asked. "You look like the straight-arrow, determined, accustomed to getting-your-way type."

"I want to take care of my dad and our ranches—we own three. No commitments beyond my family and our ranches. I want my dad to get to know his only grandchild. Pretty damn simple," Matt snapped, thinking it should not be complicated, but it was. He was playing with dynamite right now by bringing her into their family.

"I suspect there's more to it than my baby."

"I swear I'm telling you the truth."

"I know I work in a bad place and I'm looking for another job," she said, waving her slender fingers at him. "I'm holding on to my independence because that's all I really have. I don't want to have to depend on you and I don't want to have to repay you for favors."

"If it reassures you, we can put my offer in a contract. I don't want anything physical," he repeated. "I'll pay for your school and all your expenses and your baby's. I'll pay you a lump sum up front so you're not beholden to me for money. You don't have to repay any of it."

"That sounds too generous. I know you can't understand someone holding such a value on independence, but it's important to me. In spite of what you say, I can't believe there aren't strings attached to your offer."

"Listen. I'm trying to give you the help you need to become

completely independent. In exchange, I want to know my brother's child That's all there is to it."

She glowered and inhaled, and he looked down as her full breasts strained against the fabric. When he glanced up, she frowned.

"It's difficult to be convinced that you really want to know this baby—or that your father wants a grandchild badly—when Jeff so totally denied us and was emphatic he didn't want anything to do with my baby."

"None of us knew Jeff's attitude. My guess is, his reaction was to get out of his responsibility, which was typical of my younger brother."

"So what happens later when I want to move on?"

"We'll work that out when we come to it. I hope you'll stick around until you finish your education. Maybe by then you'll like us and trust us enough to stay close permanently. Do you have long-term plans?"

"I intend to finish school and get a job. I still say, you could marry again if you want kids so all-fired much."

"There is already a baby coming who is a Ransome. I'm not going to turn my back on a child who has Ransome blood. I have to keep reminding you—your baby is my relative."

Matt stared at her while she glared at him and the clash of wills was tense, but along with the contention was a sexual undercurrent of desire. Sparks danced between them, and Matt was certain she felt the same attraction he did.

Instinctively, he knew the appeal was as unwanted to her as it was to him. Trying to control his insistent lust, he made a stronger effort to think only of the future and a baby he wasn't going to surrender without the fight of his life.

"If I give you a sum of cash up front and promise to pay your expenses, you won't feel dependent on me. I'll repeat—we can sign a contract."

"I don't want to get involved with Jeff's kin," she insisted and he wondered if she had a clue how much he was willing to give her to change her grim conditions.

"Possibly my offer will help with your decision. We'll set up a trust fund for your baby. I'll cover your expenses and you'll have room and board at the ranch. Plus how's a hundred thousand dollars paid to you, half now, half in six months?"

Two

Olivia stared in disbelief at Matt Ransome as the princely sum stunned her.

"For that much money, you want me, body and soul, plus my baby," she replied curtly as she stood. "Get out!"

"Sit down," he ordered in the cold, quiet voice he had used before that sent a chill down her spine, yet made her feel that the last notion on his mind was her body. She sat.

"I keep telling you that I can have our attorney draw up a contract. If you want, you can meet my family and talk to them."

Barely considering his family, Olivia nodded stiffly while the amount of money spun in her thoughts. The sum dazzled her. Unable to stop herself, she speculated about the classes she could take, the freedom she could have, the dreadful job that she could leave. It was more money than she could ever earn at the bar. Her heart pounded, her palms had grown damp and it was an effort to resist accepting his offer blindly and instantly. She realized silence was stretching between them and he was waiting patiently.

"You're very different from your brother," she remarked.

"I hope to hell I am," he said.

She had seen Matt Ransome at the rib place hours before he had spoken to her. She had never met him, but she had seen him once when she was with Jeff and he had told her that Matt was his brother. Matt had none of Jeff's easy charm or happy-go-lucky ways. He was perhaps a couple of inches shorter, more broad-shouldered, handsome in his own way with the same dark blue eyes and thick lashes. Matt's hair was black. Jeff's had been brown.

That first moment of a close encounter with Matt Ransome had disturbed her. She had to admit that she'd had a physical reaction to him that she'd never had with Jeff or any other man. She didn't know why, either, because Matt Ransome was too forceful, too determined to get his way to suit her. He was all business, but that first moment of looking directly into his blue eyes while he gazed back at her, had taken her breath, held her totally and had steamed with sexual tension. For a few seconds, she was certain that he had been locked into the same jolting awareness that she was.

Now here was his proposition that she still found difficult to believe from a man who disturbed her physically in a way no other man ever had. With most men, she had always felt in control. But Matt Ransome demolished that sense of power. She didn't like to acknowledge it, but she had to admit to herself that she was drawn to Matt in a purely physical way. She couldn't explain why and she didn't want to be. She never again wanted to be involved with a Ransome.

At the same time, Matt's offer was tempting beyond belief, but she wasn't rushing into an agreement. She had given her trust to Jeff and he had trampled it.

She cocked her head to one side to study Matt. "You know for the money you're offering, you could adopt a child."

"Since this baby is a Ransome, I intend to take care of it and I want to get to know him or her. Do you know what you're having?"

"It's too early. I haven't decided whether I want to know or not."

"We'll say a prayer for a girl. The males in this family haven't turned out so good."

"I'll think about your offer," she said coldly, standing. "It's time for you to go."

He stood. "Look, you can mull it over, but you know you need what I'm offering. In the meantime, you should move out of this neighborhood. Come stay at the ranch tonight."

"Tonight?" Again, he startled her. "I can't possibly—"

"Of course you can," he persisted. "I'll bet you don't have more than two suitcases of stuff. Do you rent this furnished or is this your furniture?"

"I rented it furnished. Look, if you're taking charge of my life, then that settles it, I'm not going," she said, hoping her voice was forceful and trying to keep her gaze from roaming down his long legs or across his broad chest.

"I'm trying to improve your situation," he stated patiently. "What's holding you in this place?"

Her face grew hot and she glanced away, unable to meet his direct gaze. "Nothing," she admitted. "Except you're a stranger."

"Not a total stranger. You knew Jeff, so you know a lot about me. You're not safe here. This isn't a healthy place for an expectant woman. You don't need to be alone and you could be a hell of a lot more comfortable. All right?"

Annoyed, she shook her head. "You're taking charge. Back off and give me some room. I'll think it over. I'll come out in the morning and we can discuss your offer more."

He inhaled and looked as if he were trying to cling to what little patience he had. "All right, but resign and get away from the secondhand smoke. At least think of your baby."

"I do think of my baby."

"If you'll get a pencil and paper, I'll give you directions to the ranch."

She glared at him and knew he held his annoyance in check. She didn't like him taking over, yet it was for the best. If she moved to the ranch, she knew she would be making a commitment from which it might be difficult to shake free.

She didn't like Matt's forceful ways. Maybe that's why Jeff had had such a rebellious nature.

"I'm beginning to understand why your brother was like he was."

Anger flashed in Matt's blue eyes. "My youngest brother wouldn't take responsibility for anything."

She realized she had touched a nerve. Dropping remarks about Jeff, she hurried to get a pen and paper. As Matt wrote directions to his ranch, she looked at his well-shaped hands, his thick, slightly curly eyelashes and straight nose. A faint dark stubble showed on his jaw.

"After knowing Jeff, who could not be relied on, I find it difficult to trust you," she admitted.

"I'll keep reminding you, I'm not like Jeff," Matt replied quietly. They stood only inches apart and he had focused on her with that intensity he had the first time they had made eye contact. Her insides got butterflies and her gaze lowered to his mouth while she wondered what it would be like to kiss him.

When she looked up to find him gazing at her mouth, her heart missed a beat. She drew herself up. "I want one point clear—you're a take-charge person. If I move to your ranch, you agree now that you won't try to run my life."

"I wouldn't think of it," he answered with sarcasm as the fiery clash of wills continued to snap between them. "But I am going to speak up when you do things that might endanger the health of your baby."

"Right now, you can forget about ever trying to take my baby from me."

"I know a child needs its mother. I don't want to jeopardize that relationship as long as you are a loving mother. Your family has a history of neglect and abuse."

"I'm not like my parents," she snapped while anger made her hot. "My folks drank, were into drugs. They were verbally abusive. They neglected me as well as themselves and were irresponsible and it killed them. I couldn't wait to get away from them," she said flatly. She studied him for a moment. "You know a lot about me. Especially for having just met me. More than Jeff knew, I think. How'd you find out so much?"

"I wanted to know about you before I started dealing with you. I hired a P.I. to check into your life."

Her displeasure heightened that he would have her background checked, but then she knew if she were making the offer he was, she might do the same.

"You don't approve, do you?" he asked.

"No, but I can understand why you wanted to know about my past. I'll think about your offer to move into your home," she said, knowing she should accept eagerly, but she was loath to relinquish her independence.

"We won't get in each other's way. It's a big house. Also, fall enrollment is open at the university in Fort Worth." He reached into a back pocket and withdrew brochures and a catalogue. "Here, you can look at these," he said and placed them on a table. "You can become a full-time student and graduate sooner," he said.

"You've been planning this for a while. How far from Fort Worth is your ranch? I've forgotten what Jeff told me."

"Thirty miles. Not far. You can commute easily."

They stared at each other, and she wondered if he intended doing what he said. She had been surprised by men before, so if Matt Ransome didn't live up to his part of their bargain, she could deal with it. She knew he lusted after her. It showed in the way he looked at her, but his control was evident also. She had the feeling that he didn't like her at all. She suspected he didn't approve of much his younger brother had done or the women Jeff had known. Matt Ransome would have seemed like ice, real straight and arrogant, except for the smoldering looks he gave her. What astounded her was the effect he had on her. Since Jeff, she had been immune to men, but she wasn't immune to Matt. He made her pulse race, her breath catch. She didn't want to react that way to him and she knew he didn't want to respond to her, so whatever kind of chemistry there was brewing between them, it was unwanted and hopefully would evaporate.

"Are we finished for tonight?" she asked, wanting him out of her house.

"I don't think you're safe here. Anyone who wants to break into this place can do so easily if they have an ounce of skills. Do you want me to stay here? I can sleep in a chair or on your sofa."

She smiled, amused by his offer of protection. "Thanks, but no thanks. I've been taking care of myself for a long time. My dad died five years ago. My mother died two years later and I've taken care of both of them since I was twelve years old. We lived in a lot tougher neighborhoods than this. That's one reason I moved here. Cheap rent and a better area, although I'm sure it doesn't look suitable to you. One more night here is nothing to worry about."

He stared at her and she wondered if he was going to insist she let him stay. It was obvious that he disapproved of her. He probably thought she was easy. If he got to know her, he would find out he was wrong in that judgment. The last thing she wanted was to be a live-in girlfriend, going from one brother to the other.

As they gazed at each other, that searing awareness flashed between them. In spite of all her intentions to keep a wall between them, it was impossible to resist reacting to Matt. Right now her heart raced. Perspiration had broken out on his forehead, and he seemed as riveted as she was.

Inhaling deeply, he spun away to cross the room to the door. She trailed after him, pausing a few feet from him. "I gave you my cell number. Call me if you need anything," he said.

"Thanks," she replied.

"Don't worry. You'll be glad if you say yes," he said. He opened the door and strode outside. She followed, watching Matt Ransome climb into his car and drive away.

When she stepped back inside, she looked around the shabby room. By accepting Matt's offer, she could take care of her baby, get her education, live in a safer place. She was scared to celebrate because she hadn't been to the ranch yet, nor had she spent a night under the same roof with Matt Ransome. Was he leveling with her and telling her the truth? Was his sole interest in the baby?

"I hope so," she said quietly, looking around at her few possessions. She would be glad to leave this house. It would take less than a couple of hours for her to get all her possessions packed.

She switched on a bedroom light, looking at the nondescript bed and the dresser, a chest of drawers that didn't match and a torn braided rug on the floor. As she got ready for bed, she thought about Jeff Ransome. She had enrolled in a two-year college, working in a café until she had gotten the job at the Two-Steppin' Ribs. It paid more so she put up with the smoke and the leering men, but from the start, Jeff had been different from the others.

Tall, brown-haired and handsome, Jeff had gone to the Ribs to gamble. There was a high-stakes poker game in a back room that was invitation only and the night she'd met him, Jeff had been part of it. After closing he had hung around and asked her to go out with him.

Since she was twelve years old, she had known that she attracted males. Early on, she had learned to try to keep a wall around herself, but when she met Jeff Ransome, he had charmed his way past her defenses. She had been unable to resist his charismatic personality.

As Olivia pulled on cotton pajamas, gathered up the school catalog and brochure and climbed into bed, her thoughts went back to Jeff. He'd been the second man in her life, which she knew he hadn't believed. She'd had a wonderful time with him until she discovered she was pregnant. They had used birth control, but she had gotten pregnant anyway.

From that moment on, Jeff was through. And then a month ago he had left for a trek in the rugged Himalaya mountains where, in a daredevil climb, he'd had a fatal fall.

Olivia gazed into space, mulling over Matt Ransome's offer. She had to accept, but as much as possible, she wanted it on her terms, not his.

She opened the catalog and turned to the section on pre-law, her major, and for the first time allowed herself to think of the windfall Matt Ransome was providing. If only it was exactly as he said and there were no hidden agendas, no strings attached and no unpleasant surprises ahead for her. She could move to the Ransome ranch and quit her job! In the early hours of morning, the whole offer seemed surreal, and she suspected that as soon as she settled on the ranch, Matt would want to sleep with her. He was appealing, sexy and generated sparks in her the way no other man had.

Forget it, she told herself, knowing she would not go from one brother to another. "If I accept his offer, I vow I won't have sex with Matt Ransome," she said aloud, trying to stop remembering the tingles she had when she gazed into Matt's blue eyes.

Forcing her thoughts off Matt, she wondered about her future and his offer. Was there anything she could do to get Matt's proposition more on her own terms?

The next morning her palms were damp from nervousness as she drove through an open gate and passed a sign announcing the Ransome ranch. In minutes she turned a bend in the ranch road. Ahead spread houses, a barn, a corral, pens and outbuildings. A pumping windmill stood near a stock tank filled with water.

When she drew closer, she looked at an intimidating, sprawling stone ranch house with a shake shingle roof. It was surrounded by immaculate, lush green lawns and a profusion of flowers in well-tended beds that all proclaimed the wealth of the owner. She had never lived in a house that looked as grand as this one. Swallowing hard, Olivia couldn't imagine herself suddenly part of the Ransome family.

A rail fence enclosed the yard and two live oaks gave inviting shade that failed to calm Olivia's nerves. On the porch the hanging pots of yellow bougainvillea, scarlet gaillardia and purple impatiens added a dreamlike feeling. This could be her new home. She couldn't fathom it.

Adding to her jittery nerves and disbelief, Matt Ransome came striding outside. In a white T-shirt, jeans and western boots, he looked muscled, tough and electrifying. Without saying a word he created a high voltage magnetism. The sight of him did nothing to calm her nerves.

He motioned her where to park in front of a six-car garage. When she climbed out, she was conscious of her cutoffs and her white T-shirt.

"Hi there," Matt said in a deep voice as he took a box from her car. In his T-shirt that revealed sculpted muscles and his tight jeans, his sensuality jumped a notch. One look in his eyes confirmed that the sexual appeal between them burned as hot as ever. When she stepped out, she looked up to see him gazing at her waist.

"You don't look pregnant," he said.

An inner voice told her to keep everything impersonal with Matt, but she couldn't do what she knew she should. "I guess it's because I'm tall," she replied breathlessly, mindful of how close he stood. She barely knew what she said to him. He should move away. She should step aside. Instead, she gazed up at him while her heartbeat continued to accelerate.

Silence between them carried sparks. When his attention lowered to her mouth, her pulse drummed. As he gazed at her, the blatant, scalding desire in his eyes heated her.

"No physical relationship comes with this package," she repeated.

"It damn well doesn't," he replied, sounding half angry. "I don't ever want to get involved again except in the most superficial manner. You and I absolutely don't need entanglement between us."

"That's something we can agree on. It would help if you'd move away."

Something flickered in the depths of his eyes before he leaned around her to pick up another one of her boxes.

"I'll get your things and then I'll show you around. Have you quit your job?"

"No, I haven't. I figured whatever we decide to do, I'll work tonight."

Matt straightened up and she saw the hard look back in his features. He shook his head. "You quit today. You don't owe them anything and you shouldn't be there one more hour."

"I thought you weren't going to meddle in my life," she said, trying to curb her temper.

"Where the baby is concerned, I'll interfere. That nightclub isn't healthy. They'll manage without you."

"Look—"

"No, you look," he said quietly. "The bar's atmosphere isn't healthy. They're going to get along without you. If we have a deal, part of it includes you taking care of yourself and your unborn baby."

Where sexual tension had spun tightly between them only moments ago, now friction set sparks flying. She glared at him, yet she suspected she would get nowhere if she argued the rest of the day.

"Why do you want to wait tables so all-fired badly?" Matt asked her.

"I don't. That isn't it."

"There you are."

She put her hands on her hips. "I'm here tentatively. We haven't agreed on what we're going to do. I haven't accepted your offer. We need to discuss it before you start taking complete charge."

"Let me show you around, let you select your room and then we'll sit down and see if we can't come to terms," he said, lifting the last box and putting it under his arm. "Tomorrow I'll introduce you to everyone who works here. Mrs. Marley is the housekeeper and cook. You'll meet her at the end of the week. She's here two days a week. Fridays, she cooks. Saturdays, she cleans. My dad lives down the road from me. She's at his house Monday through Thursday."

Olivia nodded.

"Wait a minute," Matt said and set a box on her car. Following Matt's gaze, she watched a tall, sandy-haired man approach and shake hands with Matt.

"Olivia, this is our foreman, Sandy McDermott," Matt said easily. "Sandy, meet Olivia Brennan who will be staying with us a while."

"I'm glad to meet you, Sandy," she said, extending her hand and smiling.

"Happy to meet you, Miss Brennan. Glad to have you here."

"It's Olivia, Sandy. Call me Olivia."

Sandy nodded. "Nice meeting you, Olivia," he said, turning to talk to Matt. Olivia listened while they discussed cattle and a world she didn't know. Matt was quick and decisive and more relaxed than when he was dealing with her. As soon as Sandy told them goodbye and left, she and Matt headed for the house.

She was aware of Matt walking close beside her. Her jittery nerves kept her on edge, and she wondered what she was getting herself into.

Once again Matt took her arm and she drew a deep breath. She hadn't known him twenty-four hours, yet his slightest touch set her ablaze. She couldn't fathom the chemistry. She had known other handsome, decisive males and she had had no trouble dealing with them and no difficulty ignoring them. Until now. Even Jeff with all his charm had never carried the electricity of a bolt of lightning the way Matt did.

She wondered again what she was getting into if she accepted Matt's offer that was a windfall in her circumstances. She was heartily glad to be out of the bar and away from lustful men. At the same time, she wanted this bargain to be partially on her terms. Her queasy nerves jangled when she thought about her plan and her requests. She had no idea how Matt would react. The knowledge was constantly with her that she was taking a risk by making her own demands because if she accepted his offer and he did what he said and kept his bargain, her life would improve beyond her wildest dreams.

He held the door, following her inside an enormous kitchen with oversize windows. Sunlight streamed into the room that held maple cabinetry, granite countertops, a marble floor and maple furniture. The floor-to-ceiling windows overlooked a patio and a pool with sparkling blue water.

"This is beautiful," she said, unable to keep a breathless tone of awe out of her voice. "It doesn't look like what I imagined."

"Jeff and I must have created the wrong impression."

Her gaze flew to him and heat flooded her cheeks. Embarrassed by her reaction, she bit her lip.

"You probably thought we lived in a cabin with mounted heads and gun racks and the sort."

"No," she denied halfheartedly and then shrugged. "Maybe something like that," she admitted.

"C'mon. Let me show you this wing of the house." He took her arm lightly, yet the contact sizzled, and as they crossed the kitchen, her surroundings paled in comparison to the man beside her.

From the hall he led her into a family room and her awe returned at the sight of a twenty-foot-high cathedral ceiling, a massive stone fireplace, luxurious tan leather furniture and pictures of landscapes.

"This is a dream!" she gasped and her face flushed. "You can tell I've never lived in a house like this," she said.

"Well, now you do," he said. "It's comfortable. Across the hall are the living and dining rooms," he said, taking her arm again as they returned to the hall. "On the other side of the kitchen is a utility room, exercise room and my office. The bedrooms are in the opposite wing. Other than my bedroom, in the southeast end of the house, you can have whichever bedroom you want."

As he led her through a workout room, a media room and his office, the elegant furnishings overwhelmed Olivia. It was a dream-come-true moment to think she would live in this palace. She realized Jeff and Matt weren't the ordinary cowboys she had imagined they were. The house reeked of money and power and she wondered whether she could hold her own and govern her baby's future against the Ransomes' wishes.

"We'll have a decorator help you with the nursery." Matt's words jolted her back into awareness of the moment.

"I won't be here forever." Olivia gave him a startled, wide-eyed look.

"That's all right. You'll return to visit and bring the baby."

"You're so certain!" she exclaimed, yet now she realized part of the source of his arrogance and assurance. Growing up in a home like this, how could he be anything except confident?

"Shouldn't I be?" he asked, looking blandly at her.

Olivia stopped to face him, a frown creasing her brow. "Our lives are so different."

"It doesn't matter, Olivia," he replied easily. "We'll be related to the baby and we'll want to see him or her through the years. It'll save you money to live here until you finish your education."

She merely nodded and returned to thinking about her future while she looked at more rooms in a house that dazzled her.

"How's this for you?" he asked later, leading the way into a bedroom that took her breath and she could not imagine living in it.

She stood in the room large enough to contain the house she rented. The room was plush beyond her wildest dreams. It was ample for a king-size bed with a bronze headboard, a massive mahogany chest, bookshelves, a wide-screen television, a maroon sofa, a rocking chair and assorted tables. The decor was maroon with accents of white and beige and an oriental rug partially covering the gleaming plank floor.

She knew she wasn't hiding her amazement. She reminded herself that it was premature to celebrate her newfound fortune, her future prospects or this house that could possibly become her home. In the next few minutes, she knew, it could all disappear from her life as swiftly as it had entered.

The time had come to present her conditions.

"This is beyond anything I had imagined," she said softly, turning to face him. Her pulse drummed. She wanted to learn how earnest he really was about this whole proposition. "Shall we discuss our future and terms of a contract?" she asked, the words *our future* causing her insides to clench.

"Sure," he replied, giving her a long, speculative look that made her feel he knew her every thought. "Let's get a drink and sit in the family room."

They walked in silence back to the kitchen and she watched, barely aware of what he was doing while her pulse beat faster and her nervousness increased. At the last minute she vacillated between an overwhelming desire to accept his offer unconditionally and reap the fortune, or risk her demands that would either cause him to send her packing or solidify her prospects and fortune.

Finally, they were seated in the family room at a polished oak game table with tall, frosted glasses of ice and lemonade and a plate of cookies in front of them. She couldn't eat or drink anything. Aware that her entire prospects hung in the balance, she inhaled deeply to calm down.

"You've had time to think it over. You're here on the ranch. Does this mean you'll accept my offer?" he asked.

His blue eyes cut into her like shards of a glacier. He was formidable and determined, but she clung to her course. It was time to see how much he would commit to what he wanted. She took a deep breath and raised her chin while she locked her hands together.

"You're being very generous," she said, still awed by his offer and filled with trepidation over what she was about to demand from him for her part. "I have a counteroffer to make to you."

Fire flashed in the depths of his eyes and a muscle worked in his jaw. She suspected he was bracing for her to ask for more money.

"All right. Name your conditions and price," he said, grinding out the words. "How much Ransome money do you want?"

"You've made an overwhelmingly generous offer, but if you're truly committed to protecting this baby and raising it as a Ransome, then I want you to give my baby the Ransome name. I want a paper marriage, an in-name-only marriage that we can later dissolve." Her heart thundered so loudly that she could barely hear herself speak. "In other words, will you marry me?"

Three

Stunned, Matt stared at her. "You want me to marry you?" he repeated in amazement.

"Yes, if you're so determined to make my baby a part of your family. It'll be the same conditions you've already given me, plus marriage. This way, you're more committed. My child will legitimately be a Ransome as it should have been all along. You'll do the honorable thing that your brother would not do."

Matt stared at her. Anger and shock rocked him that she would put one more demand on him when he had given her an offer that was magnanimous beyond anything she had ever known in her life. Then he noticed her white knuckles and her hands doubled into fists. Perspiration dotted her brow and worry glazed her green eyes.

Suddenly he could see her viewpoint and why she wanted legitimacy. In the future marriage would truly tie Jeff's child into the family.

Yet it would bind Matt to Olivia in a manner he never intended. For an instant heat flashed in him at the thought of marriage to her. On a purely physical level he speculated about her shapely, naked body in his arms. With lightning speed the image aroused him.

He forced his thoughts back to business and a contract with her and a paper marriage. A marriage in name only.

"We can dissolve it as soon as I get my law degree," she added.

Could he stay under the same roof with her and keep his hands to himself? He had planned to do just that before she had come up with the proposal.

"You want it all," he said quietly, and she flushed, her cheeks turning a bright pink.

"No. I don't want sex with you," she answered bluntly. "You know it wouldn't be a true marriage. Not in any manner. But you can see that if you really want what you've been telling me, it would give my baby more protection and give me a better deal."

"Hell, yes," he snapped. "You could sue me for divorce and half of everything I own."

"You said we'd have a contract. We'll have a prenuptial agreement that will list terms as both of us want them. You can have your lawyer draw it up."

Matt was impressed. She was taking charge of part of their bargain, making some shrewd demands and she once again surprised him. He rubbed the back of his head. She had him in a corner and she knew it. He didn't want to marry her, not even a fake, paper marriage of convenience because that would be legally binding.

But if he backed out on marriage, she might refuse his deal and the baby would go out of the Ransome family.

"And you still want all the rest I've offered—the education, the cash, the trust fund for the baby?"

"I want the education and the trust fund. I'd like some cash so I can go to school full time, but if I live at the Ransome ranch, I think you could cut the amount of money in half or even less if you want. As soon as I finish my education, we can dissolve the union. I don't intend for it to be permanent."

"I've got to think about it. I hadn't planned on marriage," he said and watched her let out her breath and unclench her hands. She raised her chin.

"I didn't think you'd do it." She stood and sighed. "You were better than your brother, but it's not good enough. Since you're not interested in my terms, I'll keep my independence and move on."

"You'll be walking out on a fabulous future that's a whole hell of a lot better than you're doing now or can do. You're selling your baby short by turning down my offer."

"Perhaps, but I'm not the one who wants something here," she said. "If you're willing to commit to this baby, I want the whole deal—I want support and legitimacy and some of the things your brother should have given me." She shrugged. "I'm accustomed to tough times. You can take it or leave it."

He gazed into green eyes that were fiery and unyielding and he was certain she wasn't bluffing about turning down his offer. He believed every word she said and it increased his anger that she was being so foolish, yet at the same time, he couldn't keep from appreciating her determination to get more for her child. And deep down, Matt knew she was right. He might have done the same thing himself, had he been in her place.

"Sit down," he ordered quietly, his anger growing. "I didn't say I wouldn't do it. I simply want to think about it like you wanted to consider my offer last night."

She sat and he stared hard at her. She stared right back at him and he felt tension coil.

"I'll talk to my attorney about it," Matt finally replied, buying some time before he made any kind of commitment. "In the meantime, call and quit your job and settle in. I'll introduce you to people who live and work on the ranch."

"Until you come to a decision, I'm not leaving a job that pays better than most around here. I'm going to my room to get ready to go to work."

Matt stood and watched her walk away. He wanted to grab her and shake her and he had never felt that way with a woman before. Not even Margo before she walked out on him. Olivia Brennan got to him as no one ever had.

What was worse, was that steady, fiery sexual awareness of her, a hot attraction that kept his nerves on edge. Marry her!

His whole being wanted to yell never, but then he thought about what he would be tossing aside. He was certain she would walk right out of his life and at any point in time, she could move far from Texas. She had no roots, no ties except going to college and right now she was between semesters. Right now, she could move away without much disruption in her life. Her college credits would transfer.

"Dammit!" He pushed back his chair with a scrape and crossed the room to call the family attorney.

He presented the problem swiftly, asking questions about a prenuptial agreement, keeping his eye on the clock. While part of him listened to the lawyer speaking, part of Matt's attention was focused on hearing Olivia return.

Matt finally replaced the receiver and stared at the phone. As he suspected, marriage, even a paper-only union, would be far more binding than the bargain Matt had intended to strike with Olivia. But it could be dissolved, and he could put stipulations to try to protect himself from later demands. It didn't mean she wouldn't sue or take him to court and he would have to fight her later. On the other hand, the baby would legally be a Ransome.

Matt rubbed the back of his neck and swore under his breath. He didn't want to get bound to her. Not Olivia or any other woman.

He heard her in the hall and he crossed the family room in quick long strides. In the kitchen he caught up with her and she glanced at him as he strode into the room.

"Wait a minute!" he snapped.

Her brows lifted in question as he crossed the room to stand with only inches separating them. "I called our attorney and talked to him," Matt declared. "Marriage is a hell of a lot more commitment than you're asking me to make."

"You are the one who wants my baby in your family, remember?"

"I'm considering what you want. Call in sick tonight. You can miss one night and still keep your job."

"I can, but I don't see any reason to. I'm going to work. I need every dollar I can earn."

"I've offered you a damn good deal."

"Indeed, you have, but I told you that I want it all," she said softly. She had on her tight red T-shirt and short cutoffs.

"Hell, I'll pay your salary for tonight, but you take sick leave," he ordered, annoyed that she was uncooperative. He was as angered by her demands and stubborn will as he was by his own heated response to her.

She stared at him a moment and he thought she was going to still refuse. Instead, she nodded and crossed the room to the phone, hanging her red vinyl purse on a hook by the door.

She asked for another woman and spoke softly, turning her back to Matt, but he heard her tell her friend that something had come up and she wouldn't be there tonight.

"You could have told her you were sick," Matt said as soon as she replaced the receiver and turned around.

"I'm not sick. Kira will think of some excuse for me, no doubt. I don't think you have a very high opinion of me," she remarked. "I'm sure you think I'm cheap and easy and not too bright."

"I'll admit that I might have thought that at one time, but the P.I.'s report changed my opinion. You don't have any men in your life now. Your grades are top-notch. My opinion of you changes almost hourly. You constantly surprise me."

"The same as you astound me. So did your brother. To my misfortune, I misjudged him in too many ways. I'll never trust a Ransome again like I did Jeff."

"You want to marry a Ransome," Matt reminded her.

"That is purely a business arrangement for both of us." She took her purse off the hook. "I'm going to unpack my things, shower and change before you show me around. I'd just as soon not meet people dressed like this."

He nodded and watched her start out of the room. At the door she turned back to look at him. "Unlike Jeff Ransome, you can trust me. If I give you my word, I'll keep it." She left, and he heard the soft slap of her sneakers in the hall.

"I'll be in my office," he called after her and headed down the hall, wanting to talk to his attorney again.

Olivia closed the door to her new bedroom, walking around the room and touching the furniture lightly. She shook from pent-up nerves and her proposal to Matt Ransome. To demand that the man who owned this mansion marry her—it took her breath with its presumptuousness. How could she be that brash and calculating? Yet it would give the world to her baby.

Her proposal of marriage had jarred Matt. It wasn't what he had expected or wanted, yet he was considering it. She could detect a grudging respect growing in him.

She paused in front of an elegant rosewood-framed mirror and looked at herself. Her riot of red hair always gave the impression of a wanton woman. Her breasts were full, adding to the attraction to males. She ought to cut her hair and buy fake glasses. With the money—if she made a deal with Matt—she would be able to afford to get her hair fixed and buy new clothes.

She frowned at her image. She shouldn't think about where or how she would spend one nickel of his money. She didn't have a deal yet with Matt, and they might not ever have one.

With her proposal, had she opened it up for Matt to take control of her child? That question nagged at her. If they married, he would legally have rights and she was certain he would have all sorts of opinions on how Jeff's baby should be raised and what schools it should attend. Never would she be able to pack, divorce Matt and walk away as easily as she would if she simply accepted Matt's money offer.

At the thought of relinquishing control of all decisions concerning her child, her stomach knotted. On the other hand, giving her baby the Ransome name and making him or her an heir would offset letting Matt into their lives. And from what she could see, Matt seemed to truly want what was best for her child.

She had never had a decent home life. She glanced around

the splendid bedroom and knew she would be giving her offspring the best.

And Matt? How long could they resist the sizzling physical
attraction? She didn't want to ever love another Ransome,
another untrustworthy male and in this case, an arrogant, con-
trolling one. Yet even now when Matt was away from her, she
was hot and breathless merely thinking about him. It was a
volatile chemistry she didn't have with other men and it might
make living under the same roof with him a challenge. Seduction was unwanted, but would she be strong enough to resist
the attraction, she wondered.

Could she be uncompromising and walk away if he rejected
her proposal?

She couldn't answer her own question. She thought of the
money he offered, the chance for her to get through school
quickly, then care for herself and the baby. How could she
walk away from all that? Would it be horribly unfair to her child
to turn her back on Matt's offer?

Yet she suspected if she didn't walk away, he would never
come back with acceptance of her proposal. And she wanted
the Ransome name and all that went with it.

Her gaze drifted around the room again and the thought of her
baby being part of the fortune of this family took her breath! She
strolled to the window and looked out at grounds that were well
tended. Beyond them acres of range land stretched to the horizon.
The wealth of the place was so foreign to her, she might as well
have been in another country. Would Matt consider running the
risk of letting her lay claim to some of what he owned?

Matt wrote out a hasty prenuptial agreement, trying to think
of all the things he wanted to put into the document so he
would be prepared when he saw his attorney.

His mind kept jumping to Olivia, remembering watching her
and touching her. He groaned and rubbed the back of his neck.
He had known her less than twenty-four hours and he couldn't
get her out of his mind.

Disgusted with himself that he couldn't stop thinking about her, Matt went to look in the desk in his bedroom for a copy of the prenuptial agreement he'd had with Margo. They had married young and both had come from wealthy families so they had drawn up a prenup agreement, but when they parted, there had been no hassle over money. With her tremendous salary and her family's money, she cared nothing about demands on Matt. She simply wanted out of the marriage to pursue her career.

In the hall Matt passed Olivia's closed door and thought about her in the shower, water pouring over that lush body and down her long legs. He groaned and walked faster, suspecting he should go work out and burn some energy. A whole evening with Olivia was going to be hellish temptation.

"Matt—"

He turned as she opened her door and stepped into the hall. Her shirt was pulled out of her cutoffs and partially unbuttoned, the open V giving a tantalizing glimpse of heart-stopping curves and cleavage.

"I can't get the hot water faucet to turn," she said. "Is it broken or am I doing something wrong? I can't imagine the plumbing breaking in this castle."

"Oh, hell. Sorry, I forgot. I've intended to get that fixed. And the plumbing does break on occasion," he added with amusement. "I'll get a wrench. It won't take more than a minute to repair it. Or you can move to any of the other occupied bedrooms."

"I'll wait if you don't mind repairing it."

He left to get pliers, a washer and a wrench and returned to her room, taking a deep breath before he went inside. She stood by the window, and he hoped she stayed out of the bathroom.

The scent of her perfume hung in the air and he tried to ignore it and think about water and pipes. As he leaned over the tub, working on the faucet, he swore because he hadn't taken care of the plumbing before she arrived or remembered it and put her in a different bedroom.

In minutes the faucet functioned again, and he picked up his wrench and pliers. As he started out, she entered the room and they almost collided. Taking her arm, he steadied her. "Sorry, Olivia," he said.

She looked up at him and again, he was ensnared in wide, thickly lashed green eyes. Desire rocked him and her eyes half-closed in a sultry expression that took his breath. He placed one hand on the doorjamb beside her and leaned closer. When she inhaled deeply, his gaze lowered and then returned to her full lips. Hemming her in, he could feel the heat from her voluptuous body, detect the come-hither fragrance she wore.

"We can find out now and get this out of the way between us," he said softly, leaning closer.

Her eyelids drooped a fraction as she slanted him a sensual look that set his pulse pounding. He slipped his arm around her waist and heard her gasp. She was soft, warm, all curves. He took his time, giving her a chance to pull away or protest or whatever she wanted.

Instead, when she placed her hand on his forearm and gazed up at him with a hot look, his body responded. If he was damned for it, he was going to kiss her.

With a seductive look from her, he was hard, wanting her, wanting to plunder her swollen lips, to taste and explore and see what a storm he could stir in her. Never had he seen a woman who looked more ready for sex.

Somewhere in the depths of his being, he knew he was crossing a line, going against what he had sworn he would avoid. With the temptation of a Pandora's box, he couldn't resist even if he knew in his heart that he was opening himself up for unending trouble.

As he leaned closer, she tilted her head up. Her breath was sweet and she was soft in the curve of his arm. His mouth came down on hers, opening her lips, his tongue sliding inside her mouth. Hot and wet, his kiss demanded more. He wanted to discover her sexually and his kiss and his body pressing hers was the fiery beginning.

She wrapped her arms around his neck, leaned into him,

molding her soft curves against him as she kissed him in return. Her tongue played over his, stroking and stirring his blinding need.

His rational thought had been lost back there when she first pressed against him. He tightened his arm around her, pulling her closer into his embrace, leaning over her and taking her searing kisses, letting go the pent-up longing he had controlled until now.

His pulse roared, drowning out other sounds, and he thought she would melt him with her scalding kisses. Why was she so different? he wondered. His heart thudded and he was in flames while below his belt he was rock-hard. He pulled her up tightly against him as his hand slid down her back and then trailed over the enticing curve of her bottom.

Her softness fanned the fire that consumed him. He ached to drown in her softness and unleash all her promised passion.

Grabbing a silky handful of her hair, he held her. When her hips twisted against him, he groaned.

Their kiss had escalated and spun out of control, seconds becoming minutes, time lost in need. She was too hot to handle, yet too desirable to release. Danger, danger ran through his thoughts, but he paid no heed. He never wanted to stop kissing her, kisses that were etched in his memory. Kisses that bound him to her in spite of all his reluctance.

Dimly, he became aware of her hands pressed on his chest, lightly pushing against him.

With an effort he opened his eyes, looking down at her to see her watching him. He released her and she stepped away, her gaze raking over him. "That was pure lust," she whispered.

"There was nothing pure about the past few minutes," he retorted, breathing heavily, seeing her gasp for breath as much as he did.

"I wasn't going to do that," she said, shooting him a torrid glance and then snapping her mouth closed.

"It's not going to happen again," he said, grinding out his words, hating his loss of control. His insides churned because emotionally, he hadn't wanted to kiss her. Physically, he lusted to have her in his bed with her naked body against him. "I don't think either one of us intended that kiss to happen, but it did and it seemed inevitable. Now it's over and done and we can forget about it," he said, wondering if he was trying to convince himself. In a lifetime, could he forget her kisses?

"That wasn't what I intended," she repeated in a low voice.

"There's some chemistry that we both gave in to, but it doesn't need to happen again."

She gave him a level, direct look. "So you're sorry you kissed me."

"You know I'm not, but we'll go back like we were."

When she nodded and closed the door, he let out his breath and shook his head. Why had he kissed her? Every shred of common sense told him to keep his hands to himself.

Burning with desire, he stormed down the hall. The fire in her kisses had been even more than he had expected. And his thoughts seethed about her marriage proposal and the prenuptial agreement, because now he felt differently about her demands and expectations.

Their relationship had just changed. Whether she knew it yet or not, his feelings toward her had intensified. How easily she could wreck his peaceful life! His reaction to Olivia was lust. Lust and anger and he needed to keep tight control of both emotions. He promised himself he would never let down his guard with her again. After Margo he would never trust a woman. Margo had taken his heart and stomped it to a million pieces. He didn't ever want to risk his heart with another woman.

He charged into his bedroom and slammed the door, crossing to his desk to open a drawer and once again get the prenuptial agreement from his marriage. Margo had made no demands on him. She had wanted out of the marriage and between her job and her family, she'd had all the money she could possibly want so there had been no problems there. The only problem had been that he had thought he was in love with her and he suspected she had only briefly been in love with him.

Looking at stipulations, he pored over the agreement some more and jotted notes while he wondered how many of his demands Olivia would accept.

Thinking about Olivia, he paused. She was honest, intelligent and shrewd. Had Jeff had a clue about what she was really like or had he simply seen her as a gorgeous, sexy woman?

Matt knew his brother well enough to know the answer to his question as swiftly as the question had risen—Jeff wouldn't get beyond sex.

Matt dropped his pen. He did not want to marry Olivia and damned if he would! After the poverty she had lived in, he couldn't imagine that she would walk away from the comfort and luxury he was offering.

While a plan formed in his mind, he stared out the window. He would give her two days of fabulous living—fly her to Houston, buy her a fancy wardrobe and shower her with jewelry and clothes she had never been able to afford. He would wine and dine her at places that would impress the most hardened sophisticate. Then see if she still wanted to reject his offer when he turned down her marriage proposal.

He picked up his phone to call and change his appointment with his lawyer. Next he called to get the Ransome corporate jet ready.

He strode down the hall and knocked on her door.

"Just a minute," she called. She swung the door open to face him. She stood with a towel wrapped around her and looking at her was as jolting as getting socked in the middle and having the wind knocked out of him.

Her slender shoulders were bare and the white towel was a contrast to her creamy skin. The towel was midthigh and all he could think about was only a towel covered her naked body.

While heat flashed through him, his heart thudded. He wanted to reach for her, remove that towel and pull her into his arms. Memories of her kisses fanned the flames that consumed him and for an instant, he was tongue-tied.

Her hair tumbled over her shoulders and she still had a few

drops of water that sparkled on one shoulder. She had been sexy in the T-shirt and cutoffs. In a towel, she was gorgeous.

He realized he was staring and she shifted impatiently. "Yes?" she asked, tilting her head.

"Get dressed," he said, hating the husky scrape in his voice. "I've made arrangements for a plane and I'll take you shopping in Houston so we can get you some new clothes. You'll need them. We'll eat there tonight and then we can fly back here or get rooms there."

"You're not doing this to postpone having to reach a decision about my proposal, are you?" she asked.

"Partially," he admitted, suspecting it wouldn't fool her if he gave her any other answer. "We're making big, life-changing decisions about our futures, though, so what will a twenty-four hour postponement hurt?"

"It might get me fired from my job if I don't show up two nights in a row."

"You can be back by tomorrow night," he answered.

She stared at him while she seemed to be mulling things over and finally she nodded. "I can be ready in ten minutes," she said and closed the door.

He stared at the closed door and still saw the image of her in the white towel. He wiped his brow. How was he going to cope with her under his roof for the next several years? He wanted the baby close, but if every encounter with Olivia was like the last two, he would be a basket case in no time.

Matt charged back to his room to call his favorite hotel and reserve adjoining suites. He made dinner reservations and then hurried to shower and shave and get dressed to go.

Ten minutes later he entered the family room to find her waiting. His gaze raked over her, taking in her denim skirt and simple, sleeveless white cotton blouse and sandals. He suspected what few clothes she owned were practical and cheap. There would be no way she could afford anything fancy or expensive unless she had the good fortune to find it in a secondhand shop.

Even so, the sight of her made his pulse accelerate and he

still had to fight the urge to want to touch her as he squelched images of her without the denim skirt or white blouse.

"I've never flown before," she said.

"Good! You'll like it," he answered, taking her arm and steering her out of the house and toward his car. He wanted to dazzle her and make her want to stay so badly that she would give up all thought of marriage.

They drove in silence to Meacham International Airport in Forth Worth. As they approached the waiting plane, her eyes were larger than usual. She was pale and silent, gazing with awe in her expression at the sleek jet awaiting them.

In a short time they were buckled into their comfortable seats with Olivia near a window. She seemed overwhelmed and he hoped her life was changing forever today and she would never want to go back to the poverty and hard life she had known in the past.

The moment they sped down the runway and then lifted into the air, she flashed him a brilliant smile that set his heart pounding. "This is fabulous!" she exclaimed, and satisfaction shot through him. Hopefully, in forty-eight hours he would be able to tell her no to marriage and she would cave in to his terms. All her awe and pleasure over the trip were only beginning—he could imagine how she would feel after two days of lavishly showering her with whatever she wanted. He smiled in return.

Four hours later, his satisfaction had increased. He swam laps in the hotel pool while he waited for Olivia who was getting her hair cut and styled. He had dinner reservations and after the first hour with her he had left her to shop on her own.

He glanced at his watch and climbed out of the pool to dress for dinner. She had seemed as overwhelmed by the hotel as she had been by their flight. Matt smiled grimly. He didn't want to deal with her about anything, but at least now it would be on his terms and not hers.

No one could live like this for two days and then go back to a grinding job at a rough Texas honky-tonk.

He dressed in a navy suit for dinner. He had helped her

select a simple black dress for dinner tonight, a dress with a price that had made her eyes grow round with wonder.

Matt knocked on the door of her suite and waited. The door swung open and Olivia smiled at him.

Once again, she stunned him and threw him off guard. Drawing a deep breath, Matt stared at her.

Four

"Good evening," Olivia said with far more assurance than she felt. At the sight of Matt, who was handsome, commanding and appealing in an immaculate white shirt and navy suit, her qualms faded momentarily to be replaced by a jump in her pulse.

Matt's gaze drifted over her in a thorough assessment that was as provocative as a caress. "You look sensational," he said softly.

"Thank you," she replied, knowing they were treading dangerous ground. She reminded herself that he was a Ransome with all the complications of being Jeff's brother. Her smile faded and she inhaled, fighting that irresistible draw she experienced around Matt.

In spite of her wariness, she couldn't keep from being pleased by the admiration in his expression. She was certain that his compliment had been sincere. Earlier, she had hardly known herself after the hairstylist finished. Her hair was cut, the sides brought up and looped on her head, the rest tumbling down her back. Instead of the simple black dress Matt had selected, she had found a dark blue one she liked that had a low-cut, draped back and was sleeveless with a skirt that stopped inches above her knees. She loved the cool silk lining that was smooth against her skin when she stepped into it.

"Ready to go?" he asked, and she nodded, picking up her purse.

"So is this a truce, more or less?" she asked as they headed to the elevators.

"Might as well be," he answered easily, yet she had a suspicion his animosity toward her had changed little. "You've moved into my house and we'll be together a lot from now on so we might as well get along."

She smiled disarmingly at him, yet she couldn't get rid of her suspicions that his sudden change in attitude hid an ulterior motive. Whether it did or not, she intended to enjoy the evening. She was with a handsome, sexy man, going to an elegant restaurant and she was dressed in the most gorgeous, expensive dress she had ever owned. Tonight she was Cinderella. She would enjoy herself until the clock struck twelve or whatever happened to burst her bubble.

Today, his kisses had rocked her. Remembering caused her lips to tingle. She hated that he had stirred feelings she thought were long dormant.

His kiss had plundered and all that pent-up desire that burned in the depth of his blue eyes had poured into his kiss and demolished any resistance she might have had. Tonight she would be even more susceptible to his charm.

As they left the hotel and climbed into a limousine, it came to her what he was possibly doing—giving her a taste of a lifestyle she had never known, but soon would be able to afford if she accepted his offer.

Anger flashed at the realization of his motive. Of course that was what he was doing! His smiles held all the threat of a crouching tiger. In his own way, Matt was fighting for what he wanted. Yet she couldn't blame him, because she was doing the same with her threat to walk if he didn't accept her terms.

They rode in the back of the limo across from each other and she smiled at him.

Desire blazed in his eyes, cutting across the battle between them. While she watched, he reached into his pocket. "I bought something for you today," he said, handing a small box to her.

Surprised, she glanced at the box and then at him. She was tempted to throw it at him for what he was doing, but then she reminded herself that he was trying to win her over to agreeing to his offer just as much as she intended to persuade him to consent to her proposal.

She opened the box. Nestled inside was a gold, diamond-studded bangle. Catching the light, the diamonds sparkled. "It's beautiful!" she gasped, momentarily forgetting his motive or her caution, because she had never dreamed of owning such a piece of jewelry.

He reached over to pick it up. Taking her hand in his warm, strong fingers, he slipped the bracelet on her slender wrist.

"Thank you! It's absolutely gorgeous!" she exclaimed, her emotions churning because all at once, she was both thrilled to receive the jewelry from him and at the same time, she was annoyed. Beneath those warring emotions ran an undercurrent that saddened her that the gift held no meaning whatsoever. It was simply a beautiful bribe.

"There's something to go with it," he said, smiling at her, and her heart skipped a beat. His bone-melting smiles were irresistible, so her guard came up again because she knew she was treading on dangerous ground. In icy clarity, she realized that with this Ransome her heart was more at risk than it had been with his younger brother.

Matt withdrew another small box and handed it to her. If his motive hadn't been so underhanded, she would have been dazzled. As it was, she gazed at him solemnly, telling herself she could still refuse his offer. Cinderella for a day. She could turn her back on this and survive. But it was beginning to nag at her whether if she did, and lost her big gamble, would she be cheating her baby of a better future?

She opened the box and gasped again. Even when she knew it would hold another beautiful, expensive bauble, she stared at the golden necklace with a diamond pendant that matched her bracelet.

In a smooth movement, he slid onto the seat beside her. "Turn around," he said, taking the necklace from her hand.

When she turned her back, his warm fingers brushed her nape. Reaching behind her head, she held her hair up while he fastened the necklace and then she faced him. He sat close enough that their thighs touched and his blue eyes bore into her, causing her heart to race.

"Thank you. They're both beautiful."

"You're what's beautiful, Olivia," he said softly, brushing a stray tendril of hair away from her ear.

He was only inches away and desire, like heat lightning flashed, holding them locked in the moment. When his gaze lowered to her mouth, she thought he surely could hear her heart pounding. She should move, but it was impossible. She fought the urge to slip her arm around his neck and pull him the last few inches, to draw him close and lose herself in his hot kisses.

"I thought we both agreed we weren't going to do this," she said, as much to herself as to him. She closed her eyes and turned away.

He slipped onto the seat facing her. Even while hot desire still burned in the depths of his blue eyes, the tight clamp of his jaw reflected a tense, angry look in his expression.

"You're right. We'll eat and then get the hell back to the ranch," he said, looking out a window.

"Regrets for bringing me here?"

His head swung around and she braced against the force of his gaze. He shook his head. "Not at all. You should have this. Before long, one way or another, you get a tidy sum of money to buy whatever clothes or car you want. You might as well get some things now."

She bit back her reply when the limo stopped at the front door of a restaurant.

Even though the sun was still above the horizon, tiny lights twinkled in the bushes while large lights shone on tall pines. As she emerged from the limo, Matt took her arm.

They were led through the restaurant past a dance floor where couples already circled to piano music. The waiter seated Matt and Olivia at a table on the patio near a splashing fountain. Brightly colored lanterns were glowing overhead and red roses filled crystal vases on each linen-covered table. In the festive ambience with Matt at her side, Olivia bubbled with excitement.

Their waiter appeared, placing thick black folders with the menu in front of them. Olivia opened hers. She glanced at Matt who was reading his menu and then she looked down at her own. The dishes sounded exotic and the prices astounded her.

"I can't believe we're eating anything as expensive as these dinners," she said.

"The food here is very good," he said. "Do you like lobster?"

She shrugged. "Actually, I've never eaten lobster so I have no idea whether I'd like it or not."

"I suggest you try it and then you'll know."

"The daredevil Ransomes who will always try the unknown," she said quietly, thinking about Matt and Jeff.

"Life is exciting."

"Maybe from your perspective. From mine, life is survival."

"It doesn't have to be from now on," he said smoothly waving his hand to include their surroundings and she was aware again of the clash of wills between them. "My offer will open all the doors for you," he added.

"Marriage wouldn't be real and it wouldn't be permanent," she reminded him and they paused when the waiter appeared.

After they had ordered, she gazed across the table at Matt. "The clothes are beautiful, the jewelry breathtaking and my first flight was thrilling. My first limo ride was unforgettable. But you're not going to hold me with the life you're dangling in front of me now," she said softly. Something flickered in the depths of his eyes. Otherwise there was no reaction from him except an arch of his eyebrow.

"Don't lose sight of the fact that if you turn down my offer, you'll be taking all sorts of opportunities away from your baby. Do you want to raise a child in a neighborhood like you grew up in, instead of the Ransome ranch or a house you can afford in a prosperous neighborhood with a suitable school? You've got to think for two. It's not only you," he reminded her quietly, and her anger soared.

"Dammit, I'm taking that into consideration, but I'm not selling short of what I know my baby should have," she said, hurting because Matt was right. Pain was tight in her chest, and she fought back tears that startled her since she rarely ever cried. His accusation had been on target and hurt badly. But she wanted the Ransome heritage locked in for her baby. "You'll commit to a point and then it stops."

"It's a damn generous commitment, I'd say," he retorted.

"I'll do something to stay out of bad neighborhoods. There are some acceptable jobs out there that I can do and I'll find one. I've gotten farther now than all the odds indicated I would."

"That you have. But don't sell the baby short to try to get me to marry you. Jeff wouldn't, and I'm not going to either."

His words stabbed into her, deepening her hurt. "That's your answer?" she asked, wondering if he would abandon her on the spot. She held her breath while fear chilled her.

"No, it's not my answer. I believe you'll walk so I'm still contemplating the future. I'm not deciding something that important without giving it a lot of thought. Now, on that note, try to enjoy the evening."

"Oh, right," she answered, yet his reply rekindled her hope.

"I mean it," he said in a softer voice. "Had we met under other circumstances, we both could probably enjoy the next few hours. Neither of us will take decisive action tonight, so relax."

"That's a tall order," she remarked.

"It's simple." He stood and came around the table to take her hand. "We'll get away from our problems. Let's dance."

"I can't dance," she said.

He shook his head. "You've got two feet and you can move, so you can dance. I'll show you," he said, ignoring her protest and leading her inside to the dance floor. Her heart drummed as she looked at couples moving so easily together.

"I really can't dance. I never did get around to learning and most of my life has been spent studying and working and trying to survive."

"That's going to change," he said, pulling her into his arms. "Just move with me," he said, holding her lightly. Their proximity was volatile, and every nerve in her body quivered with awareness. As his thighs brushed hers, her desire flamed. His hand held hers against his chest.

She stepped lightly on his toe and almost stumbled, but his arm tightened around her and he held her. "Sorry. I told you—" she said.

"Don't worry. You're a feather and it doesn't matter," he said, interrupting her. "I'm holding you so you're not going to fall," he added in a husky voice.

In minutes it became easier to follow his lead. Even so, when the music stopped she stepped back. "End of first lesson. Let's sit the next one out."

"Fine," he said, taking her arm to lead her back to their table.

When they were seated, over glasses of water and tossed green salads, she paused to study him. "You know a lot about me, but I know very little about you. Jeff was a party boy—he seldom mentioned his family or background."

"He probably talked about himself and his wild exploits. My kid brother and I weren't much alike. At least, I've always hoped we weren't because Jeff was damned irresponsible. What do you want to know about me?"

"Start with telling me about your family," she asked, curious about him because whenever she had approached the subject of family with Jeff Ransome, he had talked about himself.

"There's my dad who has heart trouble and isn't in good health, but he still wants to be in charge and that's why I have my own house. The big house is down the road a ways."

"The big house!" she exclaimed. "I can't imagine one much larger than yours."

"Oh, yes. Bigger, fancier. All it needs is a moat around it and we'd have a castle. I'll take you to see it and meet Dad soon."

"So where do the other family members live? Tell me about Nick and Katherine."

"We're all close in age. I'm thirty-two, Nick is thirty-one and Katherine is twenty-eight. Business is Nick's first love. He's CEO of Ransome Energy and under Nick's control the family oil business has tripled in size, gone public and continues to grow. Nick thrives on making deals."

"Is he married?"

"No. Nick isn't the marrying kind. He's almost as wild as Jeff was, but not quite. Nick is reliable—there's the big difference."

"What about your sister?"

"Katherine has a home in Dallas and one here on the ranch. Nick has his own ranch near ours. She's single and she's a graphic artist, but she specializes in murals. At the moment she's painting one for a museum in Chicago. She's quite good."

"So how long were you married?"

To her surprise his eyes clouded over. "Two years. Margo preferred a career to marriage. Her family is wealthy, so she didn't need the money from the career, but she wanted everything else that went with it."

"What does she do now?"

"She's a news anchor in L.A. now. I suppose in the beginning, I could have gone with her if I'd been willing to leave the ranch and leave Texas, but I have my own agenda and didn't like the idea of tagging along wherever her career led her. Her career is first in her life."

"So you still love her?"

"No, I'm over Margo, but that was a bad time when we divorced. It wasn't what I'd planned."

"And what happened to your mother? Is she no longer living?"

"I don't know," he answered with a cold tone. "When we

were little kids, she walked out on us. There was another man and she married him, but it didn't last a year." Matt's brows arched. "You haven't heard any of this before?"

"No," she said. "Jeff really did focus solely on himself. In spite of that, he was charming and entertaining and drew friends like a picnic drawing ants, but then you know about him. So tell me about your mother. You didn't finish."

"My dad raised us. We've had no contact with her which is the way she obviously wanted it."

"That's dreadful. Do you even know where she lives?"

"No," he said, a shuttered look coming to his expression. "None of us want any contact now that we're grown and she certainly hasn't wanted any since she disappeared out of our lives."

"Sorry."

He shrugged. "That's the way I've grown up. I don't think about it any longer."

"So you're the cowboy in the family who loves the ranch."

"Yes. I get away occasionally. I like to ski and to escape from the ranch. Occasionally, I go to the tropics. We own three ranches, this one, one in Wyoming and one along the California coast and we're buying one we've leased in Argentina."

"As in South America?"

"Right. It's the best ranch of all. It's the one I prefer."

"And Jeff helped you here?"

"Jeff worked with me when he wasn't off gallivanting around the world. He couldn't possibly have settled and worked in an office like Nick is doing. You'll meet my family soon."

"And they approve of your offer to me?"

"Sure. Everyone is interested. A new Ransome in the family would be damn good."

"Seems to me, among the three of you, one of you could produce a grandchild."

"There's already a grandchild on the way." His gaze swept over her. "Have you felt all right?"

She nodded. "Fine. Not even any morning sickness."

"You definitely are pregnant."

"That's a statement and not a question, isn't it? I'm sure you checked that one out and you know who my doctor is."

"Sorry about checking up on you, but I had to be certain."

The waiter brought their lobster dinners. After the first bite, she looked up to find him waiting and watching her.

"It's delicious. You want me to like eating lobster. You want me to cultivate a taste for exotic food."

"I don't know that lobster is exotic. Every grocery store carries them, but I'm glad you like it," Matt answered.

"It's another sales pitch," she said, touching her diamond pendant and knowing that he was doing all in his power to get her to accept his offer and forget her proposal.

"Ma'am, I'm a plain ole cowboy," he drawled, and she had to laugh.

He gave her a wicked look. "Olivia, you're doing your own share of bribery with your smile that seduces and befuddles. You want me to succumb and accept your proposal and you're stooping to as much bribery as I am," he said softly.

"My smile seducing and befuddling?" she asked in mock disbelief, for a moment letting go worries and enjoying his company, bubbling inside because he was flirting.

"You know what you're doing," he said, inhaling deeply and she flashed him another merry smile, wishing she could befuddle him enough to get him to agree to what she wanted.

"Yes! So may the best man—or woman—win!" she exclaimed, holding her water glass up in a toast to him.

Eyes twinkling, he touched her glass with his. "You're on. But then this battle is already under way."

"And you're flirting shamelessly," she said. "Besides the gifts and dinner and clothes and the evening out."

"All my weaponry pales beside yours—your face, your body, your smile, that dress, your legs. You have the edge and you know it."

"Whoo!" She fanned herself. "I didn't know you'd noticed," she purred, enjoying flirting with him. "You have armor that protects you totally. You are shielded and immune."

"Forget dinner. Let's dance," he said, coming around the table to take her hand to lead her to the dance floor. After a few minutes he looked down at her. "You've gotten the hang of it. You're very good at this."

She laughed. "Your flattery overwhelms me! Wait until I step on your toe again."

"I mean it. You're doing fine. Don't you like this?" he asked in a silky voice.

She slanted him a look. "You're flirting again."

"So what's wrong with that? No harm done. You're a beautiful woman and a sexy one. Why shouldn't I flirt?"

"Don't expect it to lead you anywhere."

"Where did you think I want to go?" he asked.

She shook her head and laughed again. "Don't tell me you don't want me in your bed."

"I'll tell you one thing I don't want in my life—any emotional complication. Judging by your demands, I don't think you want any in your life."

"I definitely don't. Not with a Ransome, thank you."

"I take it you and I will never have a handshake deal, even if we finally do come to a mutual agreement?"

"I keep my word."

"I'll damn well keep mine," he said. "Stop mixing me up with Jeff."

The next number was a fast one and when she turned to leave, he caught her hand.

"I really can't do this—" she protested.

"You're a quick study. Watch my feet and then follow me," he said, pulling her with him.

She did what he said and soon she was dancing with him. He spun her around, caught her and then returned to the quick steps. She studied his feet for a few more minutes and then looked up to find him watching her intently. Her heartbeat skipped and she drew her breath, tossing her head and feeling her hair swing.

"Perfect," he said softly.

"Not really. I've stepped on you twice."

"Never felt it. Accept my offer, Olivia, and have a better life and an easier one," he urged. "We're a mere technicality away from what you want."

She shook her head. "That isn't quite the same."

He spun her around and yanked her up against him, his arm banding her waist instantly and holding her close while he looked down at her. She felt his hard length pressed against her and she wanted to wrap her arms around his neck and kiss him. At the same time, she looked into his eyes and felt the clash with him over their futures. She knew the light moments were gone and the flirting was over.

He spun her away from him and then the music stopped. Gasping for breath, she let him take her hand and she felt the calluses on his palm that indicated he really did do ranch work.

"Let's go back to the hotel and talk things over," he suggested.

Knowing they might as well get back to business, she nodded. At the door she glanced back over her shoulder. In the past couple of hours, she had had the time of her life, the best she could remember.

She was surprised by her own reaction and wondered if she had really been in love with Jeff at all.

In the limo she was as silent as Matt, aware they were each locked in separate worlds. At the hotel as they reached their adjoining suites, Matt shed his coat and tie and unfastened the collar of his shirt. "Let me come in for a while. I'll order tea or lemonade or whatever you'd like," he suggested.

She nodded and opened her door, moving inside. He followed and tossed his coat on a chair. "What would you like to drink?" he asked.

"Hot cocoa," she said, wondering if she could drink anything. Her nervousness had returned, but she didn't want it to show. All evening she had felt as if what she wanted was slipping through her fingers. She could feel his resistance to her offer. When he said no, was she ready to make her decision and stick by it?

He ordered a pot of hot chocolate and a cold beer. Only one lamp burned in the fancy suite and in the soft light, his appeal heightened. It would have been easier to deal with him if she hadn't had this fiery sexual reaction to him. And why the chemistry she couldn't imagine because they fought for opposing goals. She suspected he truly did not like her at all. Facing him, she knew part of his attraction was his rugged good looks and a sexiness that probably drew most females he encountered.

He moved around the room, turning on soft music, dimming the light, rolling back his cuffs, seductive moves, yet she knew seduction wasn't his goal. He wanted her to agree to his offer. His control was admirable because she guessed it was an effort for him. She suspected he usually got his way.

At a knock on the door, she watched Matt cross the room in long strides to let the bellman wheel in a cart with a silver pot, china cups and two cold beers on ice. Olivia sat on a wingback chair and crossed her legs. In minutes, Matt handed her a cup of steaming chocolate.

"It's too hot to drink right now," she said, placing it on a coffee table and then leaning back.

When he sat nearby and gave her a long look, she drew a deep breath. "I feel like the proverbial bug under a microscope," she said.

"An absolutely stunning butterfly, maybe. A bug—no," he answered quietly, his gaze drifting lazily over her while she couldn't avoid being pleased by his compliment. "Are you ready to discuss the terms of my offer?"

She shrugged. "It's not essential because I really do not intend to accept it. I prefer that you accept my proposal."

"Let's just say, 'What if?' and talk about my offer for a while. All right?"

"I suppose, as long as you don't abandon me here in Houston if we don't come to an agreement. I do want to return to Rincon."

"I promise to get you home and I don't intend to reach a decision tonight. I only want to talk things over. When I first approached you, we were complete strangers."

"And the brief time we've been together has made a difference?" she asked in surprise because it hadn't changed her opinions.

He set the bottle on a table. "We'll live in my house, but what happens if you want to go out with someone or start seeing someone regularly?"

She shook her head. "You're assuming we will go with your offer."

"Let's discuss it."

"It's pointless to, but if it makes you happy, all right," she said. "For now, I don't want any man in my life. Not at all. You're still going on the assumption that I'll accept your offer and we won't marry. Or do you intend the same agreement if we marry?"

His eyes narrowed and her heart began to thump faster at the determined expression on his face. "No. If we marry, I don't want sordid gossip floating around Cedar County about this baby's mother or stepfather."

"So what do you propose? A celibate life?" she asked, unable to imagine that he would agree.

"Hardly. If I agree to your marriage proposal, I want sex."

Heat blazed in her, and she could feel the perspiration break out on her forehead. While her emotions boiled, they stared at each other. "That isn't what I intended."

"That's what it would have to be."

"How often?" she shot back, trying to catch her breath and wondering if she could handle sex with Matt Ransome without falling head over heels in love with him—a love that she was certain he would never return. Could there be great sex and no love with a handsome man who was helping her raise her child? Hardly.

Fear curled in her, thick and as palpable as smoke from a fire. Jeff had broken her trust and trampled her feelings. Could she expect anything better from his older brother?

"Let's say after your pregnancy is over, twice a week and then we can go from there."

"And until my pregnancy is over?"

"I don't see any need to be definite except if I marry you, then I want a wedding night with sex."

She was certain he could hear her heart thudding. His demands were making both propositions, his and hers, real to her.

"You know what you want, don't you?" Agitated, she stood and moved to the floor-to-ceiling window to gaze down below at the lights on a sparkling pool. Was she ready for sex with him? Her body was more than ready. His words had set her ablaze, but sex was a fast track to heartbreak. Remembering his spectacular, sizzling kisses that had stormed her senses and had been the beginning of seduction, she knew he would be a fabulous lover. And that was what worried her because Matt Ransome seemed as hardhearted as they came.

"There's always my offer," he said quietly, standing close behind her. She hadn't heard him get up or move across the room. She turned to face him. He stood only a foot away. He had rolled back his sleeves and unfastened one more button on his shirt. All she could think of was sex with him—a wedding night.

"If I increased the amount of money, would you accept my offer? If I changed the hundred thousand dollars to a hundred and fifty thousand, how's that?"

Again, he shocked her and she stared at him while the amount spun in her thoughts. "If you're that willing to raise what you'll pay me, then marriage must be binding enough that you want to avoid it at all costs," she whispered.

Matt stood waiting quietly, letting her think about the money. He could afford what he had offered and he did not want marriage, yet standing so close to her, gazing into her wide green eyes, his pulse raced and he was hot with desire. She was stunning with her new hairdo and clothes. She had been a looker before, but now she was breathtaking. Men had watched her all evening in a restaurant where people would be far more restrained than the honky-tonk at home.

No matter how enticing she was, he didn't want a permanent entanglement. Even with the increase in his offer, he felt to his soul that she was going to hold out for marriage.

He inhaled deeply, his gaze sweeping over her slender bare shoulders and long, graceful throat, the soft curves that the dress hugged and her tiny waist. Her long legs were spectacular. He already knew that from seeing her in the towel and cutoffs. Could he take her to bed, live under the same roof, share a baby with her and still keep his heart locked away?

He had no doubt that once she got her law degree, she would be gone. He hoped by that time, she would feel that her child was part of the Ransome family. In the meantime he better worry about the present. What would he do if she turned down his offer?

"I've made you a damned handsome offer," he said aloud, half to her and half to himself.

"I know you have. It was generous before you raised the amount. It's the long-term commitment I want."

"I'll never love again," he said. "You better believe me because I do what I say."

"I imagine you do," she replied, looking up at him. "Jeff told me about how your father got lost one time when his small plane crashed in the Rocky Mountains and after the searchers gave up hunting for him, you flew up there, trekked into the mountains on your own and found him and brought him out of there on a stretcher you improvised. Jeff said you do what you say and you don't give up. Actually, he said you're stubborn as a mule."

"As if he wasn't. I knew my dad was there and I wasn't going to leave him. He had broken one leg and he couldn't get out on his own and no one else survived the crash. My dad is a tough old codger."

"I suspect you're rather tough yourself."

"If so, I've had to be sometimes," he replied, fighting an urge to reach out and touch her. In spite of the conflict between them and his anger, he wanted her. Desire was a throbbing, hot flame tormenting him. She was beautiful and he couldn't stop wanting to hold and kiss her.

"And stubborn?"

"I suppose. If it's stubborn of me to avoid falling in love

again, then so be it. I believe you have a streak of that trait yourself," he said, and she smiled at him. "So you still plan to move on someday?" he asked.

"We both know marriage will give the baby more," she said, ignoring his question.

Every minute with her he had been torn between anger and attraction and that was still true. They were at an impasse, and his desire was escalating. He knew he needed to get distance between them.

"I'll sleep on it," he said. He strode out the door into the hall, closing her door quietly behind him and going to his room.

Shedding his clothes he moved around his room. Sleep wasn't going to be part of his night. Would she walk away from all he offered simply to hold out for marriage?

He absolutely didn't want to marry again. Not even if the woman was fabulously beautiful and sexy? The question taunted him because he couldn't extinguish memories of holding her in his arms, of her scalding kisses, or how stunning she had looked tonight. How badly he had wanted to peel her out of that scrap of a dress! Marriage would mean sex with her. She had already agreed to it.

He groaned, knowing sleep was impossible. He glared at the door that led to her room. She would give up most of the cash if he would marry her, but that didn't matter because cash was no problem for him.

Coming from the background of poverty, she had a far smaller regard for money than he would have expected.

Feeling hemmed in and wishing they had flown home tonight, he paced his room and then moved to the window to stare outside. It was late and traffic had thinned. He wasn't giving up the baby. Deep down, he still felt that she would disappear if he rejected her proposal. "Dammit!" he swore, knotting his fists, wishing he could walk away. She knew she had what he wanted.

By morning, after a shave and shower, he continued to toss the choices back and forth in his mind. He went around to knock on her door and stood waiting, wondering how she had slept.

She opened the door and gazed up at him. Dressed in a white suit and red blouse, once again, she looked stunning. Her hair was looped and pinned on one side of her head, giving her a more sophisticated appearance. No amount of fancy clothes or cosmopolitan hairdos could extinguish her sultry, sexy aura and there was no stopping his body's immediate response to the sight of her.

Matt drew a deep breath. "Good morning."

"Good morning," she replied and stepped back. "Won't you come in?"

As he entered the room, he inhaled the seductive scent she wore. He wanted to tangle his fingers in her hair and pull it down. At the same time he wanted to send her packing. Never since childhood had he had to battle someone and lose as he was with her. Even when Margo left him, at the end he had been angry, but ready for her to get out of his life. He couldn't handle Olivia. It was the first time in his life he had been in this position and he didn't like it.

Staring at Olivia, he was tempted to tell her to pack and go if she wouldn't accept his terms, but when he thought about losing the baby, he clamped his jaw closed more tightly.

This morning she was gorgeous and looked as self-confident as if she already had her law degree. How much easier all this would have been if she had been as plain as a guinea hen. "You're ready to fly home?"

"Isn't that what we're doing?"

"I'm not in a rush. I'll take you to breakfast." They faced each other in a tense silence. "Have you come to a decision on my offer?" he asked and held his breath.

"I still want more than money," she replied nonchalantly as if they were discussing what to order for breakfast, and his insides clenched.

"Dammit, I don't think you know what you're doing!" he snapped, trying to hold back his fury and hating to meet her terms.

"Indeed, I do," she replied with the coolness of a card shark. "So do you have an answer for my proposal?"

He jammed his fist into his pocket. In the night he had made his decision what he would do if she turned down his offer.

"How can you reject the fortune I'm extending to you? You're not thinking about your baby."

"Oh, yes, I am. I can decline your offer because I think you want my baby in your family to such an extent that sooner or later, you'll agree to my proposal. If you do, you'll make a greater commitment than what you're now suggesting I take."

"You're damn sure of yourself," he grumbled, thinking he had misjudged her by a country mile when he first saw her. She was smart, self-possessed and quickly shedding any rough edges she had from her poverty-stricken upbringing.

She merely shrugged. "I'm more sure of you," she replied softly.

He shook his head and rubbed the back of his neck. "I have to hand it to you. I usually get my way in deals. I've bought land, horses, cattle, took over a drilling company for my dad, etc., etc. and you're the only one who's held my feet to the fire and given me something I couldn't cope with."

"Do tell," she said blithely, and he wanted to grind his teeth. At the same time, he had to hand it to her for holding out for the big deal.

"At least, it's a relief to know this baby's going to inherit some brains."

"Thank you, I think. Unless you're referring solely to your brother."

"You know I'm not talking about him."

They stared at each other while silence once again filled the passing time. She smiled at him and began to move around the room, placing her bag and a sack together in a chair so her things would be ready to go. Finally, she turned to face him. "Still debating? We can go to breakfast while you think it over."

Knowing she wasn't going to change, he shook his head. There was no need in prolonging the moment of decision because he was the only one vacillating about her proposition.

Her eyebrows arched and she slanted her head. "No? That must mean you've come to a conclusion? What are you going to do? Are you going to marry me?"

Five

Olivia's pulse jumped because the fury that burned in his gaze made her think there was a possibility he would acquiesce and do what she wanted. While she waited, she held her breath and watched the battle in his tense expression. His blue eyes flashed with pinpoints of fire.

The tension ripped at her nerves and finally she blurted, "What's your decision?"

"You win. I'll marry you," he snapped in clipped words.

Joy and relief flooded her. Her baby's future had just been sealed. It held a promise for the best possible chance for a family, a caring father-figure and education for her baby. And herself. She fought the urge to throw her arms around Matt and shout her gratitude. Instead, she merely nodded and tried to bottle her bubbling response.

"I have some stipulations." He ground out the words, and she nodded.

Like a wave pounding into shore and then receding, her relief swept away and was replaced by worry over what she had gotten herself into. What was he going to require of her in exchange? One condition he had already told her was sex with him! And soon.

"Thank you," she said quietly, feeling his anger that was almost tangible enough to spark the air around them.

He inhaled deeply and gave her another long look that burned like a streak of fire. "We'll have to work out the prenup agreement," he said.

She nodded while her heart thudded. She tried to bank her excitement and keep a lid on all her expectations of what she would gain when she married into the Ransome family.

"Let's get breakfast and make plans," he suggested. "We don't have to check out of the hotel until after lunch, so while we're here in the city, if you want to shop for a wedding dress, I'll give you a list of the stores where I have accounts and you can charge it to me, or if you prefer, I'll go along and write a check or give you a card."

"It's bad luck for the groom to see the wedding dress before the wedding."

He gave her a withering look. "I don't think that old superstition applies in this case. Business arrangements have little connection to superstition."

"I prefer to shop by myself," she answered with what she hoped was as cold a voice as his.

He nodded. "I've already made an appointment for a meeting with my attorney at three o'clock this afternoon. Right now, let's go to breakfast and negotiate the details."

She nodded. "Fine. Give me one minute here," she said, going into the bedroom. She returned shortly and smiled at him. "There. I quit my job."

"That's one good thing," he said.

Picking up her purse, she walked beside him, trying to keep quiet and let him talk. His face was still flushed and a muscle still worked in his jaw. His voice was tight and she could only guess the depth of his anger. She suspected that except for his divorce, he had rarely had to give in to something he didn't like.

Breakfast was in a solarium in the hotel. She doubted if Matt appreciated or even noticed their sunny glass-covered surroundings and tall potted palms. He drank coffee, but otherwise barely touched his breakfast.

While Matt sipped his coffee and studied notes, she remained silent.

"The first stipulation I have, is if you have an abortion or a miscarriage, the deal's off on everything. We get divorced immediately and you get nothing."

"That's fine," she agreed quickly and was surprised at quirk of his lips in a crooked smile. "What's there to smile about?" she asked.

"You won the war. Now you'll let me win the battles," he observed dryly.

She flashed a smile at him. "I can be agreeable and yes, you're right. I got what I wanted on the big issue. Now I can be cooperative on other things."

His expression softened and he studied her, his gaze roaming slowly over her features as if he were trying to memorize her looks. "I intend to get what I want, too," he drawled, and a tingle spiraled in her because she knew he was no longer referring to the prenup agreement.

"So what do you want?" she asked with a jump in her pulse.

"Forbidden fruit," he answered in a sexy tone that fanned flames of desire. "Seduction," he said, drawing out the word until it became personal and enticing.

In response, her throat went dry. "You want sex and you feel lust, but there won't be any love between us or even the illusion of it."

"That doesn't mean it won't be great sex," he replied, looking at her with blatant desire in his gaze. "Are you getting cold feet and wanting out of this marriage proposal?"

She sipped her water and prayed she looked cool and collected and that he didn't have a clue what a tempest he stirred in her. "Be warned now—no love on your part will guarantee no love on my part."

"Do you really want to fall in love with me?" he asked, leaning forward and if she hadn't known better, she would have thought that there was a trace of honesty and vulnerability in his voice.

"At this point, no, indeed not! No more than you want right now—or could—fall in love with me." She raised her glass of water. "Here's to great sex, Matthew Ransome. And a marriage made at the bargaining table."

One corner of his mouth quirked, and one dark eyebrow lifted wickedly. "You tempt me," he said, leaning even closer, "to go after your heart that you've sealed away. And I would if I didn't want to keep my own heart protected. Risk your heart and you risk heartbreak."

"So we'll both be locked in to living together and trying to resist falling in love. And you think it'll be an easy task."

"I know myself and know what heartbreak is," he said gruffly. He reached the short distance between then and drew his fingers along her cheek, sending flames of desire to a scalding temperature. "So you're willing to marry me and have sex to get what you want. You're willing to risk your future."

"I'm securing my future. Not risking it," she said, correcting him and failing to keep the breathlessness out of her voice. "The whole point of this is to take care of my baby," she added, unable to look away from his intense gaze that held her now. Her heart pounded and she suspected if there had been no table between them and they hadn't been in public, he would kiss her. And she wanted him to. Unable to resist, she reached up to stroke his cheek just as he had hers. His jaw was clean-shaven and smooth. The moment she touched him, desire enveloped her with the heat of a furnace.

"You're taking risks, too, to get what you want," she whispered. "Your heart may belong to me someday, Matt Ransome." The clash of wills between them was covered with an icing of desire, creating an emotional dessert that held the potential for spicy, red-hot sex. Goaded by his announced intention to resist falling in love when he planned to seduce her, she leaned the last bit of space and placed her lips on his. Before she closed her eyes, she saw the flash of surprise in his.

Then she was lost. His hand went behind her head and her kiss became his kiss. His tongue thrust deeply into her mouth with possessive, demanding strokes that caused her heart to pound. Her body responded fully to him, aching, on fire with wanting him. They were in public, restrained by their surroundings and with an effort she leaned away. Trying to get her breath, she opened her eyes to find him watching her.

"Sex is going to be great," he whispered.

"I'm going to make you open that vault to your heart," she flung back at him, realizing right now that if they had sex, she would want his love that he kept locked and guarded.

"No, you're not," he answered firmly, but she noticed with satisfaction the perspiration that dotted his forehead and his flushed face.

She leaned closer again. "Let's see how long you can resist me, Matt," she challenged, and he inhaled.

"Don't try to work your magic on me."

"I don't have any magic," she rejoined and his eyebrows arched.

"The hell you don't," he said, tracing her jaw with his finger. "No woman should have the effect on men that you do."

"Do I really now?" she asked, surprised that she had any remarkable impact on Matt.

"You know damn well you do! At least this marriage is going to have some real pluses and some challenges."

"And you like a challenge?"

"Of sorts. I'm not happy about being pushed into marriage."

"You're not being pushed. You can say no. You pointed that out to me on your offer."

"Dammit," he said quietly while he glared at her, and she knew even though he had accepted her proposal, he wished he didn't have to marry her. "We might as well get the questions answered and settled."

He sipped his coffee and looked at the notepad he had placed on the table beside his plate. While she ate a delicious bowl of peaches, she watched him scribble notes. The waiter brought golden omelets, but Olivia's appetite had vanished. So had Matt's because he didn't even attempt to eat, merely reading and writing notes and sipping his coffee.

Determined to avoid letting him know what butterflies she had and how uptight she was, she forced herself to take bites of her breakfast and try to get it down.

"It won't go in the prenup, but once we're married, I expect you to stay faithful. I'll do the same."

She nodded. "Our vows will cover that one."

"You said we'd dissolve our marriage after you get your law degree. As far as I'm concerned, this marriage, if we do enter into it, might as well be permanent."

"Permanent! And what do you mean—if we enter into it? I thought we agreed this is what we're doing."

"We did, but a lot of things can happen between now and weeks or months from now."

She wondered what he had in mind and was there something he was going to do to try to get her to back out of the marriage agreement. And permanent was mind-boggling. "I never planned on permanent!"

"If we're getting married, then a lasting marriage is a good business arrangement. I'll get to raise Jeff's baby, and you'll be educated and provided for and have a family for your baby. Neither of us wants an emotional entanglement, yet we'll have sex in our lives. Who knows—by then, we might be in love."

Setting down her fork with her omelet only barely touched, she drew a deep breath, suddenly feeling as if walls were closing in on her. "I can't envision being married to you for the rest of my life."

"You can always file for divorce if you want out. You know that."

"Yes, but I had no intention of going into this with permanency in mind."

"Can't you see where that would be best for your baby?"

She stared at him. Marriage to Matt Ransome. Permanent as in *forever.* Endless with no emotional entanglement, according to him. Impossible to her.

"You can't do forever?" he asked quietly, and she suspected he was pushing this condition to get her to back off from the whole marriage concept, which she had no intention of doing.

"Yes, I can do 'as long as we both shall live'," she answered, stiffening her resolve to see these nuptials through, "if everlasting is what you want." She would deal with that one as time went by.

"I would like to adopt the baby so it's mine and there's none of this stepdad stuff," Matt declared.

Joy bubbled in her over the adoption suggestion that she hadn't dreamed he would make. She nodded. "Great! That's gratifying to hear."

"I think we said the sum I'll settle on you will be one hundred thousand."

"I told you that you can cut it in half if we marry."

He shook his head. "No. We'll leave it at one hundred." His blue eyes got that piercing look that drove into her like knives. He leaned closer over the table. "One hundred thousand is enough money for you to marry, get the Ransome name and then take the money and run. You could disappear."

"I won't do that."

"Damn straight, you won't! I'll find you," he said with steel back in his voice. She had no doubt that he would do exactly as he said, but she had no intention of running out on the deal he was offering. "Part of our bargain is that you don't run out on me. My mother did that to her family. My first wife all but did that with me."

"If I repeat vows, I'll live up to my promises," she said and gazed back at him unflinchingly. He gave her a long, hard look with icy blue eyes, but instead of chilling her, she faced him and noticed his long, thick eyelashes, bedroom eyes. A lock of black hair fell on his forehead. He had thick hair that held a slight wave and a firm jaw that gave him a rugged appearance, yet at the same time, he was handsome with his straight nose and prominent cheekbones.

She wondered if she was sinking herself in a quicksand of heartbreak. How easy it was going to be to fall in love with him! For all his gruffness and reined-in anger, there had been flashes of charm when they had been out on the town last night, as well as a few minutes ago when he was flirting with her. She had vowed she would never again trust a Ransome or get involved with one, yet here she was committing to the closest possible relationship with a Ransome who had his heart locked away.

"I'll draw up a will. I own the ranches with my father, brother and sister and we want them to stay in the family. If something happens to me, my share will go directly to the baby when he or she reaches twenty-one. The money I have will be divided between you and to the baby. Fair enough?"

She nodded. "For a man not in love with me, you're making another generous offer."

As he inhaled deeply, she wondered what was running through his mind because she couldn't possibly guess. Somehow she suspected he was wishing he could have the baby and get rid of her, but then she might be wrong.

He shifted and his knee bumped hers. His eyes narrowed while she felt a tingle from the contact.

"I need to meet your family," she said.

"I know. I'll get them together."

"You're not touching your breakfast," she said quietly.

"I don't have any appetite," he replied, biting off the words abruptly. He fluctuated between flirting with her and then giving way to his suppressed fury over having to acquiesce to her wishes. In the moments when his charm and appeal surfaced, she found him irresistible.

She suspected after marriage he would accept their bargain and then she would have his charm and sex appeal to deal with daily, a possibility that gave her a tingly anticipation and at the same time, sent warnings of heartbreak pounding in her mind.

Where Matt's brother had been an engaging fun-filled boy,

Matt was a devastating man with charm and sex appeal that overwhelmed her.

"I don't think we'll have an issue about the baby's education since you fought so hard to get one," Matt said, scribbling more notes while she nodded.

"I'll still open an account for you with the one hundred thousand in it. That is your money. I'll pay the ranch expenses, etc. and open a joint account for us."

"You continue to surprise me," she said, again amazed by his magnanimity when she knew he was unhappy with her.

"We might as well work together. We're binding our lives together forever," he added and she wondered about her future with him. "Hopefully," he continued, "we'll stop fighting each other."

She laughed. "I wouldn't count on that one," she exclaimed, leaning closer. "You intend to seduce me. You want my body." She placed her hand over his on the table. "If you do, I'll warn you now—I'll seduce you because I'll want your heart."

"I thought you were going to try to avoid another heartbreak."

She shook her head. "We're on a different course since I made that declaration. We're marrying, and you're making it permanent. If that's the case, and we'll be intimate, then I want more than lust and a purely physical relationship for the rest of my life. I want love."

"Once again, you want more," he repeated, smiling at her. "Where have I heard that before? Only this time, you won't have the leverage you did about marriage." He turned his hand to take hers and rub his thumb across her knuckles, stirring tingles. "You're flirting with me, Olivia."

"So I am. Don't deny that you like it."

"Of course, I like for you to flirt and to kiss. As you said, we're stuck with each other now, so we should make—" he paused and desire heated his gaze "— love, as well as the best of it," he finished in a velvety drawl that held its own caress. "I'll have to say that you're damn cooperative now that you've got what you want."

"I try," she said, bestowing a smile.

He laughed and straightened up, releasing her hand. "I'll get you a wedding ring. We need to make some decisions about the wedding first. How about a small wedding?"

She tingled at the prospect and wondered if she could go through with this loveless marriage of convenience—even with Prince Charming, which Matt had been on occasion. "That's fine," she said, but her words were breathless and her head spun. Marriage—and then she would be in Matt's bed. Sex with Matt Ransome! Again she thought about sex with him—over and over she thought of it. Her palms felt sweaty, and she watched him writing in his notebook. If he was disturbed or gave the notion of sex with her any of his attention, he was hiding it well.

"I'll pay the wedding bills, of course," he continued. " If you don't have a particular church, we can be married at the ranch. The only people I want to invite will be our cowboys and my family."

Trying to get back to thinking about what she was doing instead of sex with Matt, she mulled over his suggestions and shook her head. "You're so concerned about my baby—which will soon be our baby. Maybe you should think about inviting a lot of your friends, too. Otherwise, I'm not too likely to be accepted by some people because of my background and where I've worked," she said, and he nodded.

"You're right. Good decision."

"Why do I get the feeling that from the first, you've expected the worst from me?" she asked.

"Maybe I misjudged you. You constantly surprise me. But it's for the good, so that should be all right," he admitted. "We'll have the whole deal, a big wedding and reception."

"Why not a small, private wedding and then the big reception?"

He shook his head. "I'd say the big wedding because I want people to accept you as much as any other member of my family and there will be a reluctance by some locals for the reasons you said and because you were close to my brother who had a reputation for being the wild man of the county."

"I'm three months pregnant."

"Won't matter. You don't look it anyway. I'll hire someone to work with you to plan this wedding."

"If we have a big wedding, it will take time to plan."

"No. I'll hire a wedding planner who can get everything ready. I'll call family and close friends. Word will get around before the invitations. You get your wedding dress right away," he said, starting a new list, writing while he talked. She wondered exactly how much wealth the Ransome family had because Matt didn't seem daunted by anything except her proposal.

She had butterflies dancing a ballet in her stomach at the thought of a big wedding with all his family and friends present. "Matt, I don't have any family and only a few friends."

"Doesn't matter. Most of the county will come to the wedding and lots of people from other counties and from Fort Worth. Matter of fact, guests will come from everywhere because my brother and sister get around. By the way, you have carte blanche on this."

"You already trust my judgment?" she asked.

His gaze drifted down over her as far as he could see with the table blocking his view and then back up in a leisurely, thorough study that curled her toes and made her forget business. "You have good taste. You look like a professional woman this morning—like the lawyer you will be someday. Last night you looked fabulous. I think I can trust you with the wedding decisions. I'll help with the wedding at the ranch because we've had so many catered parties there. I already have a battery of people who can handle all aspects of the reception. We should open an account for you today."

She nodded, growing more dazed with each of his quick decisions. It all seemed like a dream, magical, impossible, yet the man beside her was real enough. And the most fabulous, awesome aspect of all—her baby would officially be a Ransome. Matt would help raise him or her.

What was impossible to put out of mind and ran in an undercurrent of thought all the time they talked was the far more immediate prospect of sex with Matt—getting naked with each other. The thought stirred a burning low in her middle. And would there ever be more than lust and a baby between them?

He pulled out a small black book, flipped it open and scribbled in it, turning to hold it out to her. "How's this date for our wedding?"

Stunned, she stared at the black circle he had drawn and then she looked up at him.

<u>Six</u>

"I couldn't possibly!" she exclaimed while she stared at the date circled—next Saturday. "This is Monday! This week—not even a full week to get ready for the biggest event in my life, a complete life change, an enormous wedding with your relatives and friends. Impossible!" she exclaimed, trying to ignore a feeling of panic that surged while she reminded herself this had been her idea and she was getting what she desired.

Part of her wanted to ask for a year to get ready. The other part would like the wedding as soon as possible, to lock her into the Ransome family before something happened that changed Matt's mind or made the wedding impossible. Next weekend—it sounded the same as tomorrow.

His blue gaze settled on her. "You're quiet. Getting cold feet?"

"Never," she replied emphatically. "I want this with all my heart."

While they looked solemnly at each other, she knew they each had different goals for their futures. And they each would fight for what he or she wanted. She knew that, too.

He glanced at his watch. "We should select invitations today. I'll get a list of guests and get someone at the Ransome office to address the invitations and get them out at once."

"Matt, we can't do this in a few days. Give me another week at least."

"All right. The date will be the following Saturday," he said with assurance in his tone. "Let's go. I have calls to make, and you can shop for your wedding dress. We can meet back at the hotel for a late lunch around one. When we fly home, we'll go to Fort Worth and open a bank account for you. How's that?" As he talked, he fished his billfold out of his pocket, withdrew a credit card and flipped it over on the table so it landed in front of her. "Buy whatever you want," he said casually and she stared at him. "Or if you don't find what you want, we can go to Fort Worth to shop. Or Dallas."

"I'll find something," she said, quietly. "Thank you."

"And you're surprised again, aren't you? You must think I'm a green-headed ogre."

"No. I'm simply amazed you're so generous when you're angry with me. And I didn't know your family had such wealth," she said.

He gave her a dubious look. "C'mon. That's common knowledge in the county. It runs back to the fortune my great-granddaddy made on cattle and land."

She shook her head. "Your brother flashed money, but no more than a lot of other cowboys and until he left for the mountain trek, he didn't do anything that made him look particularly prosperous except play poker. He never took me home with him, so yesterday was the first time I've ever seen the Ransome ranch."

Matt shrugged and gave her a rueful smile. "You get your way on the future for both of us, so why should I stay angry or try to keep things from you when you'll be my wife next week?"

Wife next week. She was glad she was sitting down because her head spun at the thought of becoming Mrs. Matt Ransome so soon.

"We pick up and go on from here," Matt continued. "I don't want revenge because you and I are going to be a unit. From here on, it would be like fighting myself."

"And you're not?" she asked softly, unable to resist flirting with him now that their future together was sealed.

"Not what? Fighting myself?"

She smiled at him. "You don't want to be attracted to me. It aggravates you that you want to kiss me."

"Maybe so," he said, leaning close enough again to start her heart pounding. "Sooner or later, we'll work things out. I just usually manage to get my way and this is one time that I haven't."

"Maybe I can keep you from regretting your decision," she said in a throaty voice. "If we both try, Matt, we can have a good marriage."

He wrapped his fingers around her hand again. "I'd like that," he said and leaned close. "Just remember, I warned you that I'm not going to love again. And remember the old saying: 'All's fair in love and war'. You've had all the forewarning that I need to give."

"And so have you," she said with a smile. With her free hand she stroked his nape lightly.

His eyes darkened, and she knew she was taunting a tiger that could bound to life and devour her heart so easily. "I'm beginning to look forward to this, Olivia," he said softly. "And I look forward to our wedding night and having you in my arms." While he talked he reached up to wind locks of her hair in his fingers, tugging so lightly, yet making her aware of his touch.

Her pulse raced and her mouth was dry. "Twelve days from now, I hope we know each other better."

"You've learned a lot about me already and I know some about you. And I'll answer any question you want."

She tilted her head to think a moment. She was curious about him and had a multitude of questions, but she tried to choose the most urgent. "Are you still in love with your ex?" she asked, and a shake of his head gave her pleasure.

"Not even in the tiniest fraction. If she wanted to come back tomorrow, I wouldn't want her to, but she won't want to. She's in love with her job. And then with herself. When we were married, I made a threesome." He waited expectantly.

"When you were growing up, did you and your siblings get along with your father?"

"Well enough," he answered easily. "Our father can be a dictator and a lot of people are cowed when they deal with him, but we've grown up with him and his fiery temper and determination."

"Are any of you a lot like him?"

"I hope not," Matt replied. "You can ask me more later. Right now, let's go," he said, gathering his papers and standing, coming around to hold her chair.

As soon as they separated, Olivia began shopping for a wedding dress.

When she slipped the cool silk of the first one over her head, her heart thudded at the sight of her image.

The white dress was a dream. Tendrils of her hair had tumbled free and fell around her face and she had to admit that she thought she looked pretty, but it was the wedding dress and what it symbolized that held her speechless. She was dressing for her wedding for a marriage of convenience that she was going to contract to for the rest of her life. With a man who was angry with her, accustomed to getting his own way, and determined to avoid ever falling in love with her.

Would her baby's future be worth what she was willing to sacrifice, Olivia asked herself, because she suspected that no matter what she did or felt, Matt Ransome wasn't going to fall in love with her. The image in the mirror that stared back at her was a wide-eyed woman in a wedding dress about to marry—in less than two weeks—in a loveless marriage.

If she had good sense, she would guard her heart, too, she thought, turning to look over her shoulder at the dress. She guessed it would take a long, long time for Matt to forgive her for pushing him into this marriage of convenience.

Would his family accept her?

She suspected that would be one of the least of her problems.

She removed the dress and tried one that was white satin with a full skirt and cathedral train. Every moment of the past two days had held a dreamlike quality, but seeing herself in wedding dresses was surreal. She was going to marry a week from Saturday!

She ignored the pang that tore at her heart. This wasn't what she had planned for herself, but then nothing had gone as planned since she had met the first Ransome.

An hour later, she found the dress she wanted and knew she needed to look no further. She turned first one way and then another as she studied her reflection while she smoothed the skirt to a white sleeveless silk with a low-cut V-neck and straight, plain lines with a removable train. The simple elegance and flattering style made it the dress she wanted.

In another hour her head spun with her purchases of a veil, shoes and wisps of lacy undergarments. She stopped in a bookstore to select some books on pregnancy and baby care. When she glanced at her watch, she realized she would have to race to get back in time to meet Matt at the hotel.

When she arrived, he was in the lobby, seated with papers spread in his lap. At any moment she expected him to back out of their bargain. Soon she would be Mrs. Matthew Ransome. When the time came, would he go through with the ceremony?

As she approached him, his gaze assessed her, and she tucked a wayward tendril of hair behind her ear while her pulse jumped.

Watching her cross the lobby, he waited until she was only yards from him. He gathered his things and stood.

"Sorry I'm late," she said breathlessly. "I have boxes in the cab."

"You should have called," he said, walking beside her to go back outside to retrieve her packages.

"I don't own a cell phone," she replied, amused that he would automatically assume everyone he knew had a phone. He gave her a quick glance and reached into his pocket to hand her a phone.

"Take mine for now. I can get another easily." Matt took her arm and she was aware of his body warmth as she walked close beside him. She could detect a hint of barberry aftershave that was as tangible as his hostility. Yet he had accepted her terms. Marriage to a Ransome. One minute she wanted to kick her heels in the air and shout for joy. The next minute she wanted to pack and run.

He opened the cab door to retrieve her packages and move them to the waiting limo. Looking at an enormous box tied in white ribbon, he remarked: "I see you found a wedding dress."

"Yes, I did and it's bad luck for you to see me in it before the wedding."

Matt gave her a mocking grin. "You're worrying about me seeing your wedding dress?"

"All right, maybe that's foolish."

Their limo driver transferred her packages. "You should have let us pick up your wedding dress," Matt said.

"They placed it in the cab for me and I knew you would get it out," she said.

When she climbed into the waiting limo, Matt slid into the seat facing her. "Did I tell you this morning that you look beautiful?"

"Thank you," she replied.

"Perhaps we can make this arrangement halfway work."

"I hope it works completely," she admitted, wishing momentarily that she really could have it all—including a marriage with love. "It'll be a fraudulent marriage in some ways," she said quietly.

"This morning over breakfast I think we settled that we can make a marriage of convenience more palatable," he said.

"Maybe with time," she replied.

"While you shopped, I got a wedding planner," he said, handing her a slip of paper with a name, address and phone number scrawled on it. "You have an appointment in Fort Worth tomorrow afternoon at one."

"That was quick."

"For parties at the ranch we have a regular caterer and a band, so I've hired them for the wedding."

Olivia stared at him and wondered if she was getting entangled with a dynamo who would try to take charge of every aspect of her life.

"You're giving me a look," he said. "Do you disapprove?" he asked, startling her by guessing what was running through her mind.

She shook her head. "No, I'm a little overwhelmed."

"I doubt that," he remarked drily. "I've contacted our family minister and we'll have the reception at the ranch."

"You've done it all," she said. "Except buy my wedding dress."

He shook his head. "Not quite. We both need to get attendants. The wedding planner will have a florist and a photographer and you can arrange with her for the wedding cake. The big deal is telling my family. I suspect it may be a bombshell. I'll warn you right now, my dad may be difficult. Katherine might be, too, but it's dad who intimidates people. If you want, I'll see to it that you never see him without me until after the wedding."

Amused, she gazed at Matt. "You think he'll scare me out of this? If so, I'm surprised you didn't send him to talk to me before you accepted my proposal."

Matt smiled. "I don't think my dad will frighten you away, but you may not want to deal with him alone. I think you're a match for him which is saying something, believe me. Not many people can hold their own with him, but I bet you will. And if Katherine gives you a hard time, I'll deal with her, too. As soon as we get back to the ranch, I'll call them."

"Fine," Olivia said, wondering what kind of confrontations she would have with his family.

"When you become my wife, you won't need that law degree," he remarked.

Startled, she gazed back at him in silence while she thought about it. "I want to get an education. With the arrangement we have, I don't know what I'll need in the future."

"You can think about it," he said. "I moved my afternoon appointment with my attorney to tomorrow morning at ten. We'll both meet with him to go over the prenuptial agreement."

"That's fine, too."

Soon they boarded the private jet. When the plane taxied down the runway and soared into the air, she looked down at the city spread below and knew she would never forget the past night or today. Her gaze lifted to the expanse of blue sky that stretched endlessly in her view.

Once they were airborne, she heard him writing and turned away from the window to see him poring over his notes. Until he wanted her to talk to him about something specific, she was going to look out the window. It was her second flight in an airplane and she was still dazzled by it.

"Olivia," he said and a tingle spiraled in her.

"Yes?" she replied, giving him her attention.

"I want you to agree now that you'll stay with me. I don't want you to get your law degree and then take your child, divorce me and move away. Of course, if you're going, I can't hold you, but I want in the prenup that you won't get anything of mine if you leave. And I'll want joint custody."

"That's fair enough. I'm sure I can find legal work in this area. I want to practice law when I pass my bar exams."

"I can keep a child with me a lot of the time when I'm on the ranch."

"You don't know the first thing about taking care of a child, do you?" she asked.

"Nope, but I can learn. What kind of experience have you had in child care?" he asked, and her cheeks flushed hotly.

"Maybe none, but this morning I bought some baby books that I intend to study. Also, I think that child care is more likely to come to me innately than to you," she replied with a haughty air.

"We won't argue that one. Time will tell," he replied, drawing circles on her knee with his finger. She was aware of his touch and the warmth of his gaze and she wanted to lean toward him, to brush his lips with hers.

"Later this month I'm in a rodeo in Jet. The event is bronc riding. Will you come watch me ride?"

She nodded. "You always say your brother was the wild one. Seems to me bronc riding is on the wild side."

"Not so much. We do that on the ranch just for the fun of it."

She turned back to look out the window while she thought about the man she was marrying and what an enigma he was.

The rest of the day was dizzying. As soon as they landed in Fort Worth, Matt whisked her to a bank downtown and they were ushered into a thickly carpeted office where she watched with perspiring palms while Matt signed papers and deposited twenty thousand dollars into an account for her and put the remaining amount of money into a savings account. She was stunned to walk out of the bank a wealthy woman with an account and money to spend any way she so desired.

"Matt," she said, placing her hand on his arm while he stopped and looked down at her.

"Thank you. I never dreamed I would have money, not until I'd maybe practiced law forever. When I become a lawyer and pass the bar, I'll repay you," she said.

"Don't be ridiculous. We're getting married. I don't like having my money and your money. It's ours. If you contribute, fine. If you keep what you make for yourself, fine. If I marry you—even in a paper marriage, Olivia, then I'll share my bank account with you unless you go hog wild with it."

Amazed that he would allow her full access to his fortune, she could only stare in speechless wonder.

"Okay?" he asked when she didn't respond.

"Of course it's all right," she replied hastily. "I am constantly taken aback by your generosity. I can't even imagine someone sharing like you're willing to do."

He stopped and turned to her and she felt as if she were drowning in pools of blue. "Olivia, next week you'll become my wife. That's the way you wanted it. We'll have a bargain that I intend to live by for the rest of my life."

For the first time, she realized how permanent the approaching marriage of convenience would be. "Suppose you fall in love with someone?" she asked, wondering again what she had gotten herself into—for that matter, gotten both of them into.

"I won't."

"You can't know that! No one knows what will happen when love is involved."

"I'm not going to fall in love with anyone. My money will be your money as long as you handle it reasonably well. You don't have to repay the money I put in the bank account for you today."

"I'm absolutely stunned over what you're doing," she admitted, knowing every small detail of this moment would be etched in her memory forever. Wind blew locks of his black hair and his blue eyes were intent on her. A faint smile hovered, deepening creases in his cheeks. Besides Matt, the passing crowd, the sound of cars, the heat of sunshine—she would remember this event that in her wildest imaginings she had never dreamed would happen.

"Are you all right?" he asked.

"Yes. Just bowled over by your magnanimity."

"I'm just doing what I want to do. You can show me your gratitude tonight," he drawled in a husky, sensual voice that strummed across her nerves and set them quivering. As the same time, his eyes twinkled, so she didn't know whether he was teasing, goading her into something, or really meant it.

"I'll think about it," she said, giving him a saucy toss of her head.

He chuckled softly as she turned to walk to his car.

Finally they returned to the ranch and when they entered the house, Matt tossed his keys on the kitchen counter. "I'll call my brother and sister tonight. In the meantime, I'll grill steaks and we can make more plans. Where do you want this dress? You can keep it in another bedroom so it won't crowd you."

In minutes they had all her new purchases in another bedroom, and she had agreed as soon as she changed clothing, she would join him for a swim.

While she hurried to get ready for the swim, his words

echoed in her head: "You can show me your gratitude to-night." Had he meant that? Was he going to want sex before the agreed time because of the money he had given her? Or had he been teasing? If sincere, then he was in for a surprise because sex for her new bank account was not part of any bargain they had struck.

Before she left for the pool, she took a long look at herself in the mirror. She had bought a new black two-piece swimsuit that was cut low on her belly, high on her hips. She studied the changes in her body, aware that her breasts were fuller. Her stomach was still flat and she ran her hand over it, thinking about her baby. A girl or a boy? She was beginning to want to know and not wait another six months to be surprised. She wondered whether or not Matt would want to know.

Satisfied with her looks, she twisted her hair and pulled it up in a ponytail. She grabbed her cover-up, a big towel and flip-flops before going to the sparkling blue pool. Matt already had fired up the grill and the smoking mesquite smell was tantalizing.

As she walked across the patio where cool air was piped near the house, Matt bobbed up in the pool, and raked his hair away from his face, giving him a harsher, more rugged look. Water glistened on his broad shoulders, and her pulse began what was becoming a familiar racing.

He watched her approach and her heart thudded at the slow, thorough perusal he gave her from head to toe. His gaze lingered on her breasts and on her stomach, drifting down over her legs and she was on fire by the time she neared the pool.

He pulled himself up out of the water with a splash, sending cold drops sprinkling her. Her pulse was already racing, but now her heart thudded as she looked at him clad in only a scrap of black suit. His skin was tan, glistening with water, muscled, lean and hard. He was studying her, but no more than she was eyeing him and she couldn't resist staring. While her heart pounded, she marveled again that soon—tonight possibly—she would be in bed with him.

"If I hadn't seen the doctor's report myself, I'd never believe you're pregnant. You don't show at all," he said in a husky voice, walking closer.

With each step he took, her drumming pulse beat faster. She barely knew what he said as she looked up at him. They wore only bits of clothing and she knew he was as aware of her bare body as she was of his. And she wanted his lean hard body against hers. She could feel heat creep into her cheeks over the way she had been ogling him.

"How in heaven's name did you get my doctor's report? That's private," she asked, annoyed. "I may call my doctor about that."

He shrugged. "Who knows what my P.I. did, but he had the report. Your doctor may not have known someone looked at your record." Matt jerked his head toward the pool. "Come in. The water's great."

He made a running dive into the pool, swimming away from her. She followed, sliding into the cool water to swim. At the end of the pool she clung to the edge, shook water away from her face and found him beside her.

"You're beautiful, Olivia," he said in a husky voice. "I think we may have made a damn fine bargain."

"Those aren't exactly the magic words that every woman wants to hear two weeks before her wedding."

His eyebrows arched. "We're going into this like any business deal. You surely didn't expect hearts and flowers."

"No. That's not one of my stipulations. Last night was great because it was memorable to go out and not be reminded at every turn that what we have between us is a contract."

"You do want more," he observed and moved closer. "This is one thing we have between us that isn't in the contract."

Seven

He slipped his arm around her waist and drew her up against him. The moment she touched the length of his warm, hard body and legs, her stomach did flip-flops. When her hands went to his shoulders, desire exploded in her.

Sliding her arm around his neck, she looked at his lips and then glanced up to see him looking at her mouth with hungry longing. When he bent his head and covered her mouth with his, her heart pounded. Time and thought stopped. She lost all sense of where she was or what she had been doing. She was in his arms and he was kissing her senseless and she was coming apart at the seams over his kisses.

His arm tightened and his arousal was hard against her belly. Desire shook her. His free hand moved over her shoulders and throat and then slid down her front. While he continued to kiss her into oblivion, he held her away a fraction. His hand unfastened the halter top she wore and peeled it down, baring her breasts.

"Matt!" she exclaimed, ready to protest, remembering that she was going to show some restraint with this Ransome, but his fingers stroked her nipple and her protests melted. Warm and wet, his hand cupped her breast while his thumb circled her nipple slowly, making her moan softly and thrust her hips against him and want him with a need that shocked her. She twisted slightly to give herself access to him, sliding her fingers over his thick rod.

He growled deep in his throat as he kissed her. Then he leaned down to take her nipple in his mouth, teasing with his tongue, stroking and circling her taut bud.

"Matt!" she gasped again, unable to tell him to stop, knowing she was already breaking her promises to herself. How would she resist him twelve more days when she was letting him do what he wanted now? Did she want to wait until after they were married?

Desire surged, and she trembled as she kissed him and responded to his hands playing over her, first on her bare breasts and then sliding down over her belly. His hand slipped into the bottom half of her swimsuit and he found her soft folds, stroking her so lightly, yet setting off more blazing fireworks.

"You're so damn responsive to me," he whispered.

She tangled her legs with his and ran her hands over him, feeling his muscled body and firm bottom.

In minutes she knew there would be no stopping for either one of them. She pushed lightly against his chest and twisted away. He caught her arm to hold her.

"Matt, don't go so fast. I'll be in your bed soon enough."

Desire blazed in his eyes. An intense yearning that made her heart pound as violently as his passionate kisses had. He placed his hands on her waist and lifted her up out of the water and she placed her hands on his shoulders.

His gaze drifted over her bare breasts, slipping lower. "You're beautiful!" he gasped and her heart jumped.

How could she possibly keep from falling head over heels in love with him? He was devilishly handsome, rugged, sexy. He could be charming and she had the feeling that he really hadn't turned his charm and lovemaking on full force as far as she was concerned.

She didn't doubt that he meant what he said about keeping his heart locked away. Could she really scale the walls of that fortress?

She looked into his blue eyes and all she could see was desire so blatant it made her nipples tingle again. The heat low in her body intensified.

With his gaze locked with hers, he lowered her slowly, holding her closer and letting her slick, wet body slide against his. His hard shaft slipped between her legs and she gasped with desire that swept her with the force of a tidal wave. Closing her eyes and clinging to him, she knew she had to stop him right now and she needed to get out of his arms and get some distance between them.

She wasn't going to fall into his arms and into his bed and succumb to his seduction on the third night she had known him.

With an effort, as he leaned forward and his lips brushed hers, she splashed away from him and scrambled to pull her suit back into place. She looked over at him and saw him treading water while he watched her with a faint smile.

"Scared of me? Or scared about your own reactions?" He waved his hand. "Come on back. I can show restraint."

"Sure you can," she teased lightly. "Catch me," she said and turned to swim away as swiftly as possible.

He caught her easily and hauled her into his arms, laughing with her, but as their legs tangled and he held her close, their laughter vanished, replaced swiftly by need.

With pounding pulse, Olivia wriggled away. "Not yet, Matt," she said, wondering how long she could wait.

He swam past her and climbed out, grabbing up a towel and tying it around his middle. He shook water away from his face as he slicked back his hair. "I'll get out the steaks and pour glasses of iced tea."

Getting out of the pool, she watched him cross the patio and her mouth went dry as her gaze drifted over his broad, powerful shoulders and muscled back that tapered to his tiny waist and tight bottom. Abruptly, he halted and glanced at her, catching her staring at his body. He turned around to stroll back to her and each step closer he came to her, the more loudly her pulse pounded until she was certain he could hear it.

He placed his hand under her chin. "Go ahead and look. What you see will be yours to play with whenever you want," he said in a velvety voice. He stroked her cheek and let his fingers lightly slip lower, caressing her throat and pushing open the cover-up to fondle her breasts. "And what I see will be mine to play with and make love to, I hope."

"I believe that was part of our bargain," she whispered, unable to get any firmness in her voice. Was she already falling in love with him even before her wedding?

How disastrous would this bargain be to her heart? A bargain with a demon of her own creation. She could have taken the money, lived with him and waited to see if they fell in love instead of this headlong rush into marriage to get a commitment for her baby.

It was done now and she wasn't backing out, but she should take care and guard her heart more than she had so far. Two days ago she wouldn't have dreamed she would be at risk of heartbreak.

He looked over at her. "Penny for your thoughts."

"I was just mulling over what odd turns life takes and a week ago this time, my life and prospects for the future were entirely different."

"Regrets?"

"Absolutely not. Never! I couldn't possibly regret the changes. What about you? This morning you were filled with anger."

"We'll see what the future brings. Let's sit down and go over some more stipulations."

Amused, she smiled. "You're trying to think of everything. That's impossible."

"Maybe, but I want some requests. I'm in no hurry, but I want a DNA test to determine that there is no question that my brother was the father."

"That's fine," she said. "He was, so test away." She sat at a wrought-iron table on a cushioned iron chair, crossed her legs, catching Matt staring at her bare legs.

He pulled on a T-shirt over his swim trunks and then dropped the towel. The T-shirt hid his swimsuit and it was easy to imagine him without it and she hoped he had no inkling that she was doing so.

"Do I get a say in the baby's name?" he asked, pulling his chair close and stroking her knee, starting more fiery tingles.

She thought about that one. "I think we should both approve the selected name," she said breathlessly, only half aware of what she was replying to him.

He moved closer and placed his hands on her shoulders. "We've already learned that we can get along and the sex promises to be great. We both have mutual goals about the baby. But make no mistake, Olivia. I'll never fall in love again," he reminded her.

Annoyance flashed in her at his stubborn refusal to even give love a chance and then she thought how far she had already come with him. She slanted her head and smiled at him. "At the moment, I'm not after your heart. But when and if I decide I am, you may find that you don't have such a fortress as you thought."

"You've been warned."

"So have you," she said, and interest danced in his eyes. His gaze lowered to her mouth. She started to turn away, but he caught her, kissing her and lifting her onto his lap. Their legs were warm and bare and her pulse thundered while passion possessed her.

Matt leaned down to kiss her possessively. While his tongue stoked a fire in her, his arm banded her waist tightly. His other hand slipped down over her back and across her bottom, heating her desire.

Wrapping her arms around his neck, she twisted to press against him while she kissed him in return, pouring all her need into the kiss. She could feel his arousal hard against her and his free hand roamed over her while his hungry kisses demolished her intentions to resist him.

With desperation, she broke free, gasping for breath and satisfied to see his breathing was as ragged as hers as they both gazed at each other.

"Olivia, I don't think my life will ever be the same again."

"You can bet the ranch on that one," she whispered, standing and wanting to stay in his arms, wanting him to love her the rest of the night. She swept past him. "I'll dress for dinner," she called over her shoulder without looking back at him.

She hurried to her room for a cold shower, lecturing herself about resistance and caution and self-control and gaining his respect. She dressed in a denim sundress, sandals and caught her hair up in a ponytail. There was no way to stop unruly tendrils from escaping and curling around her face. She leaned forward to glare at her reflection.

"Get some control," she whispered. "You're mush when he kisses you." She didn't want to even think about his devastating kisses. But if he was leaping over barriers around her heart, she suspected she might be building bridges over his. "Just you try to resist falling in love with me, Matt Ransome," she declared.

She straightened up. "Yeah, right," she said, reminding herself that the man had iron willpower, and he could probably keep his heart locked away for a lifetime if he chose to. She thought about Jeff's story about Matt rescuing their father when all the professional rescuers had pulled out of the area. Jeff said Matt refused to give up, but he wouldn't let Jeff or Katherine search with him and Nick had a sprained ankle. She was dealing with a man who had a will of iron and would make all kinds of sacrifices to get what he wanted.

Would her heart break over this hard, tough cowboy? And beneath the wealth and sophistication, she suspected there was a cowboy who was a lot of country.

She squared her shoulders and smoothed her skirt. She was willing to take some risks. At this point she had the world to gain—and only a broken heart to lose, she reminded herself.

With a toss of her head she left to join him for dinner.

By the time she strolled onto the patio, he was grilling

steaks. A plume of gray smoke spiraled above the cooker and tantalizing smells made her mouth water, but it was the tall, handsome cook who took her breath and made her pulse jump.

He had dressed in slacks, western boots and a knit shirt, but how easily she could remember the body and muscles beneath those neat clothes. He glanced at her and then turned to give her his full attention, watching her walk toward him.

Tingling and growing hot, she sauntered up to him, stopping only inches from him. "Like what you see?" she asked in a sultry voice.

A faint smile quirked his mouth. "My anticipation about our wedding night is growing," he replied and her pulse jumped another notch.

"It'll be even better than you imagine," she said.

"You're flirting again, Olivia." He ran his finger just above the top of her sundress, drawing a line on her bare skin that made her draw her breath. "But why do I think you have an ulterior motive? I think you want me to fall in love with you so you can steal my heart away and twist me around your little finger." His fingers trailed upward to her nape where he caressed her lightly. "Am I right? Or will you admit the truth?"

"I'll answer honestly," she replied, wanting to kiss him instead of chat with him. "I hadn't thought about twisting you around my little finger and I don't really believe that I possibly can. Maybe I'm just trying to protect my heart so if I do fall in love with you, I won't be rejected."

He propped his foot on an iron chair and placed his arm on his thigh as he leaned closer. She was hemmed in by him and by his leg on one side of her, the cooker on the other and the chair behind her. His blue eyes pierced her as if he were searching for answers in her gaze. "So you're not getting cold feet yet over our deal?"

"Of course not," she said, acutely aware of his proximity and his leg touching her hip lightly. "We need to talk about the wedding. How many attendants will I need to have because you'll have groomsmen."

"Back to business? I'd rather talk about making love."

"We better take care of business if you want this wedding next week."

He smiled at her and traced the curve of her ear. "All right. How many attendants do you want?" he asked in a husky voice and she suspected he was giving little thought to the approaching nuptials.

"You're not thinking about our wedding," she said.

"I'm thinking about making passionate love to you on our wedding night," he answered in a husky voice and leaned down to brush her lips with his.

Her heart thudded, but she fought her impulse to kiss him and stepped back. "Matt, we have to make decisions about the wedding. How many groomsmen? I have three friends here, but I can well imagine that you will have a lot more close friends, plus your brother. I'll be happy to ask your sister to be an attendant."

His heated gaze kept her pulse racing. "All right. We'll discuss the wedding—for now. I've been trying to get in touch with my family to let them know. While you dressed, I tried to call Nick and Katherine. I've left messages for both of them."

"Are they here in Texas?"

"No. I called their cells. Katherine is in Chicago, and Nick is on a rig in the Gulf. I talked to my dad and of course, he wants to meet you. We're having him join us for breakfast in the morning. How's that?"

"Fine," she said, wondering if his entire family would disapprove of her and try to talk Matt out of the marriage. For an instant a surge of panic threatened, but then she reminded herself that Matt had agreed to marry her and he said he would keep his word.

Matt caressed her nape and she stopped thinking about his family. "Three attendants will be fine. If you want her, ask Katherine," he said. "I can't predict what she'll do or say."

"I hope they don't hate me."

"If they do, do you want to call off the marriage?"

"No, I don't."

He tugged on a curling lock of her hair. "Dad will be the most difficult to deal with. He's not the same since Jeff's death. Jeff was his baby and his favorite which is why he let Jeff do just what he damn well pleased."

"If I have a boy, I don't mind if you want to name him after your brother."

Matt traced his finger around the curve of her ear. "That might be a real fine thing. It would mean a lot to the whole family. 'Course you may be having a girl."

"When the time comes, I'll find out what my baby is going to be. When I have an ultrasound, you can even go with me if you want."

His eyes narrowed. "I'd like to go with you," he replied. "I'd really like it," he repeated as if surprised by his own feelings. "Something else—as soon as we marry, I wish you'd refer to this baby as 'our' baby, even though I'm not the blood father. For all intents and purposes, I will be this baby's father."

"That's wonderful!" she exclaimed, delighted with his suggestion. "Our baby," she repeated, the words thrilling her. Then she focused on him again. "You're standing close," she said quietly.

"It bothers you?"

"You know you disturb me," she replied.

"If the steaks weren't going to burn, I'd do more to disturb you right now," he said in a husky voice that was its own caress. He walked to the grill to take the steaks off and set them on the table.

Hunger pangs increased her anticipation, but when she sat down at the table across from Matt, she lost interest in food. Talking to him and making wedding plans took precedence over eating. As they chatted, she couldn't believe her good fortune.

Over dinner Matt charmed her with stories about the ranch and his brothers and sister, yet all the time he talked about them, Olivia couldn't stop wondering how much they would accept her and the approaching marriage.

She barely touched her steak and noticed that Matt didn't either. They talked about a myriad of subjects and she wondered if his life had been lonely before, but then she pushed that notion aside as ridiculous. Matt could do as he pleased and she suspected he kept busy all the time. Looking into his thickly lashed blue eyes, she couldn't imagine, in spite of what he had said, that there weren't women around often. His handsome looks and virility took her breath. If only—she dismissed that thought immediately. She was getting more than she ever dreamed possible. She had to stop looking for love.

The sun set and lights came on automatically in posts scattered around the patio. The pool sparkled with light and she was dazzled by her surroundings, but far more by Matt. He reached across the table to take her hand in his. His fingers were warm and strong. At the intense look in his eyes, her pulse speeded.

He reached into his pocket with his other hand. "I bought a ring for you today while I was waiting," he said and placed a small black velvet box in her hand.

Surprised, she opened it and her heart missed beats when she looked at the dazzling diamond that sparkled against the dark velvet. "Matt!" she gasped, stunned by his gift. She looked up at him. "It's fantastic!"

"You like it?" he asked.

"Of course, I love it!" she said. "It's magnificent! I can't believe you would do this! We barely know each other. I'm astounded—" She realized she was babbling, but she was caught off guard and never had expected any such ring.

"Olivia," he said, cutting short her words and leaning closer to slip his hand beneath her chin. "For this baby's sake, we're entering into a marriage of convenience, but as far as I'm concerned, I think it would be best for our baby if all our friends think we're in love. You'll get a hell of a lot more respect that way, and men will leave you alone. Unless you let them know they don't have to leave you alone."

"Don't worry about that one," she said. "We've already agreed to be faithful to each other."

"At this point that's merely lip service."

"Not for me," she said, solemnly, her excitement diminishing. He took the ring from her and slipped it onto her finger.

"It's a perfect fit," she said, wiggling her fingers slightly and watching the huge diamond sparkle. "This has to be the biggest diamond I've ever seen in my life."

"Good. It's eight carats and that should be big enough to keep guys away and earn you respect from the women."

She looked at the glittering diamond and then at him. He was being generous beyond her wildest dreams. She pushed back her chair and walked around the table and something flickered in the depths of his eyes. As she approached him, he scooted his chair and she sat on his lap and wrapped her arms around his neck. "Thank you," she said and leaned down to kiss him.

His arms enveloped her and he shifted her closer, kissing her in return until she forgot all about the dazzling ring and was lost in Matt's kisses.

His hands brushed her bare shoulders and nape, sliding down to twist free her buttons. He pulled down the front of her sundress to cup her breasts in his hands. When his thumbs drew circles on her nipples, she moaned with pleasure, a sound that was muffled as his tongue plunged deeply into her mouth.

Then his hand was beneath her full skirt, pushing it high while his fingers caressed the inside of her thigh. He turned her on his lap so he could slide his fingers into her lacy panties.

"Matt!" she gasped.

Shifting her over him so she was astride him, he cupped both her breasts and lowered his head to her breasts, to kiss first one and then the other. He drew his tongue in slow circles around her nipple while his thumb continued to circle her other nipple.

Bombarded by sensations and desire, she clung to his shoulders and then let her hand slide down to his hard shaft. With a pounding pulse, she unbuckled his belt and unfastened his trousers, trying to free him from the restraints of clothing. She wanted him totally, yet she clung to her resolution to wait until their wedding night to give herself fully. She refused to fall into his arms and his bed so quickly even though every caress and kiss was fueling the bonfire that consumed her.

Lost to his lovemaking, she moved her hips while trying to fight through the fog of need back to caution and patience.

Catching his wrist, she held his hand. "You're going too fast again." She swung her leg over him and straightened her clothing, trying to pull the top of her dress back in place.

His blue eyes had darkened with passion and the heated look in them made her heart pound. When he fastened his clothes, she returned to her chair and studied her new ring. "I've never dreamed of owning jewelry like this."

She looked at him and her heart missed a beat because the desire in his expression shocked her.

"I want you, Olivia. I want you in my arms in my bed and I want all that passion you have bottled up turned loose."

"You have to wait only a few more days," she reminded him, wondering if either one of them could resist that long. Already, they weren't able to keep their hands to themselves and when they started kissing, they almost lost all restraint.

"Let's clean this up—"

"Nope," he said, standing and taking her hand and crossing the patio to a cushioned glider. "Later. Let's sit and talk."

Olivia moved to a chair close to the glider and received a mocking smile from Matt. She looked at the ring again. "This is absolutely fabulous. Thank you so very much."

He nodded. "Wedding dress, ring, minister, wedding planner, caterer, band and lawyers. We need to get in touch with my family and get our attendants lined up. Your attendants will need to get dresses. As soon as we go to the courthouse tomorrow and take care of the legal stuff with the county, I think we'll have everything else in order."

"I can't believe you're getting all this done this quickly," she said, knowing she could always expect him to try to take charge and go at a gallop to get what he wanted.

"We have parties out here and some of the arrangements aren't that different," he said.

Butterflies flitted in her stomach at the thought of talking to the rest of the Ransome clan.

Matt took her hand, lacing her fingers in his. He raised her hand to brush her knuckles with kisses, his warm breath a caress that made her want back in his lap. As she talked about classes she could take in the fall, Matt scooted his chair against hers. Finally, she stood. "I insist we clean. Mrs. Marley won't be here tonight or tomorrow."

He waved his hand. "Sit and talk. I'll clean. It'll give me something to do because I'm not going to sleep."

She wrinkled her nose at him. "I'm not going to ask why you won't sleep," she said as she sat again.

"You know exactly why," he replied in a low voice. He reached over to lift her into his lap.

She wound her arms around his neck and smiled at him. "I think we did this a short time ago."

"I can't remember," he said, looking at her mouth.

She inhaled and pulled his head down as she placed her mouth on his to kiss him, knowing every kiss made her want more. "Matt," she whispered, kissing him between words, "you're making it harder to wait—"

"Darlin', you're definitely the one making it harder," he drawled in a sexy innuendo that she barely heard over her pounding pulse. Matt's arm tightened around her and his tongue went deep. He kissed her long and thoroughly before she made him stop again. Standing, she moved away. "I'll see you at breakfast."

He gazed at her with a smoldering intensity and she hurried away, knowing a few more seconds and she would have been right back in his arms.

That night she was restless, worrying about Matt's father and how his family would accept her after learning she had talked Matt into a loveless marriage of convenience.

Tuesday morning at breakfast, she could feel the tension in spite of Matt being charming and his father chatting easily. Duke Ransome was a large, powerful-looking man with shoulders as broad as Matt's and a deeply tanned complexion.

Dressed in western shirt, jeans and boots, he still was a handsome man. He had brilliant blue eyes and a scar across his temple that was a testament to his rugged ranch life. He could be as charming as Matt, but his smiles ended before ever reaching his cold blue eyes that continually bored into her.

It was no surprise to her when breakfast was over and they moved to the family room to have Duke look at his son and announce, "Matt, I'd like to talk to Olivia for a few minutes, just the two of us."

"I'd be happy to talk to you, Mr. Ransome," Olivia said, trying to sound collected. She had dressed with care and was thankful in her shopping yesterday that she had bought a new, tailored navy suit and matching silk blouse. Ignoring her churning stomach, she hoped she looked poised with her hair looped and pinned behind her head.

"Dad, I think anything you have to say might be well said with all three of us together," Matt suggested.

"Nope. I want to talk to Olivia. I'm not going to bite her head off," Duke said and smiled at her, but it was a smile that chilled her and she wondered what he intended to say.

"I'm staying to hear whatever you have to say," Matt said in a voice that was as firm and direct as his father's and she knew at this point the decision was between the two males so she remained silent.

"Very well," Duke said and nodded, motioning to her. "Please sit down."

She sat in a leather wingback chair and Matt perched on the arm of the chair beside her.

The moment Duke Ransome turned his steely gaze on her, she braced for trouble. "You know we're all interested in your baby and want the baby in this family because it's a Ransome," he began.

"Yes, sir. Matt has made that clear and that's why we're marrying," she replied, aware that Matt remained silent. She wondered if he and his father had planned this talk together and hoped to get her to back out of the pending marriage.

"Which, of course, was your idea. I know my son doesn't want to wed again, for convenience or any other reason."

Olivia merely smiled and waited. Duke Ransome moved to the window and looked out at the sprawling ranch land. "We've fought for this land and protected it and I've struggled to keep my family together. I miss Jeff. This baby is his child and is a part of him."

"Yes, sir," she said, wondering if he intended to try to stir her sympathy. Questions swirled through her thoughts and curiosity about Matt plagued her. Why was he silent? Was he hoping his father would drive her away?

Duke Ransome turned to face her and his gaze chilled her. "There's no love between you and Matt because a week ago you didn't know each other and I know you haven't fallen in love in the short time you've known each other. Matt is not in love, I'm sure."

"No, sir. We haven't fallen in love," she admitted. "But we think we have a good arrangement."

"Maybe I can give you a better one than Matt can. I don't want you messing up my son's life. And that's what you'll do." She started to speak, but he raised his hand.

"Hear me out. Give us Jeff's baby. You're a beautiful woman and you'll fall in love again. You can have a lot more babies. Give us Jeff's baby and I'll deposit in your account a half of a million dollars to let us have the baby and you get out of Matt's life permanently. You can add this amount to what Matt has offered and you can keep the ring he's given you. In total, my proposition, plus Matt's offer and his ring will be well over half a million."

Eight

Stunned, Olivia stared at him. After surprise shook her, her mind began to function. "Thank you for your generous offer, but my answer is no."

Duke's eyes narrowed. "Did you hear how much I'm willing to give you? You can't turn down that much money."

"I can and I have," she said quietly. Matt's arm curved around her shoulders and he gave her a squeeze.

"You haven't even thought it over," Duke said, scowling at her.

"I've kept quiet, Dad, to hear your offer, as well as to hear Olivia's response," Matt said in a firm voice. "Just now Olivia refused you. That's what I wanted to hear. She's honest and true and up-front about all of this. You and Jeff have both underestimated her and misjudged her just as I did before I met her. In my judgement of her, I was off a country mile and you're even more mistaken about her. Just as Jeff was. Jeff couldn't see beyond a desirable woman."

"Dammit! Neither can you!" Duke snapped, his voice rising. "Don't be taken in again. You married a woman who couldn't wait to dump you. You don't know anything about women, Matt. Stop interfering here."

"I'm not interfering. Olivia just refused your offer."

"You don't think this baby needs its mother?" Olivia asked, her anger increasing by the second.

"No," Duke replied, his attention shifting back to her. "We'll make up for that. My children grew up without their mother and they turned out fine."

"Perhaps they did," Olivia replied. "From what I knew, as charming as he was, Jeff cared about no one but himself." She glanced at Matt who gazed back with an unfathomable expression. "Matt is cynical and talks about his sister and brother being wild," she continued and turned to face Duke again. "All of your children might have benefited from a mother's influence."

"By any standards my family is a fine one," Duke said, and his face flushed a deeper red. His anger was palpable. Olivia regretted she was the cause of it, but she wasn't intimidated by Duke Ransome and she had no intention of giving up her baby for any amount.

"I didn't say they weren't a fine family, Mr. Ransome. I just think a mother might have had an additional positive impact on them. My baby is going to have its mother. Your family puts too high a priority on material things." She tried to bank her own smoldering anger and think clearly because she was making monumental decisions about her future and her baby's and she didn't want to make the wrong choice in an emotional, knee-jerk reaction.

"I think that's a bit difficult to accept coming from a person with your background and your demands on my son. You can't tell me money means nothing to you," Duke said, gruffly.

Matt stood and placed his hand on her shoulder. "That's enough, Dad. A week from Saturday Olivia and I intend to marry. We're working out a good arrangement that will give our baby a father and a mother and a family and financial support."

"Financial support! Like hell!" Duke's fiery gaze bored into Olivia. The room snapped with tension, yet she felt insulated, certain about what she wanted and reassured by Matt's stand against his father.

"The tramp will take you for as much as she can get!" Duke exclaimed, still staring at Olivia.

"Tramp?" Matt put his hands on his hips, clenching his fists and taking a step toward his father. "I don't think so," he said in a chilling tone that made Olivia draw a deep breath. "She turned down your offer of half a million dollars—that's no tramp after money, Dad, and you better face the truth. She's going to be the mother of your first grandchild. You owe Olivia an apology."

"Matt, please," Olivia said, standing and placing her hand on Matt's arm. "I don't want to cause a rift between father and son."

"Like hell you don't," Duke snapped. "In your lifetime you'll never have such wealth as I'm offering. If you marry my son, you won't be able to touch the Ransome money. Matt will see to that."

"I'm not after cash. There are other things in life that are important."

"I think you're after the Ransome fortune and I'll do everything in my power to keep you from getting a dime of it."

Olivia could feel the waves of anger emanating from Duke. His fists were clenched, and his face flushed a deeper red.

"Dad, you're on dangerous ground—" Matt said, stopping when she squeezed his arm.

"Wait, Matt," she said and turned to his father. "Mr. Ransome, it's not the Ransome money that I'm after. I'd like my baby to be part of this family that he or she belongs to by blood, although after the past few minutes, I am having second thoughts about that. From what I know so far, Matt is an honorable man. I would like a father for my child. My baby is a Ransome, therefore, I would like my baby to have the benefits of being a Ransome, but not at a price that will compromise his or her life in any manner. Frankly, you, sir, make me want to walk out of the door and never look back. Your son, on the other hand, has accepted my proposition for a marriage of convenience that will give *our* baby opportunities beyond anything I can ever offer."

"Damn straight, you little—"

"Dad!" Matt snapped in a tough, determined voice as he stepped forward with clenched fists. "Apologize to the woman I intend to marry and to the woman who is the mother of your grandson! You damn well apologize or you'll never know this child. I'll cut you off right here and now."

"Matt. Don't!" Olivia stepped in front of Matt, placing herself between the two angry men. "Stop this! Don't let me tear apart your family," she urged. Her heart pounded and she was cold with worry, wondering if Matt even saw her or knew she was in front of him. His blue eyes flashed with fire and his chest heaved.

"Get out of the way, Olivia," Matt said without taking his gaze from his father.

"No! I won't let you two destroy this family," she said.

"If you reject my offer, you'll regret it all your life," Duke said, lowering his clenched fists and turning to look at her.

"I'll never regret turning down your offer," she declared.

Duke glared at Olivia. "You're a cool customer, Miss Brennan. If you're holding out for a better offer, you won't get it."

"Sir, I've already gotten it," she said softly, and his jaw tightened. Matt stepped beside her and placed his arm around her shoulders.

"Dad, you apologize to my fiancée or don't come back to my house or to our wedding."

Olivia bit back a protest at Matt's threat because she wanted a united front with him, but his ultimatum to his father hurt. She never intended to rip apart a family.

"You have my apologies," Duke snarled in a tone that clearly indicated his insincerity. "There—you have your damned apology." He looked at his son's arm draped across her shoulders. "I hope both of you know what you're doing," Duke said.

"I think we do," Matt answered.

"You give long and thorough consideration to my offer,"

Duke said to her. "It would set you up for life. You know that you can have other babies and you know that we would provide a truly good life for Jeff's child. There's not a shred of love between you and Matt."

Olivia and Duke held each other's gaze for a tense moment. "I won't forget your offer. It was interesting to meet you, Mr. Ransome."

"You watch your step, missy. I'll do everything I can to talk my son out of marrying you."

"I think your son probably makes his own decisions."

Duke nodded. Striding from the room, he slammed the door behind him.

She let out her breath and turned to face Matt. "I hate that you and your dad had such a fight."

Shaking his head, Matt raised his eyebrows. "Dad didn't tell me what he was going to do, although I should have guessed. I'm sure he thought he'd made you an offer that you couldn't possibly refuse."

"Half a million to give you my baby and get out of your life."

"I'm a little amazed you could so quickly and easily turn down that amount."

"None of you get it—you can't hang a dollar sign on a child. I'm not giving up my baby."

"I didn't ask you to with my offer. I wanted you to let us share Jeff's child's life."

"I won't give up my baby for any amount. I didn't have to think about my answer."

Matt studied her and put his hand on her shoulder. "Dad doesn't know you at all and he thinks everyone can be bought."

She ran her hand across her brow and Matt placed his finger beneath her jaw and tilted her face up. "Upset?" he asked.

"This past hour hasn't been the easiest time in my life," she said, trying to lighten the moment, but she felt weak in the knees and anger still smoldered inside. As much as she wanted to ignore Duke Ransome and forget his hurtful words, his "tramp" accusation rang in her ears and it hurt.

"I doubt if your father will attend our wedding."

"Oh, yes, he will. I know my dad. Did it ever occur to you that you could be getting into a union that you'll hate?" Matt asked in a quiet voice while reaching out to trace his fingers along her cheek. "Soon I'll be the legal father and have as much say as you in our child's life."

Our child. The words slipped across her raw nerves, reminding her of all the changes that were soon coming because of her decisions. "I'm willing to take the chance. I think we'll work out an arrangement we can both accept," she said, hoping she sounded cool and Matt didn't have an inkling of the butterflies she had over the thought of her future shared with him and his family.

"If I ever worry about you holding your own with my family or anyone else, remind me to forget my concern," Matt said. "I've seen some tough men that couldn't cope with my dad. You won that round with the old man," Matt added. "There are a lot of people who've had tough times, and they would've taken the money and never looked back. I think Dad lumped you in with that group." Matt studied her, his gaze going slowly over her features and making her pulse drum.

"Thanks for standing up for me."

Matt shrugged. "You gave him your answer. He should've accepted it and his remarks were way out of line, but he's accustomed to getting his way and doing whatever he has to do to succeed. I misjudged you a hell of a lot more than a country mile," Matt admitted. He leaned forward to brush a light kiss on her forehead before glancing at his watch. "We need to go to town to the attorney's office. If we don't leave now, we'll be late."

"I'll get my purse," she said, gratified by Matt's remarks and his support.

"Meet you at the back door," he said and left the room with her, going the opposite direction when they reached the hall. Halfway down the hall, she glanced over her shoulder to find him still standing where she had left him. His hand was on his hip as he watched her. When she looked at him, he turned and disappeared into his office.

Matt went to his desk to get a briefcase that held papers and notes he had made for the prenuptial agreement. Half his thoughts were on the coming appointment. The other half were on Olivia and his father. He was astounded his dad offered her so much money, but by now, he wasn't surprised that Olivia had turned him down. She wanted marriage and all the commitment that went with it, even if it was going to be a business arrangement. A lot of people would have wilted with his dad and given in to him, but also, by now, Matt knew Olivia better. She was a strong woman who would not be intimidated by his dad or outsmarted by him. If the situation hadn't involved such high stakes, it would have been amusing because few people refused his dad.

Matt knew he would hear from his father soon to try to persuade him to back out of the approaching marriage.

Matt had no intention of backing out. Each day it looked like a better proposition. They would have an acceptable arrangement for living together; the baby would be his to share—he would become the adoptive father; and he would have sex on a regular basis with Olivia. If the marriage arrangement worked, he could imagine they might drift into loving each other, but in the meantime, he never wanted to go through heartbreak again.

Later, in the car as he drove into town, Olivia shifted on the seat to face Matt. "I guess your father is never going to accept me," she remarked.

"Once you present Dad with his first grandchild, he'll accept you so quickly that you'll be astounded. Believe me, I know my dad. He's wanted a grandchild, dreamed about one, harassed my sister to get married, harassed me when I was married to give him an heir. No, he's going to love your baby and you won't be able to believe that he offered you a fortune to get out of our lives. You'll see a transformation that will astound you and Dad will act as if nothing disagreeable ever happened."

"I'll believe it when it happens," she said unable to imagine Duke Ransome changing so drastically.

"My dad probably expected you to jump at the chance for a fortune because you didn't grow up in comfort."

"Comfort!" She laughed. "There were nights I slept on buses because it was safer and more peaceful than going home. My parents drank and—" she stopped abruptly. "You know all about my background. When I was in high school, I'd just ride the bus at night so I could study. I always felt education was my passport out of that life and it has been."

"That's what I mean. Dad and I misjudged you badly."

"Now I only have to face your brother and your sister."

"I still haven't been able to get in touch with Nick or with Katherine, but I'll keep leaving messages for them."

"They'll probably try to talk you out of this wedding, too. They know we're not in love." She looked at her ring and wriggled her hand. "I think the rest of the world will be fooled about it."

"Don't be surprised if you get some other kind of offer from my dad. He doesn't give up easily."

"I'm not worried."

"No, I suppose you're not," Matt said. "You continually surprise me."

"For one reason or another, most men I've met have misjudged me," she admitted. "That first night you certainly did, and I'll bet your P.I.'s report about me was not at all what you expected."

"You're right. But then, maybe I've surprised you. Because of my brother you prejudged me." Matt smiled at her. "I haven't had a chance to tell you, but you look like you're worth a million today. You look gorgeous," he said. She could see the warmth in his gaze and his compliment pleased her, taking away some of the tension of the past hour.

"You sweet-talkin' devil. You'll turn my head," she teased, momentarily forgetting the raw differences between them, giving him a mocking, coy look that made him grin.

"The more I know you the less I dread this wedding."

"Just watch out, Matthew Ransome," she said, leaning across the front seat. "First thing you know, you'll be in love with your wife," she said and laughed, straightening up and scooting back into her place.

"You would do that when I'm driving," he remarked,

shooting her a quick glance before his attention returned to the road. "Remind me later what you said. And I'll tell you again. I'm not falling in love with anyone, Olivia. All women are romantics and sometimes they pay a high price for it."

"Is that right?" she asked with such sweetness in her voice that he scowled.

"Time will tell, but you're in for more heartache if you're going into this contract thinking I'm going to fall in love soon."

"I think you've made it quite clear that you're a man with no heart. But no matter how much you declare that, Matt, you have a heart and you've loved before, so there's a chance you'll love again. You won't if you shut yourself off from everyone, and I hope you don't do that with this baby because if you want to be a real dad, then you'll have to open your heart."

"That's different and I will."

"Then just take care that if you get your heart functioning again, it doesn't do things you hoped to avoid."

"I'll take care," he answered with a cynical tone. "You better worry about protecting yourself."

"You sound defensive. You're getting angry and you're a tad beyond the speed limit. I think I see a flashing light behind us," she said, looking in an outside mirror.

"Oh, hell!" Matt snapped, and she had to bite back laughter because she knew she had goaded Matt into losing some of that iron control he had. She remained silent while he pulled off the road. When the patrolman approached the car, Matt greeted him.

"Hey, Ebby," Matt said easily, extending his hand and shaking the patrolman's hand when he leaned down to look into the open window. "Ebby, meet Olivia Brennan, my fiancée."

"You're getting married?" the man asked without hiding the surprise in his voice.

"Sure am. You'll get an invitation to the party soon," Matt said.

"Howdy, Olivia," the trooper said in a friendly voice, and she smiled at him.

"Look, my attention was on my fiancée and I just forgot

what I was doing," Matt explained easily. "You know how it is. You and Tamara just got married what—five months ago?"

"That's right. Five months and one week. Look, just slow down a little and try to think about your driving. I'll give you a warning this time, Matt."

"Thanks. I sure will go slower."

"Nice to meet you," Ebby said to Olivia and she smiled in return and twisted in the seat to watch him walk to his car and soon pull around them.

"You got yourself out of that one," she said as Matt drove onto the highway.

"Remind me to put his name on our invitation list."

"You're driving quite sedately now," she observed. "All we both have to do is to hang on to our cool through the prenup agreement."

She received a crooked grin. "You think I can't do that, don't you?"

"I don't have any idea. I don't even know what you want in the agreement."

"You know most of what I want because I've discussed it with you before."

In a downtown building in Fort Worth, she entered the large reception area and in minutes a short, blond man with lively brown eyes approached them and shook hands in greeting with Matt who then introduced her.

"Vic Waterman, this is Olivia. Olivia, meet Vic."

"Glad to meet you," he said, shaking Olivia's hand while he smiled at her. "Both of you come with me and we'll find a quiet place to work."

In a paneled conference room they sat at an oval table and Vic Waterman produced papers and a legal pad. While Matt opened his briefcase to take out his papers, she waited quietly.

For the next two hours they went over prenuptial details. At one point Matt said that he wanted it clearly stipulated that if she divorced him, she forfeited any claims on the Ransome money for herself. When he gazed directly at her, she nodded.

"I find that quite acceptable," she answered easily, watching Vic Waterman write in his tablet.

Finally they worked out an agreement that was to Matt's satisfaction as well as her own. Trying to contain her excitement, she was thrilled with the contract that would protect her in many ways and provide for her baby.

The closer she came to becoming Matt's wife, the more anticipation she experienced. She wanted the ceremony over and done, her baby's future secured. As she glanced at the handsome man she would soon marry, her pulse jumped. How much was she looking forward to the wedding for her baby and how much for herself?

How many times would she remind herself that she was going into a loveless marriage? Was she a hopeless romantic as Matt had declared? Was she dreaming of the impossible, of a man who would fall in love with her? Did she want him to and would she fall in love with him? She knew she was already doing exactly what she had promised herself she would never do—stop guarding against heartbreak.

If something happened tomorrow and she had to walk away from all this, Matt included, she could do it without hurt, she was certain. Would she feel that way in a month? She glanced at him again. Leaning back in his chair, he had pushed his coat open. His self-confidence was obvious. He was handsome, sexy and exciting. If he dreaded their approaching nuptials, he didn't show it. And she hoped she didn't show her nervousness either.

She looked into Matt's blue eyes. It was impossible to tell what he was thinking—whether he hated her for this or if he expected a satisfactory arrangement. She bent her head to skim over all the points they had thoroughly discussed.

Finally they were finished and told Vic goodbye. In the lobby of the building Matt turned her to face him. "You have the appointment this afternoon with the wedding planner. Let's grab a bite to eat and then we can separate and meet later to go home."

She nodded and walked two blocks with him to a small restaurant that was busy with a lunch crowd.

"Feel like celebrating? You're getting what you wanted," he said as soon as they were alone in their booth.

"Yes, I'll celebrate. And you protected yourself with the agreement we just signed, so you should be satisfied."

"Actually," he said, glancing at his watch, "what is going to satisfy me is my wedding night with you," he said in a husky tone that changed the conversation. He reached across the brown wooden table to draw his fingers along her arm and her heartbeat quickened while she drew a deep breath.

"See, that's what I like. You have an instant response to me." He leaned closer over the table and lowered his voice. "You're the sexiest woman I've ever known."

"I seriously doubt that one," she said, suspecting he flirted without giving it thought.

"I'm telling the truth. You're sexy and you respond to the slightest attention. Right now, you've got me aroused and hopefully, I've done the same to you."

"Please remember that we're out in public."

"Believe me, I wouldn't be sitting over here and you over there if I didn't remember that we're not alone. But that doesn't mean I can't touch you," he added. He slipped his hand beneath the table and caressed her knee, sliding higher along her thigh.

"Matt!" she exclaimed while heat rose from deep within her and her desire intensified.

"No one can see me. We're in a booth and it's dark beneath the table. No one cares what we're doing. I want you alone with me, in my arms, but more than that, I want the night to come when you're in my bed and I can make love to you."

"You stop now," she said breathlessly, knowing she had the firmness of jelly in her tone. His light strokes along her leg were stirring feelings she didn't want to have now, making her want to be in his arms and making her want to reach for him in return.

A waiter approached their table. With a mocking smile, Matt straightened and leaned back in his seat. She ordered a salad and listened to Matt order a burger. Then they made plans for the afternoon, but now she was more aware of Matt than their conversation and it was difficult to concentrate or talk about appointments and buying clothes and running errands.

After lunch they separated, agreeing to meet in three hours. She walked a short distance and turned to look in a store window, but instead of seeing the display, she watched Matt striding away. He was tall enough to spot easily in the crowd of people on the street. Wind caught locks of his black hair and he had a long purposeful stride. Saturday night and seduction. She still wondered if she would last until a week from Saturday without trying to seduce him or letting him entice her into sex.

Fishing in her purse, she produced a list of purchases to make. Her engagement ring flashed with brilliant fire in the afternoon sunshine and she was still amazed that Matt would give her such an expensive gift.

She met with the wedding planner, and then shopped and finally went back eagerly to meet Matt, hurrying because she didn't want to be late and keep him waiting.

That afternoon at the ranch Matt shut himself in his office to take care of business. In her room, she changed to cutoffs while she remembered the last few minutes with Matt. "When your wedding night comes, Matthew Ransome, I'm going to make love to you like you've never been loved before," she said, knowing she wanted this marriage to work. She crossed the room to the mirror to study her image. "Are you falling in love with your fiancé?" she asked her image softly. She looked down at the brilliant diamond he had given her. He was being too good to her, too appealing and his kisses too devastating. Was he seducing her into an illusion of love?

"You knew you were in for heartbreak," she told her image.

She pursed her lips, remembering kissing him. "But so is he," she said softly. "The men in this family have had their way far too long."

She patted her stomach. "I've turned down two fortunes for you, so I hope you know how much I already love you," she said quietly. "*Our* baby." Matt wanted her to refer to the baby as *our* baby. Excitement fluttered in her. She was going to have a family for her baby. A father, grandfather, aunt and uncle.

Staying out of Matt's way, she explored the house. In the library, she roamed around the room, looking at leather-bound volumes that were shelved along with dog-eared children's books that must have been Matt's and his siblings'. She opened cabinets to find more books and then she found a closet with shelves of scrapbooks. She looked at dates on labels on the spines of the books and pulled out some from years earlier to look at pictures of Matt as a child. She enjoyed pictures of his brothers and sister, studying them and able to pick out Jeff's cocky grin and Matt's usually solemn expression.

After she had worked her way through a stack she noticed a large gray metal box on a shelf. The box was dusty and looked as if it hadn't been touched in years. When she tried to open it, she couldn't.

Curious, she lifted it down carefully because it was heavy. She placed it on the floor and sat beside it to try to get it open, but was unable to until she discovered a tiny brass key taped to the bottom of the box. Puzzled, she stared at the key a moment. Why would someone bother to lock a box and then tape the key where anyone could find it?

She pulled the key away and unlocked the box. A chill ran down her spine and she had a premonition of disaster. Shaking away the feeling as ridiculous, she opened the box.

Nine

Four books were in the metal box. Lifting them out, she saw that they were baby books. She glanced through them and found Matt's, then replaced the others in the box. The pages in Matt's book crackled when she opened it and she wondered how long since anyone had looked inside. She read his birth announcement and then she saw baby pictures. Turning a page, Olivia looked at a stunning young woman with black hair and movie-star looks.

This was her baby's grandmother. Olivia turned the pages slowly, looking at Matt's baby pictures and his parents. Duke was thinner, younger and undeniably handsome. Matt's mother was beautiful and Olivia stared at her picture. How could this woman walk out on her four children?

Matt insisted his father would love his new grandchild. What about Matt's mother? Was there a chance she'd had regrets through the years? Would she have changed now and want to know her grandchild?

Olivia scooped up the scrapbook and headed toward Matt's

office. She knocked on the open door. Seated behind a desk with papers spread in front of him, he was talking on the phone. He had shed his coat and tie, unbuttoned his shirt, rolled up his sleeves. Her pulse quickened and she wanted to cross the room and finish unbuttoning his shirt, take it off and run her hands over his muscled chest. Momentarily, she forgot why she had come because Matt was a virile, sexy male. When he motioned her to come in, she tried to stop thinking about his hot kisses or his hard body.

She sat across the desk from him. As soon as he ended his call, he asked, "Getting tired of being on your own?"

"Not in the least."

"I'll knock off in just a few minutes and we can swim and I'll take you into town to dinner."

"Thank you." She went around the desk to place the scrapbook in front of him. Slipping his arm around her waist, he pulled her down on his lap. She arched her brows at him. "If they could see us, people would think that we're really in love."

"In just days we'll be husband and wife for real. We might as well enjoy each other," he said.

"I quite agree," she said softly and leaned forward to kiss him. He wrapped his arm around her waist again to return her kiss that swiftly escalated in passion. She wound her arms around his neck and kissed him hungrily.

His hand slid over her knee and along her thigh. As she moaned with pleasure, he tugged her T-shirt out of the cutoffs and slipped his hand beneath her shirt to cup her breast.

"Matt!" she gasped. Desire was a hot flame low inside her. The seductive onslaught increased as he leaned down to take her nipple in his mouth. He licked slowly with his tongue, circling her bud, sucking and biting lightly, a sweet torment that made her want to spread her legs and give him full access to her.

Winding her fingers in his hair, she pulled his head up so she could return to kissing him.

His arousal pressed against her thigh and she wanted him badly. She ran her hands across his broad shoulders, clinging to him as he cradled her against his shoulder and leaned over her to kiss her hungrily. She was barely aware of his hands at the waist of her cutoffs as he unbuttoned and pushed them away. His hand slid into her lace panties and he touched her intimately.

Desire flashed like fire. Eagerly, she unbuttoned his shirt and ran her tongue over his flat nipple. His fingers stroked and rubbed her, creating a stormy friction that escalated swiftly into a pounding need.

Moving her hips wildly, she twisted against him as he carried her to an edge. He kissed her, thrusting his tongue deep and then slowly withdrawing it, to thrust deeply again, mimicking the act of sex.

Gasping, she cried out, wanting infinitely more of him. "Matt!" she cried, turning to straddle him while she unfastened his belt and trousers to free him. She leaned down to take his thick, throbbing shaft in her mouth.

He closed his eyes and wound his fingers in her hair, groaning as she licked and caressed him.

He started to slide her over him, but she caught his hands. His eyes flew open and desire burned in their depths. "Olivia—"

"We can wait until after our wedding. It's not that far away." She scooted off his lap and pulled on her clothes, straightening them, meeting his hot gaze and turning to walk away from him. "We're waiting," she said again, as if to convince herself.

When she turned around, he had straightened his clothes and was sitting watching her with a smoldering gaze.

"This marriage will be good, Matt."

"Yeah, it will," he replied, but she wondered if his thoughts were on making love instead of what she said to him. "It'll be hot and sexy," he said in a husky voice that made her wonder if she could continue to wait until Saturday.

She moved back near him. "I know something we didn't put in that prenup agreement," she said, leaning one hand on his desk and bending closer to him.

He looked up at her. "Yeah, what's that?" he asked in a husky voice while he slid his fingers slowly up her arm to her throat.

"What if we want to give this baby a brother or a sister? If I want to, will that be acceptable to you?"

"Hell, yes, it would. I never dreamed I'd have a child of my own. Shortly after Margo and I married, she made it plain that she was never having children."

"How awful to not tell you until later!" Olivia exclaimed.

"Yeah. We had some real fights over it because before marriage she hadn't leveled with me about not wanting children." He slanted Olivia a look and his blue eyes filled with curiosity. "So if I want another baby, you'll agree to my getting you pregnant?"

"Yes, I will," she said. "I think it would be wonderful to have more than one."

"How many do you want?" he asked and a suspicious note crept into his voice.

"One more child would be marvelous."

"We agree on something."

She laughed. "We haven't disagreed that much. We got through the prenup without too many battles."

"More or less. What's this?" he asked, turning the baby book around. "Damn, I haven't seen this since I was a kid."

"There are baby books for all of you on a shelf in a closet in the library. They were locked in a box."

"I haven't thought about that in years. They were locked away when we were little kids so we couldn't get to them."

"Why didn't your dad want you to look at your baby books?"

"Probably just didn't want us tearing them up. By the time we were big enough to open the box to look at the pictures, I guess none of us wanted to. I never did."

Olivia opened the book and pointed to a picture. "Matt, that's your mother, isn't it?"

"That's her," he said gruffly.

"Where is she now?"

"How the hell should I know? None of us have seen her since we were little kids."

"She'll be our baby's grandmother."

He looked up and his expression was a storm cloud. "Don't get any sentimental ideas."

"She will be the grandmother. How do you know if she hasn't changed in all these years—"

"Dammit, no! Don't you contact her. She walked out on us. Do you know what that does to a little kid?"

"I can well imagine," Olivia answered solemnly, thinking about her own parents who had been a problem all her life.

"We're not contacting her or even trying to if you possibly could. She could live in Australia for all I know."

"You hired a P.I. to check into my background. Why don't you learn her whereabouts and a little about her? She might deplore what she did, Matt."

"No. And don't you even think about it."

"It doesn't matter to you that she's the grandmother?"

"It does not. She wasn't a mother to us. She's not going to be a grandmother to this baby. Understood?"

Even though she mulled over what he said, she nodded.

"Olivia, I mean it. You forget her. She didn't give a damn about us."

"She's beautiful, Matt."

"What's that got to do with anything?"

"Nothing. I just wondered how long since you've even looked at one of her pictures."

"Actually, not for years, nor do I care to now. I would think you'd understand my attitude because of your own background, although I know your parents never abandoned you."

"They might as well have," she said, looking at the window and remembering her own life. Her gaze swung back to Matt. "Very well. She's your mother, so you have the right to ignore her, but you've never heard her side of the story and your father is a strong-willed man."

"Olivia, if you were married and had four little kids, almost babies, would you walk out on them for another man?"

"Of course I wouldn't. You should know that."

"That's right. So what kind of woman abandons her family?"

"I just thought she might have regretted what she did. Or she might have tried to come back and your father wouldn't let her—have you ever thought of that?"

"I don't think so because he was hurt. As young as I was, I know he changed when she left. He's never been as carefree or good-humored since. I don't think he would have kept her away. You just said you wouldn't walk out on little kids."

"I suppose you're right," Olivia said with a sigh as she picked up the scrapbook. He caught her arm.

"Leave the scrapbook and we'll go swim now."

"I'll put it up and meet you at the pool."

"We could shower together before our swim," he suggested, trailing his fingers along her arm. She looked at him with arched eyebrows.

"I think not."

"We're going to be married soon," he replied. She suspected he was teasing her and didn't have any expectations of showering with her.

"Until then, no." She grabbed the scrapbook and left, hearing him chuckle behind her.

Matt watched the sway of her hips as she left his office. He tossed his pen on the desk and thought about his baby pictures with his mother. He didn't like looking back and remembering the hurt and longing.

"Damn, it's been a long time," he said to himself. He didn't want to contact his mother or have Olivia get in touch with her. His thoughts jumped to Olivia and desire stirred. She was sexy, gorgeous and so self-possessed it continually surprised him. Today, she had been cool, decisive and as far as he could tell, got exactly what she wanted in the prenuptial agreement. She didn't seem to care that he put a stipulation in that if they divorced, she forfeited all rights to any money from him except child support. Her attitude toward money was also amazing, but then it always dealt with her losing control of her baby.

Marriage to Olivia. It was far more palatable today than it had been yesterday. Matt strode out of the room, hurrying to change to swim because he looked forward to being with her. At the thought of her long legs and lush body, he broke out in a sweat. He moved faster, longing to get into cool water and put out the fires his imagination ignited.

When he stepped outside, she was there, stretched on a chaise longue with her eyes closed. As he approached her, his gaze ran over her and he marveled again how flat her stomach was. She didn't look one degree pregnant.

Matt was intrigued by her. Olivia was fascinating, unpredictable and he had to admire and respect her and admit that she had gotten the best of him, as well as his dad, in the contests over their futures. Maybe someday he and Olivia would love each other. It surprised him that he even considered the notion. Was her influence changing him?

Olivia had stretched on the chaise to read, but in minutes she'd shoved the book aside and closed her eyes. It was cool and pleasant by the pool. Then she heard the door slide open and she watched Matt who had changed to his brief swim trunks. A white towel was thrown casually over his broad shoulder. Like flint striking a rock, the moment their gazes locked, sparks flew. Olivia's pulse raced and she inhaled deeply. As he approached her, she could see desire heat his blue gaze.

Looking powerful, too appealing, he strolled toward her until he reached the chaise. His gaze left hers and drifted slowly over her, making every inch of her tingle. When he looked into her eyes again, she was breathless, wanting to reach for him.

Stretching out beside her, he drew her into his arms and turned her on her side to face him. Pressed against his hard length with only tiny scraps of material between them, she ached with desire. Each encounter, every hour, her need for him grew. His body was warm, hard. She could feel the rough texture of his thighs with the short dark hairs as her legs pressed against his.

"Let's swim in the nude," he suggested, unfastening her swim top to shove it away and then pushing down the skimpy scrap of material that only partially covered her bottom. With eager, trembling hands, she shoved down his trunks and pressed against his arousal. She twisted away from his kiss. "We're waiting until our wedding night."

"Sure," he whispered gruffly and covered her mouth with his again until she wriggled away and stood.

As she retrieved her suit, he watched her, his eyes taking in every naked inch of her. "I want to kiss you from head to toe and love you until you're senseless," he whispered.

She turned her head to slant him a look. Beneath his watchful gaze, she pulled on her suit. He was stretched back on the chaise, his arousal hard and ready for her. Her heart pounded and she longed to go right back into his arms.

Even though he wasn't touching her, she was in flames. Unable to resist, she walked closer and then she leaned down over him, brushing her breasts against his bare chest and raising slightly to look him straight in the eye. "Next Saturday, I'm going to love you until you're too exhausted to move," she whispered and bent down again to draw a line down his chest with her tongue, sliding lower over his flat, washboard stomach, tasting his slightly salty skin. She looked up. "I want you to want me until you're crazy with desire."

She drew the tip of her tongue lower, over his thick manhood. He groaned and sat up, sweeping her into his arms to kiss her passionately, pulling her into his embrace. Her heart thudded and she kissed him in a dizzying spiral that momentarily made everything else between them insignificant. Surroundings and circumstances vanished. His kisses changed her to a quivering, boneless mass of jelly. She wanted him as she had never wanted a man. He could drive her to a point of need that made her lose all reason.

"Later, later," she whispered, pulling her top back in place and turning to walk away from him toward the pool.

Without looking back, she went down the steps into the pool, letting the water swirl around her. As she cooled down, her racing pulse slowed to a normal beat. She swam in long strokes, in no hurry, just wanting to relax and cope with scalding desire. And try to get a wall of resistance between Matt and her.

He followed, diving into the water, swimming to catch up with her. He bobbed up beside her and moved them both where they could touch bottom and stand. He slid his arm around her waist to pull her close.

"Next Saturday, you're mine," he said, sliding his hand over her hip.

Her eyebrow arched. "It's mutual that day."

She kicked away from him, and for the next half hour any time he swam close, she turned to swim away. She kept distance between them, enjoying the water, wanting to be in his arms, excited to be with him.

Finally she climbed out. "I'll go dress for dinner," she called, hurrying to slip into her cover-up.

"As far as I'm concerned, you can eat dressed the way you are right now," he said, climbing out behind her. Water splashed off his body and her pulse jumped while she assessed him thoroughly.

She gave him an amused look. "I think I better put some clothes between us," she said and left, her back tingling because she was certain that his gaze followed her across the patio until she was out of his sight.

She let out her breath. By next Saturday night, they would be wild with desire and she intended to make love to him until he never wanted to let her out of his life.

When she returned to the patio, he was in jeans and a fresh T-shirt that clung to his muscles and revealed his powerful shoulders and biceps. Wind lifted locks of his black hair and she thought about how it felt to run her fingers through his thick hair. His gaze drifted over her T-shirt and cutoffs and as she walked up to him, she saw the approving warmth in his eyes.

"You look great," he said.

"Thank you," she answered, smiling at him. "I'm glad you approve."

"I approve except I'd like to peel you out of your T-shirt and cutoffs."

"Maybe later," she said. He smiled, but his eyes sparkled with anticipation that matched her bubbling excitement.

While a thin column of gray smoke drifted skyward, steaks sizzled on the grill. The tantalizing smell whetted her appetite. "I'm starving," she said.

"The feeling is mutual," he said in such a husky voice, she turned to look at him. "I could eat you for dinner," he said, and her pulse jumped.

"No, that comes later," she replied softly, and his chest expanded as he inhaled.

"I'm ready to cool down with some tea," she said, seeing that he had two glasses of iced tea poured. He handed one to her and in minutes they sat at the table with thick steaks and baked potatoes.

"Here's to our future together," he said, raising his glass of iced tea and she touched her glass against his with a faint clink.

"May it be less stormy than our past," she added, and he smiled. "Soon I'll enroll in the university for the fall. It's a dream come true for me to be able to do that. I'll carry a full course load. Thank you, Matt, for your generosity."

"I have to thank you in return. I'm getting a baby in my life."

"You'll be a good dad, I imagine."

He shrugged. "I don't know until I try and see how I do. At least I'll love the little boy or girl."

"Now that the prenup agreement is out of the way, I need to concentrate on the wedding arrangements. The wedding planner will be here in the morning at ten."

"All that is up to you. I'll take care of the honeymoon arrangements," he said.

"We're taking a honeymoon?" she asked, surprised. "I'm amazed we're going on a honeymoon."

"Why not take a honeymoon?" he asked and the corner of his mouth lifted slightly.

"Since we're not in love—"

"We're going to have great sex," he said, lowering his voice and leaning closer, leaving his steak untouched. "I want you all to myself. Super sex is a good reason for a honeymoon."

"I suppose," she said, but she had a pang of longing for more than lust and great sex. She wanted a honeymoon where they cared about each other, but she knew that wasn't going to be the situation and she better not delude herself. "I like surprises," she said carefully.

"Good. You'll have to wait until next Saturday to find out where we'll honeymoon."

She laughed, and he drew his finger along her cheek. "I like your laughter, Olivia. We're going to have a workable arrangement."

As she gazed into his blue eyes, desire filled his expression. She put down her fork and got up, walking around to him to sit in his lap. When she approached him, he pushed back his chair and the moment she sat down he wrapped his arms around her.

"I intend for it to be better than a 'workable arrangement,'" she said. She leaned forward to kiss him, sliding her tongue into his mouth and drawing it slowly over his. His arms went around her and he held her close, kissing her hard until she leaned back.

"How's that for 'workable'?" she whispered. "Or this?" she asked, tugging up his T-shirt so she could slide her tongue over his flat nipple and then shed kisses lower. "Or this?" she asked.

"Dammit," he said, winding his fingers in her hair and tilting her head back to give him full access to her mouth. He bent over her, molding her to him. His hand cupped her body, pulling her hips closer while he kissed her.

She pushed against him and twisted away and they gazed at each other. "It'll be workable, all right," she said, sliding off his lap and standing. "And we're waiting because it won't be many more days."

He stood to embrace her. "You're going to be mine, Olivia," he said in a raspy voice that played like a soft wind across her raw nerves.

"Be warned, Matt. Soon I may find your heart, and it'll be mine."

His eyes clouded and his jaw firmed. "You're a romantic, a

dreamer and an optimist. Watch out because I don't want to hurt you. What we're going to have will be great, but it won't be love."

She smiled at him, hiding the stab of pain his words caused and surprised by the intensity of hurt. "We'll see," she said, wondering if she was deluding herself about him. What would it take to make him fall in love with her?

"In the meantime, let's clear things up and sit down and do some wedding planning," she said, trying to keep her voice light and casual.

Matt's cell phone rang and he pulled it out of his pocket to answer. "It's Nick," he whispered. "Hi," he said. "I've got news and I know this is short notice. Olivia Brennan and I want you to come home next weekend. We're getting married."

Olivia walked away to give Matt privacy even though he was quiet and his brother had to be doing all the talking. She wondered if Nick was trying to talk Matt out of marrying her. Olivia picked up dishes to carry them to the kitchen. She knew his family didn't want him to marry her. Was she insisting on something that was going to be a disaster for all concerned, and most of all, for her?

She knew she better decide for certain because next Saturday would soon be here.

Friday evening a week later, Olivia had another attack of butterflies. Within the hour Matt's brother was arriving and in an hour and a half his sister would get in. The wedding planner had assistants getting the house ready and tonight they would have a rehearsal and then all go to Rincon to a country club for dinner. The closer the wedding, the more nervous Olivia became, assailed with doubts and last-minute jitters. Was she doing the right thing? she asked herself for what seemed like the hundredth time. Yet she was falling in love with Matt and she prayed that with this marriage, love would come to him. Then doubts would bombard her. Was she locking herself into a loveless union that would grow more difficult with time?

If she thought about walking out, though, she knew that wasn't what she wanted to do.

She slipped her red dress over her head, feeling the silky lining that was cool against her skin. Her wispy underclothes were red lace, a luxury she'd never before been able to afford. She looked around the bedroom and was reassured by the life she was giving her baby.

The moment she walked into the family room and looked at Matt in a charcoal suit and red tie, her qualms fled. When his blue eyes met her gaze, her heart thudded and her concerns about marriage vanished.

Another tall, handsome man stood beside him and they both crossed the room to her. "Olivia, meet my brother, Nick."

Extending her hand, she looked at a man with curly brown hair who stood an inch taller than Matt, as broad through the shoulders with the same straight nose and firm jaw. There the resemblances ended. Nick's dark brown eyes flashed with curiosity as she shook his hand.

"Welcome to the family," Nick said and smiled, his teeth looking a dazzling white against his dark tan.

"Thank you," she replied, relieved that he was friendly because Matt's father still was not and he had declined to join them tonight. "I'm glad you could get here and be with us for the wedding."

"Wouldn't have missed it," Nick said. "Now if we can just get my wandering sister home. Dad will come around eventually."

Unable to agree with him, Olivia nodded, but she didn't want to say so.

"Ahh, here she is," Matt said, looking over Olivia's head. She turned to see a tall, striking blonde in a sleeveless beige silk dress.

"I think all three of you had different mothers," Olivia remarked to Matt and he flashed a grin. "You don't look alike at all."

Without answering her, he was gone, crossing the room in long strides with his brother as both of them welcomed their sister. Olivia watched them hug and kiss, thinking all three could have been models. But then Duke Ransome was a handsome man and Olivia remembered the pictures in Matt's baby book of his mother who had been stunning. Why wouldn't their offspring be handsome and beautiful?

Matt approached her with his sister and brother. "Olivia, meet my sister, Katherine. Katherine, this is my fiancée, Olivia Brennan."

Gazing into crystal-blue eyes, Olivia smiled and shook Katherine's hand.

"So you're the woman who has shaken up this family? As least it put an end to mourning Jeff so much because now there's a new worry."

"And I'm the new worry?" Olivia asked with amusement.

Suddenly Katherine smiled. "I believe you are, but maybe it's not warranted. Goodness knows, this family can use new blood. And a baby is fantastic! I was beginning to give up on ever having a baby in our midst. You two didn't help the cause," she teased, looking at first Matt and then Nick.

"I don't see you helping the cause either," Matt told her in a good-natured tone.

"Don't ever hold your breath on that one," Katherine responded, turning her attention back to Olivia. "So you're going to law school?"

Olivia nodded. "I have to get my undergrad degree first." All the time she talked to Matt's brother and sister, she was aware of Matt at her side. He was friendly enough, but it should be obvious to everyone that he wasn't in love.

Within the hour the wedding party and the minister arrived and they went through a rehearsal. While they received instructions, Olivia felt a pang over the sham marriage. Yet each time she was besieged with qualms, she looked at Matt and knew she was making the best possible choice. If only…she blanked that out. Tomorrow she would be Mrs. Matthew Ransome, for better or for worse. How she wished she had his love.

As soon as they finished the brief rehearsal, they left for the Rincon country club and a catered barbecue dinner.

It was midnight before they returned to the ranch. Nick and

Katherine were staying at their father's house, so they told Matt and Olivia good-night and drove on down the road.

As Olivia walked across the porch and into the house, Matt draped his arm across her shoulders.

"Your brother and sister were wonderful to me. The way they treated me, you'd think we were in love and having a real marriage."

"Nick and Katherine are all right."

"I'm sorry for your sake that your father hasn't had a change of heart."

They entered the kitchen where only one small light was on. Matt turned to face her and put his hands on her shoulders. "Dad doesn't change easily, and he thinks I'm getting into something that's going to make me unhappy."

"I hope that isn't the case," she said, "and I'm truly sorry that he didn't join us. I know it was difficult for the three of you without him present."

"Oh, no. Dad just cut himself out of an evening with all of us. He'll be there tomorrow. You'll see."

She doubted it, but at the moment she was far more aware of Matt running his hands along her arms up to her shoulders.

"Your brother and sister were really great. I wish they stayed here."

"Got butterflies?" he asked, changing the subject abruptly and looking intently at her.

"Not badly," she replied, not wanting to admit how bad a case of nerves she had.

"C'mon. We'll sit in the kitchen and have hot chocolate. Or we could do something else," he said, leaning down to brush her lips with his.

Her heart thudded, but she held him away. "Until tomorrow night," she whispered and stood on tiptoe to kiss him long and passionately.

Finally she twisted away and gazed at him. "I'll pass on the hot chocolate and see you in the morning," she said.

She went upstairs to her room and closed the door.

Tomorrow she would get married to a man who didn't love her. She shook her head. Every time she questioned herself about the ceremony, she knew she wanted to go through with it.

The next morning Olivia could hardly believe that the time had come. This day she would become Mrs. Matthew Ransome. She still half expected his father to do something to stop the wedding.

When Olivia entered the kitchen for breakfast, she heard a knock at the back door and opened it to face Katherine who was in a T-shirt and cutoffs with her hair caught up in a clip. She carried a dress bag and Olivia knew it held the dress that Katherine would wear as one of her attendants.

"Come in. I was just starting to fix breakfast, so why don't you join me?" Olivia asked.

"Sure. That's why I came and left the men behind. Matt can go join them if he wants." She followed Olivia into the kitchen. "I'll hang up my dress in a bedroom," she said, carrying a yellow sheath encased in a clear bag.

In minutes she returned and looked around. "What can I do?"

"I guess fix coffee if you want some. Or pour orange juice."

As Katherine got out the coffeepot, she glanced at Olivia. "So no cold feet?"

"No. Maybe a few jitters, but I'm delighted with our agreement and I think we can make a good marriage of this union."

Katherine continued to study Olivia. "Just don't break my brother's heart. He's already been through that once."

"I have no intention of hurting him," Olivia replied. "Just the opposite is much more likely to happen."

Katherine's brows arched. "You're in love with my brother?"

Olivia could feel her cheeks flush. "I'm beginning to care about him," she replied cautiously.

Katherine nodded, looking lost in thought. "Well then, I hope you both fall in love. Whatever happens, I hope you have a good arrangement. I don't want to see Matt hurt. I don't want to see you hurt." Katherine studied Olivia. "I watched you two last night. You may be good for my brother."

Olivia smiled. "I hope I am," she replied, wondering if Katherine had ever been in love. Matt had talked very little about his brother or sister. She broke eggs into a skillet and stirred them. "We've been so busy all week making wedding arrangements and getting a prenuptial agreement finished that we haven't had a chance to talk about much else."

"Matt's reliable and he keeps his word," Katherine said. "And we're all thrilled about the baby. You don't look pregnant in the least."

"I definitely am," Olivia said, remembering that Jeff wasn't thrilled and hated learning that he would be a father, but she saw no point in telling Katherine. She dropped slices of bread into a toaster and returned to scrambling the eggs. In a few minutes she sat at the table across from Katherine.

"Olivia, Matt told me what Dad offered you."

"Your father may never like me or speak to me."

"He'll come around when your baby is born. That took some guts to stand up to him and it took something special to turn him down."

"You'd have turned him down, wouldn't you, Katherine?" Olivia asked, suddenly certain that Katherine would have.

"Yes. I wouldn't give up a baby of mine for money. I'm glad you didn't either. You may be really good for our family."

"Thanks," Olivia said, feeling as if she had found a friend she could trust in Matt's sister.

"Good morning," Matt said, striding into the kitchen, his gaze going to Olivia as he crossed the room to her and leaned down to brush a light kiss on her lips. He squeezed her shoulder lightly. "Do you want to get married today?" he asked, smiling at her.

"Yes, I do. I hope you're not having second thoughts," she said.

"Nope. Not at all." He turned to his sister. "Good morning, Kat," he said, crossing the kitchen to get toast and eggs.

"You can join Dad and Nick at Dad's house," she said and Matt set down the plate he held.

"I'll go do that and leave you ladies to your wedding talk." He winked at Olivia and left the room.

Katherine turned a speculative gaze on Olivia. "Maybe you're closer to Matt loving you than you think."

Olivia merely nodded because she knew she was a long way from having his love now.

By the time she and Katherine had finished breakfast and she had showed Katherine her wedding dress, the wedding planner and entourage arrived followed by the caterer and soon the house bustled with people. Katherine left to dress and in minutes Olivia's friends who would be attendants arrived to help her.

The band arrived and while they set up on the patio, Katherine joined Olivia and Olivia's friends who would be attendants.

Still caught in a dreamlike quality, Olivia dressed in the white silk. She wore white rosebuds in her hair, which was pinned on top of her head with a few locks tumbling free. Looking at herself in the mirror, she couldn't keep from staring, dazed by her reflection. Her wedding day. Marriage to Matt.

"You look beautiful," Katherine said with a cloudy look in her eyes, and Olivia wondered what had happened to Katherine in the past.

The moment was gone and it was time for the ceremony to begin.

Folding chairs had been placed in the large living room and banks of white roses were placed along the walls. As the piano player began, the groomsmen and the bridegroom entered the front of the room. Then the bridesmaids went down the aisle and finally, with a flourish of a trumpeter, Olivia knew it was time for her to proceed.

The guests stood, turning toward her. While her heart drummed, she walked with Nick who would accompany her down the aisle and then take his place beside Matt as best man.

She saw only Matt, whose blue-eyed gaze was locked with hers. And then she began walking down the aisle toward him.

Ten

Matt's blue eyes bored into her. Tall and devastatingly handsome in his black tux, he smiled at her. She smiled in return while her heart raced.

She was barely aware when Nick moved away after placing her hand in Matt's. His strong, warm fingers closed around her hand and they faced the minister.

She watched Matt as she repeated her vows. His blue eyes were brilliant, yet she couldn't guess what he was thinking— whether he was happy or angry now that the moment was actually here and he was making what they had planned to be a lifetime commitment.

"I, Olivia, take thee, Matt, to be my lawful, wedded husband," she said, dazzled by what was happening. She was marrying Matt Ransome. It was real. The whole marriage agreement had seemed a dream until this moment, but now it was coming true.

Then they were finished and the minister introduced them to the guests as Mr. and Mrs. Matthew Ransome.

"You may kiss the bride," he said to Matt and she looked up as Matt slipped his arms lightly around her and leaned close. His lips brushed hers and then were firm as they met hers in a way that seemed as binding to her heart as the vows they had just spoken. Her heart thudded and the amazement of actually being married to him rocked her. When he released her, she opened her eyes to find him watching her. He smiled and enveloped her hand in his before they turned. Hurrying beside him, she still tingled from his kiss.

As they walked up the aisle, she looked at the guests. With his jaw clamped shut Duke Ransome stared at her. He appeared as angry as he had the last time she had seen him, but her happiness was a solid wall around her emotions this day. Matt whisked her through the house to circle back to the living room for pictures.

Dressed in the pale yellow silk sheath, Katherine walked up to hug her lightly. "Welcome to our family, Mrs. Ransome," she said and smiled at Olivia.

"Thanks, Katherine. I intend for this union to last," Olivia said and Katherine nodded.

"If you ever want to talk, just call me. I know Matt pretty well. Give him time. He was hurt badly before."

Olivia nodded.

"Welcome, Olivia," Nick said, hugging her, his brown eyes twinkling. "I hope for the very best for both of you. May your future be grand."

"Thanks, Nick. You and Katherine were great to drop everything and come home on such short notice."

"I wouldn't have missed this for anything," Katherine said with a smile. Then Matt was beside her again and Katherine turned to hug him.

"You be good to her, y'hear," she said, poking her brother in the chest with her finger.

"What else would I be?" he asked Katherine with a smile.

"Bride and groom, please," the photographer called and they broke up, stepping back as Olivia and Matt posed for the first picture. As Olivia stood with Matt's arm around her waist, she saw Duke watching from the far side of the room, a scowl still on his face. Was he going to give her trouble in the future, she wondered. Then she forgot him as the photographer began giving her instructions on a pose for the next picture.

It was half an hour before they joined the guests on the patio for the reception. She unfastened and removed her train and in minutes Matt removed his coat. The sunny morning would be carved in her memory forever, more garlands of white roses, the tempting smell of roasting beef and pork, and a crowd of friends of Matt and his family. The band played, the splash of the fountain added to the festive ambience. Yet surroundings and friends faded from her notice when Olivia looked at her handsome husband.

She gazed across the patio at him as he laughed at something one of his friends said. Tall, rugged and handsome, he took her breath. The week had drawn them closer—or had she been the only one to feel that way? Would she ever look at him without a jump in her pulse?

As she watched him, he turned his head and gazed into her eyes and even across the crowd and space that separated them, sparks flew. He watched her, yet he was talking to the man beside him. Without taking his gaze from hers, Matt laughed and said something to his friend. As she watched, Matt crossed the patio and strolled toward her.

With each step closer, her pulse accelerated. He stopped only inches away, smiling down at her with that crooked, inviting smile that made her weak in the knees.

"Hi, Mrs. Ransome."

"I don't know if I'll ever become accustomed to that."

"You will someday. You look gorgeous, Olivia," he said seriously.

"Thank you. You look rather nice yourself."

"Thanks," he said and touched a lock of her hair. "I'm about ready to leave."

"We can't leave now!" she exclaimed. "Not with all these

friends you have and your sister and brother here. We have to stay for an hour or two at least."

The corner of his mouth lifted in a smile, but she could see desire burning in his blue eyes. "The very first moment we can get out of here without being rude, you come get me. Promise?"

"All right, I will. In the meantime, we should circulate." Before she could say anything else, well-wishers came up and Matt introduced her to three of his friends who were friendly, polite and respectful and made her realize how much her life had already changed.

When the band director announced that the groom would have the first dance with the bride, Matt turned her into his arms as the band began to play. He held her close, her hand wrapped in his with her other hand on his broad shoulder. He was clean-shaven, his hair slightly windblown now, so handsome she couldn't stop staring.

"I think time has stopped. I've been waiting forever to get you off to myself."

She smiled. "Not a lot longer."

"I could whisk you away after this dance," he said.

"No, you can't. We have to cut the cake and talk to more guests. Patience, patience."

"What saves me is the realization that it's going to be worth the wait," he drawled in a deep voice and she gave him another smile.

"Soon enough we will be naked in bed together and you'll forget how long you had to wait."

He inhaled deeply and his eyes darkened. "That just makes me want to get out of here more than ever."

"Think about something else." She tilted her head to study him. "I don't even know what you like to do for entertainment or what you want out of life."

"Right now, it's you."

Laughing, she glanced across the patio to see his father talking to a group of men. Duke Ransome laughed at something one of the men said to him.

"I see your father has loosened up."

"He's already had a couple of drinks so that took off the edge and now he's with some of his cronies. He's not thinking about us. At this point, it's a done deal. He'll probably settle back and accept life the way it is. When the baby comes, you'll wonder if he's the same man you know now. He'll be nuts about this grandchild."

"That's what Katherine said."

"As a matter of fact, don't be surprised if he doesn't appear with a peace offering. I heard him talking to Katherine and I think he's beginning to plan on having a couple of rooms in his house redone for a nursery and a playroom."

She glanced again at Duke. "I'll believe it when I see it. He predicted disaster if I married you and he wanted desperately to run me off."

"You'll see. He'll thaw fast now because you're family."

She looked up at Matt. "Family. That's one of the most wonderful things anyone has ever said to me."

He laughed and spun her around. His arm tightened around her waist to hold her close while they danced.

"Everyone is watching," she said.

"That's because you're beautiful."

"Thank you, but I don't think that's why." She clung to him, following his lead and thought they danced as if they had been dancing together for years. He twirled her around again and then pulled her close and she smiled up at him. He gazed down with a hungry look that increased her heartbeat. She wrapped her arms around his neck and danced with him, smiling up at him.

"This is going to be a good marriage," he said.

"Trying to convince yourself?" she asked, feeling a bubbling undercurrent of excitement.

"I think it will be good. Don't you?"

"I hope so, but who knows what the future will bring? You and I barely know each other."

He looked over her head. "I think we've got everyone convinced otherwise, except my family and whoever you've told."

The band finished and commenced a slow number. She heard a deep voice behind her.

"May I have this dance?"

She turned to face Nick, who glanced at his brother. "Get lost," he said to Matt and took her in his arms lightly.

"I'm glad you came for the wedding and Matt is glad to see you," she said, looking into his dark brown eyes and marveling how different the brothers looked.

"I wanted to come see for myself. I don't want my brother hurt," Nick said solemnly. "I didn't have a chance to talk to you alone last night. Don't hurt him, Olivia. He said that the two of you aren't in love, but seeing you together last night made me feel better."

"I don't intend to hurt him. I hope neither one of us hurts the other," she said, looking up at Nick. "Matt was the one who approached me and who wanted my baby in the Ransome family. Always remember that. I didn't come to your family or ask your family for money."

"I know. Matt told me that Jeff didn't want his baby. That's sad news for the rest of us. We need this baby in our family. I'm not the marrying kind. Jeff is gone. God knows, Katherine won't marry. Matt keeps his heart under lock and key. Your baby is the only hope for the next generation for our family."

"That's sort of a bleak outlook about you and Katherine and Matt."

"Nope. That's just the way it is. Just be good to him. He'll be good to you."

"I'm glad to hear that," she replied.

"You ever want to talk, you can call me."

"Thanks. Katherine made the same offer."

"In spite of us traveling and not seeing each other constantly, we're all close. We care about each other."

"Good. That's important."

He spun around and she saw Matt standing in a group of people while he watched her dance.

Matt dimly heard the conversation going on beside him, but

his attention was on Olivia. She was gorgeous today. As she had walked down the aisle, he thought his heart would pound out of his chest. She still exuded that earthy, sexy air, but today, she was stunning. He couldn't stop watching her, devouring her with his gaze and wanting her in his arms more than ever. He had made a bargain that just got better with each day. It was a loveless marriage of convenience, but it was a fantastic arrangement in a lot of ways and one of them was the sex he was going to have with Olivia.

His temperature climbed at the thought and he tried to focus on what was being said by friends. In minutes though, his attention was right back on his new wife. He glanced at his watch. He couldn't wait to get her out of here and off to himself.

They hadn't even cut the cake yet and the afternoon threatened to drag on forever. He suspected she was enjoying herself because her eyes sparkled and her face was flushed and she continually smiled.

He was tempted to get her away from Nick to dance with her himself, but he curbed the impulse, even though he ached to hold her. Was she becoming important to him? The notion surprised him because he didn't expect that to happen.

It was only a short leap from being essential to him to being in love with her. Was she going to slip past the barriers around his heart?

In the brief time she had known them she had charmed his brother and sister.

His gaze ran over Olivia in the long, white dress and he imagined her without it, his mouth going dry and his temperature rising again. He glanced at his watch. Time seemed to stand still. He realized the number was ending and he could go claim his bride from his brother.

He threaded his way past couples who wished him well and congratulated him and wanted to talk and finally he was there behind her and he couldn't resist reaching for her.

"Olivia."

When Olivia heard her name, she turned as Matt slipped his

arm around her waist and pulled her close against him. Katherine approached them.

"Come on, you two, before you start dancing again. They're ready for you to cut the cake and the photographer is waiting."

"Gladly," Matt said and Olivia laughed as he took her hand and they followed Katherine across the patio.

Olivia was aware of Matt's hand lightly on hers as they cut into the seven-tier cake together. She had been as dazzled by the cake as all the other details of this wedding where cost was not a problem. The entire day had seemed a dream and she couldn't get used to being Mrs. Matt Ransome. She looked up at her handsome new husband and felt a pang. Only one thing was missing to make the day perfect, but that one thing was the most important of all.

It was three in the afternoon when Matt found her. "We can get out of here now," he said, taking her arm. She smiled at him.

"Let's tell everyone goodbye," she said, and waved at his sister. He groaned and followed her across the patio to Katherine where she stood by the pool.

"We're leaving, Katherine. Thanks so much for coming for the wedding. You take care of yourself," he said and hugged his sister.

"You, too, Matt. I'm happy for you and I hope this works out for you and Olivia."

She turned to hug Olivia. "Be patient with my brother," she said, giving a toss of her head that sent her blond hair swirling across her shoulders. Olivia smiled.

"I'll try. Thanks for coming, Katherine. It meant a lot and I'm so glad to get to know you," Olivia said.

"Hey, I want a hug, too," Nick said, joining them and turning to Olivia who hugged him lightly.

"Thanks for coming to the wedding and I'm glad to meet you, Nick."

"We're happy to have you in the family, Olivia. You're the best thing that's happened to us in years and years."

"I hope so," she replied, wondering how long Nick would feel that way and wondering how much Matt shared the sentiment.

Matt embraced Katherine and then as the two brothers hugged, Matt thanked Nick for coming again. "Don't wait so long to come home, you two," he said to both of them. "Now we're getting the hell out of Dodge," he said, taking Olivia's arm and striding across the patio to a back gate. She stretched out her legs to keep up with him, her excitement mounting.

"I have a car stashed out here. A plane is waiting and we're on our way."

The moment they were in the car she turned to him. "Where are we going? You have to tell me now."

"To Ariel."

"I've never heard of it. Where is that?"

"It's a tiny island off the Yucatan Peninsula. I own it. When I bought the place, it already had a name, but it's not big enough for you to have ever heard of it. We have an airstrip on Ariel so I can fly in and out of there. It's isolated, peaceful and beautiful. I think you'll like it. I have a staff who keep it maintained when I'm there. They were there all last week getting everything ready, but we'll have the house to ourselves. Two couples live on the island who work for me and they'll come in to clean and cook part of the time."

"Aren't they isolated out there by themselves?"

"They like living there and have their own planes on the island. The Thorensons are retired stockbrokers doing just what they want. The demands of the job I hired them for aren't great. The other couple, the Ellisons, had their own business that went belly up, and they've said this job is perfect. A small paradise and a plane to get them out of there whenever they want. So far we've been fortunate during hurricane seasons. We've been hit, but most structures have weathered the storms. I've had to replace roofs and windows, but it's been worth it. You'll see."

She stared at him, amazed that he would own an island. He glanced at her. "You're staring."

"You just surprise me."

He smiled. "Good, because you've been one surprise after

another to me. We're all amazed you turned down my dad—
by all, I mean Nick and Katherine and me."

"Katherine said now that she knows me a little, she wasn't
so surprised. And she said she understood. She would have
turned him down."

"Katherine probably would, but that's different. Katherine
is unpredictable. She's grown up with a life of ease and wealth
and what she wanted, most of the time. Not so with you. You've
had a life of poverty and hardship. That should make my dad's
offer much more attractive and far more difficult to resist."

"No, it didn't. I didn't have to think about it."

"Nick couldn't imagine you turning so much down because
he had the same impression I did until I told him about you and
our first meeting. They like you."

While he talked, Olivia ran her hand over the elegant leather
seat and was amazed how swiftly her life had changed. Never had
she dreamed of living the life she was now. Even more astound-
ing was her handsome new husband. As she studied his profile,
her mouth went dry. She wanted to touch him and kiss him.

"How long?" she asked in a breathless, throaty voice that
made him glance at her and then back to his driving.

"How long *what?*"

"How long until we're on that island and alone?" she asked
softly, sliding her hand along his muscled thigh.

His fingers wrapped around hers tightly. "Not soon enough,"
he replied and his voice thickened. While he watched his
driving, he raised her hand to brush a kiss along her knuckles.

They sped to the airport in Fort Worth and soon were aboard
the Ransome jet.

When they reached cruising speed and she could move
around the plane, she unbuckled her seat belt. "I'll change out
of this dress."

"Just stay the way you are," Matt said, catching her wrist.
"We'll be there before you know it."

She sat back and buckled up again. "All right, but will I step
off the plane into sand?"

"Nope, and you can hold up your skirt. I've got a high wall around my place so soon you can go completely naked and no one will see you except me which is exactly what I intend. That's one reason I bought this particular island. Privacy and peace and I can get to it quickly and easily."

Olivia looked below at the lush green fields and then she turned back to her husband.

"Your dad congratulated me on my marriage to you today," she said.

"I saw him talking to you and would have joined you if I'd thought you needed to be rescued, but after last week, I know you can hold your own with my dad."

"I think he's just making the most of a bad situation right now."

"He'll accept you. He probably has more respect for you than he did before."

She laughed. "Like father, like son. All of you must have thought your brother got tangled with a real bimbo."

"It was easy to jump to conclusions and make hasty judgments."

"Just remember that in the future," she said, thinking again about the scrapbook of pictures of his mother. "I think there's a remote possibility you might have done that concerning your mother."

His smile vanished, and he leaned forward, catching her chin in his hand. "You leave that alone, Olivia. You're getting into something that doesn't concern you and none of us wants any contact with her. She walked out on us. Get it?"

"Yes, I do, but it was decades ago and the little I've seen of your father, you could have been told a twisted version of the truth. After all, you were little kids. How difficult would it be to bend the truth and convince all of you that you were hearing facts?"

"If you didn't know me and we weren't married, would you try to cultivate my dad's friendship because he's the grandfather of your baby?"

Startled, she gazed at Matt while she mulled over his question and she shook her head. "No, I wouldn't."

"All right. She may be a hell of a lot worse than Dad. Leave it alone. At least my dad raised all of us and he cares deeply about this grandbaby."

She could see Matt's point and she nodded. She smiled at him and leaned forward to place her hands on his knees and brush a kiss lightly on his lips. "Let's not have any cross words mar this day that has been a dream-come-true event so far. It's perfect, Matt, and I want to make you smile and then I want to kiss and love you until you will never want to let me go."

"Do tell, Mrs. Ransome," he drawled softly, leaning inches from her face. "Sounds like the best plan possible to me. We'll have our own private beach and we can stay naked. Food is already cooked, and no one is coming in to do anything unless I call and ask them to." His voice lowered while he drew his finger along the V of her neckline, stirring tingles. "I'm going to love you senseless, Olivia. I feel as if I've been waiting forever for this night."

He slipped his hand behind her head and kissed her long and passionately. As he started to unbuckle her seat belt to pick her up, she caught his hands to stop him and she pulled away. "Wait. Not here and not now."

He looked amused as he leaned back. "I'll wait, but no one is going to disturb us here."

"Just wait until we're alone."

"It already seems like I've waited eons."

She smiled at him and nodded in agreement.

When they began to fly over the Gulf, she looked out at bright blue water with an occasional boat creating a white wake. She spotted a dazzling white cruise ship and pointed each thing out to him even though he was right beside her and could see for himself.

She knew when they approached the island and at first she was astounded how small it looked but when the plane lost altitude to land, she forgot size. Her breath caught and she stared in wonder at white sand that was as dazzling in the sunshine as the cruise ship had been. Palms swayed gently and the water was a brilliant blue, lapping at the shore with tiny whitecaps. She saw the landing strip and two planes tied down and a hangar with a tin roof.

The pilot helped Matt transfer their bags to the waiting car and then Matt held the door for her. As she watched him stride around the car, she knew she was hopelessly in love with him already.

He was too sexy, too appealing, too handsome, too generous, too likeable to keep her heart sealed away. When he circled the car, wind blew locks of his black hair. How had she ever thought she could resist falling in love with him?

Sliding into the car beside her, he leaned over to brush another light kiss on her lips. "Welcome to Ariel, Mrs. Ransome."

"Thank you, Mr. Ransome," she said, trying to keep from being too solemn and losing the joy and excitement she had experienced all day, yet it was sobering to face that fact that she was in love with her virile new husband and know that he not only did not love her in return, but he might not ever stop guarding his heart.

She had locked herself into a loveless marriage. She reminded herself that this loveless marriage was going to be a far better future than she had ever dreamed of before.

She clung to that thought as they swept along a road that was made of broken shells with lush green jungle crowding them.

They rounded a bend and drove into a clearing and her heart jumped at the beauty of the house. Made of white stucco, it was a sharp contrast with the blue waters beyond it. The lawn was well tended with palms and masses of bright red hibiscus, a blooming yellow poui, red chenille plants and masses of pink oleander. Climbing yellow bougainvillea ran up porch columns and over the roof.

"It's paradise, Matt!" she gasped.

"Good. I think so, too, and I'm glad you like it. Wait until you see our ranch in Argentina. We're going to stay here four days and then fly to the ranch."

"Argentina?"

"When I met you, I told you we were buying another

ranch—it's in Argentina. We've leased it for the past five years so it won't be new to our family."

He parked and came around to open the door. As she stepped out, Matt swept her into his arms. Shrieking with surprise, she wrapped her arms around his neck.

"I'll carry my bride over the threshold," he said, going up the steps easily and crossing the porch to enter a house with a wide hallway and a gleaming plank floor. Ceiling fans turned lazily. Matt carried her to the bedroom where he slowly lowered her, letting her slide down his muscled body while he set her on her feet.

"Oh, this is fantastic!" she said, looking through floor-to-ceiling glass doors that opened onto a flower-and-palm-covered patio. White sand ran a hundred yards down to the water.

"You're what's fantastic," he said, catching her wrist and pulling her to him. Removing her veil, he tossed it aside and tugged pins out of her hair. When her hair tumbled over her shoulders, he wound his fingers in it, then tightened his fist and tilted her head to give him access to her mouth.

Her heart thudded, and she forgot their glorious surroundings.

"You're the most beautiful bride in the whole world," he said softly right behind her as he brushed a kiss on her nape and then turned her to face him. "I've been waiting for this moment far too long," he said and his voice lowered another notch.

Eleven

Olivia trembled at the sight of the blatant desire in Matt's intense gaze that lowered to her mouth and made her lips tingle. She stood on tiptoe, wrapping her arms around his neck and pulling him closer while she brushed her lips across his mouth.

With a groan he leaned down. "You'll never know how much I want you," he said, grinding out the words. His arm circled her waist, and he pulled her against him while his mouth covered hers. His tongue stroked hers, sending streaks of fire in its wake. Desire became a white-hot need as she thrust her hips against him.

Kissing her deeply, he leaned over her. Her heart thundered, drowning the sounds of the waves on the beach. She wound her fingers in his hair at his nape and then let her hand slide down to twist free the studs on his shirt. She leaned back to catch his wrist. While she watched him intently, she removed a cuff link so he could slip off his shirt. "I've waited all week, Matt," she whispered.

"I've waited a lifetime. You're what a man fantasizes and dreams about."

"I don't know that I want to be anyone's fantasy," she whispered. "I want you to desire me because I'm Olivia—my own person. One way or another, Matt, I'll get to you. You can't guard your heart against love. You may not be able to guard it against my loving. We'll see." She picked up his other wrist to remove that cuff link. He caressed her nape with his free hand and as soon as she had his shirt off, she tossed it aside.

She drank in the sight of his muscled chest, running her hands over him lightly. "I could look at and touch you forever," she whispered, trembling, on fire with longing, yet wanting to savor every moment of this night. She leaned forward to kiss his nipple while she continued to explore his chest and smooth back with her fingers.

He inhaled deeply and tangled his fingers in her hair. "Ahh, Olivia. You'll burn me to a crisp," he whispered. "I've wanted you since the first moment I saw you."

She leaned down, tracing the tip of her tongue across his flat stomach above his belt while she unfastened his belt and pushed away his trousers.

His hands slipped beneath her arms to pull her up and they looked into each other's eyes, his hungry desire blasting into her like a whirlwind. He hauled her into his embrace, holding her tightly and leaning over her while he kissed her.

In minutes or hours—time was gone and she had no idea, he turned her around and drew his tongue along her nape. His breath was warm, sexy.

He brushed his hands so lightly across the front of her dress and she gasped, feeling the faint contact on her sensitive nipples.

She inhaled and closed her eyes, reaching behind her to slide her hands along his strong thighs.

Cool air spilled across her shoulders and down her back when he unzipped her wedding dress. It fell around her ankles with a swish of silk that she barely noticed, but she was awed to see that his fingers trembled as he turned her to face him.

His burning gaze consumed her as he pushed away the

white scrap of lacy panties she wore and the thigh-high dark hose. He rested his hands on her hips and looked at her in a gaze so filled with need, it was like fingers drifting down over her and caressing her. Then he cupped her breasts, his thumbs circling her nipples leisurely in an exquisite torment that made her clutch his arms and close her eyes and try to draw him closer.

"You're beautiful!" he said in a raspy voice. "So responsive. So beautiful."

"Matt! I want you," she gasped, trembling with desire and melting from his touch. When he covered her mouth with his, kissing her hard, she shoved down his briefs. His strong arm banded her, pulling her against his hard length.

With a desperate hunger for his loving, she moaned softly, wanting all of him now. His thick shaft pressed against her belly, hot and hard for her. He picked her up while he continued to kiss her and carried her to the bed where he placed his knee and lowered her.

While she wound her arms around his neck, his hands were everywhere, exploring her body with a thoroughness that heightened her insatiable need.

His tongue traced from her ear to her breasts and he took a nipple into his mouth to bite lightly. His tongue drew slow, hot wet circles in a delicious torment around her taut bud. At the same time, he caressed her other breast, stroking her in a tantalizing feathery touch that ignited more flames. And then his hand slipped between her legs. When he kissed her inner thighs, she spread her legs for him.

Slowly, thoroughly, he trailed kisses down her legs to her ankles and then turned her over to explore the backs of her legs, kissing her behind her knees, moving higher until he reached her nape. "Every inch of you is sexy and beautiful," he whispered.

Wanting him beyond measure, she rolled over to push him onto his back and then she returned his kisses, working her way down his chest, letting her tongue circle his flat nipples. Excited by his response as he wound his hands in her hair and groaned, she kissed his muscled, washboard belly. When he started to sit up, she pushed him down. She rubbed her pouty nipples against him and then ran her tongue around his shaft, letting her warm breath tantalize while her hands stroked his thighs. When she moved between his legs, he reached for her again, but she pushed his chest.

"You have to let me kiss you the way you kissed me," she whispered, shoving him down and continuing her rain of kisses until she rolled him over and worked her way along his back. When she kissed his inner thighs and played with his hard bottom, he twisted onto his back. She took his shaft into her mouth to stroke him with her tongue, slipping her hand between his legs to caress him.

"Olivia," he whispered, grinding out her name in a voice that was gravelly and thick. He was beaded with perspiration, aroused with his shaft rock hard and ready. He stood and held her in front of him while he stepped before a full-length mirror.

"Look how beautiful you are," he whispered, playing with her breasts, his hands dark against her pale skin. He kissed her nape and rubbed his shaft against her bottom and slid it between her legs to rub her.

She moaned with desire, whirling around to hold him. "I want you!" she cried, pulling his head down to kiss him passionately.

She hadn't thought it possible to want anyone to the degree she wanted Matt. She wanted to feel him inside her, to wrap her legs around him and love him through the night. Desire enveloped her, taking her breath and making her nerves raw. How could she want anyone this badly? Her hands swept over him in a feverish need.

"You're gorgeous," he whispered in her ear. "Look at us, Olivia."

Twisting around, she opened her eyes to meet his burning gaze in the mirror. The hunger in his expression took her breath and left no doubts that he wanted her. As he turned her to face him again, his blue eyes devoured her.

"I didn't know I could ever want a woman this badly," he said, and she didn't tell him she felt the same way about him. Words were lost as he swept her into his embrace, leaned over her and kissed her with such hunger she wondered exactly what he did feel for her.

How could he kiss her so wildly and not be falling in love?

She knew that he could do exactly that and still guard his heart. His hands and mouth and hot shaft drove everything from her mind except desire.

His kisses set off fireworks low inside her and sent flashes of light bursting behind her closed eyelids while every nerve tingled. She thrust her hips against his and closed her hand around his manhood, hoping to drive him beyond control.

He picked her up and carried her to bed, lowering her gently and then moving over her.

Spreading her legs for him, she opened her eyes to feast on the sight of him while her heart thudded. She ran her hands along his rock-hard thighs and then took his shaft in one hand as she sat up to run her tongue in slow circles around the velvet tip.

His hands wound in her hair again, shaking away the last of the pins and he groaned, letting her kiss and fondle him for a moment. With a groan he pushed her down.

Watching her, he moved between her thighs and then lifted her legs over his shoulders. His dark shaft throbbed with need. She looked up to meet his fiery gaze and then he lowered his head and his tongue stroked her most intimate places while his hands slipped over her bottom and between her legs.

Closing her eyes, she cried out with passion and arched her hips, thrashing wildly as need built to a raging inferno.

"Matt, love me! I want you to make love with me now. I can't wait longer," she cried out.

He leaned down and flicked his tongue around the curve of her ear. "Yes, you can wait," he whispered and let the tip of his tongue toy with her ear. "I want you really wild with no control at all, begging for love."

She wriggled away and sat up between his legs. "Two can do that," she whispered fiercely. She took his shaft in her mouth again, sliding it in and out and stroking him with her tongue.

He gasped and shoved her down, lowering himself. "Now," he whispered and she held him as the thick tip of his hard rod touched her.

She cried out and arched her hips, trying to pull him closer and wrapping her long legs tightly around him. "Love me, Matt!" she cried. "I want you! You don't know—"

He entered her slowly, filling her, hot and hard and driving her to wild abandon. Her head thrashed and her hips undulated in a rhythm to match his in an ageless dance of passion.

She was one with him, joined in body and now in marriage, falling more and more in love by the moment and devastated by his lovemaking.

Need burned her to cinders. "Matt, love me!" she gasped as he continued his slow torment, drawing his shaft out and then sliding into her in a scalding loving that heightened desire with each stroke.

Tension wound in her like a spring coiled tighter and tighter until she felt as if she would burst with the longing that drummed through her veins.

Sweat poured off him while she cried out and thrashed and nipped his shoulder. She clung to him, her hands sliding down his back, squeezing his hard buttocks. In abandon, she rocked with him.

Knowing that she was in love with this strong, sexy man who was taking her to paradise, she wanted to declare her love, but she bit back the words. She wasn't going to let him know that she had fallen in love with him when she was certain it would not be mutual and might not ever be returned. She didn't want his pity or sympathy.

Yet how difficult it was now, in the throes of the most passionate moment of her life, to avoid crying out her feelings and being totally open and honest with him.

His control vanished and he pumped into her, filling her hot and thick as they rocked together and spun to a blinding climax.

"Matt!" she cried, unaware of anything except his manhood and the sensations exploding from his loving.

"Olivia!" he gasped and covered her mouth, devouring her with another kiss that was a storm of passion.

All she knew was Matt, his body, his arms holding her, his thick rod inside her, filling her and joining them. She held him tightly as they finally slowed and then were still.

She caressed his damp back, sliding her hands down over the curve of his buttocks, down over the backs of his thighs, feeling the short dark hairs curl against her palms.

"You demolished me," she finally whispered.

He turned his head and she looked into his eyes. When she did, he leaned forward to kiss her. In seconds he pulled away. "You're fantastic,"

"Thank you," she answered quietly. "I'll say the same for you. We're a mutual admiration couple."

"One half of this couple is boneless and unable to move," he said, placing his head down on her bare shoulder and turning her on her side to face him. Their legs were tangled together and she toyed with locks of his hair with her free hand.

"It is great sex between us," she observed.

"You think so?" he asked solemnly.

"Yes," she answered in surprise. "You don't think so?"

"I don't know," he answered carefully. "In a few minutes we'll try again and see."

She hit his shoulder lightly. "You were teasing!" she exclaimed. "And I fell for it."

He chuckled softly. "We will try again, but not until I can move and lift my head."

"Lift your what?"

He laughed in a deep, throaty chuckle that conveyed his satisfaction. "Wildcat. You're trying to arouse me again."

"No, I'm not," she protested lightly. "When I try to arouse you again, you'll know it and it won't be just 'try'."

He nuzzled her neck and pulled her more closely against him. "This is good, Olivia. Better than I dreamed possible and I had high expectations."

"'High expectations' translates into you thought I was a bawdy wench," she remarked dryly, amused.

"Could be," he admitted, trailing kisses along her ear and throat. "We're not getting out of bed the rest of the week."

"That's what you think. Hunger will soon set in. I'm eating for two, you know. Now, I want to check out the beach. The water looks like the most inviting thing around here right now."

He hugged her. "I'm beginning to think you had a very good idea when you proposed to me. I should have thought of this."

Her heart leaped even though she knew he wasn't thinking about falling in love.

"Good! I don't have to have a guilty conscience about finagling you into marriage."

"I don't know. I like you to have a guilty conscience because then you'll do more to please me."

"Is that so? I better start learning what pleases you. Let's see—how's this?" she asked, kissing his neck lightly.

He groaned and pulled her close against him. "You give me a moment to catch my breath. I don't have a bone in my body that will function now. I can't stand. I can't even move." He smiled at her and raked her damp hair away from her face. "This is good, Olivia. It's a hell of a lot better than what I had planned for us."

"Good. I quite agree, but remember that when times get tough."

"So what's going to make times get tough?" he asked, arching his eyebrows. The humor had gone from his tone of voice.

"I don't know now, but you know there will be moments we won't agree. There have been a few already and we barely know each other."

"This is a fine arrangement for both of us. You'll get your law degree, I get to be a father and we'll give our baby a family. You couldn't ask for more."

She kept her mouth closed, but she knew she wanted a whole

lot more. She wanted his heart. She wanted him to fall in love because she was falling in love. She ran her hand along his muscled shoulder and the strong column of his neck, feeling the damp sweat still at his hairline. She couldn't get enough of touching him, kissing him and she wanted so much more from him than merely a fine, workable arrangement. Maybe with time, she thought, running her finger along his jaw and then so lightly across his lips. He bit her fingers gently and then kissed her forehead.

"Later, you can practice law in Rincon or even in Fort Worth which isn't a bad commute," he said.

"I'm not worrying about that now," she said. "I have to get through years of school before that time comes."

"If there are more babies, you may change your mind completely." She smiled at him, and they gazed at each other in satisfaction. To her surprise, he rolled away, stood and picked her up.

"I thought you were weak-kneed and all that," she exclaimed.

"I'm getting my strength back," he said. "Touching and looking at you is doing all sorts of things to revive me."

"Where are we going?" she asked, alarmed as he strode outside.

"This is a very private beach, remember? The only people here are on the other side of the island, so don't worry. Unless there's a low-flying plane, which there isn't, we have this strictly to ourselves."

He carried her into the water and finally it was deep enough that he let her legs down and slowly let her slide down the length of him to stand facing him. She felt his arousal, hot and hard against her in spite of the cold water.

"You're oversexed," she accused, teasing him.

"Only because of you," he rejoined and pulled her to him to kiss her. His hands slipped over her, tantalizing strokes that re-kindled her desire and she caressed his smooth, wet body, finally slipping away from him.

"Come here," she said, laughing up at him and catching his hand.

He splashed back to the beach with her where she turned to wrap her arms around him and kiss him hungrily.

As if they hadn't made love, he swept her into his arms again and walked to a chaise. He sat and put her astride him. His hands cupped her breasts and his thumbs circled her nipples as his thick rod slid into her and filled her. She closed her eyes and gasped with pleasure, moving her hips.

Need built, driving her to move faster, tension coiling with each stroke of his manhood. She felt his fingers between her legs, rubbing her and creating more fires.

"Matt!" she cried out, moving wildly, pumping him until release burst in her with her climax. His hands held her hips as he still thrust and then he clutched her more tightly.

"Olivia! I want you!" he exclaimed deeply. He thrust rapidly, shuddering and she knew he had reached his climax.

She fell across him, gasping for breath. His breathing was as ragged as hers and she could hear her pounding pulse. Sunshine was hot on her back and he was hot beneath her.

"We need to get into the water to cool down again."

His arm circled her waist and he held her tightly against him. "Not quite yet. I want to hold you."

She smiled and raised her head to look down at him. He was bathed in sweat and his hair was a tangle of black locks across his forehead. Satisfaction filled his blue eyes and made her heart drum.

"I married a most handsome, sexy man," she said lightly, tracing her finger along his jaw.

He rolled her beside him, turning to face her. "And you're gorgeous and I don't want you to even open those bags you brought. I want you naked all week."

She laughed. "I think not! I carefully bought two new swimsuits—"

"I'll get them off you faster than you can get them on," he said, brushing hair away from her face. The ends were damp, but she hadn't done any swimming so the rest was dry.

"I've bought new clothes for this week."

"Show them to me back in Texas next week," he said.

"I'm not sitting around and eating in the nude."

"Shall we take bets?" he asked wickedly and she had to laugh.

"I'm perfectly willing to stay naked all week," he offered.

"I'll bet you are. Now that's not a bad thought but if you do, it'll mean we'll never get far from the bed or this chaise."

"I'll make that sacrifice," he teased. "It's good between us, Olivia."

She nodded. "It may just get better and better. Had you ever thought of that?"

He studied her and ran his finger down her cheek. "Maybe I can stagger into the water now if you keep me from drowning if I slide under."

"I'll keep you from drowning," she remarked and stood, walking toward the water and turning to see him sitting on the chaise watching her.

"You're not coming?"

"I was enjoying the view."

"Matt! Stop ogling me and come swim."

"I'd rather ogle," he said, standing and her gaze raked over him before she turned to go into the water. Her back tingled and her cheeks heated because she knew he was watching her closely. As soon as she was in waist deep water, she sank down to cool and turn to watch him stride casually into the water.

His body was muscled, male perfection, well-sculpted, tan. Just the sight of him made her pulse pound and rekindled her desire. "Come on in," she said.

Matt strolled leisurely out to her. He was exhausted and satisfied, but watching her just now, he knew that wasn't a condition that would last. Not with Olivia going around nude. He marveled at his good fortune. She was a fantastic lover with a body beyond belief. But he knew it was more than her body. She had a sexual air about her that was seduction just being around her.

The beach had a gradual slope and Olivia had walked out to a point where only her head and shoulders were above water. He joined her, reaching out to slip his arm around her narrow waist.

"I thought all this water would cool you down," she said, slanting him a saucy look.

"It should, but your naked body is a lot stronger influence and it heats me up. Touching you excites me," he said softly. "Looking at you excites me," he added. He gazed at her, infinitely thankful he hadn't gotten his way and settled for living under the same roof and nothing more.

And then he wondered if he was falling in love? Had she gotten past his barriers and reached his heart?

The idea startled him and he stared at her, wondering what he truly did feel for her and what it could develop into. Was he already in love with his new wife? Even when he had thought he was guarding his heart so well.

"Give me a few minutes," she said. "I recognize that look in your eye."

"You bring it on with your sexy walk and your bare bottom and long legs. Want to see?" he asked, stepping closer and rubbing against her, amazed himself at how easily she turned him on.

"I know there's something wrong with you," she remarked. "Duck yourself under the water and cool down." She turned to swim away from him and he followed, catching her and pulling her into his arms to kiss her while he treaded water and kept them both afloat.

"Don't you ever get enough?"

"I don't know," he answered. "This making love to you is all new to me, so we'll just have to see," he said before ducking his head to kiss her again.

To his surprise, he discovered that he couldn't get enough of her. They made love leisurely, and then quickly with a hungry passion that he wouldn't have thought possible when they had already loved so much.

That night, long after she had fallen asleep in his arms, he stirred and looked down at her, combing long locks of her hair away from her face while satisfaction filled him. She was sexy, beautiful and intelligent. She was going to give him babies and a marriage and solid family life. Gratitude filled him and he wondered how long it would take before he did fall in love with her. Or was he already there? Was he in love with his new wife?

They had barely eaten dinner and he was ravenous, but as he rolled over to kiss her awake, her warm, soft body aroused him and soon he was making love to her again and he forgot all about his stomach and food.

The next morning Olivia woke and shifted. She looked around, momentarily disoriented and then a strong, brown arm tightened around her waist and memories tumbled back. She looked at her sleeping husband who held her tightly. They had made love off and on since arriving and now her stomach was growling with hunger.

She slipped out of his embrace and went inside, switching on a small lamp and looking around at an inviting large bedroom with a king-size bed, bamboo furniture and a polished plank floor. She retrieved her bag, showered and pulled on a sheer black negligee she had bought and then went to the kitchen. She discovered it was fully stocked with food and dishes that had been cooked and were ready to heat. A fruit platter was in the refrigerator and she removed it, taking off the wrap that protected it and eating a thick chunk of delicious pineapple.

"There you are," Matt said and she turned to see him standing in the doorway.

He had showered and slicked back his wet hair and tied a white towel around his middle. Her pulse began to drum, but she picked up a strawberry and waved it at him.

"We are going to eat before I faint."

His mouth curved in a crooked smile as his gaze drifted down over her and she wished she had simply pulled on cutoffs and a T-shirt instead of the sheer, sexy negligee.

"Matt, we're going to eat. Did you hear me?"

"Sure. We'll eat, but you didn't dress like that and expect me to not notice, did you?" he said, strolling to her and her heart began a drumroll.

"You stay right here," she said, placing a hand against his

chest as she passed him and hurried from the room. She dashed to the bedroom, gathered clothes and changed.

Shortly she returned to the kitchen to find him getting out skewers with chunks of steak, mushrooms, onions and small tomatoes.

He placed them on plates and he already had glasses of water poured. "I heated these in the microwave. They've already been cooked and they should still be tasty."

"They'll be a feast," she said, trying to resist falling on it and devouring it as hunger tore at her. "I'm starved."

He studied her. "I liked the black thing better."

"I'll bet you did," she said, smiling at him and wondering how long the towel would stay tied around his middle, knowing if it lasted through breakfast, then she would remove it.

They were halfway through breakfast when she looked up to meet his smoldering blue gaze. She realized he was no longer eating, but looking at her with as much desire as if they had never made love. She lost all appetite and lowered her fork as he pushed away his chair and came around the table to take her into his arms.

"I feel like it's been a day instead of an hour since we made love," he said, kissing her throat.

She turned her head to kiss him, winding her arms around his neck and all thoughts of breakfast were forgotten.

Three days later Olivia was stretched beside him on a chaise after making love. "It may be difficult to return to reality."

"If you'd like to stay longer, we can, but you'll love the Argentine ranch. It's spectacular. We can stay here or on the ranch as long as we want.

"Don't you have to get back?"

"I told you that we're buying the ranch in Argentina. I stay there or on the California ranch a good part of the year."

She sat up to look at him. "What about the Texas ranch?"

He gave her a crooked smile and toyed with locks of her hair. He was stretched out with a towel across his middle and she wore a two-piece red swimsuit. "We have a foreman, but usually I go back after a few months to keep Dad happy. He wants me to run the ranch and as long as he's alive, I don't stay away more than a couple of months at a time."

Surprised, she studied him. "What do you mean by, 'As long as he's alive'?"

"After Dad's gone, I'll probably turn the Texas ranch over to Sandy full-time and move to Argentina. I love that ranch—it's beautiful country. I'll go home for board meetings for Ransome Energy, but I don't have to live there."

"You didn't tell me this," she said stiffly.

His eyes narrowed. "I think I mentioned the ranches. Besides, Dad will be around, probably until our baby is grown, so it really doesn't matter."

"It matters a lot," she said. "And you never know what tomorrow will bring. You told me about buying a ranch in Argentina, but you didn't tell me that that's where you prefer to live."

His hand stilled. "This is going to be a problem?"

"Indeed, it is," she said, her temper rising. "You should have told me."

"This won't happen for years. Look, Dad's alive. It would hurt him if I didn't run the Texas ranch, so as long as he's living, I'm not going to stay away any great length of time. He should be around many more years. You're conjuring up something that doesn't exist at the present."

"Your father has had one heart attack and you can't say what will happen to any of us on any given day. A vacation now and then would be fabulous. To live there—no way."

"It's as good a life as in Texas," he said in a cold, quiet tone that chilled her even more.

She shook her head. "No, it isn't. I want a regular life and regular school in the U.S."

"Okay, Olivia. We can settle it when the time comes."

"Somehow that's not much reassurance," she said, trying to curb her anger.

"I'm redoing an eight-bedroom ranch house in Argentina right now. Even with Dad alive and at the ranch, I intend to stay in the new ranch house, once it's finished, at least two months out of the year. I want my child to go with me. Dad knows I do this every year and that's all right. I do a couple of months on that ranch and it brings in a hell of an income so Dad's fine with it."

"That's disruptive and I can't leave school and later I can't leave a job."

"Look, we're married. You don't even have to go to school any longer and you sure as hell don't have to practice law or work for someone else."

She stood up. "You should have told me. I'm not letting you take my baby off to Argentina for months and I'm not giving up law school because you prefer that ranch to the three others that you own."

"So what the hell are you going to do?"

She stared at him with her anger boiling and hurt simmering that he hadn't told her about his preference in ranches or his plans for the future. "I'll have to figure that one out, Matt, but I'm ready to get out of here." She swept past him and into the house, going straight to get her bags, feeling she should pack and get someone to fly her away from the island before she really lost it and said things to Matt she would regret. How could he possibly think she would take her child to go live in South America, isolated on a ranch for a large part of the year? She steamed with anger because he hadn't leveled with her about his plans.

Tossing her clothes into the bag, she turned to gather more and saw Matt standing in the doorway watching her. He had tied the towel around his middle.

"Can you get a plane for me?" she asked stiffly, gathering more of her things. "I don't want to stay here any longer."

Anger flashed in his eyes and a muscle worked in his jaw. "I'll fly you back myself." He turned away and in minutes she saw him on the patio talking on his cell phone.

She wasn't giving up getting her education. She had seen the anger in his expression and she didn't think he was going to change one aspect of his life either and she realized they should have spent more time talking about their lives. She tossed her shirts and shorts into her bag. She had spent time talking to him. He knew about her law school plans and her desire to practice law. She just hadn't known anything about his goals for his future.

Anger made her shake. She didn't think he had been up-front and straight with her. She didn't know what she would do when they reached Texas. Was she walking out of this marriage already?

She knew she wouldn't do that if he went to Argentina to live forever and she never saw him again. Marriage still gave her baby a future and it gave her a chance for law school that she might not ever have worked out otherwise. No, she would stay, but she could see all hopes for love or a happy marriage smashing into a million pieces that couldn't be put together again.

Matt had acquiesced to her wishes to get the baby into the Ransome family, but he wouldn't consent to her wishes on this. She had no illusions about that. He wouldn't care what she did at this point.

She dressed in emerald slacks and a matching emerald linen top and caught her hair behind her head in a ponytail, tying it with a bright emerald scarf.

"The plane will be ready in an hour, Olivia," Matt said from the doorway.

She nodded. "Sorry, but I know what I want," she said quietly.

"You always have," he replied and they stared at each other and she could feel the clash of wills that was as strong as that first night they had met. She picked up her bag and swept past him.

"I'm out of the bedroom if you want it to yourself," she said.

She went to the front to set down her bag. Hurting, she paced the room, looking around her and suspecting she would never be back here again.

A little over an hour later, she was buckled into a seat in the plane and Matt was up front at the controls. She wondered how good a pilot he was, but then guessed that he was probably quite good. He had hardly spoken on the way to the airport and she could feel the waves of anger that buffeted her.

Tears threatened, but no matter how she looked at it, she

didn't see changing her mind about her future and tossing aside her education. If she didn't get one and Matt sent her packing one day, without an education, she would be back at jobs like she'd had in the past.

And she knew without question she wasn't letting him take her baby out of the country for months at a time, no matter how productive the ranch was or how beautiful. Not during a school year when a child would have to be tutored.

When they landed, she was no closer to solving the problems facing them and she could see he wasn't either or he wouldn't look as if he were trying to bank his fury.

At the ranch house he took the bags and she went on to her room so she could be alone.

Matt set his bag in his room and then carried hers to knock on her door. When she called to come in, he stepped inside and faced her. The tension was thick between them. His anger was palpable and she raised her chin, ready for a fight with him. She hurt and could feel something precious and vital slipping out of her life.

"Here's your bag. Where do we go from here, Olivia?"

"I don't know. I'll have to give it thought. I want to stay married."

"I'm sure you do. Well, we have a deal, and I'll stick by it," he said gruffly and then left abruptly.

Matt strode down the hall and outside, beginning to jog to work off his frustration. He wondered if she really would stay. He expected her to walk out. It hadn't ever occurred to him to talk to her about the ranch in Argentina. His dad was alive and well and Argentina on a permanent basis was far in the future. Too far to give much thought to now. She could get her degree and practice law. He hadn't foreseen that his plans to live in Argentina years from now would be a problem. To stay a couple of months a year hadn't seemed unreasonable either.

She could go on with her life and he with his, but he wanted to take the baby with him a lot of the time and she obviously was going to try to block that every way she could.

Was he wrong? He didn't think he was being unreasonable and a lot of women would have loved it if they had the opportunities that he was providing for Olivia.

"Dammit!" he snapped and kicked a rock as he jogged. Let her go and to hell with her, he told himself, but even as he did, he thought about the past days since the wedding and how great life had been with her. He hurt badly and he had to admit that he wanted her in his life.

He ran for over two hours and finally returned to the house. He had no idea where she was, but he wasn't going to pursue her when she wouldn't want him to.

For the next two days he didn't see any sign of her until he began to wonder if she had packed and moved out without telling him, but at night he could hear her moving around in her room. He had no idea where she ate or what she was doing.

Then Saturday morning, a week after their wedding, he was walking down the hall when her door swung open. She was white and her eyes were round. She grasped the doorjamb and clung to it.

"Olivia! What's wrong?" he asked, forgetting their argument.

"I'm going to the emergency room," she answered weakly and then her knees buckled.

Twelve

His heart thudded as Matt swept her up in his arms. He carried her downstairs to his car where he placed her on the backseat. With rising panic, he dashed around to climb behind the wheel and race down the drive. Terror made him cold as he picked up his cell phone and punched numbers with one hand while he steered the car with the other.

"Who's your doctor, Olivia?"

"Dr. Porter. I've called him and he's meeting me at Rincon General."

Matt called 911 and talked to the dispatcher, giving directions to the ranch.

"We're headed to town. Send an ambulance to meet us. I'll see it coming. I'm driving a black four-door." He replaced the receiver and gripped the wheel glancing in the rearview mirror.

"How're you doing?" he asked her. "What's wrong?"

"I don't know. I have cramps and I'm faint and woozy," she answered. His heart thudded. He was frightened for the baby, frightened for Olivia. He prayed they would both be all right.

He sped down the ranch road and spun out on the highway, heading into town and listening for an ambulance. He saw it coming long before he heard it and he slowed, pulling off the road and getting out to flag it down. As it approached he stepped into the road and waved his arms.

Slowing, the ambulance pulled off and in minutes they were loading Olivia into the back. Matt held her hand. "Hang on, darlin'," he said, giving her hand a squeeze. "I'll follow and I'll be there with you."

The ambulance made a slow, careful U-turn and headed back the way it had come at a much slower speed.

With a pounding heart, Matt hunched over the wheel and followed, wanting to step on the gas and get her where she would have help.

At the emergency entrance, he watched helplessly while they wheeled her inside and then directed him to a waiting room. Rubbing his neck, praying she and the baby were all right, he paced the room. Fear gripped him. It was over an hour before a nurse called his name and he hurried across the room.

"Dr. Porter can talk to you and you can go see your wife. It's the third room on the right through those double doors."

"Thanks," he called over his shoulder, already jogging the direction she had pointed. Matt found the tall, thin, brown-haired doctor coming out of a room and he introduced himself.

"She's fine," Dr. Porter said. "Or she will be."

"She didn't look or feel fine," Matt snapped, wondering if she had received the care she should have.

The physician smiled. "She hasn't been eating right. It's a matter of getting the right fluids back in her. We'll keep her tonight and release her in the morning and if she'll take care of herself—or you take care of her—she'll be back to normal in no time."

As relief poured through him, Matt felt weak in the knees. "Thanks," he said. "Can I see her?"

"Yes, but she's dozed off. She's malnourished and whatever's been bothering her, I told her she needs to stop worrying about it until after this baby arrives," he said and Matt realized the talk was directed at him.

"I understand. Thanks," Matt repeated. He moved past the doctor and went inside, walking quietly. Olivia had an IV dripping a solution that went into her arm and she lay still with her eyes closed. Matt wanted to kick himself.

He felt as if he had caused this as much as if he had withheld food and water from her. He knew that wasn't the case, she had done this to herself, but he felt responsible. And he realized she was important to him. She had given him a dreadful scare, both for her and the baby, but he had been terrified for her and he realized she was far more important to him than he had admitted to himself.

And she was more important than living on their Argentina ranch or any other damn thing like that in his life. He'd stuck it out on the Texas ranch the majority of the time for his dad. He could do that for Olivia and the baby. They were the most important people in his life now.

That thought startled him, but he realized it was true. He moved a chair beside the bed and sat down, taking her hand in his. "I love you," he said quietly, knowing she couldn't hear him, but he wanted to say it. He raised her hand to his lips and brushed a feathery kiss across her knuckles. "Get well, darlin'," he whispered.

She turned her head and opened her eyes to look at him. "Matt?"

"I'm here," he said. "Go back to sleep."

She stared at him and he leaned over the bed to kiss her lightly on the mouth. He sat down again, still holding her hand. "Go to sleep. You and the baby are going to be fine."

She nodded and closed her eyes.

Matt called the ranch and settled in the vinyl chair, watching her breathe and thinking she looked weak and vulnerable. He wanted to pull her into his arms and hold her, but he knew that wouldn't help her.

That night he slept in the chair by her bed and when he stirred the next morning, Olivia was gazing at him with curiosity.

"Hi," he said, leaning forward to kiss on her forehead. He took her hand in his.

"Hi," she answered. "You were here all night?"

"Yep. How're you feeling?"

"Better. I guess they've been giving me something."

"Your doc said you haven't been eating right."

"I suppose not."

"We'll remedy that," he said quietly. "I'll start cooking for you. But then, maybe my cooking will be an improvement and maybe it won't be," he said, and she smiled.

"I want to get out of here."

"They said you could go this morning."

The door opened and a nurse appeared and Matt stood. "I'll come back, Olivia. I'll wait in the hall." He stepped outside, going to get a cup of coffee.

The morning seemed long and tedious but by half past ten, Olivia was dismissed. They brought her down to his car in a wheelchair. She moved to the car to buckle herself into the passenger seat.

"I'm better," she said as soon as he pulled away from the hospital entrance. "Thanks for going with me."

He reached over to take her hand. "You're not going to skip any meals after this."

"No, I won't."

"Do you want something to eat now?"

"Goodness no. They removed the IV and then brought me breakfast. I couldn't eat another bite."

He glanced at her and saw to his relief, that her color was good and she looked like herself except thinner and he wondered if she had eaten at all since returning from Ariel.

He turned in the park and drove beneath a tall live oak that provided cool shade beneath it's arching branches. He cut the motor and turned to Olivia who looked at him with curiosity. "What are you doing?"

He lowered the windows to let in a morning breeze and turned in the seat to take her hand. "You gave me a hell of a scare."

"I've been eating, but I guess not enough. I thought I was taking care of myself."

He kissed her knuckles and ran them along his cheek.

Olivia could feel the rough stubble on his jaw. He hadn't shaved and his clothes were rumpled, his hair tangled. She thought she had heard him tell her that he loved her, but she wondered if she had imagined it or it had been medication they had given her that caused a delusion. Worry clouded Matt's blue eyes and she wondered what was on his mind. She wished she knew whether he had really declared his love or not.

As if reading her mind, he slipped his arm around her waist. "I love you."

She closed her eyes. How she had dreamed of him saying that! Now it didn't matter because they couldn't work out a future together. Tears threatened and she had received a lecture from her doctor about her attitude.

"Olivia," Matt said in a husky voice, "will you marry me?"

Surprised, she opened her eyes wide and stared at him. "We're married, remember?"

He gave her a faint smile. "I remember, but you proposed and I wasn't in love."

Her heart started drumming as she stared at him.

"This time, I'm proposing to the woman I love."

"What about living in Argentina on your family ranch instead of the Texas one?"

"I've always given that up for Dad. I can give it up for you and our baby. It won't mean much to me without you there. Will you marry me?"

Stunned and overwhelmed, she stared at him while tears spilled down her cheeks. He wiped them away. "Don't cry, darlin'. I didn't intend to make you cry."

She smiled and put her arms around his neck. "They're tears of joy, Matt. Of course, I'll marry you, but we don't need to do that. Your declaration of love is the world to me! I don't want to plan another wedding."

"Whatever you want. If you do, okay. If you don't, okay. I just want you to know that I love you and I want you to be my wife."

She hugged him again, feeling as if weights had been lifted from her heart. "Matt, you've just made me the happiest woman in the world!" she cried, tears spilling down her cheeks.

"You don't act happy, darlin'. You're crying—"

"I told you, they're tears of joy, believe me. I love you, too, Matt Ransome. I'm going to make you the happiest man on earth."

He chuckled. "Maybe in bed. Sometimes, though, I suspect you're going to worry the socks off me the way you've done in the short time I've known you. Since meeting you, darlin', my peaceful life has gone out the window."

She smiled at him. "I'm worth it," she said, and he laughed.

"Yes, you are," he said and then bent his head to kiss her.

Overjoyed, Olivia clung to him while her heart thudded with so much joy she felt as if she would burst. "Let's go back for another honeymoon that won't be cut short," she whispered.

"Sounds like a deal to me," he said and smiled, leaning down to kiss her again.

Epilogue

The following January as wind howled and snow swirled, blanketing Rincon, inside a hospital delivery room, a baby's cry filled the air. "Here's your boy," Dr. Porter said, placing a small baby on Olivia's stomach.

Matt leaned over the baby. "He's perfect!"

Olivia smiled. "I think so, too."

The nurse picked up the baby to clean him up.

"Jefferson Matthew Ransome," Olivia said.

Matt grinned broadly and bent to kiss his wife. "You have a perfect baby," he said softly.

"We have a perfect baby," she reminded him, and he gazed at her with love in his eyes.

He straightened up. "I've got to tell the family. They're all coming to see little Jeff Ransome."

"You'd think no one ever had a baby before," Olivia said, looking at banks of flowers that had already arrived from Matt's father and Katherine and Nick. "Look at all these flowers, and that was before Jeff was born."

"Dad's outside and can't wait to get in here to see you."

"Phooey, Matt. He doesn't want to see me. He wants to see Jeff."

"He'll be happy with you for giving him Jeff."

Olivia smiled at her tall, handsome husband and thought how good life had become for her. Now she had a baby son that she and Matt could love. Matt took Olivia's hand.

"I'm leaving for a few minutes, but I'll be back soon," he said.

She nodded and watched him stride out of the room and joy filled her over her baby and over Matt being in her life. Thirty minutes later he returned and crossed the room to her bed. "Are they finished working on you?"

"Yes, they are."

"Then Dad wants to see you. Sandy and some of the guys are here, and Katherine's flying in if the blizzard doesn't ground planes. Nick will arrive tonight."

"That's great. I'm glad Jeff has arrived in a family that will love him."

"We're going to love him so much, it'll make your head spin."

"You're not going to spoil him to pieces," Olivia said, and Matt grinned. His blue eyes twinkled as he pulled a box from his pocket and placed it in Olivia's hand.

"This is for you, darlin'," he said, and she opened a black velvet box. She gasped with surprise and delight when she lifted out a diamond and emerald bracelet.

"It's beautiful, Matt!" she exclaimed. "Just gorgeous."

He leaned down to take her in his arms and she hugged him. "Not half as beautiful as my wife," he said quietly. "I love you, Olivia. You're my world and my life now."

His words thrilled her, and Olivia clung to his broad shoulders as she turned her face up for his kiss. Her love for him made her heart pound with joy and she held him tightly, eager to be home in his arms again, knowing when she married him, she had made the best choice of her life.

* * * * *

REVENGE OF THE SECOND SON

BY
SARA ORWIG

With many thanks to Melissa Jeglinski,
to Jessica Alvarez and to Maureen Walters.

One

"Time for the kill," Nick Ransome whispered to himself. Anticipation made him eager for his dinner meeting with a corporate rival he had worked years to smash.

Steering his sleek black sports car from busy Dallas traffic into the restaurant parking lot, Nick raced toward a space along a line of cars. It was still hot in the early July evening, and waves of heat shimmered up from the pavement. Suddenly, a brown shaggy dog emerged from the row of parked cars and trotted in front of Nick's car.

A woman followed, rushing toward Nick and waving her arms.

Swearing, Nick slammed on his brakes. Tires screeched when his car skidded to a stop within a foot of the female while the aged dog ambled across the drive and disappeared behind a purple crepe myrtle bush.

Nick's annoyance melted into appreciation. Dressed in knee-length, sleeveless black, the woman was a gorgeous blonde with wide blue eyes. When she walked around to the driver's side of his car, Nick watched the sway of her hips while his pulse accelerated. With interest, he lowered his window.

"I'm sorry if I startled you, but I didn't want the dog run over," she said, leaning down to talk to him. Her voice was low, as appealing as the rest of her.

"Don't worry about it. I'm happy to stop for a beautiful woman anytime."

"Thank you." She laughed, revealing even white teeth and a warm, enticing smile that jumped his pulse. Her full, rosy lips made him wonder what it would be like to kiss her. When she waved her hands, he saw there was no wedding ring. "The dog looks old, and I imagine he's deaf," she continued. "I don't think he heard your car. As long as you avoided hitting him, I'm happy."

"Anything to oblige, but you ought to take care. The next person might not stop in time."

One eyebrow arched, and her eyes twinkled. "I doubt if the next person will be driving as fast. You're a man in a hurry."

"I'm meeting people. Just in case you hurt something when you stepped in front of my car, if you'll give me your phone number, I'll check on you later," he offered with a smile.

"You're coming on to me with the same speed you drive," she remarked.

"Not really. If you want to see coming on to you fast, you give me your phone number. Or go to dinner with me tomorrow night."

When she laughed again, he smiled, but he was curious about her answer. His pulse quickened at the thought of dinner with her. She was stunning with flawless skin and enormous, thickly lashed blue eyes.

She placed both hands on his open window and leaned closer until she was only inches away. "I'm not injured. I'm not giving you my phone number. Although I'm tempted, I'm not going to dinner with you," she said in a deep-throated, sexy drawl that sent his temperature soaring. She was inches away, flirting with him, and her mouth looked enticing.

A car drove up behind him, and she stepped back.

"You're blocking traffic," she said in a breathless voice.

"You're meeting a man for dinner, aren't you?" he asked, not caring that he held up a car behind him.

"Yes," she replied. "A man I love very much." She turned and walked away as the waiting car honked. Nick watched the sway of her hips and then took his foot off the brake and drove to a parking space.

"You may love him, but you flirted with me," Nick said quietly to no one. Nick arched an eyebrow and wondered about her.

By the time he had reached the entrance, she had disappeared inside. He wanted her name. She was dining with a man tonight, but if she wasn't married or engaged, then that was no hurdle to getting to know her. She couldn't be truly in love and act like she had. Unless the man she loved was her father. The last possibility made Nick smile.

Nick vowed he would get to know her. He laughed at himself. Why bother? Texas was filled with beautiful, sexy, interesting women. Still, when the maître d' greeted him and turned to lead him to his table, Nick scanned the room for sight of her.

"Your party is waiting, Mr. Ransome," Darrell said, threading his way across the room. Nick glanced again at well-dressed people seated at tables, adorned with white linen cloths, candles and roses in crystal vases, in one of Dallas's finest steak houses. A piano player's soft, background music was a complement to the inviting ambience. It was Wednesday, the first week of July—Nick decided it had been a very good way to start the evening.

Darrell stepped out of the way, motioning Nick to a table with three people. Both men stood, but Nick's gaze went to the blonde who remained seated and gazed back impassively.

His pulse jumped and for the second time in the past fifteen minutes, she gave him another jolt. If, in turn, his identity surprised her, she hid it well. And he knew any dinner involving just the two of them was off. His interest in her cooled to a glacial temperature.

Distaste and dull anger made Nick's throat tight as he shook hands with Rufus Holcomb, CEO of Holcomb Drilling. The white-haired man gave Nick a firm handshake and Nick gazed into calculating blue eyes beneath shaggy white brows. The old man was shrewd, scheming and stubborn; Nick could feel the invisible tangle of wills as he greeted Rufus, their smiles belying what he knew each of them felt.

"Rufus, I've been looking forward to this," Nick said, wondering why Rufus had wanted to meet for dinner.

"I can imagine," Rufus answered dryly and turned to the blonde. "Julia, this is the infamous Nick Ransome," he said. "Nick, meet my granddaughter, Julia Holcomb."

She extended her hand and smiled coolly. "We've met," she said, gazing steadfastly at Nick as she gave him a firm handshake. The moment he clasped her slender hand in his, his pulse jumped another notch and he couldn't resist a glance at her full, pouty lips.

"So we have. Protector of dogs and grandfathers," he said, releasing her hand and turning to a stocky blond man, shaking hands perfunctorily with Ransome Energy's senior vice president of marketing and his lifelong friend, Tyler Wade.

When the three men sat, the waiter appeared to take drink orders. As soon as the waiter left, Rufus glanced at Nick and Julia. "So where and how did you two meet, since it had to have been after six this evening? And what's this about protecting dogs?"

"Mr. Ransome is a fast driver and a stray wandered in front of his car tonight in the parking lot," Julia said, watching Nick. The minute their gazes locked, he inhaled and his pulse jumped. "I imagine Mr. Ransome is fast in many things he does. Am I right?"

Nick could feel the friction that he had always experienced around Rufus extend to Julia, only it was different. Julia was a desirable woman and a challenge that he couldn't ignore. "I would never tell a beautiful woman that she's wrong," Nick said smoothly, turning to Rufus. "You're a scoundrel, Rufus, bringing your granddaughter, because you're fully aware that all she has to do is bat her big blue eyes and she would tempt any man to give away the farm."

Nick knew his sexist remark would make both Holcombs bristle, particularly since Rufus was always ready to fight. Nick wondered what it was about Julia that made him want to needle her.

"Julia is a vice president in our accounting department. As you'll soon see, she's an excellent employee to have at my side."

"Thank you, Granddad. I doubt if Mr. Ransome will share your opinion or be in a position to know what kind of employee I am," she said, smiling at Nick. But it was another chilly smile that conveyed no friendliness, and nothing like the irresistible, warm smiles she had flashed when they had been in the parking lot. Her blond hair was pulled behind her head and tied with a black scarf; he wondered how she would look if it were unfastened and loose over her shoulders.

"I'm sure your granddad is correct," Nick replied. His emotions warred between competing with her and wanting to take her out and get to know her.

They paused when the sommelier appeared to uncork a bottle of wine, pour some for Nick's approval and then fill the wineglasses. As soon as he left them, Rufus picked up his menu. "I'm starving and it's been a long day. Actually, I usually eat almost two hours earlier, so let's get some food on the table."

"Fine," Nick answered, knowing what he wanted because of his familiarity with the menu. He was eager to get on with the dinner that he expected would accomplish nothing except antagonize both the old man and his granddaughter further.

There was a brief discussion of various selections before the waiter appeared to tell them about the specials and then to take orders.

"I know you've got two splendid quarter horses you race out at that ranch of yours," Rufus said. "How're they doing this season?"

"Still winning," Nick answered.

"Black Lightning won just last Saturday," Julia said.

"You go to the races?" Nick asked her.

"No. I keep up with your horses. I think it's wise to know your competitors," she said.

"What else do I do that you keep up with?" he asked, smiling at her.

"You've been very successful. Your company has tripled in size in the past five years. You recently signed a deal to drill in Russia."

"You do know about us," Nick said, surprised. Their green salads came and conversation went back to quarter horses and breeding stock. All the time they talked, whenever Nick and Julia's gazes met, he could feel electricity crackle between them. To his consternation, he acknowledged to himself that it took his breath just to look at her. Her flawless skin looked silky and soft. He wanted to sink his fingers in her golden hair. Several times, he jerked his thoughts back to the conversation when they drifted to erotic images of her.

Over thick, juicy steaks, their conversation went from Nick's horses to Rufus's hobby of sailing.

"You could retire, Rufus, and spend all your time sailing since you enjoy it so much," Nick remarked.

Rufus's mouth curled in a wolfish grin and he shook his head. "And let you steal my company? I don't think so. No, I'll continue like I am. Julia's as good a sailor as I am. With her help, I expect to win the upcoming race, just as we intend to block you in a buyout."

"So sailing is in your blood, too," Nick said to her, ignoring Rufus's remarks about business.

"Granddad's been taking me sailing since I was five years old."

"She's got her own sailboat and it's a real beauty," Rufus said.

"What's the name of your boat?" Nick asked. "I may have to come watch you race."

"Granddad is the one racing. I'll be his crew," she replied, ignoring Nick's question.

Their conversation remained neutral until coffee was served.

"Do you really think that our lawyers can sit down together Friday and hash out anything?" Julia asked, toying with her Bavarian apple tart dessert. "We don't see any point in having them meet," she added, gazing at Nick. Grudgingly, he had to admire her poise, she looked and sounded as if she had the upper hand in this struggle.

"If they meet, we might find common ground. And all of you can listen to my offer," Nick replied.

"You can keep your so-called offer," Rufus snapped. "You're trying to rob me of Holcomb Drilling."

"I have no intention of stealing your company," Nick said. "The offer we're going to bring to the table will be generous, cover your debts and give you an opportunity to retire and enjoy life."

"Granddad isn't ready to retire," Julia remarked.

"Indeed, I'm not! Whatever your offer is, I'm turning it down. You might as well know that right now, Nick. As a matter of fact, you back off, damn quick, or I'll ruin you in every way. You'll regret going after Holcomb."

Hanging on to his temper, Nick sipped his water, setting down his glass. "Don't threaten me, Rufus," he remarked quietly. "I'm not a young, green rookie just starting in business anymore."

"Doesn't matter. You back off if you know what's good for you."

"Frankly, I want what you have and you've had some setbacks that have dealt Holcomb Drilling financial blows. If I don't step in and take over, someone else will. It's inevitable."

"It's no such thing," Julia answered quietly, and Nick met her gaze. She could play poker and not give anything away, he realized. She looked as impassive as if she were discussing the weather. Her granddad was not dealing as well with the conversation, Rufus's face had reddened and his fists were clenched. "Don't come after our company," she said quietly. "It won't be in your best interests if you do."

"So you, too, are threatening me," Nick remarked, banking his anger but impressed by her confidence. He saw the flash of fire in the depths of her eyes. Would she play as dirty as her deceased father had and her granddad? "Is this why you wanted to get together—to threaten me?"

Nick leaned toward her. "You want a fight, you'll get a fight," he said quietly. When she drew a deep breath, her breasts pushed against the black fabric of her dress. Nick let his gaze roam down and then up.

"You'll know you've been in a battle, too, Mr. Ransome," she stated flatly. "Granddad," Julia said, placing her hand over his, "let's go. I don't think Mr. Ransome has any intention of cooperating or listening. There's no need in dragging out the evening." She stood and all the men came to their feet.

She looked up at Nick. "You'll never acquire anything from us," she said firmly. "You should spend your time taking care of what you have. And watching where you're going."

He was caught and held by invisible bonds, gazing back down at her and feeling the air between them crackle. He struggled to hang on to his temper, yet at the same time attraction burned hot and intense. She was desirable, beautiful and defiant and the competitor in him wanted to best her, while the healthy male that he was wanted her naked in his arms.

"Admit it, Mr. Ransome," Julia said. "Your motive is revenge for times in the past when Granddad has bested you. Revenge is what this is about."

"This will be a lucrative deal for all concerned," Nick replied, keeping calm. "You'll get rid of a lot of debt."

"We'll manage our company," Julia replied smoothly, turning to Tyler. "I'm glad to have met you."

Looping her arm through her grandfather's, she turned to Nick. "I guess if I hadn't stepped in front of you, you would have run right over that poor old dog. Manners force me to thank you for dinner, but it's been less than pleasant. You may want revenge for imagined wrongs, but you're not going to get it," she added. "Back off, or you'll regret it."

Taking her grandfather's arm, Julia started to walk away. Nick inhaled and his gaze drifted down over her, watching the sexy sway of her hips, looking at her long, shapely legs. He wanted her in an explosive way, wishing he could yank her into his embrace and kiss her into submission. At the same time, he was annoyed with himself.

He watched her walk across the restaurant until she was out of sight. Beside him, Tyler gave a long, low whistle. "She's a pistol! Wow! And a real chip off the old block. I knew the old man was grooming her to take over, but I didn't expect it this much and this soon, or his heir to be red-hot sexy and drop-dead gorgeous."

Nick turned to his vice president. "I think she brings out the Neanderthal in me," he said, and Tyler gave a dry laugh.

"She'd bring it out in any man who's not dead. Whew! She's feisty and maybe as underhanded as the rest of her family. She openly threatened you."

"That will make this all the more interesting. Too bad she's a Holcomb. Otherwise…" he let his voice trail away as he thought about Julia. "Let's have coffee," Nick said, sitting and facing Tyler. "Tell me again—we've got this takeover nailed, don't we?"

"Yes, we do," Tyler said, his gray eyes flashing with satisfaction. He poured more wine for himself and offered some to Nick, who shook his head.

"Make sure there aren't any hitches. Rufus has killer instincts and he doesn't draw the line at doing something illegal."

"As long as you live, you'll think it was one of their minions who ran you off the road back in your early days."

"I know damn well it was, but there was no way to prove it in court. None. My word against them, and they would have had an alibi."

"If that's the case, be careful now. We're going for his throat."

"I'm not a kid now. I'm not worried about Rufus or Julia and her threats. More than ever, I want to destroy Holcomb and get revenge for my family."

"Plus acquiring some real jewels," Tyler declared, taking a long drink of wine. "Rufus's sister, Helena, lives in Paris. Her health is failing and she has a nurse and companion, as well as a staff to take care of her condo. I flew over there myself to see her. She never wants to come back here."

"That surprises me," Nick said.

"She's older than Rufus and thinks it's high time he retired while he still has his health. She has definite ideas and it sounds as if the two haven't gotten along from the day Rufus was born."

"Julia isn't close to her aunt?"

"No. Helena doesn't think Julia should be at Holcomb. Helena's opinion is that Julia should be home making babies."

The image that popped into Nick's mind temporarily wiped out hearing anything else that Tyler was telling him. Julia in bed. Nick's temperature soared, and he tried to pull his thoughts back to Tyler and concentrate on his vice president's conversation. Nick wiped his damp brow and stared at Tyler.

"We own every dime's worth of Holcomb stock Helena possessed. You are now the major stockholder."

"Are there any other relatives holding stock besides Julia and Rufus?"

"No. In addition to Rufus's sister, Julia and Rufus are the only ones left. They only have each other," Tyler exclaimed with eagerness. "Julia's parents were killed in a plane crash three years ago. Between the Holcomb stocks and the bank, you've got 'em."

Nick thought about the bank he had just purchased and the Holcomb mortgages he had acquired. "We can call those mortgages in whenever we want," he said. "His family and ours have battled over horses and oil. It's time to take Miss Julia Holcomb and her grandfather out of the picture. She'll make a lot of money and so will Rufus. We're not robbing them."

A cell phone rang and Nick retrieved it from his pocket, talking softly and listening to his friend, Meredith Cates, while Tyler poured another glass of wine for himself.

"Sorry, Meredith. I'm tied up this weekend." Nick listened while she fussed.

"I can't change my plans. I'll get back with you," he said and switched off his phone.

"Another woman bites the dust," Tyler said. "You go through them like lightning. Has there ever been one you couldn't seduce?"

Nick smiled. "I'm sure there has," he answered easily. "Although I can't remember her," he added, and they both laughed.

Tyler sipped his drink and gazed at his friend. "All right," Nick said. "What's up?"

"It's after hours now, Nick. Business over."

Nick nodded. "Right. I think I should do Gina a favor and drive you home."

"Nope. I'm sober enough. I'll tell you what—I want that year-old sorrel of yours—"

"Standing Tall? He's still not for sale," Nick replied firmly. "But you have an eye for horseflesh. He's going to win me a bunch of races."

"You like my new Ferrari, don't you?"

"Yes, but I don't want to swap my horse for your car. I can buy a car. The horse takes breeding and luck."

"You might not have to have to swap your horse. You might get both if you're willing to take a risk."

Nick drank the last of his coffee and set down his cup, his curiosity growing. "So what's on your not-too-sober mind, Tyler?"

"Let me name a woman. If you can seduce her within the next two weeks, the car is yours. If you can't, the horse is mine."

Nick laughed. "You've lost it!"

"Listen to me. I'll pick someone likely—she has to be under thirty, healthy, single, a knockout, unattached and a woman of my choice."

"You're nuts. You've had enough wine. Let's go," Nick said and stood. "We've done a lot of crazy things, Ty. This is one you're not talking me into."

"Since when do you balk at seduction of a beautiful woman?" Tyler said, standing and walking out beside Nick. "Scared to risk your horse? You might get my Ferrari."

Thinking about the prize car, Nick glanced at his friend. "You'd really bet your car?"

"Yes, I will. I want that horse. I think I can name a woman you can't seduce."

"Maybe. Maybe not."

"C'mon, Nick. It'll make life interesting. Matter of fact,"

Tyler said, getting a brisk, businesslike tone back in his voice, "here's your chance to make your revenge really sweet. Miss Julia Holcomb."

"To hell with that one," Nick said.

"Scared of her? That would be the ultimate revenge, Nick. Absolute. I know your negative answer is not because she isn't attractive enough. Sparks were flying between the two of you tonight."

"Forget it, Ty. I'm not eighteen anymore, and you're not talking me into something crazy like you used to do."

Tyler kicked a small rock as they crossed the parking lot. "There goes my horse."

Nick laughed. "C'mon. I'll take you home and Gina can bring you back tomorrow to pick up your car."

As they crossed the parking lot Nick remembered Julia and their encounter. How long was it going to take him to forget her? Or his pulse to stop jumping at the mere thought of her? Seduce Julia? Just the suggestion made his breath catch. But he wasn't getting into a crazy bet with Tyler, even though it would be both a challenge and sweet revenge to seduce her.

After depositing Tyler at his house, Nick headed to his condo. While he drove, he thought about dinner and his fiery exchanges with Julia Holcomb, the sparks he could feel every time he locked gazes with her.

Beautiful, sexy, pure poison because of her family. He knew she viewed him as a monster.

I guess if I hadn't stepped in front of you, you would have run right over that poor old dog. As her words rang in his ears, Nick clamped his jaw shut. He might be ruthless at work, but he didn't run down helpless animals. He knew she'd said it to aggravate him, and his annoyance increased that she'd succeeded.

Nick drove to his condo that was the entire top floor of a twenty-story building. He moved around in the dark, enjoying the lights of the city, still unable to keep memories of Julia from tormenting him. He stood by the window and looked down on the sparkling city lights that sprawled in all directions. She was somewhere out there, probably in bed asleep. That thought made him groan, and he turned away, switching on lights as he shed clothes. He wished he were out on his ranch where he could go for night ride. Restless, he crossed to his desk and pulled out a ledger to think about work and get his mind off big blue eyes, long legs and the fiery tension between him and Julia Holcomb.

It was after three in the morning before he fell asleep, but within thirty minutes, the ringing of his phone awakened him. Immediately alert, Nick stretched out a long arm and picked up the receiver. His first thought was that something might have happened to his dad, whose health wasn't the greatest.

"Nick."

He heard Tyler's voice. "Is Dad okay?"

"Yeah, sure. Sorry. I'm not calling about your family."

Relief swamped Nick and he flopped down in bed again. "That's good. What are you calling about?"

"There was an explosion on one of our rigs in the Gulf. Now there's a fire."

"Dammit!" Nick swung out of bed. A tight knot of anger curled in his stomach. "Was anyone hurt?"

"Two men have been evacuated to a burn center."

"Get the helicopter to meet me in Galveston. I can be there within the hour," Nick said, grabbing jeans.

"Just hold tight and I'll keep you posted. You don't have to be out there fighting the fire. That'll just worry your dad more. You're going to have to break the news to him because he's going to hear it in the morning anyway."

"Tyler, you find out exactly what happened, down to the tiniest detail," Nick said, anger burning him. "If there is anything that points to the Holcombs, I'm going to sell off that company of his bit by bit and wreck what I can't sell."

"I'll get back with you."

"I'll call Dad in the morning. He doesn't get up as early as he used to. The more casual I can be about it, the less concerned he'll be. Maybe by that time, you'll know more."

"I'll keep you posted."

Nick replaced the receiver, staring at the phone speculatively. He stepped out of bed, because sleeping again was impossible. Remembering clearly Julia's and Rufus's threats, Nick doubled his fists. Had she been behind the destruction? Or had her grandfather?

At eight o'clock the next morning, Nick's intercom buzzed and he listened to his secretary's voice. "Julia Holcomb is on the phone and would like to see you today, if possible. Your calendar is clear in an hour and at two this afternoon."

Surprised, he stared across his office and seethed with anger.

"I'll see her in an hour," he said flatly, his mind racing over what he wanted to do while he was curious about what she intended. He picked up a remote, switched on the news on the flat-panel television mounted on a wall across the room, and looked at images of what had been a productive Ransome oil rig only twenty-four hours earlier.

He stared while his anger climbed. Switching off the television, he tossed down the remote, picked up his phone and dialed Tyler's cell number. In seconds, Tyler answered, static crackling.

"Any more news?" Nick asked.

"The fire expert is looking into the cause."

"Remember that offer of a bet? Is it still on?"

"Bet?" Tyler sounded perplexed momentarily. "Ah, the horse and the car."

"You're on," Nick snapped. "If the Holcombs want a fight, they'll get a fight. If I seduce Julia within two weeks, I win your prize car."

"And if you don't, I want your horse," Tyler replied, his voice fading.

"Keep me posted."

"What? I'm losing you, Nick."

Nick replaced the receiver and stared at the door, not seeing his office, but remembering Julia Holcomb's blue eyes, her long legs. Revenge would be sweet. Seduction would be just the beginning.

As his appointment with Julia Holcomb approached, Nick glanced around, hoping that his office was bigger, finer and more intimidating than her own. Immediately, he had to laugh at himself. Never in his life had he felt that way with anyone, much less someone he was going to destroy.

He looked at the walnut paneling, the thick oriental carpet in muted colors, the oversized, polished mahogany table that served as his desk and brown leather furniture. The walls of his office held original oils by famous painters, art acquired on his trips to Europe. He was located on the eighteenth floor of the Ransome Building in downtown Dallas. He knew Holcomb Drilling was in a ten-story, suburban brick building that had been built about twenty years earlier to replace the old offices in downtown Dallas.

The intercom buzzed, and his secretary announced Julia's arrival.

As the door closed behind Julia, he rose to his feet. She was as beautiful as he remembered. He hoped his features were as impassive as hers, but he couldn't resist an appreciative head-to-toe glance. Taking in her tailored black suit and blouse, her blond hair coiled and pinned on her head, he wanted to tangle his fingers in that neat hairdo and watch those silky locks fall.

"Good morning," he said, smiling at her. "Welcome to the wolf's den."

Two

"Good morning. I'm surprised you admit it," Julia said, smiling as she crossed the room and extended her hand to shake Nick's.

"Why wouldn't I think this is a good morning?" he asked, something flashing in the depths of his dark eyes.

"Since I'm paying a call," she answered.

In a long-legged easy stride, Nick came around from behind his desk. His charcoal suit added to his dark, handsome looks which she tried to avoid thinking about as much as she tried to ignore her excitement at the sight of him. She loathed dealing with Nick and beneath what she hoped was a cool, collected facade, she fought a rising panic over what Nick was about to do to her grandfather and what she could not stop.

When she shook hands with him, his fingers closed around hers, warm and firm, in a contact that sizzled to her toes. How could she be so physically drawn to him when emotionally she viewed him as a ruthless competitor? She withdrew her hand swiftly.

"Won't you be seated," he said, motioning her to a leather chair. He pulled another chair around to face her and sat only a few feet away. His brown eyes bore into her and she tried to remain cool.

She crossed her legs and noticed his gaze drifting down to her ankles. Just a look from him made her tingle. She was accustomed to having control of most aspects of her life and she was chagrined to discover her reaction to Nick Ransome today was as volatile as her response during the first few minutes in the restaurant parking lot.

"I know you won't make this easy for me," she said.

"I'm damned astounded you're here," he admitted with a frankness that took her by surprise.

Unable to avoid noticing how thickly lashed his dark eyes were, she stared back at him. "I thought we ought to get on better footing than we were last night."

"I find that also amazing," he added. He looked relaxed, sitting in the chair, one ankle on his knee, but she had a feeling that he was holding back fury. His dark brown eyes sparked with fire. His curly, dark brown hair softened his features slightly.

"I know we parted on a bad note last night—"

"That's rather an understatement."

"I thought perhaps I should try again to persuade you to let go your intentions to acquire Holcomb Drilling."

"My objectives have been reinforced since dinner."

"Your hostility has grown," she said, wondering about his barely banked fury. "Maybe there's no point in this visit."

"Are you aware that one of our rigs burned in the night?"

"No, I didn't know that." She didn't try to hide her surprise and then guessed the reason for his smoldering anger. "That's what you've been referring to—"

"An explosion of an unknown origin caused the fire." His words were clipped and his eyes blazed with anger.

"You're blaming us?"

"Did Rufus hire someone to do it?" Nick cut in with a voice as cold as ice.

"No!" she exclaimed, furious that he would jump to conclusions without proof. "Granddad would never stoop to something like that. Or risk the lives of people who have nothing to do with the fight between the two of you. Never!"

"I'm afraid it'll take more than your denial to convince me," Nick said in what she thought was an annoying stubbornness to lay blame on her family.

"If there was an explosion or fire since we were together last night, aren't you being premature in jumping to conclusions about the cause?" she asked. "I think it often takes time to discover what starts a fire."

Something flickered in the depths of his dark eyes. "You're right, of course," he said pleasantly, his anger vanishing as if she had waved a magic wand. "Until I hear from the arson experts, I'll hold my judgment about the cause."

"That's the only sensible thing to do," she replied.

"In the meantime, what brings you to my office?" he asked in a pleasant tone, ignoring her sarcasm.

He smiled and waited. She gazed back steadfastly, her anger with him rising and becoming a tight, knot inside. She didn't trust his friendliness for a second. He had turned it on like switching on a light, and the warmth in his voice couldn't conceal the fiery anger in his eyes. Determined to not let him know how disturbed she felt, she concentrated on being civil and hiding her fury.

"I want to meet with you again, informally as we did last night, and see what we can work out," she replied, hoping she sounded as relaxed and friendly as he had. "We both have old companies that were family-owned for many years. There aren't many of those around any longer. I want to keep our company intact as long as Granddad is living. This company has been his whole life."

"Perhaps your granddad shouldn't have spread himself so thin," Nick remarked dryly.

Banking her annoyance, she nodded. "Maybe, if you're willing to try, we can work something out that will be to your satisfaction and ours. You surely will be reasonable enough to discuss the matter informally before the lawyers take charge tomorrow."

She hoped she looked and sounded amiable, far from how she felt. She loved her granddad and if the company were taken from him, she was afraid it would be the end of him. He had devoted his life to it and now to see it in precarious straits kept her sleepless at night. The problem was compounded by the fact that it was Nick who was after Holcomb Drilling. The Ransomes and Holcombs were old enemies, forever business competitors. She stared into Nick's brown eyes; his bland gaze belied the chemistry between them. Her breath caught. She couldn't move or speak or think, and he was doing nothing except look at her. She was caught and held, her heart pounding loudly enough that she wondered if he could hear it. She hated her reaction, to him, yet she couldn't prevent it.

"All right," he agreed. "We'll keep it informal. You and your granddad like boats and the water. I have a twenty-footer, give or take a few feet, that sleeps six. It's docked in Galveston Bay. We can fly down there and spend the weekend on the water."

Startled, she stared at him while she mulled his offer. "A weekend together? I had dinner in mind."

He shrugged. "You wanted a casual, friendly meeting. A weekend on the water—we can stay out of each other's way or talk, whatever we want to do. The weekend would be casual— and we'll get to know each other and what each one of us wants," he said pleasantly.

Her mind raced. She had never expected several days with Nick Ransome. Yet this might give her the chance to win him over and talk him into leaving Holcomb Drilling untouched. The more she thought about it, the more she liked the idea. "What if I come without Granddad?" she asked, "I'd like to be able to speak freely without worrying him."

"Fine," Nick said, something again flickering in the depths of his eyes. "I think the weather is supposed to be good, so we should have a calm time."

"The two of us together—a 'calm' time? I don't think it's possible."

He gave her a taunting, crooked smile. "Then if not calm, interesting."

"If we're not at each other's throats, it'll be a smashing success," she said. He touched the corner of her mouth, she tingled from the contact.

"There would be only one reason for me to be 'at your throat,'" he drawled in a husky voice.

"Now you're flirting," she accused.

"Don't sound so surprised. You're a beautiful woman."

"I rather distrust your motives for turning on your charm."

"I meant what I said," he insisted.

"Very well. A weekend on the water," she said, not feeling the relief and satisfaction she had expected to feel if he agreed to getting together. "Since we're going to talk more about the company, can we postpone tomorrow's meeting and let our lawyers get together next week?"

"It's fine with me to move the meeting. Make it a week from Friday," Nick replied, flashing her a smile that curled her toes. His white teeth were a contrast with his dark skin; creases bracketed his mouth and heightened his appeal. "I'll pick you up tomorrow about four and we can fly to Galveston," he said, getting up to go around his desk for pen and paper. "Give me your address."

"Write out where to meet you at the dock. I don't mind the drive to Galveston and I have an errand to run on the way," she said, not wanting to fly with him. She watched his well-shaped hands as he wrote an address. She stood and he moved beside her to show her what he had written.

He stood close enough that his shoulder and arm brushed against her. She could detect his enticing aftershave, feel the warmth from his body. Her drumming pulse was impossible to control.

There was no denying the reaction she had to Nick. Was she making a wise move to spend the weekend on Nick's boat—just the two of them, plus his crew in the background? Yet it was the only way she could see to try to win Nick's friendship so that he would at least listen to reason when they were ready to negotiate.

As it stood now, she and Nick were at loggerheads, and that would do nothing to win Nick Ransome over to doing what she wanted.

On the other hand, to be shut away with Nick for the weekend on a boat sent her heart racing into overdrive. She reassured herself that she and Nick wouldn't really be alone, and they would be together only for the weekend.

As Nick gave her directions, she struggled to listen. He turned to face her, and they stood only inches apart.

"If you prefer, I'll send a car to pick you up tomorrow—about four and you can still do your errands."

"Thanks, but I'll drive myself," she replied, and one corner of his mouth lifted in a wicked grin.

"Scared to leave transportation behind?" he asked.

"Of course not, or I wouldn't have suggested coming by myself," she replied, trying to ignore the butterflies fluttering in her stomach. Taking the directions from his hand, she picked up her purse and headed for the door. Suddenly he was there in front of her, reaching around her. Instead of opening the door, he stepped closer and blocked her with his hand on the knob, his arm a barrier. She turned to look up at him.

"So is it going to be all business this weekend?" he asked in a husky, seductive voice that created a honeyed warmth in her.

"Probably not," she replied breathlessly, wishing she could wrap him around her little finger and get what she wanted from him. Nick leaned closer and his gaze lowered to her mouth.

Her lips parted, tingling, but she moved around him and placed her hand over his on the knob. The instant she touched him, another fiery current simmered from her fingers to her toes.

She looked up at him. "I need to open the door."

With a smile, he swung the door wide and then he followed her into the reception area. "Tomorrow afternoon about five or six."

"Fine," she said, glancing over her shoulder at him. At the outer door, she looked back to find him still watching her. The minute she was in the hallway, her smile vanished. "What have I done?" she asked herself as she stepped into the empty elevator. "The only thing you could do," she answered herself, butterflies still fluttering in her stomach, her palms sweaty from spending the past few minutes with Nick.

No man had ever disturbed her the way Nick had and that worried her most of all because she was usually in control of her responses.

All the rest of the day and far into the night, she weighed the pros and cons of spending a weekend with him. Yet she had to do something to try to get a satisfactory settlement, or even better, get Nick to back off and leave Holcomb Drilling unscathed.

The next afternoon, as she drove over the arching causeway to Galveston and looked below at sparkling blue water, she asked herself the same question worrying her constantly since leaving his office. Would this weekend help save Holcomb Drilling?

Could she resist Nick's sex appeal? She reminded herself that all she had to do was remember what he intended to do to her heritage and future.

She shook her shoulders as if she banished a problem. How easy it was to think his appeal diminished when she was miles away from him!

"Be polite, professional," she reminded herself, glancing at the rearview mirror. She wanted something from him and there was no hope of getting it if she exposed her fury.

In minutes she parked at the Galveston Yacht Club. She slipped her backpack and her purse over her shoulder and picked up her briefcase. Taking a deep breath as if going into a battle, she circled the yacht club and strolled down to the wharf to look for the slip with his boat. She spotted him in cutoffs, a T-shirt and wraparound sunglasses. He and another man were in a motorboat. When Nick saw her, he sprang to the dock and came striding forward to meet her.

It was warm and she'd worn cutoffs, a cotton shirt, deck shoes and sunglasses and she suspected that behind his dark glasses, he was giving her a quick, thorough assessment. An appraisal that she gave him in return while her pulse thudded. His T-shirt molded sculpted muscles, the short sleeves stretched by thick biceps. His chest tapered to a narrow waist, flat stomach and well-muscled legs. The cutoffs were brief and tight. She should have guessed that beneath those elegant suits he wore, he had muscles.

The same mixture of attraction and dislike gripped her. She hated his intentions to destroy her family's business but, as a woman, she responded eagerly to Nick.

"You really intend to work," he said, taking her briefcase from her.

"Certainly. That's the whole point of getting together this weekend."

"I thought my personality enticed you."

She had to laugh at him. "With the lifelong differences between us? I don't think so."

"When you weren't here half an hour ago, I thought you'd changed your mind about sailing with me," he said.

"No. Just a slight delay," she said, startled that he guessed that she'd almost canceled the weekend. Duty urged her to do what she could and spend time with him, so she was going to follow her conscience.

"Great," he said, taking her arm. He waved her briefcase slightly. "I'll make a bargain with you. In the interest of getting acquainted and laying some groundwork for keeping things civil between us, no business discussions until twenty-four hours from now. That way, we'll have a pleasant weekend, get acquainted and get down to the nuts and bolts maybe tomorrow this time. How's that for a deal?"

"Fine with me," she said, looking into his unfathomable brown eyes and wondering what was behind his suggestion. Was he laying the groundwork for seduction? The mere speculation thrilled her in a way she hated.

"Good," Nick replied cheerfully. "Come meet my captain, Luis."

Nick jumped into the motorboat, causing it to rock slightly. He set down her briefcase, took her backpack and purse. Then his hands closed around her waist and he swung her into the boat. He lifted her easily and they gazed into each other's eyes while he held her. Her hands rested on his forearms, where she detected the flex of solid muscles. Each contact heightened her reaction to him. He held her a fraction longer than necessary and she stood with her hands on his forearms when she could have stepped away. As she looked into his brown eyes, she knew he wanted her. He released her and turned to a man standing in the boat.

"Julia, this is Luis Reyna. Luis, this is Miss Holcomb."

She greeted the tall black-haired man and then she sat in the front of the boat. She watched Nick's muscles ripple and flex as he unfastened the line and pushed away, and in seconds, they chugged slowly from the dock.

"So where are we headed? I know we're not spending the weekend in this," she said, looking at a number of yachts and sailboats at anchor.

"There's my boat, *For Ransome*," he said, pointing to the southwest.

She followed his gaze to see a large, sleek yacht. "Give or take a few feet," she said, repeating what he had told her about his boat. "It has to be over forty feet long," she said, eyeing the white yacht that had teak accents and a thin gold stripe on the hull. Nick smiled and shrugged.

When they were alongside, a man dropped a ladder over the side. Nick took her backpack and purse and scrambled up, turning to help her, leaning down to circle her waist with his arm and swing her to the deck.

This time, he released her immediately. "Julia, this is Dorian Landry. Dorian, meet my guest, Miss Holcomb."

She greeted the man and then walked away while the two men talked. Nick's luxurious yacht exceeded her family's large, comfortable sailboat, reinforcing her awareness of Nick as a powerful, formidable opponent no matter how sexy and appealing he appeared.

"Let me show you your cabin," he said, catching up with her. She followed him down a companionway to a spacious starboard cabin with a cream berth in beige and white decor.

"Want to come above while we head out? We'll travel along the coast. I'll give you the official tour of my boat later."

"Sure," she said, setting down her things, aware that in spite of the roominess, Nick dominated the cabin with his height and presence. When they went above, to her surprise, Nick took the wheel and she glanced around. "Where's Luis? And Dorian?"

"They're headed back," Nick said with a jerk of his head.

Startled, she frowned at Nick. "We're *alone?*"

"Yes. I thought that's what we agreed," he replied, looking at her and his eyes narrowing. "Changed your mind? I can take you back."

"No," she answered, questions tumbling in her mind. Could they be civil to each other through the entire weekend? Would she be able to resist his charm? Could she cope with him alone for hours on end?

"Of course not," she replied, hoping her voice sounded cool and composed and far from giving away mild panic. "I was just surprised that you didn't keep a crew on board."

"No need," he answered easily, gazing ahead as if his thoughts were more on navigating than on her. "I like handling the boat and I'm sure you don't want every minute of my time," he remarked dryly, turning to meet her gaze. Electricity sparked between them and she couldn't look away. Silence stretched, crackling with tension.

His dark chocolate, thickly lashed bedroom eyes could nail her and she wondered how much he saw. He was fit, handsome and she had to admire his drive and energy, which she wished he had directed somewhere besides at her family.

Did he know how she truly felt toward him, that the weekend was a sham? She wanted something from him and she intended to get it.

She inhaled, but she still couldn't look away. Then his cell phone rang, breaking the spell. To give him privacy, she started to leave, but Nick motioned her to remain while he listened to his call.

"No, we're not losing that property, Tyler. Go as high as you need to, but you see that we're the buyers," Nick said and then was quiet again. "I don't care. Just acquire the leases, whatever you have to pay." Another moment of silence. Wind had tangled his curly hair, and unruly locks just added to his handsome looks.

"We're losing the connection, Tyler. You've got your authority and instructions." Nick turned off the phone and set it down.

As she listened to him, descriptions materialized in her thoughts—sexy, ruthless, driven, handsome, good, bad and irresistible. His hands moved lightly over the wheel and he glanced at her. "I don't exactly see approval in your expression."

She shrugged. "I don't know enough to approve or not approve."

"Oh, yes, you do. You know my company will outbid the others no matter what price. You don't approve."

"I don't know the circumstances. I just know you like to win."

"I'd guess we're cut out of the same cloth there. I don't think you like to lose, either," he said dryly.

"I doubt if winning or losing is as all-important to me as much as it is you. There are other things that I give my efforts to."

"Is that right? So how do you like to spend your time?" he asked. His voice transformed into a lower, huskier tone that gave his question a hint of sexual innuendo.

"Get your mind off sex," she said lightly. "You know that wasn't my reference."

"I can always hope," he replied, and she smiled.

"There, that would melt the hardest heart," he said, touching the corner of her mouth. "What temptation!"

"Perhaps now you should concentrate on getting your yacht into open water."

He nodded, but his gaze remained on her. With an effort, she pulled her attention from him. Breathless, she left to get distance between them, stepping out into sunshine and fresh air, wanting to fan herself and knowing that her warmth wasn't caused by the weather. Also knowing that his brief phone conversation revealed how important winning was to him.

She moved to the railing and let the wind tangle her hair as a fine spray blew back over her. She watched gulls circling, swooping down to scoop something from the water. A jellyfish, a pale transparent blob, occasionally floated near the surface and then vanished from her sight. She thought about yesterday afternoon when she had gone to see her granddad, asking him directly if he knew anything about the fire on the Ransome oil rig.

His blue eyes had widened. "No, I don't know anything about a fire." He scowled. "Why would you think I'd know? Did Ransome or some of his people accuse us of that?"

"Nick Ransome thought we might have been the reason for the fire. As of now, the cause is unknown."

"That bastard. He'll say or do anything, just like his father."

"Forget it, Granddad. I just wanted to hear you say that we had no part in it." She had wanted to be sure, but now wished she hadn't brought up the matter.

Reassured, she looked down at the blue-green water sweeping against the yacht and hoped the fire experts learned exactly what had caused the blaze. Would Nick admit to her that he had been wrong to accuse her granddad? She doubted if he would.

She glanced over her shoulder and could see Nick inside at the wheel. They were alone on this boat for the weekend. She hoped she could hide her stormy emotions from him.

The Gulf was smooth and the breeze was cool, a perfect day that appeared peaceful and gave no hint of the turmoil churning inside her. She enjoyed the ride, but knew if she wanted to win Nick over, she wouldn't succeed by avoiding him. She wondered how many women he had brought on board that had wanted all his time and attention.

She returned to the pilothouse and when she reached his side, he stepped away slightly. "Want to take the wheel?"

"Sure," she said, taking it, aware of their hands brushing before he stepped aside. Spreading his feet, he placed his hands on his hips as he watched her.

"So you've been sailing since you were five," he commented. "Is this one of your favorite pastimes or are you doing it to be nice to your granddad?"

"I enjoy sailing. I've grown up doing it. Look out there," she said, waving her hand toward the stretch of blue-green water and the lush green. "This is another world and I can forget the office."

"There are all sorts of ways to forget the office," he said in a husky voice, moving closer.

"Careful, you're coming on again," she said, smiling at him.

"Nothing wrong with that," he said, smiling in return, a devastating, knee-melting smile that made her draw her breath. Creases bracketed his mouth and, with an effort, she tried to concentrate on the boat cutting smoothly through the water. "What else have you been doing, besides sailing? I don't know much about you," he said, leaning his hip against the bulkhead and giving her his undivided attention. It made her heart race.

"I went to Rice, returned home to go to work for Granddad. I bought my own home and I sail on weekends. A simple life. That's about it."

"No special man in your life?"

"No, there isn't," she said, turning to look into his dark eyes, wondering about the women in his life. His mouth was wide, his lower lip full, sensual. What would it be like to kiss him? She struggled to get her thoughts elsewhere.

"Was there an important man?" Nick repeated.

She shook her head again. "Not really. No, there never has been anyone."

"Ah, you're particular."

She smiled. "Or busy."

"The ice princess," he said softly, his dark gaze filled with speculation. "With your heart sealed away. Who will melt your heart of ice and turn you into a warm, passionate woman?"

She laughed. "Are you trying to offer yourself for that role? If so, save your breath."

"I know better than to do that," he replied lightly. "Besides, whoever melts the ice princess then has a responsibility."

"So, Nick Ransome, you have some old-fashioned ideas lurking."

"I keep them locked away rather well," he replied.

"I imagine you do. What about you? I don't know much about you, either."

"My life is an open book. I like closing a deal that I've worked hard to get, making money, flying, sailing, swimming, passionate women, fast horses and faster cars, long, wet kisses, making love in the moonlight and touching. Pretty predictable, I'd say."

"Right, just the guy next door," she remarked facetiously, but her pulse quickened at his answers and the thoughts his remarks conjured up. If only business didn't stand between them, she thought and then realized the dangerous direction of following what-if thoughts.

"What big goals do you have?" he asked. "To be CEO of Holcomb Drilling? To destroy Ransome Energy? To fight with me and win?"

She laughed. "I think you're answering your own questions. Except I don't have ambitions to be a CEO. As for ruining Ransome Energy," she said, looking at him, "that's a tempting one. Especially when you're out to smash us. Now if we can settle our differences peacefully, I'll be quite happy. Otherwise—" She broke off and gazed out at the water, watching waves come up to meet them.

"But if we don't, you're threatening me, aren't you?"

Meeting Nick's gaze squarely, she felt the contest of wills. "We're like two sharks circling each other, part of the time swimming together, part of the time eyeing each other as dinner."

He leaned closer. "You would be the tastiest morsel I ever sunk my teeth into," he drawled in a low, husky voice.

"Careful, Nick, I might bite back," she said seductively, unable to resist dallying with him in return.

"This weekend gets to be a better idea by the second," he said, leaning closer.

She placed her hand against his chest. "You stay right where you are."

He grinned with a disarming flash of white teeth. "I'll check over the place and be back shortly," he said, leaving her at the wheel. She was surprised he trusted her because he didn't know whether she could handle his yacht. Yet in the calm sea, there would be few problems and he was probably counting on that.

Soon he returned, making her heart race as he walked up to her. "I'll take the wheel now," he said, his hands brushing hers lightly. She tingled, aware of the warmth of him as he stood close beside her. "I have a favorite cove," he continued. "It's sheltered, has a beach and we can swim."

"Sounds marvelous," she said, barely knowing how she responded as she watched him.

"See," he said waving his hand and she watched as they followed the shoreline in a sweeping curve.

"It's beautiful," she said when she saw his destination, animosity momentarily forgotten as she turned her attention to the breathtaking view of blue water, white sand and tall, swaying palms. "Your cove is paradise," she said quietly, wishing she were with a companion to share the beauty of the place and make it a weekend of warm memories instead of a chess match with high stakes.

"This is a special escape. I've been sailing here for several years."

"I'm surprised there isn't anyone else here."

"That's part of the charm. Most of the time, this inlet is secluded. And in a few minutes, we can drop anchor," he said, taking the wheel from her and brushing his hands over hers. "I'll give you a tour of my boat and then we can swim," he said.

A few minutes later, he took her arm to go down the companionway to show her the cherrywood and stainless steel galley that opened into the saloon. The galley held a refrigerator, a freezer, a four-burner stove, a built-in table and bench.

"Hopefully, everything we need or want."

"That's your life, isn't it, Nick," she declared. "Everything you need or want at your fingertips. You have to get your way."

He turned his attention to her and arched an eyebrow. He placed his hand on her shoulder. "I suspect in a few areas, we're too much alike. So far, you seem accustomed to getting your way and determined to continue to do so."

"So I guess we're locked in a contest of wills."

"This should be the most delicious, hottest challenge I've ever faced."

"Don't make me a challenge," she cautioned. Aware of his smoldering gaze on her, she moved around the galley, lightly touching the gleaming cherrywood cabinets. "This is a beautiful yacht."

"I like beautiful things, particularly beautiful women," he said in a low voice.

"Well, now that doesn't surprise me one degree." She turned to study him, sensing the sparks flying between them. "I hope this weekend thing was a good idea," she said quietly, her pulse quickening as he stepped closer. When he brushed a tendril of hair away from her face, his fingers skimmed her cheek lightly.

"This weekend is going to be sweet. The wise choice is always to get to know each other and to garner a clear understanding of what your opponent wants."

"We don't have to be opponents, Nick."

"No, we don't," he replied, his voice thick and husky.

"That was not a come-on. Don't mistake it for one," she stated and wished her voice held more force. "If we can just work it out where you don't hurt Granddad," she said, trying to get back to the purpose of her being on Nick's yacht, "I'll try to see that you get business concessions in return that satisfy you completely."

"You want to satisfy me completely?" he said huskily, sending her temperature soaring. Fire danced in the depths of his eyes, and her pulse pounded. He looked at her as if he were about to kiss her.

"Did you even hear the word *business*? I still feel as if I'm swimming with a shark that is eyeing me for dinner," she stated breathlessly.

"There is nothing like a shark about what I want. 'Satisfy me completely'…that opens visions of possibilities."

"You know what I meant! I'm not talking about in bed," she said bluntly. "I meant absolutely no reference to anything personal."

"Too bad. If you had, I might be more easily persuaded." His hand rested on her shoulder and his thumb lightly rubbed her throat, then paused. "It isn't problems with work that has your pulse racing," he drawled, and her heart thumped. Nick saw too much, understood too clearly, guessed too accurately about her. She was held immobile by his hungry, steadfast gaze. That first searing attraction when they met was escalating at an alarming rate.

"We both know that we have some chemistry between us— it doesn't mean a thing," she said.

"I beg to differ," he said softly. "From the moment you ran in front of my car and stopped me, the attraction has been undeniable. My curiosity's stirred. I want to discover the depth of this fire that's between us."

"There is nothing between us except a disagreement we're trying to solve," she argued breathlessly.

"You know better than that," he responded with a wicked arch of one dark eyebrow. "Right now, your pulse races and so does mine."

"I think I'll go on instinct here. Beware the circling shark."

"You're the one who wanted to get close," he reminded her.

"Not quite as close as you have in mind. You're going way too fast. Slow down, Nick. This time two nights ago, we were barely speaking."

She was hot—her heart thudding, her breathing ragged—but she knew she had to get control of herself as well as cool him down. She couldn't stop her body from responding to him, but she should maintain distance between them. A degree of aloofness was becoming increasingly more vital to her well-being. She didn't want to end up two days from now with her heart lost to Nick Ransome. He was everything she didn't want in her life. Business rival. Ambitious, ruthless and into risks. She knew he had been in Special Forces, knew he had a reputation for doing as many wild things as his mountain-climbing brother, who had recently died in an accident.

With effort, she turned away. "Let's finish this tour or the sun will set before we can swim. I like to see what I'm swimming in." When he didn't answer and silence stretched, she was compelled to glance back at him.

As soon as she turned, she found him watching her intently, that smoldering anger back in his expression. Comparing him to a shark was apt—he looked like a predator, a danger to her heart. She had to put distance between them. She didn't trust his motives and his smooth talk. Seduction? The thought shook her, but she reminded herself that if she let him seduce her, she would probably regret it forever because her emotions would be entangled in the act while she was certain his would not.

"Are we going to continue the tour?"

"Sure," he said and led the way below to his forward stateroom. In his stateroom, she stepped away from him while she gazed at the king-size berth, navy and white decor and mirrors on the bulkhead. Too clearly, she could imagine him sprawled out in that bed. The image of his broad, bare chest, lean length, hard muscles, flashed hotly, making her grit her teeth.

Drawing a deep breath, she turned to see two large hanging lockers, plush chairs and a desk.

"As you already know, your stateroom is luxurious and beautiful," she said, glancing at him.

He stood with one shoulder braced against a bulkhead while he watched her. He shrugged lightly. "I don't spend a lot of time in here. C'mon. I'll show you the rest."

She drew a quick breath. The yacht that had appeared so large and accommodating was shrinking with each passing hour. She suspected she and Nick would be together nearly every waking minute and the thought of spending the entire weekend near each other fueled her burning desire.

More aware of Nick than her surroundings, she followed him while he showed her the salon where sunlight streamed in through portholes. He had a game room with a pool table and a plasma television.

When they finished the tour, she returned to her cabin to change to her swimsuit, a black two-piece cut inches below her waist, high over each thigh. It was no more revealing than what many other women wore, but now she longed for a one piece that covered as much of her as possible. The expanses of bare flesh she was presenting would be a come on to Nick.

Why had this weekend seemed such a good idea when she had been alone at home? At that time, she hadn't factored in the scalding response she had to Nick, a reaction that heightened steadily.

"He's just another man and one you don't like very much anyway," she whispered to herself, yet she knew that wasn't true. But he wasn't just another man, and while he angered her, he also appealed to her.

Plaiting her hair into one thick braid, she studied herself in a mirror, turning first one way and then another, knowing she was locked in a contest of wills with him. The outcome of their battle would probably be determined this weekend, no matter what transpired between their lawyers. This was one struggle she intended to win, and the unwanted steamy attraction between her and Nick wasn't going to get in her way or defeat her.

He was a sexy male with a strong liking for women, so he was approachable. She intended to win him over without selling her soul—or her body—to do it.

"You're playing with dynamite," she whispered to herself.

She could resist him because their families had feuded for generations. Her granddad despised Nick, his brother, his father and his grandfather when he had been alive. With that history, she could withstand Nick Ransome's charm. She just hoped he couldn't resist cooperating with her.

She wondered what the evening would bring as she went to

join him, feeling as if she were diving into water that held a shark.

Her conscience told her that Nick would never resort to a shark's tactics. He would never attack and devour. There was never need to. Nick's appeal was the most dangerous kind of all to resist—pure seduction.

Three

As Julia emerged onto the deck, Nick's dark gaze drifted over her like a caress, a slow perusal that sent tingles dancing in its wake. His approval was obvious.

At the same time, she was mesmerized, unable to keep from returning his study, letting her gaze lower across his bare, muscled chest with a mat of brown curly hair. Sunlight splashed over his tanned body, with golden highlights on the swell of hard muscles. His broad chest tapered to a tiny waist and slim hips and a black strip of swimsuit that bulged with his masculinity. His long, muscular legs were covered lightly in short brown hairs. She imagined what it would feel like to be in his arms, pressed against his strong, warm length.

"You're beautiful, Julia," he said quietly. "Definitely an unfair advantage in this battle between us." Moving closer, he reached out to tug lightly on her braid and his knuckles brushed her bare shoulder.

"We're not in a battle today," she said.

"Liar," he accused lightly. "You're taking unfair advantage here."

She stepped closer, looking up at him, only inches of space between them. "No more unfair advantage than you do when you flirt," she said in a sultry voice.

Desire smoldered in his dark eyes. He dropped his towel before placing his hands on her waist. "I have that effect on you?" he asked.

"You know you do. Don't act surprised," she chided, more aware of his hands on her than of what she was saying.

"You're keeping a barrier between us. I want to scale that wall you've surrounded yourself with. I want to get to know you."

"Nick," she cautioned. "We have to step back and get a lid on the sex and emotion."

"Let go a little and let's see where they take us," he coaxed. He reached out to let his fingers slowly trace her jawline. "Let's start with a swim."

She was tempted to tell him to turn the yacht around and head back. She didn't want a weekend with him coming on to her and turning her into breathless mush, a melting, responsive female who boosted his ego and gave him the upper hand in their dealings. She knew enough about him to know there was a steady stream of women in his life. She didn't want to fall into his arms and his bed, and then be tossed aside like an old shoe. Only an old shoe didn't feel anything. She had always avoided heartbreak, and she could imagine the casualties in Nick's background.

He lowered the ladder over the side and stepped back. "You can go into the water this way," he said, motioning with a wave of his hand.

"Do you climb down that?"

"I dive."

"Then I will, too," she said. He laughed, touching her cheek lightly with his forefinger.

"Ever competitive. Let's go." He stepped to the side, going over in a smooth dive, his muscles flexing. Her mouth went dry as she looked at his long, powerful body in prime physical condition.

Trying to stop her flood of thoughts about him, she followed him, feeling refreshingly cool water closing over her. She came up to find him swimming away from her, parallel to the beach, and she followed, catching up with him and swimming beside him. What compelled her to compete with him on every level? She wanted to best him in every way, wring what she wanted out of him, make him as breathless when they flirted as he made her. She suspected on the last, she did. Only she knew his flirting might have a deeper effect on her. She was certain that she couldn't be as casual about sex as he could be.

He turned to swim back to her. "Want to snorkel or just swim?"

"Snorkel," she replied.

Nick splashed out of the water, clambering back on board to return in minutes with breathing equipment for both of them.

As she swam under the surface, she looked with wonder at the world of water she had entered. Brightly colored fish, in deep blues and bright yellows swam gracefully near. She clutched Nick's arm to look at one with brilliant orange-and-black stripes. Then she forgot the water and the dazzling array of fish as her hand closed on his arm. He was sleek and warm and muscular. She released him immediately, but he caught her arm and pulled her close again.

While her heart raced, she looked into his eyes. They couldn't talk and even submerged in cool water, she was hot, burning with desire that was a constant torment.

She pushed away from him and went to the surface. Nick splashed up beside her. Breathless, she stared at him. "It's beautiful down there," she gasped.

"It's beautiful up here," he said solemnly.

She placed her finger over his lips, conscious of a current that tingled through her hand. She went under again, gliding away from him. They swam close together, looking at tropical, salt-water fish that were a myriad of bright colors.

When they put away their snorkeling equipment, Nick swam away from her, heading out toward the open water where waves were choppier. She wondered how well he knew the water they were in. Even though he hadn't said anything, she felt as if he were daring her to follow him.

Wisdom told her to stay in the cove where they had been swimming and where the water was more calm, but her competitiveness made her want to keep up with him.

She swam out beside him and treaded water, thankful there wasn't a stronger chop and wondering how deep the water was. The yacht and shoreline appeared to be a long way back.

"You're a damn good swimmer," he said, moving beside her. "And either not scared of this or determined to keep up with me."

"I figured you hoped to drown me," she said, and he laughed while they bobbed in the water.

"Not at all. You're far too interesting alive. Let's race back."

"You know you'll win. You want to win every time, don't you?"

"No more than you do. I'll give you a head start."

She was getting tired of treading water and the open water was choppier than it had looked when they were on the boat. She turned to swim back slowly, watching him slice through the water spreading the distance between them. She wondered why he swam out so far, but then decided he liked challenges. Did he view her as a challenge? she wondered. Probably not.

She swam to him as he waited.

"Have you worked up an appetite for dinner yet?" he asked.

She was standing flat-footed in water that came to her shoulders, and he stood only a few feet away. Water droplets sparkled on his bare shoulders and his curly brown hair was plastered to his head, making him appear sleek and dangerous. Drops of water sparkled on his thick eyelashes and were sprinkled over his skin.

"Now that you mention it, yes. By the time we dress and cook dinner, definitely," she answered, wondering if she was going to have this heart-pounding reaction to him the entire weekend—or longer.

"Let's head for my boat," he said, turning to swim away. When they climbed back on board, he said he would get dinner.

In minutes, their suits were dry, and she pulled on her low-cut, hip-hugging cutoffs and a T-shirt, turning to find him watching her.

"I was hoping you'd eat like you were," he said.

"No way. You can."

"That's definitely not the same." He vanished inside and returned shortly in a T-shirt and cutoffs and his deck shoes. As the orange sun slanted low in the west sending a golden streak of fire across the surface of the blue water, Nick put steaks on to grill and served her a glass of red wine.

Tempting smells made her mouth water and the quiet was relaxing, wrapping around them. On the deck overlooking the water, four chairs with tables between two of them were in a small circle. She sat on a chair and he sat facing her and raised his glass. "Here's to mutual satisfaction in our endeavor."

"I'll drink to that," she said, raising her drink in a toast and taking only a small sip.

"Tell me about your life, Julia," he said, studying her with that dark-eyed intensity that gave her goose bumps. He set his glass on a table. "What do you want in the future?"

"That's an easy question. I want to marry and have a family, although I'm only twenty-eight, so I'm not in a rush."

"I'm thirty-two, and not only in no rush, my freedom is essential," he replied firmly. "No marriage for me."

"That sounds final and bitter," she said, wondering why he was so sour on marriage. "I know you like women."

"I just want my freedom. I come from a family of nonmarrying people except for my brother, who has had one disastrous union and is married again. My parent's marriage was even more of a calamity than my brother's. I say no thanks to the ball and chain."

"You view someone you love as a 'ball and chain,'" she repeated with amusement. "You may have a lonely life," she predicted, yet she knew the handsome man she faced would never be lonely. "I want a family because I have almost none. My only living relatives are my granddad and my granddad's sister. I want a big family. You have a brother and sister—aren't you close to them?"

He shrugged one muscled shoulder. "I suppose, but we go for periods of time without seeing each other. We keep in touch."

"I'm sorry about the brother you lost—the one that died in the mountain climbing accident."

"Yeah. We all miss Jeff. Well, good luck with getting married and having kids. With your looks, there'll be no problem about marrying."

"Thank you, I think."

"You're beautiful, but your brain may scare off some guys."

"Not the right one," she answered with amusement. "He'll be smarter than I am, I imagine."

"I'd take bets on that," he said, and she smiled. He touched her cheek, and she felt a frisson of excitement from the slight contact. "That smile should get you everything in life you want."

She flashed him another broad smile. "Do you think so? Will it get what I want from you?"

"I walked right into that one," he remarked, leaning closer. He was only inches from her. "It probably will," he said in a husky voice as he looked at her mouth. She wanted to kiss him, even though she knew she should keep her distance.

"So what do you want, Nick? No family. Freedom to do what?" she asked too breathlessly, but hoping to get back to more impersonal topics.

"To build an oil empire," he said immediately. "To have the toys and homes I want. I want success."

"We measure success differently, Nick. To you, it's money and acquisitions and a career. I measure success in love and family and relationships and people. We're worlds apart."

He gave her a mocking smile and traced his forefinger back and forth on her forearm, distracting her from what he was saying.

"You'd like to accomplish what you set out to achieve or you wouldn't be with me right now," he observed. "You're out here because you intend to fight for your company and your grandfather. We're the same."

"No, we're not," she argued quietly. "If it weren't for Granddad, I wouldn't be here. I can give up the company. I'd just move on. It's for him. We're not remotely the same, Nick. What you value in life is not what I hold dear."

Nick picked up her hand and spread her fingers against his, examining her hand and running his fingers lightly over her knuckles. She knew she should move her hand away, but she couldn't.

"I like challenges and winning. That's not so bad," he said, watching her.

"Whether it's bad or good depends on how you go about acquiring what you want."

"I'm sure to you and your family, it's bad. I'd guess you view me as Mr. Greed," he said. When his gaze ran the length of her, she tingled from head to toe.

"Business aside, we might do all right," he speculated, looking at her mouth and then letting his gaze slide slowly to her legs.

"Oh, sure," she said facetiously, knowing he knew as well as she did the impossibility of what he suggested. "As if either one of us could forget that I'm a Holcomb and you're a Ransome. The animosity between our families goes back too many generations for that to happen. Plus, I see marriage in my future. I don't take relationships lightly. I'm sure you're the opposite."

"You and I could change the dynamics between our families and end the fuss."

"Like you're suddenly going to love Granddad, and I'll be ever so happy with your family. I wouldn't count on it," she said.

"I suppose you're right. I'll check on the steaks." He stood and she watched him cross the deck. On his boat, he had a rolling gait and kept his balance well, moving around with ease. Another big plume of smoke rose from the grill and the smells made her mouth water. She surmised the weekend would be a bust. She couldn't imagine Nick changing his views about her family or their company any more than she intended to change her opinions of him or his family. They had agreed to not discuss business for the first twenty-four hours, yet so far, they had hassled over everything they did, including something as simple as swimming. How could she hope for a business compromise or an agreement from him?

She scanned his bare legs. One thing was certain—he was too sexy to easily resist.

Julia went to offer her help. When he turned her down, she moved to the rail to sip her wine and lookout at the beach and the water, thinking that all the beauty of their surroundings was being wasted on two people who were at cross-purposes.

"Enjoying the view?" he said softly behind her.

She turned to face him, leaning back with her elbows on the rail. "Yes. It's enchanting here."

"I like charming places and gorgeous women." He moved closer and put his hands on the rail, hemming her in.

"Nick—"

"Scared of me?"

"No, I'm not. But we're very different and I don't want to get closely involved with you."

"Do you tell this to all the guys?"

"No," she replied. "I don't go out with ones where we're 'very different.' This weekend with you is unique," she said, aware of his proximity, the breeze catching locks of his curly hair and blowing them slightly. She looked at his brown hair framing his face and could imagine her fingers tangled in its thick softness. What was it about him that constantly drew her?

"This weekend is singular," he agreed in a low voice, "and I still insist that we can be friends." His hands slid from the rail to her waist and she inhaled deeply while her heart skipped a beat.

"Careful, Nick," she warned, trying to ignore her racing pulse. "I imagine you rarely play by the rules."

"*Au contraire!* I certainly do follow rules. Pay my taxes, help little old ladies across the street, take my dad fishing," he said while his gaze roamed over her features.

"What an upstanding, law-abiding citizen—most of the time. But then there are the moments when you are over the speed limit, when you turn on your sexy charm and when you devour your competitors," she declared.

His hands rested lightly on her waist and his thumbs moved languidly back and forth on her ribs. His touch created havoc with her concentration.

He laughed. "Sexy charm? Guilty as charged, I hope! I'm not going to stop coming on to a gorgeous blonde. Not in this lifetime. It's far too interesting, and who knows where it might lead? Now here's where I hope it leads. I hope said blonde has to succumb to the flirting, and I do believe there is a bit of flirting in return from this beautiful blonde."

Amused, she smiled at him. "It will lead nowhere. Is dinner burning?"

"Probably," he said, studying her and not moving.

Her pulse drummed because he stood too close and was looking at her too intently. She placed her hand against his chest, feeling the warmth of him beneath the cotton T-shirt. "Dinner, Nick," she reminded him. "I don't want charred steak."

"If I got something else instead, I wouldn't care," he said in a husky voice.

"If the something else is a hamburger or some such, I'd just as soon have my steak," she said, trying to keep the moment light. She stepped away at the same time he turned and strode back to the grill.

Watching his sure-footed stride, she drifted along behind him, taking in his cutoffs, his trim backside. She inhaled while desire coiled like a dangerous flame low inside her.

Trying to focus on something besides Nick, she saw the steaks were ready and she helped him get everything on a table. As they ate, a breeze blew over them and the sun was a mere orange slice on the horizon.

She bit into the thick, juicy steak and wished she and Nick had known each other under other circumstances. But such was not the case, and nothing could take away the past or change how she felt about him.

"I'll admit, this has been a wonderful day, Nick."

"Good. See, it's possible to get along."

"Yes—as long as not one word is said about business," she

added with amusement. "Tell me about yourself. Where did you go to school and where were you stationed with Special Forces?"

"I went to Texas University. In the military, I was stationed several places, but spent most of my time in North Carolina."

"Is your dad active in Ransome Energy now?"

"No. Dad retired to his ranch the minute I could take charge. He and my brother run the family place—mostly my brother Matt. Dad just enjoys himself. His health hasn't been so great. I have the feeling that you already know all that about me and my family."

"Only the most general information. You said your father divorced. Do you see your mother often?"

A shuttered look crossed Nick's features and he glanced away. "I haven't seen her since I was very small and she walked out on us. She made it absolutely clear that she didn't want to see any of us."

"Sorry," Julia replied. "I can't imagine a mother doing that," she added, wondering how much that event contributed to his grim outlook on marriage. She tilted her head. "I saw her once."

His dark eyebrow arched quizzically, but the flash of surprise was gone instantly. "How would you even know her?"

"Granddad. I was a teen traveling with Granddad and we were at the airport when Granddad said hello to her and they talked briefly. At the time, I thought she was incredibly beautiful."

He merely shrugged.

"Granddad said she was hurt by the breakup."

"Your grandfather doesn't know at all. She was far from hurt."

"None of you have ever had any contact with her since that time?"

"No. Julia, she left us—not the other way around," he stated flatly with a harsh note in his voice and she suspected he had been badly hurt at the time.

"You were little children. Maybe your father didn't tell you the whole story."

"He might not have told us the whole story, but he told us enough. Forget her. She's no part of our lives and never will be."

"She was a big part at one time."

His annoyance heightened and his dark eyes flashed. "I don't care to even think about her. Subject closed."

"Sorry, Nick. I didn't intend to intrude."

He shrugged and placed his hand on her shoulder, massaging it lightly. "And I came on too strong, but she's no part of our lives."

"You're strong-willed. My guess is that you've surrounded yourself with people who do what you want constantly and with women who are gaga and likewise try to please you. You're not accustomed to dealing with someone who doesn't follow your express wishes."

"And you're going to oppose me every way you can," he said, a twinkle appearing in his eyes.

"I think it just comes naturally," she replied, amused in turn. "We're opposites, Nick. There's no common ground."

"There a delicious common ground that is the chemistry boiling between us. Sparks dance and you can't deny that you feel them. Every time I get your pulse, it's racing. Is that a permanent condition? Or the result of us?"

Her pulse quickened at his words, but she didn't want to admit the truth to him.

"I don't know what you plan for Ransome Energy. What direction do you plan to take it?"

"You're running, Julia. Scared to face the truth about what you feel right now? Or scared to admit it? You're changing the subject."

"It's time we changed it. Answer my question, please."

He stared at her a moment while her pulse drummed because every word he said was true. "I want a worldwide company that will grow," he finally said.

They talked and ate little of their dinners. Afterwards, she helped him clean up.

"It's been more than an hour since we ate," he said finally. "Let's go in for a quick dip. We have a full moon coming up over the horizon and the water is cool."

She looked at the dark water and shivered slightly. She didn't like to swim in water that wasn't clear and she didn't like to swim at night, which frightened her as much as opaque, muddy water, but she didn't want to admit her vulnerability to a man whom she suspected feared very few things.

"Talked me into it," she said standing, trying to keep in mind how swimming had been earlier with golden sunlight streaming through the crystal depths. "I will race you into the water," she said, peeling her shirt off and tossing it aside before she glanced at him. Her hands were on her shorts as she paused.

He watched her without moving. Desire burned hotly in his brown eyes.

"There are other things we could do," he said in a husky voice and she tingled. His hungry gaze held her and the smoldering attraction blazed, threatening the control she was trying to maintain.

"Julia," he said softly, taking a step toward her.

Her mouth went dry and desire shook her, but common sense held sway. She waved her hand at him, motioning him to stop. "I vote for the race and this time I have a chance of winning," she said, unfastening her shorts with shaking fingers, too aware of his scalding gaze. She dropped the shorts as fast as possible, stepped out of them, kicked off the deck shoes and rushed to jump overboard. She didn't want to think about how Nick was looking at her, about peeling off her outer layer of clothes right in front of him, or about jumping into black Gulf waters that held a myriad of creatures.

Cool water closed over her and then she pushed up and burst to the surface. Shaking her head and slicking back her hair, she treaded water, fighting a sense of panic about the inky water surrounding her. Then she glanced back at the yacht and her fears evaporated.

Backlit by lamps on the boat, Nick stood poised at the side. The impact of the view was broad shoulders, long legs, a man who was strong and desirable. The last few minutes had made her blood run hot with longing. She wished she knew him under other circumstances.

Nick sliced into the water and came up close beside her. "I'll race you to the beach. It'll give us a workout."

"You're on," she replied, wondering on how many levels she would compete with him during the weekend.

"I'll give you a head start. You go," he said.

"I'll go when you do. You can beat me, but I don't want a head start."

He laughed and began swimming toward the beach. She tried to keep up with him, but he soon widened the distance between them. She swam enough at home that she was fast and in good physical shape, but his powerful muscles told her the same was true of Nick. His arms sliced through the water and he won easily, walking up on the sandy beach and sitting down.

She followed, knowing he was watching her walk toward him. Silvery moonlight splashed over him, highlighting powerful muscles, revealing his long, bare body. The scrap of swimsuit looked like a dark shadow. Everything they did stirred her desire, making her more and more conscious of him. This moment was one more scalding temptation.

She sat beside him to look at the water with a slash of a brilliant moonlight streaming across it. Even so, the dark water sent a shiver down her spine. "You win again, if you're keeping score."

"No. I don't keep score in little things. It's the big things that matter."

"Why do I doubt that?" she asked, leaning back on her hands and still looking at the water, amazed she had been able to swim in it and, for a few minutes, lose her apprehension.

"You were right behind me."

"Trailing you quite a bit," she remarked. "Earlier today, I thought maybe there was hope for us to reach a state where we're on friendly footing. Since sailing with you this afternoon, it's beginning to look hopeless. We compete in everything."

"No, we don't. There are some things we do great together," he said.

"Like what—eat steaks and drink wine?" she said.

"There's this," he said, drawing his fingers in a feathery

caress along her ear and throat and down her arm. Inhaling deeply, she turned her head to look at him and her heartbeat raced.

He leaned closer and placed his hand on her throat. "You and I have the same response to each other. Admit it," he demanded softly.

Excitement built inside her as she was locked in his stare. "Mine is unwanted," she whispered. "We're poles apart in too many ways and in one of the most important aspects of all." She pulled away from his touch even though desire flamed through her veins. She couldn't keep from looking at his mouth. Her breath caught, and with an effort she tore her gaze away.

"Business is nothing next to this," he said and his words cut through the haze of wanting him, the temptation to lean closer and kiss him.

"I think there is never a moment when victory is nothing to you," she whispered, unable to draw a deep breath, physically responding to him, yet mentally fighting herself.

"Dammit, there are times when I forget ambition," he argued in a low voice as he turned to face her and scooted close. He slid his hand behind her head. His fingers were warm on her nape. He was too close, his mouth only inches away. They were both almost naked—warm, bare bodies with his knee touching her, his hand caressing her. He wanted her and the hungry longing in his eyes made his desire plain to see.

She ached to kiss him. He was only inches from her. What would a kiss hurt? He searched her gaze and pulled lightly on the back of her head.

Closing her eyes, she twisted away and stood. "Dark water scares me," she said softly, "but I think I'm a lot safer out there than here."

"*Safe?* I'd never hurt you," he said, standing and placing his hand on her waist.

"You can break my heart and you know it," she replied, her voice as raspy and breathless as his.

"You're a beautiful, desirable woman. I know men have been

in your life before, so you're not going to get a broken heart if we kiss a few times this weekend," he persisted.

His arm slid around her waist. "I don't have that big an effect on you, do I?" he asked in a teasing voice, but he watched her closely.

She shook her head. "No, you don't. I wouldn't tell you if you did and you know it."

She placed her hand against his bare chest to stop him from drawing her into his embrace, but the moment she touched his rock-hard muscles and felt his heart pounding, she wanted him more than ever.

"No!" she whispered and stepped back, turning to dash into the water to cool her scorching body. She splashed away, swimming toward the boat, for the first time that she could remember, she forgot her fear of opaque water.

Soon he swam beside her. He brushed against her. "Want to get back on board?"

"Yes," she replied.

He swam ahead, scrambled up the ladder and turned to lean down when she climbed up. He lifted her easily to the deck and watched her, keeping his hands on her waist. She caught his wrists and removed his hands.

"Nick," she said quietly.

"I'm curious. I want to know what it's like to kiss you. I want to see how much response I can evoke from you. I want you in my arms where I can feel your softness," he said, his voice dropping back to that husky tone that made her toes curl while his words drew pictures in her mind and made her want him to do just what he said.

"Instead, I'm going to get dressed," she replied with that same breathlessness that he could constantly stir. She hurried away to her cabin.

As she dressed in fresh cutoffs and a T-shirt, she wished she could develop an immunity to him. She couldn't put his sexy drawl or what he said to her out of mind, hearing it over and over. He was trying to seduce her. He had said "a few kisses," but she knew once she started, it would never stop at kisses. The attraction between them was too hot and too strong. Why did it have to be Nick Ransome who turned her into a quivering, melting woman with an insatiable craving for what he offered?

She reminded herself of all the reasons to resist. "He's a playboy," she said to herself. "A man driven by ambition and a compulsion to win and conquer challenges and women." She dried her hair, staring at her reflection, but seeing Nick and his fit, powerful body. "He's too desirable, too seductive, too smart. He goes after what he wants and right now what he wants—" she paused and leaned closer to the mirror, looking herself in the eye "—is me."

"He wants me and he's turning all his sexy charm on to get his way. And it's working too darn well." Thinking about him, she tingled. She wanted to join him on deck. She was playing with fire and he had her wanting him passionately. She should go to bed, alone, and stay away from him for the rest of the night. She should, but she couldn't. The man was too exciting, and maybe he had some of the same need and longing.

"Oh, right!" she said aloud. "How many women have thought that one!"

She intended to soften him up with this weekend together, get him more willing to compromise on a deal. Soften Nick? Ridiculous! The man was hard inside and out! His body was as hard as his feelings for business rivals.

All the time she argued with herself, Julia continued getting ready to join him again.

Before she left her cabin, she paused to look at herself and give herself one last admonition. "Beware of charm," she said. "Resist him no matter how sexy and hot he is, in spite of how much you want him." Trying to rein in her eagerness, she headed above to join him.

Since part of her couldn't wait to see him, she wondered if she could resist him.

Four

She found him sitting on deck. He had cut the lights except the ones needed for safety, but moonlight illuminated the night, giving the boat a cozy, dreamlike ambience. The moment she appeared, Nick came to his feet.

He wore only cutoffs and his muscles were highlighted by the moonlight. At the sight of him, Julia's mouth went dry. She hoped he couldn't hear her pounding heartbeat.

When he reached out to lift locks of her hair, she thrilled at the faint tugs on her scalp. "Your hair is soft," he whispered, letting it slide through his fingers. "Come sit with me," he said, taking her arm to walk a few feet to deck chairs.

A barrel table with a cleared surface was between two chairs. Nick took a cushion from a chair and placed it on the top of the table and sat on it to face her, putting him close to her.

"What are you doing?" she asked in amusement. "The chair looks more comfortable."

"But this is more interesting. It puts me nearer to you, and I can touch you a little," he said, drawing his forefinger over the back of her hand that rested on the arm of her chair.

"You never stop!" she exclaimed, smiling at him.

"I'm fascinated."

"Oh, please. You're after my family's company."

"When I sat down here, there was not one thought in my mind about business," he drawled in a velvety tone. "You're beautiful, sexy and I want to sit close and touch a little and maybe I'll get to kiss you."

His voice dropped a notch. "Sooner or later, Julia, we're going to discover how much fire there really is between us."

She hoped he didn't guess how excited she was. "Sit in your chair, Nick, and look at the stars."

"You want me to keep my distance?" Before she could reply, he slipped his hand behind her head to caress her nape in feathery touches that fanned flames higher in her. "I don't think so," he continued. "When we're together, I know your pulse quickens. I know you breathe faster. I know—"

"You're too observant," she whispered, on the verge of leaning the last few inches and drawing him to her to kiss him. Instead, she removed his hand and wiggled her fingers at him. "You back off. You may make my pulse race, but I know what's good for me."

Smiling at her, he straightened and kept his hands to himself. "You eat right, you exercise, you don't take risks—I don't believe it, Julia. You're at sea alone with me. You swim with me in your scrap of a suit that is a red-hot invitation and branded into my memory."

"When I bought this suit, I didn't know you."

"You knew me when you packed it. I'm not complaining, believe me. It's the best-looking swimsuit I've ever seen."

"You're absolutely incorrigible!"

"Your protests have nothing to do with the way you react to me," he observed dryly. "I can wait. I'm patient." He leaned close again and his warm breath fanned her ear. "We're going to kiss. I'll bet the boat on that one." Before she could tell him to get away, he took her wrist, felt her pulse and gave her a mocking smile. Then he slid into the empty chair.

"I suspect you are far too accustomed to women succumbing to your every whim."

"How I wish!"

"When I look at you, I see a man driven by ambition. Your life is wrapped around your career. That's cold companionship, Nick."

"I want good friends, beautiful women and good times together, but I'll admit I like the wheeling and dealing in business. I told you, I like success."

"I'm sure you *love* success."

He leaned forward and reached out to draw circles on her knee. "Today you said you didn't want to be CEO of Holcomb, so in the big picture, what do you want?" he asked, watching her closely.

"That's an easy question. I want people in my life I can love. I hope I have children. If it works out, I want a man who loves me above all else. I want him to be the most important person in my life and I want to be the most essential person in his life. And I want *us*, together, to be foremost always."

"So someone can come before your love for Rufus."

"That's different and you know it. You'll always love your family, won't you?"

"Oh, sure."

"So why do I suspect that the deepest love of your life is yourself?" she asked softly.

"Ouch! That hurt! Damn, do I act that egotistical and self-centered?" he asked, narrowing his eyes.

"No, in fairness, you don't, but you don't care to have the love of one particular woman forever—"

"Drop the *forever*," he said, watching her. "I'd like to have the love of one particular woman," he added huskily.

More tingles spiraled in Julia because she knew he directed the statement at her. She laughed softly, trying to defuse the impact of his words. "You flirt shamelessly!"

"Shamelessly is more exciting. C'mon and enjoy yourself.

You like being here with me. We're clicking. I don't think you know how to enjoy life."

"And you're going to show me?" she asked, shaking her head.

"Anytime and anyway you let me," he drawled in that velvety tone again. She was tempted to give in and just enjoy him and the weekend without any thought for tomorrow.

He leaned closer, reached out and touched her throat lightly. "Be friends with me, Julia."

She gazed into his dark eyes and wondered if she would feel the same with a tiger purring beside her—strong, beautiful, inviting to pet, but with claws hidden and power leashed. Nick was the same. How far could she trust him? How involved should she get and how much would she regret it later?

The last question brought reality crashing back. She pulled her gaze away from him. When she did, he stood.

"Can I get you something to drink? Either hot or cold?"

"Just some iced tea," she replied. He nodded and left her alone. She let out her breath, feeling her heartbeat slow and her temperature drop to normal. He knew she reacted to him, but did he have a clue about how strongly she responded? She hoped not. She would bet money that he kept his word and sooner or later, they would kiss. He had come close to goading her into it tonight. Actually, closer than before. If he were anyone else—

She stopped that train of thought and looked around. The night was beautiful, with a moonbeam reflecting on the dark surface of the water. Overhead millions of stars twinkled, a sight impossible to view in town. Everything was perfect except the unbridgeable chasm between them. It went beyond business competition—their personalities clashed. His dreams and goals were what she wanted to avoid in any male she got deeply involved with. Her dreams and aspirations probably made him want to run. Actually, she suspected he ignored her views of commitment, considering them insignificant. He had probably had relationships with women before who had wanted exactly what she herself did—marriage, family, abiding love. Nick wanted none of them, and he easily dismissed her goals and dreams.

She needed to remember their differences all the time because on a purely physical level, their desire was mutual, compelling.

Interrupting her thoughts, he returned with their drinks.

When he handed her a glass, his warm fingers brushed hers. He set his tea on the table between them and sat in the chair.

"Thanks," she said.

"Why the fear of dark water?" he asked casually.

She shivered. "I don't even like to talk about it."

"Then don't. I can't keep from wanting to know all about you," he added quietly.

"How can I resist telling you now?" she asked. Before he could answer, she continued, "My fear isn't a secret, just unpleasant to recall. When I was a kid, I fell into some muddy water with a friend. We were on a rickety log over a brown creek. She tumbled into a nest of snakes and was bitten and had to go to the hospital. I wasn't tangled in the snakes, but it terrified me. Since that time, I've never liked opaque water. A childish fear that hangs on."

"If that's the case, you hid it well. If you hadn't told me, I wouldn't have known it. And you should've told me. We can do other things that you'll enjoy more."

"Actually, you took my mind off the water and my fears several times."

"Did I now?" he asked with great innocence, and she laughed.

"You know you did! Anyway, if I don't want to swim, I'll tell you. So now you tell me—what do you fear, Nick?"

"Losing. I don't like to lose," he said. His tone was light, but she knew he gave her a truthful answer.

"We all lose at one time or another," she said. "I suspect you've lost very few times in your life."

"That doesn't make me like it," he replied, and she heard the note of steely determination in his tone. "Most of the time I'm happy with what I'm doing."

"You have a boat and a plane and a ranch. What else do you enjoy, Nick?"

"Bronc riding," he said, surprising her. She figured he would prefer city life and everything connected with it, and very little about the country. "I like racing horses."

"I'm sure you mean winning races."

"Of course. At the ranch, I raise quarter horses and race them. So what do you like?"

"I think you already know. I sail. I work out, and I imagine you do also. I love opera."

"Favorite composer?" he asked, taking her hand and threading his fingers through hers.

"What are you doing?" she asked immediately.

"Just holding your hand. It's as pleasant as looking at the stars and just as harmless. What composer do you prefer?"

"Mozart, definitely," she replied, tingling from his thumb lightly rubbing back and forth over her hand. He disturbed her, kept her physically aware of him every minute, fanned the attraction that grew hotter by the hour.

"Good choice. Verdi is another fine choice. Mozart's *Magic Flute* will be performed at the Santa Fe Opera next week. Want to fly out with me and see it?"

Her immediate inclination was to accept his offer. The prospect of flying to Santa Fe with Nick and attending the opera, spending another weekend with him, dangled like a golden gift. Her eagerness bubbled, but common sense prevailed. The last thing she should do would be fly out of state with him and spend another couple of days in his company. She was enjoying this weekend beyond her wildest expectations. Another weekend, and she would want to be with him all the time.

"Thanks so much for the invitation, but I have to pass. When we part Sunday, we might not be on good terms," she replied while her heart thumped.

"Scaredy-cat," he teased lightly, caressing her cheek. "We're getting along fine now, and we have since the moment you arrived at the yacht club. There's no reason to think that will change. We enjoy each other." His voice lowered. "I get the feeling that you're very careful about what you do."

"Being careful keeps me out of trouble. There's no way that you and I should spend more time together than we will this weekend."

"The invitation stands. If you change your mind, just say so."

"Thank you," she answered politely, wanting to get off the topic of spending more time with him or speculating on how well they could get along. "Tell me about your quarter horses."

"Do you have one degree of interest in horses, or is this a mere tactic to get the conversation back on an impersonal level?"

"Definitely a tactic to get back on the impersonal," she answered bluntly. "Therefore, tell me about your horses. Which one are you running this season?"

"Willow Wind will be running in Ruidoso next and he's good. He's undefeated so far. That's the way I want his races to continue."

"Well, you said you don't like to lose at anything," she said, watching him while he reached down to trace circles on her knee and rev up her pulse.

"No, I don't, and neither do you."

"Compulsive personality, Nick. Have to be the best, don't want to lose, determined to get your way."

"Normal, just like everybody else, impressed with beautiful blondes who are equally resolute."

She laughed. "Not in this lifetime have I ever been as firm about getting what I want as you are!"

"You firm? You're as soft as warm butter," he said quietly. "At least I made you laugh. That's good. You're too serious, Julia."

"It's the circumstances that make me solemn. A lot is on the line."

"Not tonight, it isn't."

"Just stick to horses, Nick," she urged, continuing to try to keep the conversation away from the difficulty between them.

For the next hour, she listened while he talked about his horses. All the time they chatted, he touched her casually. Conversation drifted from horses to their childhoods and then to other topics. All the while, Nick continued to rub his fingers on her hand, or trail them along her arm or through her hair.

Each stroke of his fingers built responding need in her until she was on fire with wanting him. In the darkness, she could see his profile and his long, bare body covered only by his cutoffs. As he talked, she noticed his thick lashes that were dark shadows above his prominent cheekbones. There was a dangerous, predatory air about him, a rugged edge to his handsomeness that hinted at what she suspected was a ruthless streak in him. Brown curls had fallen across his forehead and she was tempted to reach up and push his hair back. What would he do if she touched him? To resist the temptation, she locked her fingers together in her lap.

They talked, skipping from topic to topic, avoiding any reference to the big issue between them.

Nick stood, disappearing into the pilothouse and returning as music played. He took her hand. "Come dance with me."

Laughing, she stood. "In deck shoes?"

"It'll work if you pick up your feet," he said, and she wondered how many times and with how many different women he had danced on his yacht. He pulled her to him and wrapped an arm around her waist, holding her close against his bare chest. Her T-shirt and lacy bra were a thin barrier between them, and contact with him heated her. She moved with him, their legs brushing, her hand held in his.

"So what are your favorite things, Julia?" he asked softly, his warm breath fanning over her. "Every time I try to get to know you, you steer conversation back to horses or me or something impersonal."

"Impersonal is safer, innocuous and forgettable."

"And that's what you want your evening with me to be—innocuous and forgettable? I think not!"

"That's *exactly* what I want this night together to be," she answered, and he shook his head.

"Oh, no," he murmured. "Not when we can have so much

more. I want to satisfy all my curiosity about you," he said, drawing his fingers down her cheek. "What do you like best in daily life?"

He was close to her, inches away, speaking lowly as his gaze drifted over her features. Then he looked into her eyes. His hand slipped to her nape again, brushing her with the same feathery touches that wreaked so much emotional havoc. She looked at his full underlip, his sculpted mouth, and wondered again what it would feel like to kiss him. He had asked her a question, and she struggled to concentrate on what he had said.

"My favorite things are being with my family or my closest friends, bluebonnets, Mozart, skiing, walking in the snow," she replied. "It's your turn to tell me your favorites in life."

"My favorites are making love to a passionate woman, deep kisses, success, meeting a challenge and winning, racing horses."

"And winning at it," she finished for him. "Winning, winning, winning. I think we could have answered for each other." She tilted her head. "Perhaps you couldn't have guessed my answer, but I could have predicted yours."

"Ouch! I'm predictable?"

"Absolutely! When it comes to women and business and what you hold dear, you've made it abundantly clear what you like."

He spun her around and bent over her, dipping deeply so that she tightened her grip on his shoulder. He held her that way, leaning over her as if he were going to kiss her and her heart pounded.

He swung her up and they continued dancing, desire, hot and thrumming, building between them.

"I'll have to work on that one and see if I can't surprise you. Predictable is dull. Like being nice and being good. You've given me another challenge."

"A quite unintentional one, Nick. It's not so bad that we're beginning to know each other and what the other one likes. By now, you know I put family as my top priority. I know you put winning."

"I don't believe I said winning as my number one choice."

She smiled. "You would never consider making love as important as winning a business deal you've fought for. I can well imagine how your mind works on it. There are always beautiful women in your life, so the real challenge is in your work. Don't deny it. I'm certain I'm right."

He gave her a mocking smile. "If women succumb to my charms constantly and easily, why don't you?" he asked huskily.

She inhaled and smiled and hoped she could keep her voice light. "Not every woman you encounter is going to be swept off her feet. There might be one or two of us, Nick, that don't wait breathlessly for your attention."

He laughed. "Damn straight you don't! I can't get to first base with you. Which just makes you all the more interesting. That, plus the chemistry is volatile. And so obvious that even you can't deny it."

"No, but I don't have to yield to it and I have no curiosity about it and no inclination to follow up on it. Chemistry is physical. My emotions and my intellect are still motoring along. Sorry, Nick. Stop making me one of your projects."

He smiled at her. "A luscious, irresistible, impossible challenge—the best of all possible 'projects,' I'd say."

His words heated her. She smiled in return, but the tension between them still dangled in the air.

The music changed to a fast number and in spite of the deck shoes, they danced around each other, moving fast, her pulse throbbing faster as she watched his lithe, muscled body and his sexy movements.

She was aware of his smoldering look following her, his eyes traveling over her, speculation and desire burning in the depths of brown eyes. Fast or slow, the dances were seduction, more kindling on an already searing fire.

Another slow dance began and he enfolded her in his embrace, pressing her against his length and barely moving while he feathered kisses over her ear. She ached with desire. She longed to wrap her arms around his neck and pull his head down to kiss him. Instead, she pushed against his chest and stepped back when he loosened his hold on her.

"I think it's time to sit out a few dances," she said breathlessly and turned away without waiting for his answer as she headed back to a chair and sat down.

Facing her, he sat and rested his elbows on his knees. "Why do I think you really could dance the night away and not sit out any dances?"

She shrugged. "Nonetheless, here we are. No more dancing for now. Back to some impersonal topic."

Leaning closer, he ran his fingers over her knuckles and she inhaled swiftly. "When we get home, go out with me. How about dinner Sunday night?"

"Sorry, Nick. I have a date with Granddad. I told him I'd come by when I get home. I won't let him down."

"So I strike out again with you."

"Something you're completely unaccustomed to having happen in your successful life."

"That sentence had a bit of a bite to it, Julia," he said quietly. "You know you're just throwing more challenges at me. I want nothing more than to hold you in my arms, in my bed, and have you tell me you want my kisses." He slipped his hand behind her neck and caressed her nape. "And it's going to happen. You'll be mine."

"Nick! Dream on at your own risk," she exclaimed.

"I'll take that chance."

"Let's try a safer subject. Tell me some more about the quarter horses," she said, trying to pay attention while he talked. He leaned closer and his fingers tangled in her hair and caressed her nape, feathery strokes fueling her desire.

They talked, argued, teased. Time passed, and she had to admit she could too easily continue chatting with him the rest of the night. Effortlessly, Nick charmed and beguiled.

She took his wrist and looked at his watch. "Nick, it's after three in the morning!" she exclaimed, standing. "I think I should turn in," she said. The night was over, but Nick had stirred her up and her nerves were raw. Even at this hour, she knew she wouldn't sleep. She wanted him desperately.

She pulled her hand away from his and stood. He came to his feet at once.

"Then I'll walk you to your room."

She laughed. "All twenty steps with me? I can find my way."

He placed his arm across her shoulders. "I want to be with you as long as possible," he said seductively.

His warm body was close beside hers and he smelled of a tangy, inviting aftershave. His arm tightened and he pulled her closer against him.

"When I said we should get to know each other better, this isn't what I had in mind," she stated, trying to ignore her tingly awareness.

"It's exactly what I had in mind and I think it's grand," he said.

They walked along the deck, moving in the moonlight and then they were in the shadow of the pilothouse. It was darker, the passageway more narrow. Nick stopped and turned to face her, resting his hands on her waist. "It's been a good day, Julia. Better than I ever thought possible."

As she looked up at him she placed her hands on his forearms. "Nick, there's an invisible line that I don't want to cross."

"You know I'm going to kiss you. Sooner or later," he said quietly in a low drawl, and her heartbeat quickened. "I don't like later. I want now." His face was in shadow and she couldn't see his dark eyes, but she knew he watched her, and she imagined the intensity of his gaze.

"We need space between us, Nick."

"Why? We agreed no business. It's just a man and a woman. You and I have been headed this way since the dog ran in front of my car in the parking lot."

Her heart thudded as Nick drew her into his arms. He leaned down and brushed a kiss on her lips. Featherlight, yet his warm lips melted her.

"Nick," she whispered, but her protest faded as his mouth closed on hers. When his tongue slipped into her mouth, playing over her tongue, every stroke shot fiery sparks through her. Sliding his arm around her waist, he drew her closer.

All she was aware of was him, his strong arm circling her waist, his lips on hers, his tongue in her mouth. With the first slight contact, caution took wing and flew away.

As she pressed more fully against his long, hard length, his arm tightened around her. Bending over her and holding her close, Nick flexed his powerful muscles. She ached to devour this vital, sexy male.

His kiss consumed her while she shook with passion. Desire flared hot and low in her, and she thrust her hips against him.

All their touches, the flirting, the feathery contacts and double entendres burst into thundering longing. He had her primed and ready for his kiss, yet she dimly realized that she also had a devastating effect on him.

His thick, hard shaft pressed hotly against her. Wanting to demolish him as much as he destroyed her, she wound one arm around his neck and she rubbed against him, slowly.

While her pulse raced, he gasped for breath, a tremor shaking him. His passionate kisses demanded her response, and her need for more of him built rapidly.

She had guessed accurately that his kisses would be devastating. Each stroke of his tongue sent her pulse galloping. Just his kisses set off fireworks inside her. She responded, kissing him while moving seductively against him and wanting him more than she had thought possible.

She moaned with pleasure, the sound lost in his kiss. Stroking his muscled back, she relished the hard feel of him against her. A sheen of sweat covered his smooth, warm skin.

As he wound his other hand in her hair, he pulled her head back so he could kiss her.

Standing in his arms, kissing him, was a dream come true, or was it a nightmare unfolding? She wanted his kisses, but at the same time she realized that she had opened Pandora's box of problems.

She leaned away to run her hands across his chest, sliding them slowly over sculpted muscles. Delighting in him, she tangled her fingers in the thick mat of curly hair across his chest.

Then he wrapped her in his embrace, leaned over her, molding her against him as he kissed her. Arching up against him, she clung and returned his kisses, hoping she overwhelmed him as he did her. She wanted to set him on fire, make him remember her, be more than just another woman for him to conquer.

Releasing her pent-up hunger, she let passion run riot. Her fiery response to his sex appeal mixed with her anger over his arrogance and ambition.

For this moment, like sunshine on fog, their kisses burned away the discord between them. Desire consumed her and she wanted him as she had never wanted a man before. At this instant, Nick was special, the most exciting man on earth, and, her hunger to hold and kiss him overcame judgment.

Passion escalated with breathtaking swiftness. Far too fast, desire flamed.

As she explored him, his hands slipped up from her waist to touch the underside of her breasts. His fingers brushed across her breasts, so lightly, yet his touch was a white-hot brand. She gasped with pleasure, catching his wrists and pulling his hands down. "No," she whispered.

Pushing against him, she turned her head. On fire with wanting him, she gasped for breath. While her entire body tingled, she wanted to go right back into his embrace, but she knew better than to do so. "We stop now," she said hoarsely, unable to resist drawing her fingers across his rock-hard chest.

She shouldn't have ever let things get as out of hand between them, but she liked kissing him, liked it too much. She wanted to make love to him and have him love her in return. And that could be something that could wreck and destroy too much in her life in the future. Regret threatened to be enormous.

"We traveled where we don't belong. There's no forgetting the enormous differences between us."

"The differences lie in business," he whispered, leaning forward to brush kisses along her throat. "They have nothing to do with us right now. I can keep work and pleasure separate."

She stepped back out of his embrace. The rail was at her back as she gazed up at him and placed her hands on both sides of his face

"Nick, it isn't business and pleasure—it's lifestyles and values. We each measure success differently. To you, it's money and acquisitions and a career. I value love and family and lasting relationships. We're worlds apart. You know we can't separate our personal lives and what we hold worthy."

"It's just kisses, Julia," he replied quietly while he caressed her throat.

"We can't resolve the friction between us with kisses. I don't want to get emotionally involved and compound our battle. And it is a battle. You know that without hearing it from me," she added.

"Are you trying to convince me or yourself?" he asked softly, tucking a tendril of her hair behind her ear.

"Maybe both of us," she admitted. "We both know there is chemistry between us."

"A damn hot one," he said in that seductive drawl that made her knees weak. "It's a weekend together. Relax, enjoy it, some dancing, some kisses—don't be so uptight about them. I'm not propositioning you. C'mon, lighten up."

"I don't want to fall in love with you," she stated bluntly. Anger heated her that he would so blithely pass off the attraction between them. His statement reinforced her determination to resist his charms.

"I didn't say one word about anyone falling in love," he said quietly. "We can have a wonderful, intimate relationship—"

"Not I, Nick!" she snapped. "There's no such thing as a wonderful, intimate relationship without love. That's a hollow, empty life."

"You're missing out on some great moments, Julia," he said

in a velvety rasp that was seduction all by itself. "Don't take life so seriously."

"As if you don't take it seriously when you lose a business deal. And you occasionally have lost, haven't you, Nick? Somewhere back in the history of Ransome, you've lost?"

Anger flashed but was gone so swiftly from his expression that if she hadn't known him as well as she did now, she wouldn't have caught it. She knew she had struck a nerve—he not only took losing seriously, he loathed it and didn't want to acknowledge it.

"When did you lose last, Nick?" she asked softly, unable to resist needling him but fully aware that she was toying with a tiger that had incredibly sharp claws. "How civilized and lighthearted were you then?"

He stepped closer, wound his fingers in her hair and tilted her head back. He was breathing heavily and anger burned in his brown eyes. "You're pushing me and you know it. You're doing it deliberately."

"You're the one who said to lighten up and not take life so seriously," she reminded him, hoping he couldn't hear her pounding heartbeat or realize how much she wanted to kiss him. He was after her body and she wasn't going to satisfy him because she knew he had no interest in her heart. His love was making deals, power and financial success.

He inhaled and leaned down, tightening his arm around her to pull her tightly against him. "You're going to be mine. We've got this fire and it's too rare to ignore. Sometime soon, you're going to stop being cautious and careful and throw yourself into life just the way you threw yourself in front of my car to protect that dog. All this caution isn't your natural self. And the more you goad me, the more I'm coming after you, Julia. The more you challenge me, the more I intend to seduce. You've had your warning."

"So do you always get your way? I don't think so, Nick. And this is one time you won't. You want my body. You practice seduction and chase success. Just beware, that you don't discover there are other values more important in life. Mess with me and you'll proceed at your own risk," she warned him.

He gave her a mocking smile. "I'll remember your warning and take my chances. And I'll start now." He hauled her close suddenly and bent to kiss her hard and long.

His kiss electrified her, demolishing her ability to coolly stand back and merely observe what he was doing.

She kissed him in return, her tongue stroking his with the same fury that he had given her. When he leaned over her, she tightened her arms around his neck.

"You'll be mine, Julia," he vowed. He ducked his head to kiss her hard, silencing any answer she might have given him.

With her thoughts spinning, she held him while she arched her hips against him. Purpose and resolutions vanished. There was only Nick and his devastating kisses. Desire pounded in her, hot demanding, her body craving more.

They were locked in battle and she knew it was too late to turn back. She leaned away and opened her eyes. "This is one fight you won't win, Nick," she whispered.

"Yes, I will," he answered and then kissed her and silenced her. He drove thoughts of competition, threats and warnings out of mind. She kissed him recklessly, wanting him wildly.

She slid her hand down his back to his waist, feeling his smooth back, and then let her hand slide down his hip. She heard a growl in his throat. He tightened his arm around her, and his thick rod pressed against her.

He set her ablaze, but his response to her was evident, too. She could feel his arousal, as well as the tremors that shook him and the damp sweat on his skin. His breath was as ragged as hers. His kisses this time around were more fiery than last time.

His hand tugged her T-shirt out of her shorts and he slid his fingers up over her ribs. Then his large hand cupped her breast through her bra and his thumb played back and forth lightly over her nipple.

She gasped with pleasure, her desire escalating in quantum leaps. He slipped his fingers beneath her bra.

She caught his hand, opening her eyes slowly, dazed and aching with need. "Now we stop, Nick. I'm not getting on your yacht and falling into your arms and into your bed within hours of sailing."

"You like my hands on you, Julia," he said softly as he nuzzled her neck and ran his hand lightly down her back and over the curve of her bottom.

She twisted away. "I'm calling it a night," she announced. She hated her breathless voice for giving away the effect he'd had on her. His gaze traveled over her and she was aware of her taut nipples pushing against the cotton fabric of her T-shift. Her pulse pounded and she ached for more of him.

"I'll walk you to your cabin."

"No need for that," she replied dryly. "I couldn't possibly get lost. You know I've had a good time, Nick. Far too good."

"Admit it, Julia," he said, stepping closer and touching the neckline of her shirt. "The evening was hot, sexy and exciting. Wasn't it?"

"You just have to hear me admit it, don't you? All right, Nick. You're sexy and you're exciting. The day and night have been fabulous," she admitted, watching him draw a deep breath and realizing her words were fueling his desire as much as caresses would have. "My heart is pounding. I'm breathless, on fire and I doubt if I'll sleep because of you and your incredible body. There. I said it. I'll see you in the morning."

He caught her arm and hauled her into his arms again. "How do you expect me to let you walk away when you tell me things like that?"

"Easily, Nick. I didn't tell you one thing you didn't already know and you pushed me to tell you. 'Night."

She wriggled free and hurried away from him without looking back. Her heart beat swiftly and she could feel his heated gaze as strongly as his consuming lust. She could imagine him debating silently with himself about coming after her.

Then she was shut away in her cabin, and she let out her breath. Her image in the mirror showed her tousled hair, her erect nipples, her red mouth that was rosier from his kisses. She ached with wanting him and wondered how she would sleep even an hour in the short time that was left of the night.

In spite of knowing full well that it was merely lust and determination to best her in business that motivated him, she liked being with him. He was an exciting, desirable man who could charm and kiss and captivate. If only—as always, she stopped that thought immediately.

She needed to constantly remember that Nick was after something she had. His lust and seductive ways had no effect on his heart. Women were objects of lust to him and that was all.

Moving automatically, Julia finally climbed into her bunk to stay awake, thinking about Nick, wanting him and lecturing herself. If she had good sense, she would go home tomorrow. She hadn't accomplished one thing and swaying Nick to her cause looked hopeless. The man seemed as stubborn as the proverbial mule.

She turned over, closed her eyes and tried to forget him, willing sleep to come. Instead, all she could think about was dancing with him, kissing him, flirting with him.

She had warned him to beware of losing his heart, but her heart was the one in jeopardy. Nick's pleasure was beating a competitor. Ambitious, out to win for the sake of winning, ruthless—all described Nick and she should remind herself of that constantly.

She stirred and woke with sun streaming in the portholes. For a moment, she was disoriented, but then she remembered where she was. She sat up and stretched and stood to get ready for another day with Nick.

Half an hour later, she found him cooking breakfast in the galley. Tempting smells of bacon and coffee wafted in the air. As she entered the galley, Nick set down a pot and it clanged lightly.

"Good morning," she said and he turned abruptly. For an instant, there was a flash of anger in his expression. Just as it had happened in his office, it was gone immediately and she wondered if she had imagined it both times. Why would he be furious now?

Five

As soon as she said good morning to him, Nick's pulse quickened. Her big blue eyes burned like a flame. Momentarily, his anger vanished. He forgot deals and rigs and business and threats. Desire blazed, hot and intense.

When she faced him, her eyes widened and she scanned his features. She tossed her head and her hair swung over her shoulder.

"What's wrong, Nick? You're solemn and quiet this morning."

He barely heard her question. When had he wanted a woman with this heart-pounding, breath-stopping intensity? He reached out to take her arm and closed the distance between them as he slid his other arm around her waist. Her eyes widened and then he looked at her mouth. When he did, her lips parted and she tilted her head back.

His heart thudded in his chest. To know that she felt what he did carried its own excitement.

She half closed her eyes and wound her arm around his neck.

"I want you, Julia," he whispered. "And you want me to kiss you."

"You're a danger to me. Because of business, we should keep our distance. Yet you are a temptation," she said, drawing out her words. She stood on tiptoe and pressed her mouth against his. With a groan, he slipped his arm around her tiny waist, marveling how she could look so small and fragile, yet be so sexy and strong. And her mouth was soft, sending molten fire down his insides, along his veins and into the center of his being. He leaned over her, kissing her hard while he tangled his fingers in her hair.

She clung to his shoulders and arched up beneath him. When her hips shifted against him, he slid his hand down the length of her from her throat, lightly, slowly over her breast, brushing her nipple that was taut and pointy. His hand slipped down over her hip and then along her thigh.

Her body pressing against his made him rock-hard. Mere anticipation aroused him. She kissed him while she combed her fingers in his hair. Then she wriggled away, her breasts rising and falling as she gulped for air.

"You're going too fast again."

"Seems to me you're the one who started this."

"I might have been," she admitted with a sly, coaxing smile that made him want to pull her right back into his embrace. "I'll help get breakfast while you tell me what's bothering you."

He turned to fix toast, debating whether to share his news with her. "I had some e-mails from Tyler that were about business deals that have problems. I didn't know my feelings were showing."

She placed one hand on her hip and studied him. "So is one of the problems Holcomb Drilling?"

Again, he was tempted to tell her the truth, to let her know the reason for his fury. But it was his nature to keep things to himself and he clamped his lips closed. "This morning, my e-mails were far removed from Holcomb Drilling," he said, knowing there was nothing yet that revealed with certainty that Holcomb people had any part in the rig fire. But now, from Tyler's messages, Nick knew that the oil rig fire had been deliberately set. Tyler had made it clear that the investigator didn't have any leads yet on the arsonist, but the authorities had fingerprints now, as well as a picture from a security camera of a man running across the rig. With so much evidence, they hoped they could identify the criminal.

Nick had no doubt the information would lead back to Rufus Holcomb. Or maybe Julia herself. She had threatened him and she could have easily given the orders.

She set out orange juice and glasses and mugs.

He watched her moving around the galley as she poured coffee and a tumbler of orange juice. She was graceful and sexy in her movements.

In spite of his anger, the feud between their families and the possibility she was behind the rig sabotage, he wanted Julia more than he could recall wanting any woman.

Even if there hadn't been all those differences between them, they clashed because they both were strong-willed. If they got into any kind of relationship, even briefly, he knew her goal would be marriage while his would be gratification and enjoyment. The satisfaction of lust and the pleasure of each other's company were sufficient for him. He didn't want permanent commitment. He couldn't cope with it.

Forgetting his problems, he watched her and he wiped his damp brow. The temperature was rising. He knew it was the direction of his thoughts about her that had him sweating. She had a more intense effect on him than other women did. He was surprised by his reaction, because he didn't want her to stir him so easily.

When his gaze ran down her long, shapely legs, his pulse climbed another notch. Her silky blond hair fell freely over her shoulders. She wore cutoffs and a short blue cami that left a bare midriff. Her cutoffs hugged her hips and rode low beneath her navel, revealing her flat stomach.

The cami had spaghetti straps and lace across the low neckline. More enticing bare skin and luscious curves were revealed. He studied her appreciatively. She was the best-looking woman he had ever known. And the sexiest. Too bad she was from a family that his had feuded with through three generations. Even worse, she was so tied up in family and marriage. Otherwise, what a time they could have!

Still, he intended to have a damn fine time with her anyway. It just wouldn't last as long as he wanted because the time to deal with Holcomb was looming, and then she would be furious with him forever after. He was going to take Rufus's company and enjoy doing it. He wasn't going to ruin the old man, but Julia would never view the purchase of their business as anything except evil, no matter how much money she got from the buyout. Drawing a deep breath, Nick controlled the urge to take her in his arms and kiss her until he could carry her to bed. He was certain he could seduce her.

Who was the man in her life? Nick wondered. She had said none and maybe she truly was like he was—and hadn't been seeing anyone lately, but he couldn't imagine that. She was far too beautiful, far too sexy to sit home alone at night.

He look at the slight sway of her hair as she walked around the galley. He could watch her all day because she was fascinating to him. He wanted to reach for her now and forget cooking and breakfast. He wanted to get right to his plans for the day—her seduction.

She stopped to pour two mugs of coffee.

Walking over to her, Nick stood close behind her and inhaled her perfume, smelling the clean, soapy scent of her hair. He placed his hands on her shoulders. She glanced over her shoulder at him and smiled. His heartbeat quickened.

"Maybe we should skip breakfast," he said. His voice had thickened and he let his desire for her show. He slid his hands slowly down her arms to her elbows and then back up again to her shoulders. Her skin was smooth and warm, silky to his touch.

Her expression changed as she inhaled and turned to face him. "Great minds think alike. Or something like that," she said, her voice trailing away. She placed her hand behind his head, winding her fingers in his hair, and he had to draw a shaky breath.

She got that hot, lethargic glaze in her eyes that excited him. She stood on tiptoe, pulled his head down and kissed him.

Instantly, he wrapped his arms around her and his mouth came down hard on hers. He let go his pent-up longing and kissed her passionately, wanting her naked now but knowing he had to wait. His blood pounded hotly in his veins. He wondered if he could ever get enough of her. When they made love, he vowed silently that it would be long, slow, thorough. He wanted to take forever to kiss and caress her. He wanted her softness wrapped all around him, enveloping him.

She was the most exciting woman he had ever known and it surprised him. So far, her hot kisses burned him to cinders and she responded passionately to his kisses.

As he kissed her, he inhaled, shaking with his effort to control the urge to start peeling her out of her clothes. He had to take time, to take care, he reminded himself, but he wanted her and she was driving him wild. His blood thundered hotly through his veins.

"Julia," he whispered, wrapping his arms around her tightly to kiss her. He needed her softness and her sweetness. He wanted her fire. She took his breath away with her beauty and sexiness.

His need compounded swiftly, a hot flame low between his legs. He throbbed with desire, aching while he tried to maintain his control. Her softness pressed against him, burning him like a brand. He wound one hand in her hair. He leaned away to pull the cami over her head, tossing it aside. His breath caught as he looked at her lush breasts.

With a raspy breath he leaned back and cupped her breasts in his hands. She was soft, warm, burning him. He groaned as he leaned down to take her breast in his mouth and his tongue circled her nipple. He heard her moan, felt her fingers winding in his hair.

Her waist was incredibly tiny. She felt fragile, so dainty, yet he knew from swimming with her that she was far from delicate. How could she be so tiny, yet so strong? Her body amazed him. Her breasts were full, beautiful, and his pulse thundered in his ears as he drew his tongue over her nipple again.

"Nick!" she gasped and clung to him.

She straightened and caught his hands, moving them and then turning to yank up her clothes.

Her back was to him and he stepped close behind her, sliding his arms around her while his tongue traced the curve of her ear. He whispered in her ear, "I want you. I want to shower kisses all over you from your head to your toe. I want to see what makes you respond and what drives you wild with passion."

She stopped his words, kissing him as if he were the last man on earth and this was the last kiss. He groaned, but the sound was lost in her kisses.

He unfastened the waist of his cutoffs and then she caught his hands. She gasped for breath as she stepped back.

"Nick. Slow down. We barely know each other. We're going to be enemies in a few days—"

"No, we're not, Julia. Not in a few days, not ever," he said, knowing that his fury with her was temporarily banked, but it would return. Yet at this moment, he couldn't imagine staying angry with her. All he wanted was her in his arms. "I have to love you, darlin'. Make love to every beautiful inch of you," he murmured. "The sooner we do, the more time we'll have—"

"Shh, Nick," she said softly, placing her finger on his mouth. "Hush! We're not making love. We've kissed too much already. I don't live like you do, love like you do. I can never be casual about a physical relationship."

He smiled at her, listening to her protests, yet watching the vein in her throat pulse at an accelerated rate. She was breathless. Her nipples were taut. Her lips looked swollen, ready for more kisses. "We will make love, Julia. I promise you. After the kisses we've shared, I'm not walking away and neither are you. Our kisses promise fiery sex beyond all imagination. I'm not letting that escape me and you won't, either."

"You slow down," she argued, stepping back while her eyes remained locked with his. She moved slowly, carefully. She desired him. He saw it in her blue eyes, knew it from her kisses. She was fighting yielding to her desire, but he was certain she wanted to make love as badly as he did.

He knew she was scared of his motives and she had good reason to be. Yet she was a strong woman and knew what she wanted. He wouldn't be taking advantage of anyone because she would never let him.

Turning her back, she slithered into her cami. As she crossed the galley, she straightened her clothes and drank some of her orange juice. She set down the glass and studied him from a distance. He turned to put on eggs, making an omelet. As she watched him flip the omelet, she spoke up.

"Nick, something's bothering you. What is it?"

She surprised him. He didn't think he ever let his feelings show. He couldn't remember anyone else knowing when something was bothering him unless he wanted that person to know. He paused and gave her a level look. She stared back unflinchingly.

"I heard from Tyler. The rig fire was deliberately set."

"How awful! Do they—" She stopped abruptly and her eyes widened. "You still think we did it, don't you?"

"Who else has threatened me within the month?"

"I can't imagine, but no one from Holcomb has done anything to your blasted rig. You're way too suspicious, Nick!"

Her blue eyes blazed and she caught her lower lip in her even white teeth while she stared at him. His anger heightened because he was absolutely certain that Holcomb people were behind the fire.

"C'mon, Julia. You have no idea what your granddad has ordered. You swear you weren't involved in any way?"

His question hung in the air. Her face flushed and she glared at him.

"I swear I was not!" She ground out the words. "I know you want to blame us since Granddad and I both threatened you, but that wasn't the kind of threat I was making and neither was he. You know we aren't behind setting your rig on fire or any other sabotage to your company!"

Nick walked up to her. Her eyes were clear and her gaze steady. If she was lying, she was damn good at it. But he had been lied to before in a very convincing manner and he wasn't going to be taken in now by big blue eyes and a beautiful face. He slipped his hand behind her head.

"All right, I'll accept that, but if I find out you or your granddad were behind it, I'll destroy Holcomb bit by bit."

She shrugged. "That means nothing to me, Nick. We didn't set your fire so that's the end of it."

He looked down into her guileless expression and wondered if he could trust her. He would get to the truth. It was just a matter of time. Until then, he would try to curb his anger. But he was certain either Julia or her granddad or both were behind the fire. He was tempted to believe she really didn't know and it was just her granddad, but he wasn't going to be now, no matter how beautiful and beguiling she was.

"They'll find out who did it eventually. They have prints and our security camera caught a picture of a man running across the rig."

"Good. Then you'll know for sure."

"We'll see, Julia. I have a reward that ought to flush out the guilty party. Someone is going to be happy to tell what he knows."

"I hope you find out exactly who did it," she said. "In the meantime, if you're going to stay angry all day, there's little point in us continuing here. We might as well weigh anchor and go."

Amused, he relaxed and forgot business. "We're not going to weigh anchor yet. We have a beautiful day ahead of us. Let's have breakfast and swim and plan what we'll do." He leaned down. "I'll forget differences for now if you will," he coaxed and she nodded.

They ate leisurely and talked, avoiding the topic of business. Part of the time, he didn't even hear what she was telling him except he knew vaguely that it was about her years at college. His thoughts were on kissing her and peeling those clothes off her. Soon he was getting aroused by his imagination, so he tried to concentrate on what she was saying.

"This is paradise Nick. No cell phones—no phones. I don't have any electronic gadgets with me right now."

"I can see you don't," he said, looking her over slowly. Revenge couldn't possibly be sweeter than his would be. He had waited and worked for years, but had never dreamed it would involve the seduction of a drop-dead gorgeous woman who fascinated him. Yet once the buyout occurred, he was going to sever all chances of ever making love to her again.

The realization gave him pause for thought, but then he shrugged it away. He would forget her. There were other beauties in the world. Take away the sex, and he'd had a good time anyway, he had to admit it. She was good company, a great dancer, could swim, challenged him constantly and wasn't intimidated by him.

Nor was she dazzled by him as some women so obviously were. They wanted to please him at all costs. Julia would never be that way. Far from it.

For the first time, his thirst for revenge wavered. He didn't even know if she was involved. Surprising himself, he stared at her and realized he didn't want revenge to get in the way of a relationship with Julia.

An hour later, they sat on the deck in a light, early morning breeze. Nick wanted to reach for her again, but he curbed the impulse.

"It's beautiful out here," she murmured.

He glanced at her long, bare legs appreciatively. "It's gorgeous," he agreed.

She gave him a sharp look and then smiled at him. "Thanks, Nick," she said patiently. "The water is beautiful."

"You're thinking about it the way it was last night in the dark," he said quietly, surprised that she still had the fear from childhood. He doubted if she feared much else in life.

She shook her shoulders slightly. "I know. A silly fear, but one that I can't get rid of, although I did for a few moments last night. You made me forget it."

"When you say things like that to me, I want to take you in my arms and kiss you senseless," he said, his voice hoarse.

She placed her hand on his arm and his heart raced. "You stay right where you are," she said. She tilted her head to study him. "Last night, you said you feared losing. Why, Nick? What happened to you somewhere in your past that made you to lose so much? No one likes to lose, but most of us know we're going to lose off and on during our lifetime, so we accept it."

He thought about winning and losing and knew it ran deeper than that. And it was a subject he never talked about. It was one he didn't like to think about.

"You still don't have to like it when you lose, just because it happens once in a while," he said lightly.

"I'll bet it's happened very little to you."

"It happens," he said and looked away.

There was a steady slap of small waves against the hull, a reminder that they were on water.

"Sorry, I shouldn't have asked you a personal question," she said quietly, and he turned to look at her.

She had her lower lip caught in her teeth, and she shrugged. "How much time do you spend on your ranch?" she asked and he knew she was trying to steer the conversation away from the topic of losing. He thought about why he hated losing. He had hated it all his life.

"You can ask me about losing." He stared beyond her, remembering moments when he was a child, remembering hurts and longings. "As a kid when I did, Dad made me miserable. And I never could please him, no matter what I won. I've never been able to be good enough for him."

"That can't be true now since you're grown," Julia said. "You've built Ransome Enterprises into a much larger company. I know you have made some terrific deals. I know you have more than a few trophies from riding in rodeos. You have a reputation for succeeding at everything you do."

"It's still not good enough," Nick said, feeling old hurts stir and knowing he was foolish to let his father and childhood hurts get him down.

"I can't believe that!" she exclaimed, leaning forward to put her hand on his. He forgot about the conversation momentarily.

"That's awful," she said. "My whole family always praised me—often far more than I deserved, but I knew they approved of me all my life. It would be dreadful to never get that approval from a parent."

He picked up her hand to brush a light kiss across her knuckles.

"Don't stare at me like I just announced I've been an orphan and living on the streets. Of course, I'm happy to have your sympathy and attention," he said, lowering his voice and picking her hand up again to rub along his jaw.

She let him and he realized she was feeling sorry for him and allowing him more liberties because of her sympathy.

"I can't believe you've grown up that way," she said.

"Well, I did. Maybe I'm the proverbial 'middle child.' Dad always threw Matt up to me as so successful—Matt could ride broncs better, throw a ball better."

Nick brushed kisses lightly along her knuckles and then turned her hand and let his tongue play in her palm. His thumb was on her wrist and he felt her pulse race. She leaned toward him, listening to him talk as if what he was saying was the most important thing she'd ever heard.

"For years Matt was bigger because we were growing boys and I was younger. It was always something," Nick said.

"That's dreadful! You've been far more successful than your father was."

"Maybe not in his eyes. I don't ever remember high praise from him. He praised Matt and he adored Jeff. Those were the years when we were growing up and I was a year younger. Matt was the oldest son, the firstborn, able to do things before I could. Jeff was the youngest son, Dad's delight, the son he spoiled. Katherine is the only girl."

"You seem to get along with your brother now."

"I do. In the first place, Matt never worried about the competition. He was older and for years, he was bigger. Jeff was spoiled by Dad and he didn't worry about competing with either Matt or me.

"So that left me. Actually, for years it's been my dad, not Matt, that I've always wanted to best. When we were grown, I could beat Matt at some things, but I've always been driven to top Dad. The biggest way of all to surpass him is to do better in business. That used to get to him. Now that his health is poor and he's older, he's mellowed a degree, maybe. He's a tough one."

"Maybe he didn't know a lot about raising children."

"Probably didn't know a damn thing about it. He had no experience until he had us and then he had to raise us single-handedly. I competed with Dad, but then once I found I could make deals, I liked what I was doing and Dad was no longer a part of it. Or maybe not as big a part. Somewhere in me, there's always the son who wants to hear some praise from his father."

"Sounds as if you both are too much alike," she said, remembering Granddad telling her how Nick's father had threatened him on more than one occasion. She had heard him talk about the time they had a shouting match in a shopping center. She had already discovered that Nick was competitive in everything he did.

Nick shifted his focus back to her. "You're probably right. We're the most alike—aggressive, operating a little on the edge, determined and ambitious. Business is the most important aspect of what we are and do. Business defines us."

"Business and success," she replied. "Ah, Nick. You can't imagine what you're missing in life."

"Feel sorry for me?" he asked with amusement.

"No, I don't. You're conscious of your choice and doing what you want."

"You're right there. At the moment, I'm overwhelmed by a blonde who has the ability to make me forget everything else."

"I don't think so." She stood. "I think it's time to swim."

He suspected she wanted to get away from the intimate, personal conversation.

Smiling, he stood. "You don't have your suit on under those clothes. Are we skinny-dipping?"

"Absolutely not!" she snapped and left swiftly. He chuckled, watching her stride away, his pulse beating fast in anticipation of a day with her.

* * *

For an hour they swam and then Nick piled picnic provisions into a fiberglass dinghy and they rowed to the beach.

"Pick a spot and we'll have a picnic and tour the beach," he said.

He watched her look around. She was in her swimsuit with a black, sheer cover-up that still gave him an enticing view. He wore a T-shirt over his suit.

"There," she said, picking up an armload to help him carry their things to the palm she had selected. They spread a blanket and put everything down on it. He took her hand.

"It's too early to eat. Let's look around."

She was dazzled by the place while he was dazzled by her. He watched her, laughed with her. She had caught her hair up in a ponytail clipped behind her head. They wandered along the white beach beneath swaying palms, hearing the rustle of the fronds.

"This is so beautiful!" she said, touching a low-hanging frond and turning to look at him. "We should have known each other somewhere else, Nick. Some other time in life."

"Do I hear regrets?" he asked. She stood near a tall, graceful palm tree. He walked over to her and placed his hands on her shoulders.

"Yes. I have regrets because this weekend is turning out to be—" she paused a heartbeat "—a very good time," she finished, her gaze sliding away. He brushed a kiss on her cheek and then her temple.

"It doesn't have to end," he declared.

She smiled at him. "Yes, it'll end like smashing a glass."

"In the meantime, here we are with the day spreading before us and the best company possible for me. This is great, Julia. I want our friendship to last when we go back."

"We'll see."

"That's a no. Let's prolong what we have. We won't talk business until tomorrow. Another evening that is sexy and exciting and full of great feelings, fine food and terrific dancing. How about it, Julia?" he coaxed.

That's what he wanted. He had no interest in business this weekend. He no longer had interest in revenge. He was having a fabulous time with her, and he wanted another twenty-four hours like the past hours. He brushed a kiss on her throat.

"C'mon, say yes. Let me have my way. I'll try to make it an evening to remember," he whispered, his tongue tracing the curve of her ear. "Give me what I want."

She smiled up at him, a heated, sexy look that made his blood thicken. "I suspect you get too much of what you want all the time, Nick. Someone should say no to you."

"I get plenty of no's. And I don't want any from you, especially not now." He raised his head. "Look at this—we're in paradise and we have it all to ourselves. Palms, water, sunshine, perfect weather, privacy." He looked down at her and slid his arm around her waist, hauling her up against him to wrap his arms around her.

"Hot, steamy sex that you won't forget. See if I can't make your pulse pound."

"You know you can," she whispered.

He felt as if he were drowning in depths of blue as she looked wide-eyed at him. He leaned down to kiss her, his mouth covering hers and his tongue thrusting into her mouth.

She wrapped her arms around his neck and he caressed her throat, making her arch against him and tighten her arms. He leaned back and peeled away her flimsy cover-up and the top scrap of her swimsuit to cup her breasts.

He gave her a heavy-lidded, smoldering look and then lowered his attention. "You're gorgeous!" he murmured, cupping her breasts in his large hands, circling his thumbs over her nipples until he bent his head to take one taut bud in his mouth.

"Nick!" she gasped, winding her fingers in his hair while her other hand slid down, to caress his chest. Her fingers slid lightly over him and his heart pounded. He wanted her now, yet he wanted to savor their time together and make love for hours.

He kissed her throat. His tongue traced over her ear. "We're going to make love," he said softly in her ear. He brushed kisses along her throat. "I'm going to make you let go and love until passion is a raging fire."

He stepped back to look at her and slide his hands to her waist. "Now, Julia, now say yes to me. I want you to say yes."

Six

Julia barely heard him. Her heart pounded, and she opened her eyelids that suddenly felt heavy. She wanted Nick and from the first moment they'd met, desire had been burning brighter, hotter, a flame that licked along her veins and throbbed inside.

She ran her hands across his strong chest, feeling the sculpted, hard muscles, tangling her fingers in the mat of his chest hair while she was consumed by his dark stare.

She looked lower. Her gaze slid down across his powerful chest, and her hands drifted lightly to his narrow waist and then along his slim hips. She gasped when he cupped her breasts again and ran his thumb in lazy circles over each nipple. She moved her hips, wanting him, desperation building. She lost all sense of time and all arguments of logic that declared Nick off limits and dangerous territory.

Gone were the barriers, common sense, caution. They were replaced by a driving hunger that had built hourly. Desire filled her, burning away everything else. She wanted Nick to make love to her. She wanted to touch him and kiss him. She hooked her fingers in his narrow strip of swim trunks and tugged them down to free him.

Her pulse pounded as she gazed at him. He was muscled, aroused, tan and fit. His body was male perfection, and she leaned forward to trace her fingers across his chest.

He pulled away the bottom of her swimsuit and held her away from him, his eyes moving hotly over her, making her nerves tingle as much as if he had been running his fingers over her.

"Beautiful, darlin'. You're fantastic," he murmured. He leaned down to cup her breast and take her nipple in his mouth, sucking and running his tongue slowly over her pouty bud.

"Nick!" she gasped, closing her eyes and clinging to his waist, her hips moving as she pulled him to her. She knelt in the sand, moving down slowly and letting her tongue trail down over his flat, washboard stomach and then she took his hot shaft in her hand. With the tip of her tongue, she traced his thick rod up to the velvet tip, letting her warm breath drift over him, relishing his fingers tangling in her hair and his groans of pleasure.

"Like that?" she whispered. "And that? I want to pleasure you, to demolish you, to finish the storm you started when we met."

She took him into her mouth, running her tongue over him while her hand slid low between his legs and caressed him.

His hands went beneath her arms and he lifted her up. Desire made him heavy-lidded. His lips were wet and red from kisses and he was gasping for breath. He looked at her mouth, then wrapped her in his embrace and kissed her hard and long.

Kneeling in the sand, he lowered her easily and turned her over. "I'm going to touch and kiss every gorgeous inch of you. You're beautiful," he said softly, brushing feathery kisses on her ankle, then up over her calf to the back of her knee. His tongue drew lazy circles that were erotic and she tried to turn to reach for him, but his hand in the small of her back pushed gently.

"Let me kiss and love you," he cooed. His breath was tantalizing and warm behind her knee, another blaze igniting in her, adding to the wildfire.

Then he moved higher, his tongue drifting along the back of her thigh, his breath hot on her bare skin. His hands played over her naked bottom, stroking, teasing.

He straddled her and moved higher. By the time he kissed her nape and then her ear, she was moaning with desire. She turned over, reaching for him while he started again at her feet while his hands caressed her inner thighs.

Sensations bombarded her. She couldn't be still. She wanted him and he was building her need by the second.

She turned and sat up, pulling him to her to kiss him passionately while her hand went to his manhood and caressed him. Then she pushed him and leaned down to kiss and lick him again.

"I want you, Nick. I want you now," she said, pausing to look up at him. The desire in his gaze took her breath and then they were in each other's embrace and she felt his thudding heart pounding against hers.

As he leaned over her and she clung to him, kissing him back, one of his hands slid down her back. He shifted her, placing her back on the sand. He moved between her legs, lifting them over his shoulders to give him access to her.

She was drowning in need for him, wanting his lovemaking, gasping and stroking his thighs. Watching her steadily, he leaned forward, sliding his tongue over her intimately, finding her feminine bud, kissing and nipping and teasing until she was on fire and tugging at him, trying to get him to make love and end the exquisite torment.

He lowered her, pulling her close while his fingers went between her legs to rub her and stir a storm that drove every thought from mind.

There was no turning back now. She had to have Nick, all of him. They were on the sand in the sun, and she didn't care. She didn't know how private the cove was, if they would be alone.

But at the moment, nothing mattered except Nick—his irresistible body, his devastating hands, his possessive mouth. He was magic, hot sex, hard male.

"I want you," she choked out. She wanted him now and

wanted him to possess her, hot and hard and fast. "Nick," she urged, catching his arm. His fingers were still on her feminine bud, rubbing her and building a blaze.

Desire pounded with each of her heartbeats. She had to have release, had to have Nick! Clinging to him, she thrashed wildly to a sexual crescendo—higher, more urgent and then release that made her want all of him, not just his mouth and hands.

"Nick, love me," she said, opening her legs wide.

She pulled on him, and he moved between her legs. "Are you protected?" he asked, and she shook her head.

He stood, walked over to their picnic things and grabbed up his shorts to reach into a pocket. He returned, striding to her and she drew a deep breath as she looked at him. He was naked, virile, aroused. Strong, muscled and desirable beyond her wildest dreams.

She wanted him inside her. She wanted his hardness, his strength. And she wanted to make love to him in return. To drive him beyond rational thinking just as he had her.

With his gaze locked with hers, he knelt between her legs and opened the packet. She took the condom to put it on him until his shaking hands brushed hers lightly away.

"You're way too slow," he said hoarsely. "I want you more than I've ever wanted anyone," he admitted, and her heart pounded.

"If only that were true," she whispered. Oblivious of the warm sand beneath her, she watched him kneeling between her legs. He slid his hands lightly, slowly, along the inside of her thighs and she gasped, opening herself more to him. She raised her legs to lock them around his waist as she tried to draw him to her.

He was poised, ready, his shaft thick and hard. She stroked his thighs and watched while he lowered himself. Wrapping his arms around her, he kissed her. When he eased into her, she arched her hips and held him tightly.

Pausing, he raised his head, his eyes narrowing. "Julia—" His voice was hoarse.

She whispered, "I want you now."

"You're a virgin," he said flatly, starting to pull away.

Julia tightened her arms and legs around him and raised to
kiss him, pulling him down again as she thrust her tongue into
his mouth to kiss him passionately.

"Love me, Nick!" she demanded, tugging on him. He gave
her one long, searching look before he groaned and then eased
into her again. She held him tightly, kissing him, feeling a flash
of pain that was gone as she moved with him.

"Julia!" he breathed and then returned to kissing her. They
moved together, bonded, their rhythm increasing. She was lost
to the moment, giving herself to him totally. Urgency drove
them. Desire for him overwhelmed her, and sensations rocked
her as she moved her hips with him.

Then he slowed, almost withdrawing, filling her. She cried
out, tugging on him and arching against him. "Nick!" she
gasped, her voice hoarse as she thrashed wildly beneath him.

And then he plunged hard and fast, and she spun off into a
world of sensation.

Her climax burst in a release that blinded her. Within seconds,
he shuddered as he thrust hard and cried her name again.

He pumped faster and she moved with him until he slowed
and their ragged breathing began to return to normal.

Finally he lay still, his weight still held slightly off her. He
scattered kisses over her face and then rose on his elbows to look
down at her. "You should've told me you were a virgin."

"No," she said softly. "I know what I wanted." His dark eyes
still blazed with desire, and he leaned down to kiss her long and
passionately while she ran her fingers through his hair and kept
her other arm wrapped tightly around him. His weight was
heavy on her, but it was good and she liked holding him. Fleetingly, they were united, one together.

He turned on his side, keeping her with him as he stroked her
hair away from her face and tucked strands behind her ear.
"You're fabulous," he said and leaned forward to kiss her again.

She curled her arm around his neck and kissed him in return,
a kiss of satisfaction. It was minutes before he leaned away. "I
hope you know what you want."

"I do," she answered solemnly. "I know exactly," she said softly with more assurance than she truly felt. She had wanted him, badly enough to give herself to him physically in the most intimate way possible.

"You're gorgeous, sexy, enticing," he said, brushing kisses over her between each word.

"Thank you. You're not so bad yourself," she added, trying to keep the moment light, as much to convince herself that she hadn't committed her heart to him as to prove that any relationship between them would be casual and brief.

She ran her hands over him, delighting in his hard, muscled body. He was a marvel to her—fit, healthy and too sexy to resist.

"Next time will be better for you, I promise," he said.

"If we're in bed instead of hot sand, it'll be better," she teased.

"I could have gotten the blanket I brought for our picnic."

"Maybe next time," she said lazily, running her hands across his chest and tangling her fingers in the short hair on his chest.

"I've never made love to a virgin," he said, caressing her throat. "That's special, Julia."

"You didn't want to," she reminded him.

"I was surprised. And then I wanted you to be sure. I'm a little awed," he said solemnly, and she wondered what was running through his mind. He was making more of an issue about it than she had expected him to. "You're my woman now," he added.

"Yes, for now maybe, Nick. It's not a big deal."

"Yes it is, if you've waited this long. I'm amazed you've waited. You surprise me constantly."

"Maybe that's good."

He looked at her with so much warm satisfaction, her heart thudded. She couldn't imagine a groom looking at his bride with much more warmth and pleasure. She hugged him in return and kissed him lightly on the mouth.

"I have an idea," he said and she leaned back to look up at him. "Let's get back to the boat and satin sheets and comfort."

"Best idea you've had in the last two minutes," she said, smiling at him. He laughed and hugged her lightly.

He stood and pulled her up. She yanked on her swimsuit, turning to find him watching her. He walked to her silently, every step ratcheting up her pulse because of the hungry look in his eyes. He picked her up and carried her back to their picnic place. She wrapped her arms around his neck. At their basket, he set her on her feet and she turned, keeping her arm around his neck while she stood on tiptoe to kiss him. Desire fanned to life again, a fire licking along her veins, making her want him as if they hadn't just made love.

She kissed him passionately, wanting to steal his heart, afraid to study her own actions or probe too deeply yet about what she truly felt for him. Finally, she pushed against his chest.

"Let's get back to the boat," he said, gathering up their things. They loaded the dinghy and pushed off.

The sun was still high in the sky and once they had gotten their picnic things back on board his yacht, they spent the next hour languidly in bed until Nick talked her into a swim.

When she told him she was getting out, he swam closer and slipped his arm around her waist, pulling her to him so he could kiss her.

Her pulse hummed as she felt his hand caressing her, sliding over her back and bottom, up to her breasts to touch her nipples. She didn't know when he whisked away her suit or his, but she realized they were naked, pressed together in water deep enough that he held her and his feet probably barely touched the bottom.

He was warm, nude and wet, awakening her desire swiftly.

He raised his head. "C'mon. Let's get out," he said. His voice was gravelly, a rasp that conveyed his need for her had returned full-force.

She shut her mind to tomorrows or consequences, knowing she had never wanted a man as she did Nick. He climbed out and turned to lift her up onto the deck. He was wet, sunlight reflecting off tiny drops of water all over his shoulders and body, his face, everywhere. His hair was plastered to his scalp. Water still clung to his thick lashes.

He reached for her, drawing her to him to wrap his arms

around her and kiss her. His body was nude and warm, pressed against hers. He was aroused, and his thick shaft pushed hotly against her stomach. He picked her up and carried her to his large stateroom. A shaft of golden sunlight streamed through a porthole and spilled over the cabin. He stood her on her feet in the sunlight, holding her waist while his gaze traveled languidly over her.

"I want to kiss every gorgeous inch of you," he murmured.

He cupped her breasts in his hands. "So soft and warm," he whispered and bent to take a nipple in his mouth while he sucked and teased.

Sensations raced from his touch, fanning out to set every nerve ablaze. She quivered with wanting him, reaching for him and running her fingers over him.

She caressed him, her fingers drifting over hard muscles down along his strong thighs. She knelt to take him into her mouth, letting her tongue slide over him until he groaned and hauled her up to kiss her thoroughly.

"Nick," she sighed, astounded at how intensely she wanted him when they had just made love earlier. Yet his body dazzled her, and his hands and mouth set her ablaze.

He framed her face with his hands, looking at her solemnly. "You can't ever guess how much I want you."

She knew she would remember the moment forever. "Oh, Nick, if only…" He kissed her and her words were lost, but she wouldn't have finished her sentence because loving forever wasn't Nick's intention.

He picked her up again to carry her to his broad bunk, where he placed her down gently. Then he turned her and began showering slow kisses and feathery caresses, teasing and tantalizing, until she was quivering and tugging on him.

"Love me, Nick!" She pushed him down to straddle him, playing with his flat male nipples, letting her fingers flit over his chest while he caressed her breasts and then slipped his hands between her legs to rub and tease and find her erotic hidden places.

She gasped with pleasure throwing her head back, giving him access to her, yielding to the sensations that held her in their grip. She moved her hips until she leaned down to kiss him.

He rolled her over and reached out to get protection. Sunlight streamed across the center of the bunk, splashing over Nick and giving golden highlights to the bulge of his muscles. Her pulse raced as she watched him he put on a condom and move between her legs.

"This time we'll go slow and take our time."

As their eyes locked, she wrapped her long legs around him, pulling him to her. At this moment, he made her feel as if she were the most desirable woman on earth. His dark gaze burned into her, hot, eager, hungry. She tingled, aching and wanting him as she ran her hands over his slender hips, feeling the jutting bones. Then he leaned down to kiss her and she closed her eyes, wrapping her arms and holding him tightly.

He thrust slowly into her. Hot and thick, he filled her.

Her blood thickened, pounded, burning through her veins while she moved her hips.

He withdrew just as slowly, entering her again, taking his time, Again and again he repeated slow thrusts until she was wild, thrashing and tugging on him, need building and thundering in her ears.

Finally he moved, fast and hard. She cried out as lights exploded behind her closed lids while she climaxed. Ecstasy enveloped her, and she rocked with him until he climaxed and slowed.

"Julia, Julia," he murmured her name softly. She barely heard him and then he rolled over, keeping her with him so he could face her while he smiled at her again.

"It's good between us. All that it promised to be. I want to keep you here in my arms for the rest of our time together."

"That's not possible," she whispered.

"I'm going to make you want the same thing," he said, drawing his fingers along her arm. "I don't want to let you go."

"You'll change your mind when your stomach starts growling with hunger," she said in amusement. But his words thrilled her even though she knew she shouldn't give them much credence in the aftermath of passion.

His dark brown eyes searched her gaze and he studied her solemnly. Brown curls were damp on his forehead, and she pushed them back slightly.

"Julia, I want to keep seeing you. Go out with me Monday night," he said gazing solemnly at her.

She placed her finger on his lips. "Shh. We're worlds apart, Nick, in what we want."

"Ah, that business deal—"

"Not that," she said, interrupting him. "A year from now, that won't even be an issue. I'm talking about lifetime differences, our values and goals. Lifestyles."

"I just want you to go to dinner with me Monday night," he said tightly.

"No, you don't," she said, tracing her forefinger along his jaw. "You want more than Monday night. A vast chasm stands between us. You have your future mapped out and know what you want, and it's definitely not what I want in any man I get deeply involved with," she replied and her insides clenched. Was she so certain she wanted to toss his offer aside?

He stroked her face. "So you're just waiting for Mr. Right to come along?"

"Hardly. And don't worry, Nick. I know you're not into long commitments of any sort. No. If he does, then I want marriage and family. But that doesn't always work out and if it doesn't, I'll find a way to work with children. There are endless volunteer things I can do."

"And I'm sure there has never been a dearth of guys wanting to take you out," he said with a gruffness that surprised her. She couldn't imagine a shred of jealousy in Nick. "I'll bet you've already turned down proposals."

"I'm particular and I've never found anyone that I wanted to live with the rest of my life."

"'The rest of my life' sounds like a hell of a long time."

She laughed. "You talk about it as if it were a prison sentence.

With the right person, it will be the most wonderful relationship possible." She traced her finger through the hair on his chest and then slid her hand down over his bony hip and his muscled thigh.

"See what you do to me with just the slightest touch," he said, leaning down to kiss her throat.

"You can't want to make love again!" she exclaimed and then kissed him. His answer was lost as she wrapped her arms around his neck and he rolled over, pulling her on top of him while they kissed.

They explored each other, long and slow and leisurely. She didn't think about his offer or the future. She took today and knew that that was all she could be concerned about. Tomorrow was for later, when she could think clearly.

This time, she straddled him and he pulled her down on his thick shaft and she moved with him as urgency built to the same blinding, white-hot need that sent her spiraling into space with rockets exploding inside her. He rolled her over suddenly and reached his climax as he pumped into her. "I want you. You're mine, Julia. You belong to me now."

"And you belong to me, Nick," she whispered back. "This moment we've given to each other without holding back. Make love to me, Nick!"

She felt his shuddering release and then she was enveloped in his embrace as he turned on his side and pulled her close, wrapping his legs with hers and running his hand down her side. "Fantastic long legs," he said, caressing her leg.

His seduction had been intoxicating. She marveled over it. She never wanted to be out of his arms, but she knew that was impossible.

Just as impossible as a long-term relationship with him. Their family differences loomed large, but she knew that was just the tip of an iceberg of differences that would separate them forever. Even so, she wanted to make love with Nick. She had waited, hoping to wait for marriage, for one particular man who was incredibly special. She had found the one particular man who was special—he just wouldn't be part of her future.

She leaned forward to kiss Nick's throat and then lay back in his arms and looked at him. "You're special, Nick. Very special."

He pulled her close against him and they lay side by side. "Tell me what you want in life besides family and kids."

"I want it all, I guess," she admitted quietly. "I want to get Holcomb back making solid profits and in the black and keep it running for Granddad until he retires. Actually, keep it going as long as he lives. I want to do my accounting, what I've been trained to do. I want to spend time with my family, too. I want at least three children. I want to live right where I do now or near there, but that's because of Granddad."

"I want to see you and have you in my life. I want to take you to the opera, the rodeo, bring you back here with me. Instead of going to Santa Fe, we could come again next weekend. If you'll agree to come, I'll clear my schedule."

She shook her head. "Sorry. I don't think it's wise for us to plan any long-term time together."

He raised up to look at her, turning on his side and propping his head on his hand. "You mean it, don't you? You're not going to come back here with me anytime in the future, are you?"

"You won't care, Nick. There'll always be someone else," she answered lightly, but it stung her to tell him. She wound her fingers in locks of his hair and then drew her hand along his jaw and felt the short stubble of his beard. "You and I want different things so we'll go in different directions."

She pulled his head down to kiss him to stop the trend of the conversation.

Later, Nick grilled shrimp kabobs and they ate on deck while they watched the sun slip beneath the horizon. They danced until they drifted back to Nick's stateroom where they made love far into the night.

Nick fell asleep holding Julia in his arms. She lay on her side and watched the steady rise and fall of his chest. Her gaze traveled beyond him as she looked around the stateroom. Now moonlight spilled through the portholes and gave a silvery illumination to her surroundings. When her attention returned to Nick, her pulse drummed. They had loved most of the day and night. In a few hours, it would be dawn again.

Julia wished she could hold back the dawn and delay the intrusion of the world and problems and differences. She wanted to say yes to Nick's offers. She wanted badly to be with him and the thought of spending next weekend the same way as she had this one tore at her heart. Everything inside her screamed at her to accept.

If she continued to see him and it developed into a long-term relationship, Nick might fall in love with her.

She had to laugh at herself. How many women had succumbed to his charms with that very same reasoning, she wondered. Nick would always be Nick, and that meant single, center of his own world, steeped in ambition and driven to succeed and compete.

Not what she wanted in her life. Why did she have to keep reminding herself of that? His offers were pure temptation of the strongest kind. He was sexy, charming, everything she had suspected he would be when she had first encountered him in the restaurant parking lot.

He was so handsome it made her knees weak, and she could look at him for hours on end. He was so sexy, he had melted all her resistance and gotten past every barrier that had protected her heart all these years.

She wanted to continue to see him and she ached to have him in her life. She wanted to go with him on his travels, watch him ride in a rodeo. And she knew she couldn't do any of it. As it was, he was going to give her a heartache, but how much worse it would be if she spent more time with him? He could shatter her heart into a million pieces.

She traced her fingers across his broad chest, feeling the regular strong beat of his heart, tangling her fingers lightly in his chest hair. "Nick," she whispered, wondering how long it would take her to forget him. How long would it take her to get over him?

How could she ever forget this weekend? Nick was the first in her life. The first man she had given herself to completely in making love.

She wouldn't have regrets there. He had been a consummate lover—sexy, considerate, passionate, unforgettable.

And for that, he would forever be in her memory. She had only herself to blame. She could have said no or resisted him or waited.

Yet she suspected she and Nick would have little time together in the future. She had a bad feeling about what the future held for them.

"Nick," she whispered. At least at this point, she hoped she wasn't wildly in love. She couldn't possibly be because she hadn't known him long enough to be in love.

A tiny voice taunted her about the first encounter she'd had with Nick and how she had floated into the restaurant and wondered if they would ever see each other again. At that moment, she thought he was the most handsome, sexiest man she had ever encountered and she had hoped someday they would get together again and she would get to out with him.

"You're not sleeping," he said quietly. He hadn't moved, but his eyes were open and he was watching her. He surprised her.

"No. I'm watching you sleep."

"That means you can't sleep. What're you thinking about?"

"Remembering that first meeting we had when I tried to keep you from running over the dog."

"I was determined to find you in the restaurant and ask you to go out with me again."

"So here we are."

"I think you're worrying about something and that's why you haven't gone to sleep. You should be relaxed. So whatever's on your mind and creating worries for you—maybe we can do something about that."

"Nick, we've loved for hours."

"Not nearly as much as I want to," he said as he kissed her

throat and made her heartbeat quicken. "See what your pulse does when I kiss you?"

She turned to kiss him and their conversation ended.

It was another hour before she finally did fall asleep in his arms.

The next time she opened her eyes, sunlight poured into the stateroom and Nick was nowhere around.

She showered, dressed in faded cutoffs, a blouse that tied above her bare midriff and sneakers. She found Nick lounging on deck with a steaming pot of coffee, almond biscotti and bright red strawberries. He stood, his gaze drifting over her as he came to meet her. He wrapped her in his arms and smiled. "Good morning," he said, desire twinkling in the depths of his dark brown eyes.

"Good morning," she said, her mouth going dry as want enveloped her and she forgot about the enticing smell of coffee and the delicious fruit. She gazed up at him, needing him as if they hadn't made love yesterday and all through the night.

"Nick," she murmured and stood on tiptoe to wrap her arms around his neck.

He leaned down and his mouth covered hers while his arms tightened around her.

When he released her, he smiled at her. "Come have breakfast."

As she chewed biscotti and sipped her coffee, Nick glanced at his watch. "We'll have to start back." He leaned close and took her hand, rubbing his thumb across her knuckles. "I'll tell you what—why don't we push our conversation about business to dinner tonight. I'll pick you up at seven."

"I have to go see Granddad."

"Go see him. You'll have time to see him and still have dinner with me."

His voice was hoarse, his fingers warm and stirring emotions in her. He leaned close and she looked at his mouth. She nodded. "Yes, I'll go to dinner with you," she said breathlessly, feeling giddy and eager to continue being with him. She knew the time was narrowing until they would be on opposite sides of a big issue. After that was settled, the ill will might be insurmountable.

"All right. Let's have one more swim, a few minutes on the beach and then we'll head home."

She glanced around. "I wondered how much this place influenced us," she said. "You have a movie setting here with the palms, the isolated cove that we have completely to ourselves, the sparkling blue water—it's paradise. Plus your beautiful yacht all to ourselves. Maybe it's all this that seems magical and removed from everyday problems and our world at home."

"It wouldn't have mattered if we'd been in a dark cave that smelled dank. I would have wanted you just as much," he said softly, drawing his fingers across her nape and stirring her.

"I think it would have made a difference. This is enchanted," she said, looking around, memorizing details, yet knowing what would be with her forever were images and memories of Nick. "We're away from our regular lives. It matters, Nick."

"So you'd rather change it?" he asked, his dark eyes watching her closely.

She shook her head. "No. It's just an observation. You're able to compartmentalize your life more easily, I think."

He brushed kisses along her shoulder and then to her ear. "All I know is that I'm with a gorgeous, desirable woman." He raised his head to look intently at her. "I want you more than I did early today. That isn't the way it's supposed to work. You're the one weaving a spell of enchantment, not a bunch of palm fronds, sand and water."

He sounded almost gruff and had a solemn expression that made her heart pound while his words sent her spirits soaring.

"I'm glad it works that way and that I have some effect on you that might be stronger than mere lust."

His eyes narrowed a fraction. "I haven't changed, Julia."

"I know you haven't. Tigers never change their stripes, but it's nice to think when we get home, you aren't going to forget me by this time tomorrow."

His mouth curved in a lazy, crooked grin. "What you're doing to me, I couldn't forget, ever," he said softly, cupping her breast and leaning down to kiss her and start another giddy spiral of love-making. Yet his words spun in her mind and she was thrilled by them.

Was she already falling deeply in love with him? Could she admit the truth to herself? As she kissed him and wound her fingers in his thick hair and ran her other hand over his lean, muscular body, she dismissed her questions as swiftly as they came. She gave herself completely to kissing Nick, wanting to make him hers, wanting him to remember and desire her and melt from her kisses.

She leaned away and framed his face with her hands. "Have you ever really been in love, Nick?"

"Of course, I have," he said, twisting to kiss her fingers while he caressed her breast.

He turned to kiss her again and she forgot questions as she kissed and caressed him.

When they started home, it was later in the day than he had told her. As they sailed out of the cove, she watched the receding beach, wondering if she had lost her heart there along with her virginity.

She turned to look at Nick, who stood at the wheel. She went in to join him, coming up behind him and drinking in the sight of his broad, bare shoulders, narrow hips, long legs, knowing exactly how he felt and tasted and looked beneath the cutoffs he wore.

She wanted to slide her arms around his waist and hug him, but she could feel subtle changes already in both of them. They were heading home, back to real life. They'd had a brief idyll that had been a dream come true, but Nick's heart was already given to driving ambition. What she wanted in the man she loved was permanency, love, devotion. A man who put family first and Nick never would.

She felt a pang, knowing she would continue to see him for a time because she couldn't resist him. She hoped she wasn't really in love with him, that she had been wrapped in a dream world because of the time and place.

Silently, she left the pilothouse and walked to the rail to watch as they rounded a bend and moved out into open water. A wind had sprung up, and there was a chop that was rougher than the sea had been on Friday.

"We're in for a bit of rough riding. Nothing too bad," he said. "There are life jackets here in that locker if you want to wear one."

She nodded and went to put one on. "And you never wear one, do you?"

"Of course, I do. Not right now, but I've been in some big storms. I lost one boat."

"So that reckless streak your younger brother had runs in the family."

Nick grinned and shrugged, turning his attention back to steering. She went outside, standing in the bow riding the rough waves.

They would rise and slap back down. Cool spray blew over her. She looked at the whitecaps and gulls swooping over the water. When she joined Nick again, he reached out to snag her around the waist, pulling her close to kiss her.

She held him tightly, feeling as if he were slipping away from her, having a premonition of disaster waiting at home. Finally, she pushed lightly against his chest and he released her.

"I could drop anchor again," he said in a low voice, placing his hand against her nape.

She shook her head. "We should get home," she said softly and left, knowing she should put distance between them now.

When they stepped back on the dock, Nick carried her briefcase and strode ashore with her, going with her to her parked car. He set her briefcase in her car and then turned to place his hands on her shoulders.

"See you at seven," he said, tracing his forefinger along her chin. "The weekend has been unforgettable—something I never expected," he said in a tone of voice that sounded as if something puzzled him.

"I agree. This week will be something entirely different, Nick."

"Maybe. We can discuss it tonight if you want."

She nodded and slid behind the wheel. "Thanks for the weekend," she said lightly and he leaned down to brush a kiss on her lips.

She drove away without looking back, knowing she would be with Nick again in just hours.

Seven

At six Julia swung open the door and looked up into Nick's dark eyes. Longing for him took her breath away. In a navy suit, a snowy shirt and a navy tie, he was handsome.

His gaze took her in, drifting languidly over her and setting her on fire. He stepped inside to take her into his arms and kiss her while he kicked the door closed behind him. He leaned back against it, pulling her tightly against him.

He was hard, handsome, irresistible. She wanted him with a desperation that shook her. It was as if they had loved and then been separated a year instead of hours. And he had the same hunger. He startled her with his shaking hands as he ran them in her hair that was looped and pinned on her head. Pins flew and she didn't care. She shoved away his coat.

"I want you, Julia!" he rasped. "All I've been able to think about is being with you!" His words increased her eagerness. His hands fluttered over her shoulders and bare back until he found her zipper at her waist. He slid it down while he kissed her and pushed away her sleeveless black silk dress. It fell in a whisper and cool air spilled over her, but she was too hot to notice.

Groaning, Nick leaned back to look at her. She wasn't wearing a bra and his chest expanded when he inhaled. His tan hands cupped her breasts lightly while his thumbs played over her nipples and she gasped with pleasure. As she twisted free the small buttons of his shirt and pushed the starched, cotton shirt off, her hands were as fluttery as his. She unbuckled his belt, unfastening the button at his waist, pulling down the zipper to push away his trousers.

"I couldn't wait to see you," he said. He leaned down to take her breast in his mouth and kiss her. "Beautiful."

"Bedroom?" he queried and she pointed.

They walked backward, a meandering walk with her directing him breathlessly between kisses while clothes were strewn along the way. His briefs and socks were tossed aside; her panty hose and her black thong lay in a heap.

They never reached her bed. Nick leaned against the bedroom wall, picked her up and she locked her long, bare legs around him, sliding down on his throbbing, rock-hard shaft.

With abandon they made love and then sank to the floor exhausted while Nick wrapped her in his tight embrace. He tangled his legs with hers and held her close.

"I'll feed you tonight. We'll dress and go back to plan one."

She laughed against his throat while her fingers skimmed across his smooth jaw. "I think I'll shower first."

"Give me a minute. My legs won't work right now," he said.

Soon they showered together and dressed, and by nine o'clock, they were locked in each other's arms on the dance floor at Nick's petroleum club high above the city on the top floor of the tallest building.

They hardly touched their salmon dinners. They danced to slow numbers wrapped in each other's embrace, barely moving, merely swaying to the music. Her hand was enclosed in his, held against his heart and she had her arm around his neck. She snuggled close, relishing the warmth of his body, pushing aside all warnings that she was involving herself more and more with a man who didn't view life in the manner she did.

By ten, Nick leaned back to look at her. "Want to see my house?"

"Yes," she answered, knowing he implied more than he asked. If they went to his house, they would make love again, maybe through the night, but she knew tomorrow would come too soon.

She also knew that neither one would change the other, not on business, not on lifestyles—the real unbridgeable chasm, even if they settled their business differences amicably.

They passed her house on their way to his and in a few blocks turned to wait while tall, black iron gates swung open. Nick drove up a wide, winding drive to a tall Georgian mansion with a fountain in front of the porch that was graced with half a dozen mammoth Corinthian columns.

Nick circled the house, parking in front of the eight-car garage.

She didn't see any more of his house than she guessed he had of hers because they moment they stepped inside the entryway at the back, they were in each other's arms and made it no farther than the thick carpet in front of a fireplace in the kitchen.

Later, Nick carried her to bed and she spent most of the night in his arms, but by four in the morning, she slipped out of bed to gather her clothes.

"I can take you home anytime. Come back to bed," Nick said in a seductive voice that slithered hotly her. He lay sprawled on his side, long and powerful, and she was tempted to go flying back to him. His chest hair was a dark mat in contrast to the creamy satin sheet that lay in folds across his hips and long legs. Locks of his dark hair fell over his forehead, adding to his appeal. It was pure temptation to do what he asked.

Taking a deep breath and reminding herself what she should do, she shook her head. "No. For once I'm going to resist your charms. I have to go home, Nick."

He swung out of bed and she inhaled. He was aroused, sexy, naked.

She turned away swiftly and stepped into her dress pulling it up.

When she reached for the zipper, he already had it in his fingers and he leaned down to shower kisses across her back as he tugged up the zipper. As he caressed her, she glanced over her shoulder at him.

"We have to go," she whispered, wondering if he had any idea how difficult he was making it for her to leave. He pulled on clothes while she finished dressing.

"Want a tour of my house before you go?" he asked. She glanced beyond him at the enormous master bedroom that was a suite. He had a king-size four-poster that looked over two hundred years old. Both a tall dresser and an ornately carved armoire matched the bed and a gilt floor-to-ceiling mirror was across from the bed.

"You surprise me with your beautiful antiques, Nick."

"Why the surprise? I like beautiful things," he stated in a velvet tone while he caressed her nape.

"You just don't seem the type to give much time or attention to your surroundings." She turned away, crossing the polished oak floor and heading for the hall.

"I give a lot of attention to my surroundings." Nick caught up with her and held her arm as they walked down a sweeping staircase that curved to an entrance hall below. "We can take a quick tour. I want you to see my house. I want to know you, and I want you to know me," he added.

"I should go," she said, glancing through double doors into a formal room that had Corinthian columns, oriental rugs and gilt-framed oil paintings on the walls. "And you do have a beautiful home."

"Thank you. This house is the formal one. My ranch house is casual. So is the villa at Cozumel and the cabin in the Rockies. I hope I get to show you all of them," he said and her pulse quickened at all he implied. At the same time, she reminded herself that they really didn't have a future together.

He slipped his arm around her waist and they walked to the

back door where he readied the alarm before he locked the door behind them.

They waited for the gates at the end of his drive to swing open. She rode in silence, knowing every tick of the clock was taking them closer to saying goodbye forever.

He drove the short distance to pull up in her driveway where he got out to accompany her to her door. They stood on her wraparound porch while he brushed her hair away from her face. "It's been another fabulous night."

"We'll see each other in a few hours."

"You don't mind that we never discussed business?"

"What good would it have done either one of us?" she asked with amusement.

"I can listen and change sometimes. If there is a good reason."

"I rather doubt your answer. And I'm sure it doesn't apply in this situation."

"Four days until we all meet. That means you and I can continue to go without a storm between us for the next few days. So let me pick you up tomorrow night."

"We can eat here," she said.

He smiled and nodded. "And since I can't wait until evening to see you, meet me for lunch. Where will you be around noon?"

She laughed. "Nick, you're impossible. I have a ten o'clock appointment at State Bank, the branch on Highland."

"Meet me at Gregory's Café at half-past eleven. That will give you time, won't it? You can call me if you're earlier or later. I'll be there." He leaned down and brushed a kiss on her cheek before he turned to walk to his car. She watched his long-legged purposeful stride, wondering if Thursday night he would walk right out of her life forever.

She gave a small shake of her shoulders and stepped inside, turning off the alarm and locking up, and then setting the alarm again before she went to her bedroom. As she walked through her house, she looked at the polished oak floors, the oil paintings she owned, her formal living room that was furnished in cherrywood and a pale blue decor. Her home was attractive, livable. His was magnificent and a museum. Hers was kid-friendly and his was not, but then Nick didn't intend to have any kids running through his house. Four more days of Nick. How long would it take to get over him?

She set the alarm, knowing if she could catch even thirty minutes of sleep she would feel more refreshed and ready for the day. They had this week until Friday to make a last-ditch effort to save the company; for her grandfather's sake, she would try as hard as she could to thwart Nick.

She imagined the dealings Friday would cause a split with Nick, but it was a split that was inevitable; business just moved up the timetable slightly. Nick was blind with ambition, chasing success, and not the man for her. If only her heart could get the message!

She had an appointment at ten with Leon Jefferson, a banker her grandfather had known for years. Because the vice president was running late with another appointment, the receptionist asked her to wait with an apology, so Julia sat in a tan wingback chair in the lobby and picked up a magazine. While customers moved around her, she turned pages until she was startled to hear a familiar voice.

She recognized the voice of Tyler Wade, Nick's vice president, and turned in her chair to say hello. When she saw him greet a friend of his, she didn't speak. Wanting to avoid interrupting the two men, she settled in her chair and planned to say hello to Tyler when he finished his conversation. As she glanced through the magazine, Tyler's mention of Nick caught her attention, and she couldn't resist listening.

"You've got to come out and see this yearling," Tyler said.

"I thought that damn sorrel was Nick Ransome's prize. I've offered him a small fortune to buy it."

Tyler laughed. "I proposed something better. I thought I might have a chance to win his colt if he made a bet with me."

"What the hell did Nick bet with you and lose?"

"I bet him I could name a woman he couldn't seduce within two weeks." Julia stiffened and chilled, unable now to stop listening to Tyler.

"Yeah, I'll bet she was over ninety," the stranger scoffed.

Tyler chuckled. "Nope. Just beautiful, single, under thirty, a knockout, unattached and a woman of my choice."

"Sounds like Nick Ransome's type. What did you stand to lose?"

"My Ferrari," Tyler replied, and Julia wondered who the woman was that Tyler was talking about.

"I can't imagine that either one of you would take a bet like that."

"I really thought I had a chance. The lady doesn't like Nick. They're business rivals," he said, and another icy jolt hit Julia. She listened as Tyler continued. "I chose a woman who could resist him and collected royally. He tried to seduce her for revenge over business deals and took her sailing for the weekend. But surprise, surprise—the lady withstood Nick's charms. I should take her out for a steak dinner at Fort Worth's best. Anyway, come watch Standing Tall."

"I will. Maybe I can name a price that you'd take for the colt."

"Not in a million years. This horse is going to be a winner and Nick knew it, too. Come to my place eleven Saturday morning and we'll go to lunch after you've seen my horses."

"Great, Tyler. I'll see you Saturday."

"Miss Holcomb," the smiling receptionist said as she approached Julia, "please come with me." No longer caring to be seen by Tyler, she followed the receptionist to a corner office, and as she shook hands with Leon Jefferson, she couldn't get her thoughts off Nick and his bet.

In spite of the working relationship between her grandfather and the banker, Leon Jefferson politely turned down her request for an extension on their loan.

Her grandfather had gotten too extended, too bogged down in loans and exploration, and was now vulnerable, especially to Nick.

Numb, Julia stepped into the sunshine following her meeting and crossed the expanse of paving, not noticing the immaculate flowerbeds filled with bright yellow marigolds and red and white periwinkles.

Worry nagged at her, but along with it her fury was hot and thick. She was supposed to have lunch with Nick. She could cancel by phone or just stand him up.

Anger rocked her and she debated whether to go to the office or just go home to be alone and cool down.

She opted for the office, where hopefully she could get her mind off Nick. She turned her sports car onto a boulevard, moving into a stream of traffic.

Nick had told Tyler he had lost the bet, but that didn't matter. Seduction had been revenge for him. Waves of anger buffeted her, and she forced herself to concentrate on her driving.

In minutes, she pulled into the tree-shaded office parking lot and climbed out to hurry to her large, corner office on the tenth floor. She told her brunette secretary, Angela, that she didn't want to be disturbed and she wasn't taking phone calls for the next hour. Let Nick cool his heels at the restaurant; she didn't care.

She closed the door to her office and glanced around at familiar surroundings that usually gave her a sense of satisfaction. Green plants, oil paintings, a floor with a thick beige carpet and comfortable leather furniture filled the room. Near floor-to-ceiling windows was a large ebony table that she used for a desk. She had an adjoining bathroom, small sitting room, closet and a tiny wet bar in a corner of her office.

She walked to the closet to toss her purse inside a built-in drawer. She shed the jacket to her suit and then walked to the window to look outside. From the tenth floor she had a good view of the city. Nick was out there, waiting at a restaurant for her. At the thought of him, her cell phone rang. She ignored it.

Seduction for revenge and she had succumbed eagerly! She clung to fury because her anger covered her hurt.

After ten minutes and two more calls on her cell, she moved away from the window. She had to forget Nick. Do something that would take her mind off him. She could see no way of stopping him from acquiring Holcomb, but she pulled out the books to look at figures to see if she could think of any possibilities. She withdrew a ledger of possible places they could get more financing, knowing this had been gone over and over long ago.

As she looked at the books, her thoughts still spun around Nick. She couldn't get him out of mind and that added to her anger.

A commotion in the reception room caught her attention and she saw her secretary standing, arguing with someone and waving her hands. Then Angela walked around her desk, heading toward Julia's door and Julia lost sight of her. She could guess who was arguing with Angela and she moved around in front of her desk, wondering if Angela could manage to keep Nick out.

The door swung open and Angela tried to pass Nick, thrusting her head around him. "I'm sorry. He insisted—"

"That's all right, Angela. You can close the door please," Julia said, barely aware of what she'd told her secretary. Her gaze was locked with Nick's.

In spite of her anger, the moment she spotted him in his navy suit and tie, her pulse raced. Too often her desire was tangled with her anger where Nick was concerned. As he approached her, his eyes narrowed.

"Something's wrong," he said quietly stopping within inches of her and placing on hand on her shoulder. "Why didn't you show up for lunch or call me? You aren't taking your calls. What's happened?"

She felt as if his probing brown eyes were going straight through her and that he knew her every thought. Her anger boiled over again. "I saw Tyler at the bank, but he didn't see me."

"And?" Nick asked, sounding puzzled.

"And I overheard him talking about you wanting revenge."

Nick grimaced, his eyes now flashing with fire. "Dammit! Julia—"

"My seduction was a bet with Tyler to get revenge on my family in just one more way," she said, keeping her voice down, but unable to bank the fury rocking her.

Taking her arm, Nick inhaled. "Damn Tyler anyway! I told him that I lost the bet."

"That hardly matters. What matters is that you took me with you for a weekend to seduce me with cold calculation and get some more revenge for old hurts. That's the lowest—"

"Listen to me," Nick ordered in a firm voice, squeezing her shoulder lightly. "I was angry with your grandfather and wanted revenge. I'll admit it. I still think if they find the culprit that sabotaged our rig, there will be a connection to Holcomb."

"If there is, Granddad knows nothing about it," she said and Nick shrugged.

"I was angry and wanted revenge and made the damn bet with Tyler. After spending time with you, revenge and anger toward you went out of mind."

"You're a very smooth talker, Nick. You know how to manipulate and charm people and get what you want. But this bet tramples all over my trust." She looked into his brown eyes that gazed unwaveringly at her and she wondered how much she could ever trust him from here on. She would never know the truth about his declaration because it was all past and done now.

"Do you think I would have told Tyler I lost my bet and give up my prize horse if I still wanted revenge? Do you, Julia?" Nick insisted.

She sighed and shook her head and felt some of her anger with him subside. "I suppose not."

"Hardly. Tyler is ecstatic to get my horse. I could have had his Ferarri and kept my damn horse. He's filled with glee because he thinks I struck out with you. Does that sound as if I'm lying to you about the bet?"

"No, it doesn't," she admitted. She stared at him, wishing they could settle all the differences between them as easily. "There's a ruthless streak in you, Nick, to make the bet in the first place and try and get revenge in seduction that is so tied with someone's—in this case, my—emotions."

"All right. I shouldn't have even toyed with the idea, but I dropped it totally. I told you that I was angry and made the bet in the heat of anger. Just keep that in mind. When we made love, there was not one degree of revenge in my thought. I wanted you, Julia," he said hoarsely, sliding his hand to her nape. "I wanted you more than I've ever wanted a woman in my life."

She ached to believe him, but she couldn't believe the last statement. She couldn't imagine evoking such desire in a man like Nick.

"Nick!" she exclaimed in an exasperated sigh. "What can I believe? You're a charmer and you weave spells. Your reason for the past weekend was—"

"I told you. I tossed that aside before we made love. Forget it, Julia. It had nothing to do with what took place between us. I swear I'm telling you the truth."

His voice was earnest, his expression solemn and desire burned as hotly in his brown eyes as ever. Despite her anger and their arguments and opposing goals, he took her breath away and she wanted him right now, with more urgent desperation than ever.

Something flickered in the depths of his eyes and he inhaled, his chest expanding with his breath. He slid his arm around her waist and her heart raced. "I wanted you when we were out there. I wanted you with all my being more than I've ever wanted anyone. That's the damn truth, Julia."

His words burned her anger to cinders. He was believable, totally convincing. Dazed, she looked up at him and trembled from her toes to her head. "You can always tell what I'm thinking."

"See? We're in sync sometimes." He pulled her to him and leaned down to kiss her, a hard, possessive kiss that made her forget her surroundings, her arguments, her hurt and anger. His kiss was a brand and a declaration that left no doubt that he wanted her. His lips moved on hers and his tongue thrust deep, awakening every nerve. He groaned and leaned over her and she arched against him eagerly. This kiss was different, more intense, as if his kiss would convince that his words were true.

And it made her feel wanted by him totally, urgently enough to turn her knees to mush and build her desire to a raging fire.

"Nick," she whispered, trying to think and regain some control. "We're in my office. We're not—"

"Where can we go?" he murmured, looking around. He dropped his arm around her waist and pulled her into her sitting room, shutting the door. Windows spilled sunshine from the outside, but otherwise they were closed off. He pulled her into his embrace and leaned over her, kissing her as possessively as before.

"I want you more than you can ever know," he said softly and then his mouth came down on hers again.

She wound her fingers in his hair, kissing him back with the same fiery passion, letting her desire for him run rampant.

With shaking hands, he peeled her out of her tailored suit skirt and panty hose while she unfastened his belt and freed him from his slacks.

"You're crazy, Nick," she sighed, wanting him, knowing they were in her office and should wait. His words and kisses had set her on fire. How could she resist or wait when he made her feel as if he had to have her to survive?

Standing on tiptoe and wrapping her arms around his neck, she responded, kissing him passionately. He moved to lean back against a wall and picked her up. She wrapped her legs around him while she kissed him and he slid her down on his hard shaft.

He groaned, kissing her with the same urgent fervor as before. Desire consumed her. She moved her hips with him, hearing him call her name dimly above the roaring of her pulse in her ears.

"Julia, love!" he gasped and his tongue thrust into her mouth.

Frantically she moved with him, seeking release while tension coiled and burned inside her.

Her climax exploded in fury; then his release came, and he pumped fast and hard. Knowing their loving forged another link in a chain binding her heart to him, she held him tightly and wished she never had to let go.

They gasped for breath while they clung to each other.

"Thank heaven, there's a shower in my bathroom. It's small, but it works."

He kissed her throat and gazed into her eyes while he still held her. "I meant everything I said to you. I want you more than I've ever wanted anyone."

Her heart skipped a beat and she thrilled at his words, even though she knew they were headed for calamity no matter what each of them wanted.

"We have such differences, Nick. Sooner or later, they're going to matter."

"Just take today," he said in a gruff voice. "Let's not worry about the future."

She slid her legs down him and stood, but he didn't release her. Brown curls clung damply to his forehead and she pushed them back while she shook her head. "Nick, this is outrageous! We're in my office and I should go shower and dress."

"Let me just hold you a minute," he whispered and she couldn't refuse. Her arms were under his white cotton shirt, locked around his waist.

"Julia, we can weather the business deal. You told me all that matters is your grandfather and in the long run, he's going to be better off and have fewer worries."

"We'll see. You just told me to take one day at a time."

"So I did and I will. This day is turning out to be a fine one." Nick raked his fingers through her hair slowly. "Julia, I lost my prize racehorse to Tyler. You should have an inkling of what that horse means to me. It was Standing Tall, my best horse and one I had great expectations pinned on. I could have had Tyler's Ferrari if I'd wanted. Instead, he has my dream horse."

Startled, she stared at him. "Standing Tall? Your best horse?" The implications of what Nick had been telling her began to sink in. "You did that?"

"Yes, I did."

His sacrifice stunned her. As badly as Nick liked to win, how could he have given away his best horse when he actually won the bet? She took a deep breath and wondered how deep Nick's feelings really ran for her.

"I need to get on some clothes," she said, trying to remember they should dress.

"We'll shower together," he said, scooping her into his arms. She pointed toward the bathroom and Nick set her down in the narrow shower stall.

"I'm not sure this together is a good idea, Nick, and I want to keep my hair dry."

"It's a fabulous idea. Afterwards, we'll go to lunch," he said as he turned on a spray of warm water and began to lightly soap her with his hands, running them slowly over her breasts.

She inhaled with pleasure and closed her eyes, catching his wrists. "Nick, stop. I have an appointment at two and I want that lunch before then."

"All right if you'll promise to let me do this tonight," he said softly, kissing her neck and sliding his hand down over her bottom.

"I promise," she breathed, her thoughts still mulling over Nick giving up his horse. She would never have figured he'd do such a thing and it made her wonder about him. "We're getting bound more and more together with chains that are going to hurt when they break. But then you never have known heartbreak."

"Have you?" he asked.

"No, and I don't want to now," she replied.

"Back to one day at a time, remember?"

"For now, but pretty soon, Nick, we have to talk about what we each want."

"That's incredibly easy. What I want is you, delicious," he murmured, kissing the corner of her mouth, "beautiful," he added, kissing her breast, "soft and curvy and exciting."

His words wove a spell of magic. "Stop your seduction," she murmured. "I have to work today and we're not making love again in my little shower."

"Nope, but you promised tonight…" His voice faded away. She soaped him, unable to resist and in minutes they both kissed passionately while water poured over them.

She wriggled away and stepped out of the shower. "That's it, Nick. I'm getting ready for lunch."

They dressed swiftly and when she left her office, Julia felt her cheeks flush as Angela looked back and forth between them. "I'm sure you met Nick Ransome," Julia said.

Angela reached out to shake hands with him. "I've heard so much about you," she said. "I'm glad to meet you."

"I hope what you heard was good," Nick said lightly, glancing at Julia before taking Angela's hand and shaking it briefly. "It's nice to meet you."

"I'll be gone until four," Julia said. "I'm going to lunch and then I have a two o'clock appointment. I have my cell phone."

Her secretary nodded and looked back at Nick, smiling at him.

As Julia walked down the hall with him, she said. "I'm sure she realizes you may be her new employer starting Friday, so I doubt if she put up much fight to keep you out of my office."

"I was so busy thinking about seeing you, I didn't notice," Nick said. He punched the button for the elevator and turned to look at Julia. There was speculation in his gaze and she wondered what was running through his mind.

They had the elevator to themselves and Nick pulled her into his arms for a quick kiss. As they stopped and the doors opened, he took her arm. "There aren't nearly enough floors in this building."

"You do just as you please. I can't believe we made love in the middle of the day in my office. That's as public as this lobby."

"No, it wasn't. Might be sometimes, but it wasn't today. We had it to ourselves."

"Angela had to know what we were doing," she replied.

"Doesn't matter. I could happily kiss you right here and now."

"Don't you think about it!" she snapped, and he grinned and shrugged.

"Why not? I want you to be my woman."

"'My woman?' That sounds like something out of the Dark Ages," she protested.

"Not at all."

She stopped and tilted her head and looked up at him. "Nick Ransome, is this a proposal?"

He grinned and shook his head. "Not the kind you have in mind." His smile faded and he studied her solemnly. "Julia, I'm asking you to move into my house. Have you thought of that possibility? We could make love all we want when we want. We could hold each other through the night every night."

"You know that's not what I want."

"You act like you might want it," he said.

She was aware they stood in the busy lobby of her office building. People walked past them without a glance. "Why are we into this very private conversation now?"

"Because it came up and it's important. What do you want, Julia?"

"You know what I want. I told you when we were on your yacht. I want it all, the ring, the permanency, the babies, lifelong commitment."

"I can't do that and I think I made that clear before."

"You did, so there's no future for us."

"But there's today. Stay at my house tonight. Come over and I'll cook and you stay and let me love you all night and hold you close for hours." His voice lowered and became silky and ran over her like a caress.

What temptation he flung at her! She wanted to say yes to whatever she could have of him. If she were with him constantly, he might fall in love with her later. She stopped that train of thought that could delude her and lead to more trouble than she already had.

"C'mon. Agree with me," he coaxed. "You want to. I can see it in your expression and we'll have a fabulous night. Say, yes, Julia," he said, stroking her cheek.

"Yes, tonight, but there will come a tomorrow."

"You're right, of course, but for now I can look forward with anticipation for tonight and I don't have to think about the future."

"Someday, Nick, you're going to get in too deep to get out and you'll wonder what you've done to yourself," she said. She wanted to kiss him—hot, passionately—make him think of her the rest of the day and be anxious to be with her. But she was in her company's lobby with familiar people passing them. This wasn't the time or place.

They went to lunch and parted with Julia agreeing to be at his house at seven. She worked through most of the afternoon, keeping appointments she had made before she knew Nick, trying to get Holcomb solvent and knowing it was impossible.

Discouraged, hoping tomorrow would bring some kind of response, she talked briefly to her grandfather and to company accountants. Then she left for home. With every turn of the tires taking her closer to her house, her excitement grew. She would be with Nick tonight and he had a point about taking things one day at a time. In bubbling eagerness, she dressed in emerald slacks and an emerald shirt.

When she drove up Nick's drive, he was standing outside. At the sight of him, her pulse leaped. Dressed in tight jeans and a T-shirt that clung to his sculpted muscles, he motioned her to the back. When she stepped out of the car, he strolled up.

Nick enveloped her in his embrace. "I've been waiting forever," he said in a husky voice.

"Liar!" she accused, knowing Nick did not stand around and wait for anything.

He ended the conversation as he kissed her. "Now my evening begins," he said when he leaned back to look down at her. "Come in and see my house."

It was hours later before he gave her a tour of his house, and they ate dinner after ten that night. She sat in a kitchen alcove, looking out at a dazzling blue swimming pool that had a sparkling fountain in the center.

They had both showered and dressed and she gazed outside at the patio with its baskets of colorful flowers. Nick sipped a glass of water, ice cubes clinking slightly as he set the glass back on the table.

"Wednesday night Matt wants to have us out to his ranch for dinner. My dad will be there and my sister is coming in. The whole family tries as much as we can to get together at least once a month."

"So, you're close with your family?"

"Yes. We've tried to do this since we got out of college, but there are times some of us are away. We bring friends, too. It's casual." He gave her a long level look, and she wondered what was on his mind. She waited in silence. "Will you go with me Wednesday night?" he asked finally. "I'd like you to meet my family. I like to have you with me as much as I can, so why not take you to our family gathering? I'll enjoy the evening more if you're there."

Her heart swelled with his declaration of wanting her with him. She stared at him and wondered if he really wanted to have her with him. "I'd be delighted to go," she said carefully, and he smiled.

"You sound as if I asked you to eat in a burning house."

She laughed in return and shook her head. "No, you just surprised me."

"Don't worry, my family is just getting together for dinner and I want you with me whether we're with my family or somewhere else. Besides, we've always brought friends with us."

Julia nodded, but as they ate and she listened to Nick talk, she wondered about the approaching family dinner. He made it sound casual and as if the Ransomes invited outsiders regularly, but a family dinner meant she was getting to know Nick and those close to him. And he wanted her with him as much as possible—how deep did that go?

She felt as if she were sinking into an abyss where she couldn't escape with her heart intact. The family dinner might mean nothing to Nick or any of his siblings and father, but it meant a lot to her. She would know his family, know him better, be closer to all of them, be more familiar with the Ransome homes and lives. It was definitely moving her into their inner circle and she knew it wasn't wise on her part. But as always, Nick was impossible to resist.

Wednesday night, her curiosity grew with each mile as they sped through the Texas country, leaving the city for the wide-open spaces. As they raced along a highway that had little traffic, she watched Nick drive. Nick's strong hands moved on the wheel, but all she could recall was his hands moving over her. His fingers were well-shaped, the nails blunt. He was in slacks and a Polo, and she wore her yellow slacks and yellow silk shirt. She wanted to reach over and touch him, but he was concentrating on his driving and she left him alone.

She thought about their time together. Only one more day stood between them and a showdown over the Holcomb company.

After Friday morning, Julia wondered if she would see Nick again. She suspected she would not, but life was filled with unexpected twists and turns.

As Nick raced over the cattle guard, she knew she was the first member of her family to ever set foot on the Ransome ranch.

"Stop looking worried. My family is friendly. Matt and his wife have a baby, little Jeff. Dad has mellowed. Katherine is too busy to notice much of anything."

"You see too much. Most people can't guess whether I'm worried or sad or happy if I don't want them to," Julia answered.

"First of all, you don't have to hide your feelings from me, and second of all, I can tell by looking at you."

"Scary," she teased, but she wondered about his answer. And then it was forgotten.

When they pulled up to a sprawling ranch house, her trepidation increased. She was reluctant to meet his family. They didn't know each other that well, and generations of hate had existed between the men in their two families. As Nick slammed the car door and came around the car to open her door, she wished she could skip this night.

He held open the door and she stepped outside. Nick slipped his arm around her waist. "Come meet everyone," he said.

Eight

They crossed a green lawn that had a profusion of flowers in well-tended beds. On the porch, the hanging pots of yellow bougainvillea, scarlet gaillardia and purple impatiens couldn't cheer Julia.

When they entered the house through the kitchen, Julia met his family. His brother Matt bore a family resemblance; he shook her hand warmly while he kept his arm around the shoulders of his wife. Holding a sleeping baby, Olivia Ransome flashed a warm smile and greeted Julia. Katherine Ransome was equally welcoming, studying Julia with the same intentness that Nick sometimes did.

It was Duke Ransome, whose blue eyes were glacial, who stared at her as if she were in an enemy camp. His handshake was perfunctory, and she suspected he didn't approve of his son seeing her or of her being included in a family dinner.

"How's your grandfather?" Duke asked.

"He's fine," she replied, and Duke nodded, turning to talk to Nick. It was the last time Duke gave her any attention or talked to her. Later in the evening. when she was alone in the kitchen with Katherine, Nick's sister stepped close.

"Don't worry about Dad. When he meets people, he's cold at first."

"I'll bet not all people. I know we go way back with lots of animosity between our families, so I'm not surprised."

Katherine leaned against the kitchen counter, her crystal blue eyes sparkling as she studied Julia. "Can I ask you a question?"

"Sure, go ahead," Julia responded, wondering what Katherine had in mind that she felt she needed permission to ask.

"Are you serious about Nick?"

Startled, Julia stared at her and shook her head. "No," she said, turning away before she revealed more than she wanted it to. Katherine might have the same keen perception about people that her older brother did.

"I think Nick's serious about you," Katherine said in a quiet voice, and Julia turned around to stare at her again.

"Oh, I don't think Nick gets serious about any woman. You of all people, should know that."

"He sure hasn't before, but I've seen the way he looks at you. He isn't casual with you. He's intense."

"I don't think it means anything."

"I know my brother. Your relationship with Nick may be more serious than you realize."

Julia shook her head. "No, I can promise you it's not. We have a lot of business differences, but those aren't really important. It's our lifestyles and goals that will always cause a rift between us. Nick is not a marrying man."

"That's exactly what my brother Matt said. Now look at him. Married and loving it. Nick might change his mind, but then again, he might not. You could live with him and take your chances if y'all have a thing going between you."

"No. That life isn't for me. Absolutely not," she said, surprised at how easy it was to talk to Katherine. She felt as if Katherine was her friend, and it seemed as if she had known her for years instead of hours. "I know what I want and I'm not settling for something partial or temporary," Julia said quietly.

Katherine gave her a long look before she pushed away from the counter. "Too bad. Nick hasn't wanted to marry. After the way he grew up, there's not much appeal in it. I hope the business deal works out for you, too. I don't keep up with Nick's work, even when it's the energy company. I've got enough to worry about with my own company and I know Nick will take care of things."

"Yes, he will."

"Well, it's been nice to meet you."

"I don't think your dad wanted to meet me at all."

"That's just Dad. He holds old grudges." Katherine brushed locks of hair out of her eyes.

"Has my sister pinned you to the wall?" Nick asked, sauntering into the room and looking warmly at Julia as he crossed the room to her.

"Uh-oh," Katherine said. "Time to exit," she added and disappeared through the door.

Nick wrapped his hands around Julia's waist. "Having a good time? Katherine probably was Miss Twenty Questions."

"Yes, I am having a fine time. You have an interesting, friendly family."

"Good. I like them and I'm glad you do. If you can tear yourself away, it's time to start home. Ready?"

"Yes, I am," she said. His words *it's time to start home* gave her a thrill and a pang at the same time. It sounded as if they were a married couple; how she wished that were so. She looked up into Nick's dark eyes, letting her gaze drift down to his mouth. She realized in that moment that she was in love with him. Hopelessly lost. After Thursday night, she would move out of his house and get back on her own, but she was in love with him. What would it hurt if she stayed longer?

Just a bigger heartbreak. She knew tomorrow night was the last. Thursday was time to end it. They would disagree on the business deal, so this would be a good time to break away even though the break was caused by something far removed from business.

They told the family goodbye and Julia gave Matt and Olivia her thanks for a wonderful evening and repeated how cute their baby was. Duke Ransome's expression was as cold as it had been early in the evening. Katherine gave Julia a light hug. "Come see us again," she exclaimed.

Nick held Julia's arm and they hurried to the car.

In the dark as he drove back to Dallas, Julia pondered what Katherine had said about Nick being intense.

She watched him drive just as she had earlier. Now lights from the dash splashed over him and highlighted his prominent cheekbones, the long, straight slope of his nose, his sculpted mouth.

"You have a great family."

"Dad's probably a little like your granddad. They're another generation from another time. They're cranky sometimes, stubborn, smart. Wiley old codgers who have survived all these years. Dad sees you as a Holcomb. He's not going to warm up to you instantly."

"If ever," she added dryly. "I don't think he will any more than my grandfather will welcome you into our midst. It's just as well we're not going further, Nick, you and I, because members of both our families wouldn't like it."

"And would that really matter to you?" he asked her.

"Yes, it would. Granddad and I are close. I want the man in my life to get along with Granddad and vice versa."

"I'll admit I used to have animosity toward him and your dad, but it's gone now."

She studied him and wondered if he had really lost the ill will. "Probably because you finally won."

"Probably because of daughter and granddaughter," Nick added dryly. "They're part of you. That makes a difference."

She was surprised that it would make a difference or that she might be that important in Nick's life. What did he feel for her?

"Your sister is very pretty."

"Katie—I guess. She's my sister and that's all I ever see. Kid sister, at that. She had a bum romance and she's a little bitter now."

"Too bad. All of you are a little sour on marriage."

"But not on love," he drawled softly, brushing kisses across her knuckles again. His breath was warm. "I know you have to stay buckled in, but I'd like you in my lap."

"Soon enough, Nick. I'm going home with you."

"Don't say it reluctantly. I think my family visit worried you."

"No, I just think they got all excited because they think you're serious about somebody, and that isn't the case."

"I'm fairly serious."

She had to laugh. "As serious as a tiger about a chunk of meat."

He smiled and this time traced his tongue over her palm. She withdrew her hand. "Wait until we're at your house. You keep your attention on the road."

"Much more inviting to keep it on you. I know this road like my own hand and we're still almost an hour away from our houses and from me getting to make love to you," he said in a low voice that thrilled her.

She couldn't resist and placed her hand on his warm thigh. He immediately covered her hand with his. "I want you home. I want you in my bed. I just want you."

"I don't think your attention is totally on your driving."

"Sure as hell isn't," he said. "We could pull off the road into the bushes."

When she laughed, he glanced at her. "I'm serious."

"Home, please. Maybe we'll even get as far as a bed. I'm going to miss you, Nick. Miss you badly."

"So where are you going? And when?"

"I figure probably tomorrow night is our last night together."

"How in sweet hell do you figure that?"

"Friday, you buy out Holcomb and my grandfather will be in a rage. I'll have to move on. And I would have to eventually anyway."

"Back to long-term commitment, aren't we?"

"Not necessarily," she answered with a lightness she was far from feeling. But she didn't want him to know she had fallen in love with him. She didn't want him to ever know it. When she walked out of his life, she didn't want to give him a guilt trip. And sooner or later, if she didn't walk, he would. Better her, and the sooner the better.

"Nick, you're going to break the sound barrier," she said, glancing at the speedometer.

"This is a straight road that I know absolutely and I can't wait to get you home into my arms so I can kiss you the rest of the night."

She looked out the dark window and anticipation curled in her. She wanted the same thing he did, to make love until morning.

When they reached his house, the minute the door closed behind him, she reached for him. Clothing was strewn across the back entryway through the kitchen and into the hall. Nick turned her into the family room and they made love on the thick carpet.

Later, he held her close and combed her hair from her face. "There are some thirty-six rooms in this house and I want to make love to you in every one of them," he murmured.

"Ridiculous!" she said, laughing.

"I love it when you laugh. I don't want tomorrow night to be our last night. Not that soon, Julia."

She looked away from his velvety dark eyes and thought about their future. "I think after tomorrow, you'll feel differently about it."

"You barely have anything here of yours. Wait until tomorrow and let's see how you feel. Until a week ago, none of this would have been an issue. Just wait. Don't do anything."

"Nick, you're prolonging what's inevitable. You and I are on different wavelengths about our futures."

He wrapped his arms around her and pulled her tightly into his embrace, wrapping his long, bare legs with hers.

She ran her fingers over him, down across his washboard belly, his muscled thigh. "Are we going to argue all night?" she asked.

"Sure as hell not," he said, pulling her closer again so he could kiss her.

Through the night, they made love, showered and talked, and every moment held a bittersweet edge because she was certain she was moving closer to saying goodbye.

Thursday passed in a blur and that night she was back in Nick's arms and bed, loving him wildly, savoring each moment.

She was learning more about him and now everything he wanted was tied directly to success in some business endeavor. She tried to make the most of the moment and bank her mounting disappointment. Finally, near dawn, he fell asleep in her arms. She watched him for a long time, looking at his chest rise and fall, the thick mat of hair that covered his chest, his tangled hair that fell over his forehead.

She finally drifted to sleep and woke in his arms to find him watching her. "It's early," she murmured drowsily, glancing at the gray light in the windows. "We don't have to stir yet."

"Then come here," he said, pulling her closer. "I'm sure that we can find something entertaining to do until the sun is fully up."

"Speaking about something being up—" she said playfully, running her hands over him.

She caressed him, moving over him as they began making love again. This time she threw herself into the passion more than ever, shaking with desire, knowing this might be their last time together.

It was another two hours before they showered and dressed. As Nick tied his necktie, he turned to her. "I want to have lunch with you."

"Sorry, I promised Granddad a long time ago. Let's not set plans, Nick."

He shrugged and turned back and she watched him dress for a moment. He was as darkly handsome as ever and she wanted to walk right back into his arms, but she knew she couldn't.

She realized he was watching her in the mirror, staring at her as she dressed. She moved away because they needed to get going. Nick had promised to take her home so she could get her own car.

In another hour, they had dressed and eaten. Nick pulled into her driveway to let her out. "I want to take you to dinner—how's that, instead of lunch?"

"We'll see, Nick, how things go. I'm not promising anything at this point."

He climbed out of the car to walk her to her door. "Remember, this is just business. It has nothing to do with our private lives."

"It does with yours because it's be-all and end-all to you, everything."

"I can compartmentalize it, Julia. I have a private life, a personal life. I can shut off the other."

"I doubt if they've often been in conflict," she answered coolly. "I'll see you with your lawyers at ten, Nick."

"Look," he said, placing his hand over her head on the doorjamb and leaning closer, hemming her in. He ran his other hand back and forth beneath her collar. "I don't want to call it quits. I don't want to stop seeing each other. We set each other on fire. Why give that up?"

"There are other considerations and you know it. That's lust, Nick. I keep telling you—I want it all. I want more than lust and your desire. I want the total, lifetime commitment. We're not even in love," she said, her words sounding hollow.

"Dammit, I'm in love!" he snapped. He pulled her to him and kissed her hard, another demanding, possessive kiss that rocked her and left no doubt that he wanted her desperately. She wound her arms around his neck and kissed him back. Their physical relationship was good and she wondered if she was doing something she would regret forever.

He leaned back. "I want you. You're mine."

She shook her head. "I'm not yours and you're not mine. You know that. Love is union, but it's not possession. I have to go, Nick." She brushed past him and opened her door and stepped inside.

She turned to look at him, finding him watching her intently.

"At least give me a chance and say you'll go to dinner with me tonight," he said. "You can do that much. One more dinner isn't going to do you in."

"Promise to bring me right back here when I'm ready."

"Of course I will," he answered solemnly.

"All right. I'll go with you."

He let out his breath and then raised his head to look at her. "How about seven? Pick you up here."

"Fine. But it might be subject to change."

He ground his jaw closed and stared at her. "I'll see you soon."

She closed the door and sagged against it. Her lips tingled from his kiss and she burned with desire. She could never get enough of him!

At the sound of his car driving away, she opened her eyes and went to her room to change clothes. She just hoped the buyout wasn't a total disaster.

Swiftly, she dressed with care, choosing a tailored black suit and white silk blouse. She looped and pinned her hair behind her head, gathered her papers and headed for the Holcomb office. Sunshine spilled over traffic and the blue sky and busy street made it seem like any other day, but she knew this day would go down in the history of her family as one of the worst.

She drove to the back to her special parking place, noticing her grandfather's long, black sedan already in his reserved place on the other side of the door, opposite hers.

She entered the brick building for a short meeting before they would meet with Nick and the Ransome people. She closed her eyes, praying swiftly for a miracle to save them, and then went to the meeting to hear the last-ditch efforts of their lawyers and accountants. But if any miracle had occurred, she would have heard about it before now. There was a remote possibility because the attorneys had found a slim chance they could get financing if they could meet certain requirements, but it would take a month or two that they didn't have.

Promptly at fifteen minutes before ten o'clock, she arrived at the Ransome Energy building. She rode up in the elevator with her granddad and their people, but her thoughts were on her first visit to Ransome Energy, when she had asked Nick if they could get together privately.

She had never expected what had resulted. That morning when she had walked into his office, she wouldn't have guessed it possible. When she saw him, her pulse had jumped and she knew with certainty the same reaction would occur today.

She emerged from the elevator, walked down the hall and
entered a reception area filled with people, but she didn't see
Nick. She guessed that he was still in his office.

"Good morning," she heard a familiar deep voice behind her
say, and she turned.

Nine

Nick sauntered toward her and there was no way to stop her physical reaction to him. Her heartbeat quickened and her mouth went dry. Desire burned as hotly as ever and she forgot about any meeting.

How devilishly handsome he looked in his charcoal suit and red tie! His hair was neatly combed, but unruly curls still tangled. Memories of her fingers winding in his thick locks taunted her. In spite of the differences between them, she melted at the sight of him. From the start, she had known that she shouldn't succumb to his charm, but it was too late for regrets now.

Ten minutes into the meeting, Julia realized she was in trouble. For the first time in her life, she couldn't keep her mind on business at hand. Never had she had difficulty concentrating in a meeting, but now all she could think about was Nick, their dinner together tonight, the essential, unbridgeable differences between them. While her thoughts swirled about her personal life, she looked to the end of the table at Nick.

He could turn off everything else. Watching and listening to him, she knew his focus was totally on the matter at hand. When his gaze met hers, his dark eyes were impersonal, unfathomable.

He was cold, ruthlessly efficient and going ahead with his plans in spite of their attorneys' suggestions and offers. Holcomb was vulnerable, and Nick was taking advantage of it to acquire their company.

She knew that was a biased opinion. He was making a savvy business deal and if it hadn't been Holcomb and her family's business, she had to admit that she would agree with what he was doing. He was acquiring rigs for his company that would enlarge his profits enormously. He was making his company stronger, and she reluctantly had to admit he was paying them more than Holcomb was currently worth and a generous sum that few would find complaint with. An amount he didn't have to pay to get what he wanted.

She was hurt and angry and it was difficult to think reasonably or to pay attention to what was happening—a problem she had never had before in her life.

Her grandfather's face was flushed, his fists were clenched and at any minute she expected him to walk out because he couldn't do anything to change the outcome. It was no longer necessary for him to be there, either, because the Holcomb attorneys could handle the details.

"If you'll give us a month more," Rufus said, "we can come up with the money. If you're truly not out for revenge, you'll do this. Tell him, Julia."

She heard her name, but she hadn't heard another word her granddad had spoken. All eyes were on her and her face flushed hotly. She had no idea what had just been said.

"It won't matter what you tell us about holding off for a month," Nick said quietly, letting her know what she had been asked. Embarrassed, she felt foolish, yet business didn't matter right now as much as other aspects of her life. Success was all-important to Nick, also to her grandfather. To her, other facets of her life were far more important. She listened as Nick continued smoothly and again she wondered about him and what he truly felt.

"You win, Nick," her granddad said. "All your life you've been aiming for this moment, and your dad before you. I'm surprised he isn't here to gloat this morning. You've taken advantage of us in every way possible," he snapped, startling Julia.

"It's a fair offer," Nick said quietly.

"You're a shark going in for the kill. Go ahead. Finish me off, but I won't stay and watch." He stood and the others came to their feet. Julia met Nick's cool gaze. She knew there was no point in her staying and listening to them hash out the details.

"I suspect our attorneys can handle the rest. Tyler—" Nick said. His words were clipped and there was no exaltation in the tone of his voice. She followed her grandfather. Nick reached the door before she did and held it open for her. She detected his aftershave as she passed him and it triggered unwanted memories that taunted her.

Her grandfather had already taken the elevator down. She followed and caught up with her grandfather in the lobby. "Granddad! Wait," she called.

"I'm getting out of here," Rufus said, glaring at Nick who emerged from an elevator and approached them.

"I'll see you at home," she said.

When Rufus hurried away, she turned to Nick as he walked up to stand only inches from her.

"You won in every area. You seduced me. You've taken over Holcomb. You've beaten Granddad. You must be planning to celebrate, Nick."

"That wasn't why I made love to you," he declared solemnly, "and you damn well know it. And this buyout is a generous purchase. When the dust settles you and your grandfather will see that you got a profitable bargain."

He took her arm and pulled her closer. "In the meantime, I still want to have dinner together tonight."

The slight contact of his hand on her arm sent her heart racing and she stared up at him, torn by conflicting emotions.

During the past hour, she had hurt for her grandfather and the meeting had been a reminder of how cold and ruthless Nick could be.

At the same time, her heart raced and her breathing suffered and she reacted to Nick merely telling her that he wanted to see her. He wound his fingers in her hair and tilted her head back. Pins and locks of her hair tumbled over his hand, but she didn't care. She slid her hands up his arms, feeling the luxurious soft wool of his sleeves.

"I want you. I want to see you and I want to love you and I know you want me. Don't take us away from each other, Julia," he urged.

Her heart slammed against her ribs. Before she could answer him, the elevator doors behind them opened and Tyler stepped into the lobby. "We want you in the meeting, Nick."

"You'll have to wait," Nick replied. "This is urgent. You take care of it."

Tyler shot her a quizzical look. He left and she heard the door close, but she wasn't thinking about Tyler or watching him.

"I want to come see you and talk to you tonight. All right?" Nick asked.

"No, it's no longer what I want to do," she said, ignoring her racing pulse, trying to keep a barrier of refusal between them. "This evening isn't a good time."

"Julia, I won't give up like this," he declared firmly. He stepped closer and lowered his voice, but she could still hear the urgent note in his tone. "It's too important that I see you. I have to get back to the meeting, but I'd like to see you. How about seven at your place? I'll bring something to eat. Let me come talk to you."

In spite of the emotional upheaval of the morning, she couldn't resist him. "All right. Seven."

"Don't do anything. I'll bring what we need for dinner." As she looked into his dark eyes, she was drawn by the same hot desire she saw in his gaze. People milled in the lobby, but they ceased to exist to her. There was only Nick. Julia tightened her fingers on his arm slightly. Nick inhaled and then he leaned down to place his mouth on hers and kiss her. Torn between wanting to kiss him and wanting to push him away, she lost the battle and returned his kiss.

The moment she did, she forgot the differences between them. She knew each kiss was kindling for a bonfire of wanting Nick. It steadily burned higher and hotter and she wasn't helping herself now.

He straightened, and she opened her eyes. Nick touched her chin. "Seven. Give me a break here. Holcomb got a good deal and if it hadn't been Ransome Energy, it would have been someone else buying you out."

"I know you're right," she admitted.

"I'm glad to hear you agree. Tonight, darlin'," he said, striding away from her.

She watched him with churning emotions while his endearment echoed in her mind, "...darlin'..." If only—she thrust the thought out of mind. Nick was who he was and he wasn't going to change because of her.

He got what he had wanted from her, from her family. Yet at the same time, he felt something strongly, too, or he wouldn't make such an effort to see her again.

"He's already breaking my heart," she said softly to herself, knowing she should tell him goodbye tonight. She was in love with him. She hoped it wasn't irrevocable, but at the moment, she felt as if she would love him the rest of her life.

As he stood in front of the elevators, he looked back at her. They stared at each other for a moment before she walked away. She emerged out into hot July sunshine and walked to her car.

She needed to see her grandfather first and then go home. Nick was coming tonight and bringing dinner. The knowledge excited her and she shook her head. "You're hopelessly in love with him," she whispered, "while he's in love with what he's doing up there in that meeting right now."

To her surprise, her grandfather stood beside her car.

"I didn't know you were waiting," she said, rushing to him.

"I figured you'd be worried and hurry over to the house." He gave her a hug. "Don't worry, honey. The dust hasn't settled. We've got money again and a lot of it. We made a large amount of money this morning."

Startled, she stepped back to study him. "You're taking this well," she said.

His blue eyes crackled with anger and his face was still flushed, so she knew he wasn't happy despite his words.

"My family started the drilling company with one wildcat well. We've got money now and I can begin again. There are little companies that we can buy, rigs out there. Nick's young and I've got some years left in me. I can still give him competition and by Jupiter, I intend to!"

"Just don't let your blood pressure go sky high while you think about it and plan, Granddad." She gave him a squeeze and stepped back to look at him. She loved him and didn't want to see him hurt. "We'll meet with our officers and the legal staff this afternoon and map out what we'll do. Maybe Nick will give us some time for the transition."

"Don't count on it," Rufus remarked darkly.

"I'll see you at the office," she said and watched her grandfather stride around to his car. She wished he'd retire and take it easy, but she knew that wasn't his nature. The feud between the two families had just escalated. In spite of it, she was seeing Nick again tonight. She hadn't told her grandfather about seeing Nick, because she expected her relationship with Nick to be brief, over with tonight if she could stick to what she planned.

As she climbed into her car, she glanced back at the building, knowing Nick was doing what he liked best—achieving success in an endeavor he had given years to. Revenge was his today. Success, revenge—how much more important were they to him than love?

Nick stood at a window in a hall and gazed at Julia's car. She hadn't driven away yet and he wondered how hurt she was. Victory over Holcomb was empty, and revenge no longer mattered. He wouldn't back out of the deal because it was a good one for all concerned, whether Rufus saw it that way or not, but there was no satisfaction in smashing Rufus. Not if it hurt Julia.

Nick reminded himself that he would see her this evening. He wanted Julia to move in with him and he would ask her again tonight. He glanced at his watch and decided he would go to a jewelry store and get her a gift. He wanted the day to fly by so it would be time to see her.

"Nick?" Tyler's tone was quizzical and he frowned, studying Nick as he walked up to him. "We're waiting."

"Yeah. Tyler, I want you to offer Rufus a vice presidency with us. We'll absorb his company, but there's room for him."

"You've lost it, Nick! Bringing Rufus in with us is crazy after—"

"Do it, Tyler," Nick ordered flatly in a tone that made Tyler close his mouth. "I think you can handle the meeting from here on. None of you need me. I've already signed the papers I need to sign."

"You're going soft on this deal of acquiring Holcomb! And it's because of Julia. You're in love with her and not using your brain," Tyler snapped, his face flushed. "You worked to demolish that old man and now you want to turn around and offer him a job with us so he can continue with his old projects."

"That's right, Tyler. And it's my prerogative to do all of that," Nick said, pushing his coat open to place his hands on his hips.

"I don't give a damn what you do when you're out of here, but you're making a mistake to offer Holcomb anything. Crush him like you planned. Here's why."

Tyler held out a manila folder. Nick took it and opened it to see the picture of the man running across the Ransome rig in the Gulf. "We've got an identification," Tyler continued. "He's a Holcomb employee."

Nick drew a deep breath and anger stabbed him that Rufus had lied about involvement, but he wasn't surprised. He had known all along that the culprit would turn out to be someone hired by Rufus.

"Rufus knew about it and hired him himself," Tyler said.

"We've got the whole story from another guy who's his friend—in a manner of speaking, since he turned the arsonist in for the reward money. He's friends with this guy and he helped him. We promised anyone who gave us information immunity, so we have to stick with it."

Nick nodded and took the manila folder.

"Now, forget the offer to Rufus and fling that picture at him," Tyler urged. "I'll tell him that we have a confession and know the culprits."

"No. I'll deal with Rufus. Leave this to me. We own his company and all this is over."

"You can't be serious!" Tyler exclaimed. "It's a criminal act."

"It's done. Let it go. Let the guy know that we have evidence and a picture so he won't do it again, but drop it, Tyler," Nick ordered firmly.

"Damn, you really are in love with Julia. Never before in your life would you have made a decision like this."

Startled, Nick stared at his vice president. "I guess I do love her, but it's not the first time I've been in love," he said, knowing when he said the words that they didn't apply to how he felt about Julia. It was the first time he'd felt his way, but he wasn't about to admit the truth to Tyler.

"And she's in love with you," Tyler said with a note of disgust. "She was lost in the meeting. She didn't hear anything we said. Every time the two of you look at each other, the air all but bursts into flames. I'm surprised you lost our bet."

"Well, I did."

"There's always a woman in your life, but this is different," Tyler said and Nick stared at him. "She distracts you from business. That's a first."

"It's none of your business, Tyler," Nick said in a cold voice.

"Dammit, it's my business when you start making bad business calls because of it. You've gone soft and you're gaga over a chick."

"Don't call her a chick. You wind up, Tyler. I have something more important to do," Nick said, turning and walking away. He stopped and faced Tyler again. "Don't show that picture and we're not telling Julia that her grandfather hired the man. The old man lied to her. Just leave it alone. She worships him."

"She's wound you around her little finger. I never thought I'd see the time that a woman had you tied in knots or jumping through hoops."

Nick shrugged. He didn't care what Tyler thought. He just didn't want Julia hurt unnecessarily or disillusioned about her grandfather because there was nothing to gain from it.

He turned his back on Tyler and strode toward the entrance.

"Nick, dammit! You're not thinking straight. Start thinking with your brain. It would have been better if she'd let you seduce her because then you'd have gotten her out of your system."

While Tyler was still ranting, Nick left. Thinking about tonight, he strode outside into hot sunshine. He glanced again at his watch, wishing he could be with Julia right now. He climbed into his car, drove to Holcomb Drilling and was ushered into Rufus's cluttered office.

Rufus stood behind a desk piled high with papers. More papers, ledgers and books were strewn on the floor around the desk. Sunlight spilled through the long windows behind him.

With his blue eyes flashing fire, Rufus glared at Nick. "So you came to gloat. I might have known," Rufus said in disgust.

"No, sir," Nick replied, holding his temper. "I came to tell you that we have a photograph and a witness who is willing to testify that you personally ordered the arson on our rig."

"You're bluffing and wasting my time and yours. There's no such proof or witness."

"I'm telling the truth and you know it," Nick said quietly. "I can produce the photograph, the witness and his sworn statement if I want," Nick said, holding out the manilla folder he carried.

Rufus grabbed the folder from him and opened it, pulling out the photographs of the arsonist running across the Ransome rig. Dropping the pictures on his desk, Rufus looked up. "You bastard!" he snapped, clenching his fists and charging around his desk toward Nick, who stepped back quickly.

"Sir, I won't fight with you," Nick said, holding up both hands, palms toward Rufus in a show of peace.

Suddenly Rufus stopped and all color drained from his face.

Afraid Rufus was having a heart attack, Nick stepped forward to catch him if he collapsed. "Are you all right?" Nick asked.

"You're going to tell Julia," Rufus said, his shoulders slumping. "You're going to destroy me in her eyes and get revenge for everything."

Concerned, Nick shook his head. "No, sir. I'm not going to tell Julia. No charges will be pressed. This matter is between you and me."

"You're lying. I don't believe you," Rufus said, sitting in the closest chair. He trembled and his voice lost its force. Nick's worry increased because Rufus seemed to be aging before his eyes. He looked old, frail and frightened.

"I mean what I say," Nick assured him. "We'll warn your employee never to do it again. That's all. Julia will never know."

With a perplexed expression, Rufus gazed up at Nick. "Why? Why are you backing off when Tyler can finally destroy me and get revenge for all I've done?"

Nick looked down into the blue eyes of the man who had caused him so much trouble through the years. Revenge no longer mattered and he knew why.

"I love Julia," Nick declared quietly, and Rufus flinched as if Nick had struck him. "I want to avoid hurting her."

While Rufus blinked and stared at him, Nick was relieved to see a little color return to Rufus's face. "Are you all right?" Nick asked again.

"Yes. Does she love you?"

"I hope so, sir," Nick said.

Taking a deep breath, Rufus stood. "Don't you ever hurt her."

"I don't intend to," Nick said.

"Now get the hell out," Rufus said, beginning to sound more like the man Nick had always known.

Glad to go, Nick turned and hurried to his car while he thought about what had just passed between Julia's grandfather and him.

As he climbed into his car and made his way to the highway, Nick had forgotten Rufus and was thinking only about Julia. He was in love with her.

He couldn't commit to marriage, which was what she wanted, but he loved her and he wanted her to move in with him. His pulse raced at the thought. She had given him her virginity—a first in his life. It surprised him that it was important to him and made him feel special in her life. He would have never guessed he would feel that way about it, but he did.

She was vital to him and he loved her. More than he had ever loved anyone else.

He entered the flow of traffic and headed for his favorite jeweler. He wanted to buy something for her. Eager to please her and to be with her, he wished the hours would fly past.

"Julia, darlin'," he sighed. "I love you." He needed to tell her that he wanted her to live with him. Would she accept life and love on his terms?

The thought of coming home each night to her built his anticipation. He wanted her in his bed every night. Excitement bubbled in him and he drummed his fingers impatiently on the steering wheel while he thought about holding her close in his arms in his bed tonight. "Julia, Julia," he whispered.

By five o'clock Julia was surprised at the turn her life had taken. Nick had offered to keep Holcomb intact, just absorb it into Ransome Energy. He had offered Rufus a vice presidency in drilling, but her grandfather didn't want to cooperate. It would mean few changes and Holcomb would be part of a profitable larger company and she wanted her grandfather to accept, but he refused to listen.

She drove home at five to get ready to see Nick. Dazed, she entered her house.

Her anger with Nick evaporated earlier. He had mollified her feelings about the bet, made her grandfather an overwhelmingly generous offer. How could she stay angry with him or even think about business? Her usual excitement over seeing Nick was tempered by her resolution to break off with him tonight.

She didn't want to settle down on his terms. Every day she was with him, she was falling deeper in love with him. She wanted everything—not just part of him. And she knew the time had come to tell him.

If they never saw each other again, she would pay that price because she wasn't going to live with him, love him with her whole heart, become accustomed to him in her life and then have him walk away and leave her with only heartbreak.

Solemnly, she dressed in her green silk slacks and green sleeveless blouse. She caught her hair behind her head, tying it with a scarf.

When the doorbell rang, she dashed to open the door. Nick stood patiently waiting and the sight of him took her breath as always. He gave her a glance that held warm approval.

"Are you going to invite me in?" he asked.

In brown slacks and a tan knit shirt, he stood with his hands filled with a sack of food and covered dishes.

"Of course," she said, touching his wrist. "Let me get that." She took a dish from him and carried it to the kitchen.

She was excited. Her resolve to end it with him wavered as it had each day because she wanted to be with him more than anything else she had ever desired in her life. There was no way she could refuse to see him yet. In that moment, she wondered if she would stay and let Nick break her heart.

She turned to face him and he placed his hands on her shoulders. "Still angry with me?"

"No. I was at Granddad's when Tyler called and offered him a place in your business and told him what you were going to do."

"He didn't want any part of it."

"No, but you offered, Nick. That's what mattered to me. I'm not angry and Granddad is busy plotting how he can start up a new company."

"That old pirate!" Nick let out his breath and stared at her. "You're not concerned now about your grandfather. Business is behind us. There's something worrying you and I want to erase it completely. Save it for later. For now, let's have everything I've waited for all day long," he said quietly, running his hands up and down her back. His touch was light, slow and tantalizing. His brown gaze bore into her, and desire consumed her.

"You're wonderful and you're necessary to my existence," he said softly, leaning down to kiss her throat. His words fueled her hot desire. Unable to wait or resist, she stepped into his arms and stood on tiptoe to kiss him passionately; she forgot about dinner or decisions.

With shaking hands, she unfastened his clothes, tugging on him as she led him while they kissed. They got as far as the hall when Nick peeled away the last of her clothes, tossing her lacy panties aside. Desperation shook her and she knelt to take him into her mouth and lick and kiss him while her hands played lightly between his legs.

"Julia, I want you," he ground out the words and picked her up.

"My bedroom," she said hoarsely, waving her hand as he carried her in the direction she had pointed while she wrapped herself around him and kissed him as if this were the last kiss they would ever have.

They fell across her bed. "Nick, protection—" she reminded him. He left her, but return swiftly.

She watched him striding toward her, virile, nude and aroused. Her heartbeat thundered and she slid off the bed, throwing herself into his arms.

He caught her easily as she wrapped her long legs around him and then he placed her in bed again and moved between her legs, pausing to put on a condom. She ran her hands over his thighs, feeling the strong muscles, the hair on his legs.

He lowered himself to thrust into her. "I love you, Julia," he murmured.

She thrilled to his declaration, taking it now without question. "I love you," she whispered in return as she showered his face with kisses. "Love me, Nick. Make love to me all night."

He groaned and slowed, thrusting and then easing back while she thrashed beneath him and pulled him closer. Her legs tightened around him. "I love you, Nick, with all my heart. Absolutely," she said softly, wanting to add *forever,* but refraining because she knew it wouldn't be what he wanted to hear.

As he plunged into her, he kissed her, and they moved together. She stopped thinking, drowning in sensations, aware of his strength and hardness, for a moment feeling as if they both wanted each other with equal urgency and depth.

Release was a starburst, carrying her over the moon. Clinging to him, she cried his name. "Nick!"

He reached a furious climax, his hips thrusting hard as he gasped. "My love!" His words were a husky rasp, but she heard him. He held her tightly and kissed her. Her happiness was a bright, fragile bauble. Her breathing became regular, her heartbeat calm. Wanting to prolong the moment and shut out the problems, she held his damp body close against her. For now, Nick was in her arms; he had told her he loved her, and her heart thudded with joy.

Still holding her close, he shifted, turning on his side. She could feel his heart beating when she ran her hand slowly down the smooth curve of his back. "This is paradise, Nick. It's perfection."

"You're what's perfection," he said in a throaty voice. "I think I should find that furry mutt and give him a home for life and all the bones he can chew. I'll be eternally grateful to him."

She smiled and ran her fingers along Nick's smooth jaw. "You just shaved."

"I planned to see someone special."

"We would have met with or without the dog. You were having dinner with me."

"But if we'd just met at dinner, I wouldn't have felt the same, and neither would you. There was too much animosity steaming through dinner. But out there in the parking lot because of that mutt, we were just two strangers. A man and woman, with chemistry like dynamite between us. No, I owe that mutt, but hopefully he has a home."

"If he has a home, he should have been there instead of wandering in front of speeding cars."

"You always make it sound as if I raced through the parking lot like a criminal."

"Not a criminal, Nick. But you did race. You were in a big rush and I was frightened for the dog because I saw you coming."

"I'm glad I didn't run over you. But you knew you were safe. You knew any man on earth would stop on a dime if you stepped in front of his car."

She smiled at him. "This is good, Nick. This week has been the best in my life."

His eyes darkened as he held her. "It's been the best in mine, too."

"Even if I have missed a few meals."

"So let me see, are you getting too skinny anywhere?" he asked, running his hands over her.

"Nick!" she caught his hands as she laughed. "Speaking of food, I'm getting hungry."

"Very well. First, there's something I want to show you. Promise to sit right where you are and let me get it."

"I promise," she said with a smile.

He slid off the bed and strode from the room to return in seconds. "Close your eyes," he said.

She closed her eyes, wondering what he was doing. She felt the shift of the bed with his weight. "Okay, open your eyes."

He sat in front of her holding out a long, black box. "Nick!" she exclaimed, guessing he had bought her a gift. She opened the lid and looked at a diamond pendant snug against a cream-colored lining.

"Nick, it's beautiful!" she exclaimed.

"Turn around," he said, taking the pendant from her and dropping it over her head before he fastened it. The large diamond was cool against her skin, dazzling in the light. She touched it and was astounded he had gotten it for her.

She turned around, looking into his eyes and feeling as much one with him as she had in the throes of passion and making love to him. "Thank you," she said softly. "I love it, and I'll always treasure it. It's an heirloom, a keeper, Nick, like you." He wrapped her in his arms, sinking down on the bed and leaning over her to kiss her.

He finally raised his head. "It's just a symbol, Julia. My love is as lasting."

She wanted to cry out that he didn't mean what he said, because his love wouldn't last. Instead she kissed him again.

Finally, she pushed against his chest. "Nick, I have to eat. I feel faint," she said.

"Wimp. All right. Point us in the direction of the shower and we'll get ready again for dinner."

"Right through that door and I can walk all by myself."

He stood and reached down to pick her up. "Not while I'm around. You're a feather and I want to carry you. It's a treat to have a gorgeous, naked woman in my arms. There are few things better. Not many, but a few."

"I'm not asking what," she said with amusement. He carried her to the shower to set her on her feet and they showered together.

Afterwards, when they sat in the kitchen alcove to eat tilapia fillets Nick had helped Julia grill, Julia was still torn between what she knew she should do and what she wanted to do.

"Julia," he said, taking her hand in his across the table. "The necklace is a bribe. I want something."

Her pulse jumped and she held her breath. The moment became etched in her memory for all time—Nick in his tan shirt, curly locks of his dark hair falling over his forehead. His chocolate eyes were intent and his expression solemn. She became aware of every detail of the moment—the smell of their steaks, the music playing softly, the flickering candlelight in her quiet kitchen. Her gaze roamed over his features that she now knew so well—his sensual, full underlip, his smooth jaw and strong column of his neck. While her heart drummed, she knew what she hoped he would ask. "What is it, Nick?" she asked quietly, thinking her heartbeat was a drumroll for his announcement.

"Julia, I love you. I want you with me all the time. I want you in my bed every night, in my arms. I was serious today when I asked. Will you move in with me?"

Ten

While her heartbeat raced, his words both thrilled and disappointed her. "Nick, love to you is so casual. 'I love you' rolls easily off your tongue and you've told me that you've been in love lots of times."

"Not like this," he answered solemnly while he ran his thumbs lightly back and forth over her knuckles. "You're different, Julia. I've never wanted a woman like I want you."

Magic words that made her pulse quicken, yet how easily he said them. How many others had he said them to, she wondered. She looked down at their hands together, her fingers wrapped in his while she mulled his offer, knowing it wasn't what she had hoped it would be.

"Nick, where are we going? I move in for how long—a year? A month?"

"You know it'll be longer than a month. Who knows how long? It's good between us and you know it. No one can predict the future. I've told you from the first that I'm not a marrying man," he said, the first note of chill coming into his voice.

"And I made it clear from the first that I am a marrying woman. I want it all, Nick. I want the in-laws, the vows, the permanency. Don't you want kids and a family?"

"Not necessarily. I don't know anything about raising kids, and Matt will have the children in the family."

His request was temptation beyond measure to her. She wanted him, wanted to live with him and love him daily. It could grow into permanency. "Nick, I want you in my life so badly," she said softly.

He took her hand and pulled her on to his lap. "If you're not ready to answer, you think about it, Julia. And let's stay together tonight. I've been waiting all day for this time with you. It's special. Don't take it away from me."

"This is the best!" he said quietly. "You in my arms. That's what I want."

Stay, take another week with him and then break off. Or stay indefinitely and let life unfold. Nick might want her with him so badly, he would ask her to stay forever. She knew she could stay to see if she liked life on his terms. The possibilities danced before her, dazzling in the prospect of being in his arms every night, sharing kisses and passion.

For a few minutes, she gave herself over to thinking about how exciting living with him would be and how much she would like it, but then she faced reality. She couldn't imagine being happy for long when love might be fleeting, and she definitely wanted children.

With sadness, she knew it wouldn't work for her. Their lives were on divergent tracks. She couldn't change and he couldn't change.

She pulled back to look at him. "I'm with you tonight."

He placed his fingers on her mouth. "Whatever your answer. Tell me in the morning. Give me tonight for certain, Julia," he said and she nodded, relief surging in her because it would be one more night with him.

"Very well," she said and held him tightly

That night they loved until dawn streaked the sky. She slept a brief time and woke in his arms. She turned to look at Nick. He was naked, warm, pressed tightly against her with his arm around her. Her hair spilled over his shoulder.

He opened his eyes to look at her. "Good morning," he said in a husky voice that held a note of intimacy. Her pulse raced and she leaned down to kiss him lightly on the mouth.

"Good morning yourself," she replied, tingling as he traced his forefinger over the curves of her breasts.

"Did you think about what I want? Will you move in with me, Julia? It's not far from your house."

"It's a heartbreak away. Nick, I can't. I told you that from the very first," she said.

To her surprise, he winced as if he'd received a blow. Then he drew her into his arms and kissed her passionately. He stopped abruptly and raised his head. "I want you. I need you in my life." Desire burned in his brown eyes and his voice was earnest.

"Nick, I don't want the temporary agreement," she explained, looking into his dark eyes while she felt as if her heart were splintering into a million shards of glass. "I love you. I may love you the rest of my life. Right now, I feel like I will."

"Then, dammit, move in with me. Maybe I'll want to marry after a time. Take a chance here, Julia. Let go your rigid rules."

"It isn't rules. I just think that your way holds much more chance for a dreadful heartbreak whereas now, I think I'll survive."

"You don't have to survive heartbreak," he persisted. "I love you and want you and maybe it'll turn into marriage. Give us a chance."

She hurt badly, wanting him and knowing everything he was telling her might be the best possible solution, but she didn't want to take that chance.

"What about children? You don't want them. I do. That's pretty simple and poles apart."

He inhaled and studied her. "I've never thought of myself in relation to having a family. It's been out from day one, but if you want a child—I'd think about it."

"That's not good enough," she said. "I want a child with the man I love more than I want anything else in life. You don't and that's your choice and you'll be happy with what you've chosen, but I can't change what I feel just so I can live with you and have the pleasure of your company for the next year."

He looked at her and desire blazed in his dark eyes. He tightened his arms and pulled her into his embrace while he kissed her until she shook and her head reeled and she wanted him to the exclusion of every other thought.

She wanted him inside her, wanted his strength and vitality and loving. But their values had come between them. She pushed against his chest.

He leaned away. "Julia—"

She placed her fingers on his lips. "Shh, Nick. Not now. We're on divergent paths, want different things in life. It's been wonderful. I'll give you back your pendant," she said, reaching behind her neck to unfasten the chain.

He caught her hands. "You keep it. I bought it for you and I want you to have it. You want me to walk out of your life, just like that?"

"It hurts to lose you and I think it's going to hurt for a long time, but I have to say goodbye."

"Dammit, Julia! Stop hurting both of us."

"It's a smaller hurt compared to a larger one later on," she said, struggling to hold back tears, letting her gaze roam over him, memorizing the sight of him.

"You don't know that. Give us a chance. I may change and want children. It's something I hadn't ever considered doing. Let me get used to the idea but don't leave me while I do."

"Nick, if you really loved me the way I love you and the way I want to be loved, we wouldn't be having this conversation," she said softly. "'I love you' rolls off your tongue with ease because you're practiced at it, but it's superficial. You don't love in life-and-death, love-forever way. That's what I want."

While silence stretched between them, they stared into each other's eyes. Nick inhaled and turned. "I guess it's time for me to get my things and go." She watched him leave the room.

She brushed back tears, hating that she couldn't control her emotions, hurting and feeling as if her insides were shattering. It was her heart breaking into pieces, she knew. She had loved him in spite of all her logic, common sense and warnings to herself. But who could stop love when it happened and when it was true and special and right?

"Nick," she cried lowly, letting tears fall and wondering how many years it had been since she had shed tears over anything.

She wiped away her tears and walked toward the front as he appeared. A muscle worked in his jaw and he was solemn, gazing intently at her. He crossed the hall to her and placed his hands on her waist. "So you're not giving us a chance? Or giving me a chance?"

"People don't change, Nick."

"They change constantly. I just can't promise anything more right now except that I love you and want you with me. That's a helluva lot, Julia," he added tightly.

Her insides clenched and she hurt. She didn't want him to go because when he went through the door, she knew he wouldn't be back. She flung her arms around his neck to kiss him hard and long.

He leaned over her, thrusting his tongue deep, a kiss that she would remember always. His tongue stroked hers, explored her mouth, firing up desire into fiery need. Suddenly he released her, his dark eyes searching hers.

"If that's what you want," he said. He walked past her, opened the door and strode outside. She couldn't see for a blur of tears. She hurt. She wanted to run to call him back. She felt as if he had yanked her heart out and was carrying it away with him.

But she let him go because she knew what she wanted wasn't what he wanted.

His car motor roared to life. She heard it fade away and then he was gone.

For one of the few times in her adult life, she sobbed. She hurt and she already missed him, and she wondered if she would hurt over him the rest of her life.

* * *

The next week Julia threw herself into her job because the transition would take a month. At present, all Holcomb employees were continuing with their regular tasks. She still worked in their building, but it would close at the end of the month. She had an offer from Nick's company, but the thought of seeing him daily at work was something she didn't want to deal with so, she had started sending out her résumé and making contacts for another job.

Wednesday morning, she stopped at her granddad's. She had never told him about Nick and there was no need to now. He knew something was wrong in her life, but he credited it to the buyout of Holcomb and she hadn't enlightened him about it.

As they sat over cups of coffee, he stared at her with a frown. "You're thinner. Don't take this so hard, honey. We'll get along and we're well fixed."

"I know. I've gotten some good job offers. Henry Banks wants me to work for them."

"Ah, that's good. Is it a good offer?"

"Yes, it is."

"You going to take it?"

"I have to interview with them and I want to take my time. I've signed up to tutor kids with reading two afternoons a week. I'll work my schedule around it."

"Julia, are you seeing Nick Ransome?"

Startled, she shook her head. "No, I'm not. I was, but I'm not any longer. It's over."

Rufus scowled at her. "Has he hurt you?"

"How did you know we've been seeing each other?" she asked, wondering who had told her grandfather and how long ago.

"I just heard you were," Rufus said, and she guessed that one of his friends had seen her out with Nick and told him.

She shrugged. "Well, we aren't anymore and I'm fine."

"No, you're not fine. You don't seem happy and you're losing weight. You're busier and busier, like you're trying to forget something."

"It was my choice, Granddad. Don't worry about it."

"Your not seeing him any longer—it's not because of me, is it?" Rufus asked.

"No!" Julia smiled and patted his hand. "Not at all." Glancing at her watch, she said, "I better go."

"You're getting your schedule solidly booked. Still working out?"

She nodded and stood, carrying her cup to the sink. "Yes, and I have to go now. I'll see you later this week."

"Pretty soon, you won't be able to work me into your busy schedule."

She smiled and hugged him. "Yes, I will. I'll always have time for you." She kissed his cheek and left to drive to work, thinking about her volunteer jobs. No matter how busy she kept, she missed Nick. It was worse than she had dreamed it would be.

She didn't want to eat. She couldn't sleep, no matter how hard she worked out or how many miles a day she ran.

She turned into her parking place and rushed to her office, pulling out ledgers and switching on her computer, trying to concentrate on figures and charts, but seeing dark brown eyes and remembering Nick and wanting him. Was life now so much better without him? She had to be honest with herself—there was nothing better about it.

Nick had transformed her world, making it into a special place. Her life had more zest, more excitement, with Nick in it. What happened each day was more interesting when she discussed it with him. And the hours of lovemaking—she ached for his kisses and his arms around her. She wanted his strong body pressed against hers.

With a groan, she ran her hand through her hair and wondered what she had settled for? An empty life with no children and no Nick? She knew she would never meet a man who excited her like Nick had. It had been a once-in-a-lifetime attraction.

Had she made the biggest mistake of her life? The question plagued her daily, and her longing for Nick increased instead of diminishing. She saw him everywhere she went, only it always turned out to be a stranger. She would glimpse a tall, dark-haired man in a crowd and her pulse would quicken. But when she looked, it would be someone else who really bore little resemblance to Nick.

He was in her thoughts most of the time. She desperately tried whatever she could do to think of other things. Nothing worked. Not going out with friends. Not throwing herself into exercise or work.

Nights were the worst time of all. She couldn't sleep and her big empty bed held too many memories of that last night with Nick. Too clearly, she remembered his strong, lithe body sprawled in her bed after making love. She remembered him crossing the room, naked, aroused, breathtaking.

She groaned and rolled over, getting out of bed and raking her hair away from her face. It had been three weeks and she was going crazy. She hurt, she missed him and she was beginning to wonder if that had been the worst mistake of her life.

She wondered about Nick. Did he even miss her? Had he suffered in the least? Did he have any regrets?

When Nick parted with Julia, he sped away without looking back. He could forget her. In his adult life, he had never had a broken heart, heartache, anyone he couldn't do without in his life. He wasn't going to now. The past was past, and he usually could shrug it away and never think about what might have been.

For the next week he worked in a frenzy, trying to shut out nagging thoughts and memories of Julia. By the week's end, he had to admit to himself that he failed miserably and still missed her. He was making mistakes at work because his mind was elsewhere, something that he had never done before in his life.

He packed and flew to his villa in Cozumel, running several hours a day, swimming, working out, trying to exhaust himself and get his mind off Julia. He did no better there about forgetting her or getting over her than he had at home.

He packed and flew back home, going to work grimly, passing her house each day without a glance, until he found a new route that was longer but disturbed him less.

Three weeks later, he stared out across his desk while he mulled over his life and his future.

Marriage with Julia. It was the first time he had considered it as a possibility. And it made his pulse race to think of her always there for him. Restless, he moved to the window and stood staring at traffic below, but seeing her in his arms. Marry Julia. Babies with Julia. He couldn't imagine. He didn't know kids or anything about them. But Julia in his life permanently—the thought made him feel better than he had since the day he had walked out of her house.

He rubbed his jaw and thought about his future. He didn't want to go out with another woman. He wanted Julia only. He had never felt this way in his life. From the very first meeting, everything with Julia had been different, an attraction that bound his heart with golden chains.

Business no longer mattered, and he was beginning to see what she was talking about when she said success wasn't everything. It wasn't anything without her.

"Nick?" Tyler said from the doorway.

"Yes?" Nick turned to stare at Tyler, trying to focus on him and get his thoughts off Julia.

"Do you have the letter you were going to send to Consolidated?"

"Consolidated?" Nick's mind went blank. He inhaled and shook his head. "Refresh my memory."

Frowning, Tyler came into the room and closed the door. "I don't know what's the matter with you—well, yes, I do. Dammit, Nick, go back to Mexico or call Julia Holcomb. You're going to hell in a handbasket here, and you'll take the company with you if you don't watch out."

"Sorry, Tyler. I may take a few days off."

"Take a month. I'll take care of things," Tyler said in a strained tone. "Dammit, go find another woman. Want me to introduce you to someone tonight? Someone that can take your mind off Julia?"

"No, but thanks," Nick answered. "I'll get that letter."

"Let me write it. No telling what you'd put in it," Tyler said darkly.

"You write it. I'm leaving the office."

Tyler nodded and stomped out, slamming the door behind him.

Nick rubbed his neck and glanced at his watch and thought about what he would like to do. He closed his computer and strode out, telling his secretary that he would check back with her, but he would be out of touch for a while and to let Tyler handle everything.

While his heart raced, he pulled out his cell phone to call Julia. Disappointment filled him when she didn't answer. Nor did he get a machine where he could leave a message. Annoyed, he broke the connection and climbed into his car, driving out of the lot and forgetting about the office immediately.

Nick ran errands and periodically tried to call Julia, but no answer. When he drove home, he passed her house, but he couldn't tell whether anyone was home or not. He sped up his drive and parked, striding into the house to strip and shower, his pulse humming. He intended to call her and see her. It was just a matter of time until he got in touch with her.

He dressed in navy slacks and a navy knit shirt. Whistling, on edge and wondering where she was, he tried again to call her.

He heard a car coming up the drive and went striding down to the door. Salesmen weren't allowed in the area, and his family never came without calling.

The engine stopped outside and he heard a car door slam. He went to the door and swung it wide. His heart thudded as he stared at Julia.

In the shade of his porch, the late-afternoon sunlight caught golden highlights in her hair. She looked pale and thinner. Her blue eyes were enormous as she gazed at him.

His insides clutched tightly. "Julia?"

Eleven

When Nick swung open the door, Julia's heart skipped a beat and words failed her. He was a darker tan, fit, so handsome he took her breath.

"Julia?" he repeated. "Come in. I tried to call you."

She stepped inside his quiet entryway, oblivious to her surroundings, seeing only Nick. Her heart pounded and she could only stare at him. "You called me?" she asked, wondering if she had heard correctly above the pounding of her heart. It had been a full three weeks and for all she knew, there could be someone else in Nick's life now. Solemnly, she gazed at him.

They stared at each other, sparks dancing between them. She wanted him as she had never wanted anyone or dreamed she could want someone.

"I was wrong," she said, the words tumbling out quickly. "I want you in my life whatever way I can."

He looked as if she had knocked the breath out of him. He rocked back and blinked. Then he closed the space between them, taking her in his arms to kiss her.

The minute his mouth covered hers and his tongue thrust into her mouth, she knew what he wanted. There was no question of his desire, no doubt he had missed her as much as she had missed him.

"Nick!" she cried, flinging her arms around his neck and kissing him with a hungry desperation that matched his own. He leaned over her, his tongue stroking hers while his hands slid all over her as if he were reassuring himself that she was really there.

She tugged free his buttons and they undressed each other frantically. Nick shook as much as she did.

"It's been forever," she whispered, her hands playing over his strong, naked body. "I'm on the Pill now—" she said softly and then words were gone as he lowered her to the floor and moved between her legs.

"You're my love, Julia," he rasped the words and thrust into her. She wrapped her legs around him, holding him fiercely, moving with him while joy filled her. Nick was in her arms and he wanted her!

Their lovemaking was frantic and when release came, she held him tightly.

"I love you, darlin'," he choked out. Sweat beaded his brow, and he thrust fast and hard, carrying her to a second climax.

"Ah, darlin'." She came down from over the moon, floating in ecstasy, her rapture complete in the knowledge that he wanted her as badly as she wanted him.

"Nick, I missed you," she said, showering kisses on his face, biting his shoulder lightly, running her hands over him as if she still couldn't believe that he was in her arms.

"You couldn't have missed me as much as I did you," Nick protested, drawing his fingers along her cheek. Their breathing was ragged, and she could still feel his heart pounding. "I've thought about you constantly," he said.

His words thrilled her and she buried her face against his throat, breathing the scent of him, relishing every inch of him. "Nick, Nick," she said, over and over, delirious with joy to be in his arms and be able to love him again.

He turned on his side, taking her with him. He glanced around. "We're on the marble floor. Next time, I promise a bed."

"Don't make promises you can't keep. Next time may be in your shower," she said lightly, feeling giddy with happiness. "And I know we're on a marble floor. Now I know it—I didn't until a few seconds ago."

"You were my cushion," he said, stroking her hair away from her face and tucking strands behind her ear.

She framed his face with her hand. "I was wrong, Nick. I can't get along without you. My life was empty and lonely and dreadful without you in it. I'll move in with you if you want me."

"Ah, darlin', if I want you. I don't want to let go of you at all. Let's go see about that shower and whatever else we can do. I'm not sure my knees will work yet, but I'll try."

"You feel as if you've been working out big-time," she said, running her hands down his arms.

"I have," he said, standing and lifting her in his arms easily. "I swim, I jog, I ride, I've done everything I can to exhaust myself and to try to forget you for a few minutes each day."

"Have you really?" she asked, amazed by his declaration.

"Don't act so surprised," he said. "You left a void in my life that was enormous."

"I find that difficult to believe," she said. "At least the last part. You must have been working out to take the stairs the way you just did."

He set her down in his shower and turned warm water over both of them. They showered and dried each other. He drew the towel slowly over her, inching his way down her backside and then just as leisurely down her front.

"Nick!" she gasped, winding her fingers in his hair.

"We just set a record for fast. Now we'll try to set one for slow," he said, nuzzling her throat and moving slowly down her body.

They made love leisurely, moving to the bedroom, loving in his big bed.

Afterwards, they held each other tightly.

"We shouldn't have waited so long," she whispered. "I've been miserable."

He propped himself up to look down at her while she pulled the sheet up beneath her arms. "You'll move in with me?" he asked, watching her closely.

She placed her hand against his face. "Yes, I will. Life was nothing without you, Nick," she said solemnly. Something flickered in the depths of his eyes before he leaned down to kiss her for a long time, a kiss of satisfaction and union.

When he raised his head, he stood. "Don't go away," he said, and turned to cross the room to his dresser.

She watched him, her gaze drifting over his nude body that was superbly fit. "You were sexy and had muscles before. Now you really do."

"I glad you like what you see because it's yours." He sat beside her and pulled the sheet across his hips. "I missed you more than you could possibly have missed me. You said you were wrong. I was the one who was wrong, Julia," he said solemnly and her breath caught.

"I thought about life without you, about marriage, about children. I don't know anything about children, so that's a blank, but I don't want life without you. I want to marry you. Will you marry me?"

Stunned, joy filled her and she gasped, crying out and throwing her arms around his neck, knocking him off balance. She shrieked as they tumbled to the floor and she fell on top of him. Laughing, they rolled over. "Yes! Yes, I'll marry you!" she cried, hugging his neck and then kissing him hard.

In minutes, he sat up while she wriggled to sit on the floor facing him. She yanked the sheet up beneath her arms and gazed into his warm, brown eyes. "You will marry me?" he asked again.

"Yes, Nick, I'll marry you," she replied, happiness keeping her from sitting still as she wriggled and bounced slightly. He took her hand and hunted around on the floor, picked up a ring and slid it on her finger.

She gasped at the sight of the huge diamond that sparkled and caught the light. "Nick! It's gorgeous! It's fantastic!"

"Good. I'm glad you like it," he said with satisfaction.

She tore her attention from her ring to look at him and placed her hand against his cheek again. "You're sure that you want marriage?"

"Positively. I was the one who was wrong, Julia. I want it permanent. I don't ever want to be without you and your love."

"We can have children?" she asked cautiously.

"As many as you want," he said.

"Oh, Nick!" Sliding into his lap, she wrapped her arms around his neck as she let out a sigh. "This is the best day of my life."

"It'll just get better," he said, brushing kisses on her temple.

"I'll have to tell Granddad. Someone told him we were seeing each other. And your family—your father will hate me."

"No, he won't. Once you're in our family, you'll be a Ransome and he'll like you. Now your granddad is another matter. If those two old coots don't want to come to our wedding, I don't care."

"Granddad will come. He'll walk down the aisle with me."

"You want a big wedding?"

"Yes! I want the world to come! Actually, not that big."

"How long is this going to take, Julia? I want to get married tomorrow."

She grinned at him, feeling giddy still. "I can do the whole thing in a month."

"A month!" He groaned. "I don't want to wait."

"You can wait that long and part of the time, I'll be right here, waiting with you," she said, wiggling her hand and looking at her dazzling ring. She smiled at him and ran her fingers through his thick curls. "It's gorgeous, Nick! I never dreamed this was possible."

"Whatever you want, sweetie," he drawled, running his finger across the top of the sheet and over the full curve of her breasts. "I love you, Julia. I want you always."

"Thank goodness, you do! Let's go tell our families and plan this wedding."

He grinned and shook his head as she stood, tugged on his wrist and reached for the phone.

Epilogue

The last week of August, Julia dressed with care, her heart beating eagerly as she smoothed the white satin skirt over her hips. Katherine shook Julia's train and shifted the veil. Katherine was a bridesmaid and wore a simple red dress with a long skirt and spaghetti straps. "You look beautiful," Katherine said solemnly.

Julia gazed at her reflection, unable to believe the day had finally arrived. Her engagement ring caught reflections of light, sparkling as she moved her hands.

"You do look gorgeous," Olivia said. Her red dress was identical to Katherine's.

"Everyone looks beautiful," the tall, black-haired wedding planner said, beaming at them and smoothing Olivia's skirt.

"I can't believe both my brothers will be married," Katherine remarked. "Somehow, I never expected it from Nick, but I'm glad. He'll be a nicer person."

"I think so," Julia said, laughing and feeling giddy. Her pulse skipped and raced with excitement. Tingles danced in her and she couldn't stop smiling. She also couldn't wait to see Nick and was glad they were having a morning wedding.

"It's time to go," the wedding planner said, and the bridesmaids went out ahead of Julia. She had three friends who were attendants, plus Olivia and Katherine who would soon be in-laws. Her granddad met her in the foyer and she smiled at him. She paused to straighten his tie and the photographer took their picture.

"How handsome you look!" she exclaimed.

"Hmmph! I probably should be packing with that scoundrel Duke Ransome here."

"Granddad, you promised!" Julia said, giving him a harsh look.

He clamped his mouth shut. "I'll remember and be nice to the Ransomes, although how you could marry one, I don't know."

"I hope you give Nick a chance," she said lightly. "Ready?"

He looked at her and placed his hands on her shoulders. "You're lovely, Julia. All grown up and a beautiful woman. I wish your momma and daddy could see you. And your grandmomma."

"I know," she said quietly. She brushed a kiss on his cheek. "At least I have you."

"Time, Miss Holcomb," the wedding planner said.

Julia turned and linked her arm through her grandfather's. She waited to begin, but already her gaze had gone to the tall, handsome man who waited at the altar and who was watching her now.

The moment she met his gaze, her heart leaped. Joy filled her and she couldn't wait to walk down the aisle, repeat vows and become his wife.

Then they were moving, walking past guests and flowers and garlands, but all she could see was Nick and his dark eyes on her. She might as well have been alone with him. Love for him filled her, and she felt as if she were the luckiest woman on earth that morning.

Her grandfather placed her hand in Nick's warm hand. Nick smiled at her and she smiled in turn. "I love you," she silently mouthed the words to him and he winked at her.

Then they turned to repeat their vows. She stood in a dream world, only it was real—she was actually going to be Nick's wife in minutes.

"I now declare you man and wife," the minister finally announced, introducing them to the guests as Mr. and Mrs. Nicholas Ransome.

"You may kiss the bride."

She turned to Nick, who raised her veil and placed his hand lightly on her waist. His brown eyes were warm with love, and her happiness bubbled in her. When he leaned down to kiss her lightly, his lips were a warm promise. "I love you," he whispered. "You've made me the happiest man on earth today," he said.

"Nick, it's fabulous!" she exclaimed, smiling at him.

Taking her arm, he walked up the aisle beside her. As she passed him, she glanced into Duke's cold blue eyes and wondered if she would ever win over Nick's father. Then the thought was gone, and she didn't care. She couldn't worry about him when Nick kept repeating he loved her.

With a fanfare of trumpets, they rushed up the aisle and into the narthex. Immediately, friends showered them with congratulations until Nick led her through a door. "We have to go back around for pictures," he said, leading her through another door.

"I don't think you're going the way they told us to," she said. He entered a small office and closed the door.

"I'm sure as hell not. I wanted you to myself for a minute," he said, pulling her into his arms, bending over her until she had to cling to his shoulders as she was almost off her feet. His love poured into his kiss while she held him and kissed him in return.

Finally she pulled away slightly. "Let me up, Nick! They'll be searching all over for us and I'll be all rumpled."

He laughed and swung her up. "I can't wait to get you alone and peel you out of everything. I want you naked in my arms for the entire honeymoon!"

She wiggled her hips. "Just you wait," she purred seductively. "I'll make you want to keep your clothes off for the honeymoon, too."

He inhaled and his smile vanished, fires of longing flashing in the depths of his brown eyes. "Dammit, Julia, do you know what you're doing to me!" he growled reaching for her.

With an impish grin, she dodged his grasp. "We better go, Mr. Ransome, so you can get your picture taken with your new wife who can't wait to get your pants off."

"Julia!"

Laughing, she opened the door and stepped into the hall. "Now where do we go to get to the front of the church for pictures."

"You bawdy wench!" Nick growled and turned her to kiss her passionately until she pushed against him.

"Now you've done it! Look at my veil."

He straightened it. "You asked for that kiss."

"I most certainly did not, but we're going to be late—"

"Nick!" came a call.

"That's Katherine. C'mon," Nick said taking her hand.

They posed for pictures and then left for the reception at a country club. A band played, tables were laden with food and the room was filled with the scent of garlands of white roses that decorated the large reception room. From the moment they arrived, Nick and Julia were besieged by well-wishing friends.

Later, Nick led Julia onto the dance floor for the first dance. "Don't be surprised if my father wants a dance."

"I'll faint in shock. He is glaring arrows through me."

"No. He'll change. You're in the family now. Just like Olivia. He tried to buy her off to keep her from marrying Matt."

"No!" Julia exclaimed, realizing where Nick might have gotten his ruthless streak.

Nick nodded. "Matt told me. My dad will go to great lengths to get what he wants."

"I'm not saying anything bad about anybody on this very special day in our lives. Nick, I love you," she said. "You're going to have to get used to hearing me say that over and over."

"I'll never hear it too much," he answered solemnly. "It scares me when I think I almost lost you. If you'd met someone else and fallen in love—"

"That was impossible, so forget it. I was already madly, madly in love with you."

"Good thing," he said, swirling her around on the dance floor. As the number ended, Nick looked over her head. "Here comes my brother."

"Will you give up your bride for one dance with her new brother-in-law?" Matt asked and, without waiting for Nick's answer, looked at Julia. "May I have this dance, sis?"

She laughed and took his hand. As they danced away from Nick, she looked up at Matt. "'Sis.' That sounds wonderful. I'm an only child. I've always longed for a family and finally, now I have one."

"You'll be good for Nick. I've never seen him this relaxed and happy."

"Your dad, on the other hand, wishes the ground would swallow me."

"He'll come around, maybe faster than your grandfather who hasn't shaken hands with any of us yet."

"He hasn't?" she asked, surprised after her lecture to her grandfather.

"Uh-oh. Shouldn't have told you. Don't go fuss at him. He doesn't have to be buddies with us."

"No, but he needs to be civil."

"Leave him alone. We'll all get along. And Dad will thaw. He always does. Watch him with Olivia. He wouldn't speak to her when we married."

"You'd never know it now," Julia said, thinking how she had seen Duke Ransome talking to Olivia often during the wedding activities.

"That's because she has the first Ransome grandbaby. Now he's as good as he can be to her. He comes by the house with baby presents, built a nursery in his house. He can do an about-face before you know it. Now on another subject, I hope you're happy, Julia. I know Nick is."

"I'm deliriously happy. I love him with all my heart."

"Good." Matt spun her around and they danced easily together. The minute the music stopped, she turned to face her grandfather.

"My turn next," he said, nodding at Matt.

She stepped into his arms and danced, and then Nick claimed her. "I know we have to stay for a couple of hours, but then we're out of here."

"Sounds fine to me," she replied, looking up at her handsome husband and wanting to be alone with him.

She drifted through the reception in euphoria, constantly looking at Nick when he was away from her, touching him if he stood close. Joy bubbled in her and she knew she would remember this day all her life.

It was three hours before Nick appeared at her side and took her hand.

"Now's the time, Mrs. Ransome. We're making a break for it. Don't stop for anything."

"Nick. I need to change and we need to tell the family goodbye."

"I told everyone for both of us except your grandfather. We can catch him on the way out, and you leave in your wedding dress. You can change later."

"I have a gorgeous dress in the dressing room."

"I'm sure you do and after we get back from our honeymoon, I'll really appreciate it when I take you out, but right now, we're going to escape. That means we run just as we are. The limo is ready and waiting."

"Nick, we can't—"

"Yes, we can," he said, taking a tighter grip on her hand. "Let's tell Granddad goodbye."

Laughing, she hurried with him to kiss her grandfather. Then they went out through the kitchen and into a delivery area behind. A white stretch limo waited, and a chauffeur opened the door. She climbed in, dropping into a seat and laughing as Nick climbed in and sat beside her.

In minutes, they were moving through traffic. "A perfect getaway."

"Now where are we going?" she asked. "You said you had a surprise."

"How's the Plaza in New York and then on to a villa on the Mediterranean?"

"Fabulous," she said, running her hand along his thigh and swinging her legs across his. "I'll never see any of it."

"You will when we go back on our anniversaries," he said as he wrapped his arms around her and leaned forward to kiss her. He slid his hand down the neck of her dress, caressing her breast until she grasped his wrist.

"Nick, we're not alone here."

"We can be, almost," he said, closing the partition between them and the chauffeur. He turned back to kiss her and she wrapped her arms around his neck.

"I'm not sure I can wait until we get to New York," she said softly.

"You're not going to have to. Tonight is the bridal suite at the Fairmont in Dallas only a short drive away from the country club."

"Why, bless you, Mr. Ransome!" she drawled in a throaty voice. "You do think of everything."

He laughed and tightened his arm around her waist. "It's going to be wonderful, Julia."

"It is, Nick."

Just as he promised, they reached the hotel in a short time. She was aware of heads turning as they crossed the lobby to the elevators. "Everyone is staring at us."

"No, they're drooling over you. The women are thinking how beautiful you are and I don't want to tell you what the men are thinking, but I'm getting you out of here as fast as I possibly can."

Laughing, she walked closely beside him as they followed a bellhop to their suite on the top floor. As soon as they were alone and the door closed behind them, Nick reached to pull her into his arms.

"Welcome home, Mrs. Ransome."

"I love you, Nick. This has been the most wonderful day of my life."

"I want to try to make it the most wonderful night," he said softly, trailing kisses along her throat as he carefully unfastened her veil and tossed it on a chair while he kissed her. His kiss was reassurance, satisfaction, promises, as seductive as ever. She kissed him in return as her heart pounded with joy.

Standing on her toes, she kicked off her shoes and wrapped one arm around his neck while she unfastened his shirt with her other hand. "I love you, love you," she whispered, embracing her tall, handsome husband. Her joy was complete. "Life will be good, Nick," she said and kissed away his answer.

* * * * *

SCANDALS FROM THE THIRD BRIDE

BY
SARA ORWIG

Special thanks to my editors,
Jessica Alvarez and Melissa Jeglinski.

One

After a short drumroll from the band, the emcee, Lance Wocek, stepped forward. "Here's our own beautiful Katherine Ransome," he announced, taking her hand, "talented artist, successful businesswoman and stunning bachelorette."

Smiling into the ring of bright spotlights on Fort Worth's Oak Hill Country Club's impromptu stage, Katherine waved to no one in particular. The patrons in tuxes and designer dresses made a ritzy gala of the elegant charity benefit for homeless children. Katherine was in sympathy with the cause, but she wished again that she had written a check instead of participating herself.

"Gentlemen, for an evening with the charming and beautiful Miss Ransome, what am I bid?" Lance asked. "Who'll start the bidding?"

"One thousand dollars," called a male voice and guests applauded. Trying to gaze beyond the lights, Katherine looked at a blur of faces turned in her direction, probably men she had known all her life.

"One thousand dollars! Good start! What am I bid?" Lance asked, circling and smiling at his audience.

"Two thousand," a man called, and she recognized local attorney Wes Trentwood's voice. She was glad men were bidding, remembering her brothers teasing her that no one would bid because she had been so cool in the past to the local males. So far, between the two bidders, she preferred an evening with Wes to anyone else.

"Two thousand dollars," Lance repeated. "We have a bid of two thousand dollars. Who'll make it three thousand for an evening with one of the most gorgeous ladies in the county?"

"Three thousand," came another bid that was raised immediately to four.

"I bid five hundred thousand dollars," a deep male voice said.

While an audible gasp rippled through the room, heads turned. Stunned that anyone would pay so much for an evening with her, Katherine peered in the direction of the voice.

As she watched, a man stood and applause broke out over his bid. He threaded his way between the tables of onlookers. Unable to distinguish his features because of the lights, Katherine could see his black hair and broad shoulders. He wasn't local, yet something about him struck a chord of familiarity. She could only stare in amazement, and then she reminded herself the money went to a good cause and his bid was a magnanimous donation.

As he approached the stage, even though she couldn't see him well because of the blinding lights, she discerned that he was tall and moved with the grace of a panther.

As he narrowed the distance between them, her heart thudded.

Katherine's pulse roared in her ears. Time hung suspended while she was flung back nine years. For an infinitesimal second, everything in her cried out to throw her arms around his neck and hug him. He stood as still as she, and the electricity jumping between them made her wonder why flames didn't scorch the air.

Her brain began to function, and the moment was gone. Longing vanished, replaced by surprise.

Dressed in a black tux and a snowy white shirt, he stopped in front of her and looked at her solemnly. "You're more beautiful than ever."

She knew his voice, knew the pitch and timbre, knew his brown eyes. Even if he had changed in appearance and manner, his voice was the same and sent tingles spiraling through her as if he had touched her.

Dismayed, she gazed at him while her head spun and her heart pounded, drowning out all noise. For an instant she thought she would faint.

"Cade," she whispered. Cade Logan, the man she had planned to marry was standing in front of her, close enough for her to touch. It was her first time to see him in nine long years, since the week before their wedding.

Lance spoke to Cade or to her. She had no idea which one. Someone called Lance's name and he excused himself, leaving without either one of them answering him.

She was held in a gaze that shut off the rest of the world. Nine years ago and suddenly, here Cade was standing before her. She had thought about this occasion over and over again, and played multiple versions of it in her mind. Now that it was actually happening, she was unprepared, and the moment wasn't like anything she had rehearsed in her fantasies.

Everything in her screamed a protest. And deep down, most disturbing of all, her first thought was, he was too handsome for words. She had a response to him that she despised, yet could not control. Her reaction rocked her because she had thought she was over him long ago and immune to ever seeing him again. There was nothing resistant in her system. Every nerve was raw; the beat of her heart was faster.

He stood holding out his hand to her. She moved automatically, going through the motions without thinking about them, numb as she offered her hand. His warm hand enveloped hers in a surprisingly gentle shake, and the moment they touched, an electric jolt went to her toes.

She yanked her hand away and narrowed her eyes, while her anger surfaced and overrode other emotions.

Rage, pure and deep, shook Katherine, sending tremors through her body. She wanted to wave her fists and shout at Cade, to scream at him and pound on his chest. Instead, she lifted her chin and gazed away coolly in disdain as if she hadn't even recognized him.

"This is Friday night. As I understand it, I've acquired the privilege of taking you to dinner tomorrow night," Cade said. She ached to decline. But she had made a commitment and little kids were depending on her.

"How dare you! How can you show up here like this?" she hissed between clenched teeth unable to hold back, yet aware they still stood spotlighted on stage. Her fists doubled and she shook. "You can't possibly expect me to go out with you, of all people."

"I not only expect it, I just paid a hell of a lot of money for the evening with you," he answered quietly, thoroughly scrutinizing her, which only heightened her fury.

"There are several others you can take to dinner tomorrow night who will be much more receptive. Perhaps you'd rather go with someone else."

"No, Katherine. I knew what I was doing when I bid for an evening with you," he answered with a note of steel in his voice. Beneath her anger was a dim awareness that he was far more self-assured and confident than he had been nine years ago. He had to be worth a royal fortune to have tossed away five hundred thousand dollars to go out for a few hours with her. Occasionally, she had read about him in newspapers or seen articles or pictures in magazines and she knew he was a successful business entrepreneur, but she hadn't dreamed the extent of his fortune. How had he made so much money in such a short time? Why was he back? Questions buzzed in her head.

Lance returned and his voice finally penetrated her shock. Lance extended his hand toward Cade and they shook hands.

"Thank you, sir, for your overwhelming donation to this fine cause. Your generosity will be deeply appreciated for years to come. You'll change many children's lives. And in return, you get an evening out with one of Fort Worth's most beautiful women, Katherine Ransome.

"Before we go any further, let me introduce myself. I'm Lance Wocek. We're overwhelmed by your donation that's the largest we've ever had in any local charity event from a single donor that I recall." He looked expectantly at Cade.

"Lance, you two know each other," Katherine interjected in a tight voice. The two men had grown up in Cedar County and gone through Rincon High School together and she had been four years behind them. "Remember Cade Logan?" she asked. "Cade, I'm sure you recall Lance."

Lance's jaw dropped, and his eyes grew round while he stared at Cade. "Cade Logan? From high school? You've changed," he stammered. "I didn't recognize you," Lance said as if talking to himself, and Katherine remembered the wild, slender boy who had won her love.

She could clearly see his shaggy long hair, tattered T-shirts and faded jeans and she had to concede that he did look different. She herself hadn't recognized him at first. She surveyed the differences, noticing he had filled out his lanky six-foot-four-inch frame with broad shoulders. His black hair was neatly trimmed and combed. There was a subtle difference in his demeanor, a presence about him that indicated a "take charge" personality that hadn't been there before.

But the sexy bedroom eyes with thick lashes were the same. He could still flash the penetrating look that always made her feel as if he knew her every thought. His full, sensual lower lip was the same, as was his wide, sculpted mouth.

"I'm the same Cade Logan," Cade said easily. "It's been a while."

"None of us—" Suddenly Lance broke off and looked back and forth between Katherine and Cade. "You two..." His voice trailed away, and he looked stricken.

"I'll make arrangements with Katherine for our evening together," Cade said smoothly. "I have a check here for the five hundred thousand. Shall I make it out to the Slade House Children's Foundation?" Cade asked, pulling out his checkbook and pen.

"That'll be fine," Lance said, staring at Cade until someone spoke to him and he had to turn away again.

Katherine couldn't believe what was happening. She hoped it was a nightmare that would vanish upon waking.

Only it wasn't disappearing. Cade gazed at her with unfathomable brown eyes, and she didn't have any idea what was running through his mind.

"Why are you doing this? You can't possibly want to go out with me."

"I think I've shown that I do want to go out with you. I want to see you and this was the quickest, simplest way to do so."

"It was rather costly."

"I didn't want to hassle over you with someone, nor did I want you to back out of the evening. It's far more difficult to change your mind and your promise when so much is at stake for the kids."

"Your donation will be wonderful for the charity."

"I was happy to help that cause. Where should I pick you up and how is six?"

"Six is way too early," she said, hoping she could go late and come home early. You can pick me up at this address," she said, opening a small, black bag and producing one of her business cards. She turned it over, retrieved a pen and scribbled her address before handing the card to him. Again his fingers brushed hers and sent another electrifying jolt to her system.

He glanced at it, looking from it to her in a curious scrutiny that made her want to fidget and ask him what he was thinking.

Instead, she gazed coolly back at him and hoped he couldn't detect her racing pulse or ragged breathing or any other reaction she was having to seeing him. Why was he here? The big question had always been why had he left, but now, the answer to why he had returned was more pressing.

"Have you had dinner tonight?" he asked.

"No, I haven't, but if we go out tonight, that's the night you just bid for and won."

"That's fair enough," he said. "Can you leave now?"

"Leave? They'll serve a very elegant dinner here. That's part of the evening. Then there's dancing afterward," she said, unable to think about dancing with him and being in his arms again.

"I'd rather get out of here where we can be to ourselves. I don't care to be interrupted all evening. Is there any arrangement that as a participant you have to stay?"

"No, not at all. My part in the auction is over. I'll tell them I'm leaving and join you at the door," she said, both relieved they would get the evening together over quickly and on edge about going out with him.

If she ever saw him again, she had always expected that she would hate him, but that wasn't what she felt. Fury was dominant, but she responded to him as a female would to a sexy, appealing male. The evening alone with him made her tingly and excited even though she didn't want it to.

After telling a coordinator she was leaving, Katherine hurried to one of the private rooms that the bachelorettes had been given to use as a dressing room. She paused to look at herself in the mirror, glancing swiftly over her sequined sleeveless black dress with a low-cut vee neckline. She wore high-heeled black pumps.

Taking a deep breath, she left, hurrying toward the exit and experiencing another jolt when her gaze met Cade's as he watched her approach. A few hours with him and the evening would be over, she reminded herself. She could guard her heart and emotions for that long, surely.

He held the door open for her and then walked beside her, sliding his arm around her waist while they stepped outside into a cool October night. She felt the light contact with Cade as if it were a burning brand. She was prickly with raw awareness of his shoulder against hers, his arm circling her waist and her hip lightly touching his.

In the front of the club at the porte cochere, a limousine waited with a driver, who opened the door for her. Cade climbed in and sat beside her, turning slightly to face her.

Gazing back at him, she almost felt as if she were with a stranger. She didn't know Cade any longer. There was only a dim connection to the boy he once was and the person she knew. Yet there was no way to wipe out memories or her hurt or her anger.

"Why are you here?" she asked bluntly.

"Reasonable question. Some curiosity about you and my past. But that part is minor."

"So what's the big reason?" she persisted.

"I've found that ninety-nine percent of the time, when you purchase something, it's worth the difference to get the best."

"So you're here in Fort Worth to get the best of whatever it is you want."

"That's right. Why were you in the bachelorette auction?"

"The Slade Home is one of my favorite projects. Little children shouldn't be on the streets. You helped the children enormously tonight," she said, aware that he deserved thanks for what he had done for the kids.

"But, at the same time, you'd rather I hadn't bid."

"No. The money is more important and it'll do many needed things," she said, thinking how bland their conversation was while sparks ignited the air between them, and she fought the attraction for him that pulled at her as if he had never walked out and the past hadn't been filled with hurt.

"You could have written a check to the charity, so I'll inquire again, why did you participate?" he persisted.

"I've been asking myself that all evening," she remarked dryly, still having the feeling of talking to a stranger, except for his voice. She knew his voice. Even his hands were different—larger, less roughened.

"So the men who bid didn't particularly mean anything to you?"

"Not at all. I recognized one man and we're friends. Where do you live?" she asked, curious in spite of wanting to ignore Cade.

"I live most of the year in Los Angeles, part of the time in Pebble Beach, part of the time in Switzerland. I'm building a house in Houston."

"You've done well. Sometimes I've read about you," she said. "According to the papers, you're an entrepreneur involved in investments and finance," she said, leaving out that every time she had read about him, she had wondered how someone who had been penniless and a high school dropout— a mechanic whose expertise had been bikes and cars—could have investments, but she didn't want to give him the satisfaction of asking about his life.

"Katie," he said, reverting back to the name he had always called her.

"It's Katherine," she snapped. "I don't care to be called Katie by anyone."

"Very well, Katherine," he said in a flat tone of voice that gave no indication of what he really felt.

There was no wedding ring on his finger, nor would there have been if he'd bid for her time for an evening. Cade had been wild, the local bad boy. Friends had warned her he would never settle and he wouldn't go through with the wedding. And they had been correct in their dire predictions.

"You've done well," he remarked.

"I enjoy my work," she said, wondering how he knew anything about her business. She became silently aware they were in downtown Fort Worth now. She gazed at the tall building that held Ransome Design, Incorporated. She had two floors and sixty employees and she dreamed of opening more offices. Her company was growing fast and she usually experienced a rush of pleasure on viewing the building with her office, but her emotions churned over Cade, and she didn't feel the customary satisfaction. Thanks partially to the man seated facing her, her work was her life.

She turned to find him watching her.

"A penny for your thoughts," he said quietly. "As the old saying goes."

"It won't cost you even a cent. I was looking at the building where I have my business."

"Ransome Design, Incorporated had a very impressive twenty percent growth over a year ago. You've made a name for yourself, too."

"My job is my whole life," she said. "I suspect you can understand that."

He shrugged one shoulder casually. "There are other things more important," he said, his dark gaze boring into her.

"Not in my life," she answered and turned away to look out the window again. She could feel his gaze remaining on her and she wished she could lose the prickly awareness of him, the attraction that made him larger-than-life in too many ways.

She had no inclination to engage in conversation with Cade. She stayed on a raw edge, hanging on to her temper and all the accusations she had accumulated over time.

She wondered what was going through his mind, because he was quiet and didn't try to engage her in any polite conversation, which would have been pointless.

She didn't want to be alone with him. She didn't want to be with him, period. In her peripheral vision, she could see him, and while she tried to ignore him, it was impossible. His long legs were stretched out near hers.

In minutes they stopped in front of another tall building and she realized their destination was the exclusive and prestigious Millington Club on the twenty-sixth floor. Her father belonged to the Millington, as well as the Petroleum Club, and she was surprised Cade even knew about it. She was certain he had known nothing about the exclusive clubs when he was growing up in Rincon in Cedar County, Texas.

They rode the elevator and emerged at a reception area with a thick navy carpet and mahogany furniture. To her surprise, she realized Cade had reservations. She watched while he talked to the maitre d'. As the two men conversed briefly, her gaze ran down the length of Cade, and she remembered exactly how it felt to be in his arms, pressed against that strong, hard body, his legs tangled with hers. Heat coiled low inside her and she clenched her fists, trying to ignore feelings and banish memories and desire.

He wore a simple watch with a leather band, but in the limo she had seen his watch was one of the most expensive brands. She suspected he'd meant what he'd said about having the best. And who was the woman in his life now? Cade wouldn't be without one.

When he turned to take her arm, his hand touching her was as electrifying as any other contact they had had tonight. Trying to ignore everything about him and continually failing,

Katherine walked beside him as they were shown to a linen-covered table beside floor-to-ceiling windows that overlooked the bright city lights. Soft piano music played and couples already were on the dance floor. She gazed across the table into Cade's dark eyes.

"As I recall you like prime rib and they serve it here," he said, and she drew a deep breath. Pain and fury and surprise mixed in her that he would remember. "We weren't into drinking wine, so I don't know your preference there," he said.

"My tastes have changed and tonight, I think I'll start with a cup of black coffee," Katherine said, intending to keep as clear a head as possible around Cade. She saw a flare of amusement in his dark eyes as he ordered white wine for himself.

"You're an entrepreneur, so what's your latest project?" she asked, not caring, just wanting to get to an impersonal topic.

"I just acquired a film company. The news became public yesterday."

She remembered seeing an article in the paper that she had merely glanced at without making the connection to Cade. She did remember it was one of the oldest and one of the last still family-owned. "I saw that the studio sold," she admitted, "but I didn't take the time to read about who had bought the business. I didn't think about it being you. You're going into show business—are you seeing an actress?"

"No. It was good investment and the company was on shaky footing and about to go under. As far as an actress is concerned, at the moment there's no woman in my life."

"I find that difficult to imagine," she remarked dryly and he smiled, a smile that took her breath and hurt. Creases bracketed his mouth and memories tore at her. To escape from her tormenting thoughts, she picked up a thick black folder and opened it to study the menu.

"It's true, there's nobody," he commented. "Who's the man in your life, Katherine?"

"There isn't one. I wouldn't have been in the bachelorette auction if there was anyone on a serious basis. There isn't even anyone on a not-so-serious basis. I spend most of my time involved in my work."

"Then we're alike there," he said. "I could have given you the same answer. So there's no particular man in your life right now and no woman in mine."

"Don't make anything of that," she said sharply. "For me, it means nothing. And it doesn't matter."

His gaze caught and held hers in another penetrating look that made her wonder what he was thinking. Could he feel her rage? If he did, it didn't disturb him, but then, why should it? He hadn't cared when he had walked out on her without a word only a week before their wedding.

"I can't believe you would come back to Texas. When I look at you, Cade, all I feel is hurt and anger and hate!" she admitted, the words pouring out, yet an inner voice screamed she felt something else, too. Attraction was hot, volatile, impossible to ignore.

She became silent when the sommelier came to the table to open wine for Cade and let him approve the selection. While Cade's wine was being poured, a waiter came to pour her steaming black coffee and ice water for both Cade and her.

Once they were alone again, Cade raised his wineglass. "Here's to our efforts tonight to help children." His dark eyes were riveting and held her, fanning her desire. It was an effort to tear her gaze from him.

"I'll drink to that," she said, picking up her water and reaching out to touch Cade's goblet lightly. His hand touched hers and he watched her as they sipped.

"How civilized we're being," she said in a tight voice, grinding out the words and unable to contain her fury. "All I want to do is shout and scream at you."

"I can understand. We hurt each other, Katherine," he said solemnly.

"Then why did you come back here to open it all up?" she asked, wondering again where *each other* came in and how she could possibly have hurt him? She couldn't guess how he had twisted the past in his mind because there was no earthly way she had done anything at the time to cause him pain and she wanted to fling that fact right back at him, but she clamped her mouth shut.

"The past is far behind us and we've both moved on," he said. "I expected to find you married with a family."

"I'm married to my work," she remarked. "You gave me a convoluted answer when I asked why you're here and why you wanted an evening with me. What's the real reason?"

TWO

"I've seen some of the work you've done. It's fabulous," Cade said. "I have a project I want to discuss. I hope to hire you."

She gazed at him coolly. "I won't work for you, Cade. How dare you waltz in and expect to hire me!"

"I could have sent someone with a corporation name you'd never have recognized. You would have taken the job. As a matter of fact, until a few days ago, that's what I intended to do. At first, I thought it would be best if our paths never crossed. I wasn't any more eager to see you than you have been to see me."

"So what made you change your mind?"

"I realized that as soon as you learned who owned the house, you might have walked out. Of course, I could have kept you from ever knowing. I have companies that you'd have to investigate to know that I own them, and I doubt if you check on all your clients."

"No. I've never seen any need to do so."

"I considered the possibility of staying out of it and keeping you from knowing, but later, it would come up sometime that there's a house in Houston with your murals and a reporter would dig through the facts to find out who the homeowner is. Also, if I'm here, I can make sure I get what I want."

"So you chose to come yourself. You want to hire my company's services. Cade, I'm not for hire where you're concerned. Get another ad agency. The world is filled with them."

"They don't all paint house murals and I don't want your agency. It's you I want to hire."

"No! I won't work for you."

"I've been told by people in Houston, Chicago and L.A., that you're the best in the country at painting murals, interior or exterior."

"That's good to hear," she said, not really caring at the moment what he'd learned about her company or her. Why did he have to come back so damned handsome and so self-assured?

"I've heard that from people who had no idea where I grew up or that I knew you. You're recommended by gallery people, museums and your former customers. I've seen your work and it's top-notch. I told you, I prefer the best."

"That's flattering, but there are others who are skilled at their craft and they can create scenes that will be as artistic as any I paint," she replied, certain that there was no way he could talk her into working for him.

"I've heard differently."

"I promise you, there are others who can paint as well. Graham Trevor is one. He's excellent, and there are plenty of examples of his work for you to view. A mural is a simple thing to do."

"Right, Katherine, if you're good at doing them. Otherwise, it's a difficult challenge." Cade leaned back in his chair with one hand on his hip. "I don't want Graham Trevor or anyone else except you. Surely we can both get past what happened nine years ago."

"No, I can't! I don't want to. I hate you for what you did and I don't want to work with you now. How plain do I have to say it?" she cried. She hurt and he was opening old wounds. Worst of all, right now in the midst of all their bickering, she wanted his arms around her.

"I figured by now that you would have let go of the past. It's been over a long time," he said and his words cut like a knife. How could he dismiss the past so easily when it had hurt so badly? But maybe it hadn't hurt him at all, she reminded herself.

"I'm sure it's forgotten for you. Obviously, it was over for you before you left Texas nine years ago."

"We don't have to be together for you to accept me as your client. I'll pay you well."

"I'm sure you would, but I don't want your money, your business or anything to do with you," she said, absolutely certain that there weren't any circumstances in which she would agree to work for him.

They halted their discussion because the waiter came to take their dinner order. Even though she preferred prime rib, she didn't want to give Cade the satisfaction of thinking she was the same person as she used to be. "I'll have the pecan-crusted trout," she said and the waiter nodded. She glanced at Cade to see a questioning expression as he ordered lobster. As soon as the waiter left, Cade leaned forward.

"So prime rib is no longer first choice with you?"

"No. Most all of my choices have changed through the years."

He stared at her with a look of speculation. "There's no reason to argue all evening. Let's settle this right now." While he continued to watch her, he took out a cellular phone and spoke so quietly, she could barely hear him. He put away the phone and stood, coming around to hold her chair.

"Let me show you something," he said, and her curiosity was stirred because she couldn't imagine what he intended. Walking close beside her, he took her arm. Before they left the restaurant, Cade paused to tell the maitre d' to delay their dinners until they returned. Her curiosity grew over where they were going. They left the building and crossed the street to one of Fort Worth's best hotels.

"I have a room here. That's why we're eating at the Milington Club instead of the Petroleum Club tonight. The Milington is closer. I want to show you something that I intended to show you after dinner."

She balked and stopped walking. "Your hotel room?"

"That's where we're going. I have blueprints of the home I'm building. It won't hurt you to come up and look and then we'll go right back for dinner."

"I don't need to see any blueprints," she insisted. "We have nothing to discuss."

"Yes, we do. I want to talk to you about murals for my house."

"There isn't enough money in the world for you to hire me to paint for you," she said, facing him and touching his chest with her index finger. "No, Cade." Seething, she burned and perspiration dotted her forehead. She wanted away from him. At any moment she was afraid she would lose the iron control she was exercising and let fly all the accusations she had stored up for nine long years. And that last day was as fresh in her mind as if it had happened yesterday. To her surprise, Cade's appearance had brought back the monumental hurt when she had thought she had finally been free of it.

"There might be a price that you'd agree to," he answered quietly. "I have blueprints. At least look at what I want."

"No!" she cried. "There's no point in it. None! I'm not working for you and opening up old wounds or causing myself anguish. You've hurt me enough, dammit!"

"'Dammit' is right," he charged in a low voice. "This is

work, not our private lives. It's just that everyone—I mean all the galleries and the ad people and the artists—says that you're the best. Start being the professional that I know you are," he ordered. "We have the rest of the evening and nothing to do except eat or shout at each other about past hurts or discuss the paintings I intend to have in my new house. Come look at my blueprints." He tugged lightly on her arm. "You're the expert. Come look."

Reluctantly, she nodded and got another warm smile. As they crossed the lobby, he stopped at the desk to pick up a large roll of papers.

In silence they took the elevator to a suite on the top floor of the hotel. Cade unlocked the door and held it open for her.

She entered a large living area with beige and white decor. An adjoining dining area held a table with chairs for eight. Through open doors she could see two bedrooms and beyond sliding glass doors was a balcony with an iron table and chairs.

Cade shed his coat, and she remembered times he had taken off his coat before turning to make love to her. Her mouth went dry as he slipped out of the coat and draped it over a chair. When she had known him before he had been fit, muscled and strong. She guessed that hadn't changed.

As she watched, Cade cleared a crystal vase of fresh flowers off the dining table and she joined him while he opened the blueprints. No way did she want to work for him or even have someone else in her firm hired by him. She was conscious he stood only a couple of feet away. She looked at his well-shaped hands as he smoothed out the stiff paper. He had become far more appealing, but she supposed she saw some of the same things in him now that she had when they had been younger and madly in love.

In another reminder of how successful he had become, she looked down at the prints that held a drawing of a Greek Revival mansion that had two immense wings and was three stories tall. Surprised, she glanced into his dark eyes that as so often before, caught and held her, making her forget what she had intended to say. His dark eyebrows arched questioningly.

"What is it, Katherine?" he asked.

She didn't want to admit that she had lost her train of thought. "You left here without funds. You've done well, Cade."

"I've been lucky," he said in an offhand manner as if he hadn't done anything more than the next person. "Here's my house. It's under construction and I'm not living there now. I want murals in six of the rooms."

"Cade, this is such a waste of time," she said in exasperation. She couldn't imagine working for him because she was having difficulty getting through an evening with him.

"Give me a price," he urged, facing her. His calmness and persistence were wearing her patience thin.

"No, I won't. Don't you realize that I absolutely have hated you for walking out on our wedding? Do you have any idea how that hurt?" she asked, shaking as she let go some of her restraint. His patient silence irritated her even further.

"You humiliated me and broke my heart!" she cried out. "I was devastated. I didn't imagine anything could hurt like I did!" she exclaimed. The words came tumbling out and now that she'd started, she couldn't stop. "You didn't give me one reason why, or one scrap of a warning. You were gone. Running out on me in the worst, cruelest possible way."

He flinched and paled beneath his tan, but he had an inscrutable expression that hid his feelings.

Suddenly she let go, all the pent-up fury boiling to the surface, and she reached out to slap him.

Like lightning he caught her wrist and held her firmly, but not tightly enough to hurt her. "You're not going to strike me when you don't know why or what occurred back then," he said.

They were both breathing hard, tension drawn tightly between them while he held her wrist. Rage consumed her.

Fire flashed in his dark eyes and the clash between them was tangible. While they stared at each other, he clamped his jaw tightly shut as if holding back harsh words, which was exactly what she was trying to do. The moment drew out and then, as they stared at each other, her anger changed.

While she gazed into depths of brown, he looked at her mouth. When he did, her lips tingled. From the very first his kisses always melted her and erased any resistance to him.

Desire flamed, building heat inside her. They both were breathing hard. For an instant, everything else fell away except hunger for his kiss. She almost leaned toward him, started to and then realized what she was doing. She yanked her head back and shook her shoulders.

"Damn you, Cade. And you're still not going to explain why you walked out."

"I didn't come back to Texas to dredge up old hurts and fling accusations. That's over," he said, releasing her wrist. "I'm not going there because we could hurt each other more than ever. There's no point in stirring up resentment over the past. Not now. You were hurt at the time and for that I'm sorry," he said with a dismissal that added to her fury. Yet even as his voice remained calm, she could feel the tension stretching and fiery sparks flying between them, invisible, yet tangible.

"Sorry is so completely inadequate!" she cried, jerking her arm free and spinning away from him to walk to the window again. Tears threatened, and she fought to get a grip because she didn't intend to shed one tear over him. Not after all this time and all the control she had achieved. Where was all that restraint she had maintained through the years?

She wrapped her arms around her middle and hugged herself. "I don't want to have anything to do with you, Cade," she said.

"You can look at my house plans for a minute. There's no commitment in looking. Come back over here, Katherine."

She turned to glare at him and he stood, impassively

waiting until it seemed ridiculous and childish to refuse to look at his blueprints. She crossed the room to stand a few feet away from him.

As she gazed at the drawing of the house, she was again amazed by his success, which was greater than the news articles or the magazines had indicated.

"This is the dinning room and I want a mural on this wall," he said, pointing with his index finger. "One of the other walls will have mullioned windows that will prevent a clear view of the outside, so I want a landscape."

She examined a drawing of a room with a cathedral ceiling and an enormous stone fireplace that had a medieval flair, and she could imagine a scene of a European countryside on one wall. He wanted six murals. Her usual price popped into mind and she suspected that she could easily get more from Cade. She tried to stifle any thoughts about the income and what she could do with it for her company. What a windfall the job would be if it had been anyone else who wanted to hire her!

Cade shifted papers and she watched his well-shaped hands as he carefully smoothed a print. She could remember those hands on her body, moving over her seductively, magic hands that had set her aflame. Everything he did provoked memories that were too vivid. Attempting to focus totally on his plans, she leaned over the table to peer at the drawings. Cade moved closer beside her and turned over a page to look at the next drawing. "Here's the kitchen and dining area and I want a painting in here."

"Why are you showing me these pictures? The answer is no," she repeated, wondering if he ever heard "no" any longer.

"You're letting your emotions rule your judgment because you're turning down good business. My house will get attention and it would be advertising for you," he said, turning to study her. He stood only a couple of feet from her and she drew a deep breath. Why couldn't she handle being near him?

When she was so angry with him, she hated to discover that she was still incredibly attracted to him.

"This is one time I don't want the business," she said, wishing her racing pulse would slow.

"Let me show you the other rooms," he said, shifting pages around. He leaned over the table to point with his finger. "I want a mural on this wall. You can select the subject. Of course, I have to approve what you propose before you do it."

"You don't trust me, either."

"Yes, I trust you. I want to see what you have in mind. I'm the one who'll have to live with it. Give me a price, Katherine," he said softly. "You have to be enough of a businesswoman and professional to look at what I have and give me a bid. Don't say no over old hurts. There is surely some point where it would become worth your while."

As he stared at her, their clash of wills was offset by her attraction, and she guessed he felt it, too. "No, there isn't because I don't want to work for you in any manner," she said tightly and turned to walk away. For one fleeting second she was tempted to fling some impossible price at him, like five hundred thousand per mural, and see if he would back down. The money was a temptation because she was ambitious, but she put the possibility out of mind.

She walked to the balcony door, opened it and stepped outside without allowing herself to think about what the job would mean to her. A cold gust of wind whipped around her and she wrapped her arms around her middle.

"All right," he said. She turned to find him standing in the doorway, leaning one shoulder against the jamb as he faced her. "I'll make you an offer."

She shook her head. "There's no point in it."

"I've told you that I want six murals. How's eight million dollars for all of them?"

She lost her breath as if she had received a blow. Stunned,

she stared at him. "Eight million dollars?" she gasped over the amount. She couldn't imagine such extravagance.

"That's too much!" The words were out before she thought.

"No, the price isn't too high if I get what I want," he replied smoothly. "I'll pay all your expenses, of course."

Again, he had shocked her profoundly. Never had she commanded such a price for her paintings. Her head spun over the amount and what she could do with it.

"You surely can use the income for something," he remarked dryly.

"Yes, I can," she said, barely able to get out the words. "Cade, I can't believe you'd pay so much to get my art. You can hire perfectly good painters who will do a fine job for you for vastly less."

"Maybe I owe you, Katherine," he said quietly.

"A payoff," she snapped, her temper rising, but there was no way to get the amount that he had offered her out of mind. Her plans for the future of her advertising company flashed, impossible to ignore. His murals would enable her to do what she wanted years sooner than she had expected. "Eight million for six murals," she repeated as if she couldn't believe what she'd heard.

He crossed the balcony to her and placed his hands on her shoulders.

Even though her pulse jumped, she shook her head at him. "No, no. You're not buying my body with that offer."

"I'm only standing here with my hands on your shoulders," he replied in a husky voice that made her forget the money and the murals and everything except Cade. Wind blew locks of his black hair and she remembered how it felt to run her hands through his hair. His hands were warm and he ran them up and down her upper arms, sliding his fingers slowly, lightly in a provocative touch.

"You're more beautiful than ever," he whispered.

"Stop, Cade. We're not going back there," she said, but her heart thudded and she trembled, aching for him as if it were yesterday when she had last seen him.

He ran his finger across her lower lip. "Beautiful, Katherine."

Tingles spiraled from his touch and her lips parted. The moment she realized her reaction, she twisted away to walk around him. "Let's go inside."

He followed her in and closed the door. "You know you can take the money, invest it and retire."

"Never!" she exclaimed, frowning at him as he joined her at the table again. "My work is my life. I thrive on painting and would never consider quitting."

He tilted his head to one side. "I know you took art classes, but I don't recall that you had any burning ambition."

"I threw myself into work to get over being hurt when you left, and then I discovered that I like success. All my life I've competed with my brothers. I want to make more money than they do, and now I might be able to do so."

"You'll have to go some to top your brother Nick. If you accept my offer, you might pass Matt."

She studied the drawings spread in front of her.

"Here they are," he said, leaning slightly over the table to spread more drawings out. "Here's each room that I'd like to have murals in. I don't have any idea what to put in these rooms. It's up to you to select the picture."

"I usually furnish the ideas about three quarters of the time," she said. "Occasionally, someone knows exactly what he wants," she answered without thinking about what she was saying to him. The amount of money dazed her. She turned to him. "You can afford to toss out eight million to get these murals?"

"Yes, I can. I've been fortunate."

She had been adamant that she wouldn't work for him, but his offer was impossible to refuse. She would be certifiable if she turned him down. She could do his murals without succumbing to his charm, she promised herself. And she knew there would be charm. He had melted her heart before when he had been rough and a boy and without means. Now he would be irresistible.

She moved along the table, spreading papers and looking at precise line drawings of floor plans, but she was doing it merely as an excuse to buy time while she mulled over his offer. Could she do the murals and resist Cade at the same time? Maybe he would go back to California or wherever he worked most of the time. As swiftly as she thought about it, she dismissed it. No matter what he said, she knew he would oversee the project.

Eight million dollars for his murals. The offer was temptation with no way to refuse. Yet she could not keep from wondering how badly he wanted her. Curiosity tempted her. With her heart pounding, she looked up at him, wondering if she dared raise the amount. If he refused, she would back down instantly. "I'll do your six murals for ten million," she offered.

Holding her breath and frightened by her own audacity, she saw amusement flash in the depths of his dark eyes, which surprised her. She had expected almost any other kind of reaction from him. "A few minutes ago you told me that I proposed too much."

"I was in shock over your offer. Now, I'm thinking about business."

"Then we've got a deal," he said, and she let out her breath. "Ten million it is."

Ten million! Her reputation would be instantly established by the price. Soon, she could do the ambitious projects she had only dreamed about before.

"How do you want payment?" he asked. "How's half now and half when you finish?"

She inhaled deeply. "You're one surprise after another," she admitted. "Why would you pay so much up front?"

"I'm certain you'll deliver, so why not? You can put the

cash to use right away. I can write you a check now for the first half, or Monday morning we can go to a bank and have the funds transferred to your account."

"Let's go to the bank Monday morning," she said, unable to believe such a thing was actually happening.

"Let me show you the rest," he said, stepping close beside her and pointing to blue lines on another page. "This is a recreation room. It'll have a pool table. This is an interior room, so I want something in here, too, that will bring in the outdoors. I want the mural along this wall," he said, drawing his finger in a line across the blueprint. "Something festive."

"I'll give you several choices and if you don't like any of them, I'll do more."

"Fair enough," he said and she realized she would be working with him constantly until he approved the murals she would paint.

"Then this room," he said, reaching for another sheet and brushing against her arm as he pulled the blueprint in front of them. "This is an exercise room. Do something to liven it up. Something cheerful. Nothing is more monotonous than a treadmill, so give me a picture along this wall that I can enjoy viewing."

She knew she would have to give thought and planning to what she would paint. She couldn't make any suggestions at this point and she was certain he didn't expect her to.

"Then over here," he said, reaching beyond her and brushing against her again. Catching a whiff of his aftershave, she could see the faint dark stubble of his beard that was beginning to show as he leaned forward, close in front of her. Did he even notice when they touched each other? Was he doing it deliberately or without thought? She couldn't keep from noticing and tingling as if the contact had been a caress.

"There's no woman who should have a say in this?"

Katherine asked, wishing she could take back the personal question the moment it was out.

He straightened and focused intently on her. "I told you before that there isn't a woman. The only person who has a say in this is me." He rested his hand on her shoulder again, but this time, he rubbed it slightly, touching a lock of her hair. "But as long as you brought it up—"

"Cade, I'm taking this job when I never intended to, but I want us to leave the past out of it. I don't want to go into personal things. Let's work as if we were two strangers who met tonight for the first time."

"If I'd met you tonight for the first time, I'd be flirting with you every minute of the evening," he said solemnly, his gaze drifting lazily over her features. His fingers trailed along her jaw.

Ignoring him, she turned back to the blueprints. "All right, we've looked at the dining room, the exercise room and the rec room."

"I want murals in my bedroom, a utility room and the kitchen dining area. That should cover it."

His bedroom. Her stomach grew fluttery at the thought. If only he would return to work in another city instead of staying at his Houston house, but she expected him to stick around to see what she was doing. She wished his bedroom wasn't one of the rooms.

"How soon can you start?" he asked. "I'd like to have them started right away."

"I have a job that's pending, but it's something someone in my office can handle," she said.

"Don't give my projects to someone else in your office. I'll have a contract drawn up and I want your efforts exclusively."

"I'm the only one doing the murals. That's something I've specialized in and I enjoy, so of course, I'll do the design and drawings myself. The work will go faster if someone helps me with the painting."

He shook his head. "No, unless it's errands and setting up equipment and that type of thing. Otherwise, I'm paying for you only," he said firmly.

"Fair enough," she replied.

A look passed between them that made her sizzle. Then he stepped closer to place his hands on her waist. "This is good. I've seen your work and you're talented. I admire the mural you did in San Francisco at the Haywind store and I saw a couple you did in Kansas City and one in San Antonio."

"I'm glad you liked what you saw," she said. She was aware of Cade's hands resting lightly on her waist as she looked up at him. They stood too close, conjuring up memories of other times she had stood with him like this.

"You can start right away?" he asked and his voice had dropped a notch, the only indication that he noticed anything else between them.

"Yes, I can," she said, stepping away from him. "Is your house far enough along for me to start drawing?"

"Yes," he replied, pulling on his coat. "We can talk about it while we eat dinner. Let's get back to the club," he said, and she crossed the room to pick up her purse, relieved that they were leaving his hotel suite and she would once again be out in public where the situation could not get intensely personal.

They had been seated only a short time back in the Millington Club when a first course of pan-seared crab cakes was served.

"We're so civilized," she said quietly while she ate a small bite. "I want to scream at you and throw things at you instead of work for you. As it is, you've bought yourself peace because I can't do that and work for you afterward."

He arched an eyebrow and his gaze drifted over her features. "For right now, perhaps we can both put the past on hold. It may not last, but we can try."

She inhaled, thought about the price he was willing to pay her and what she could do with the fortune. All her life she had been in competition with her brothers and even with her father. Now, her earnings would equal theirs. The mural earnings would give her a chance for spectacular accomplishments in her career.

If only she could hold to those thoughts and shove the past into oblivion, she might get through this assignment without unleashing all her pent-up fury that increased every time Cade indicated that there was reason for him to be angry with her over the past.

He couldn't have a single reason to have any bitterness on his part and it mystified her and infuriated her when he said that he did, but she didn't want to go into it because she'd already lost control once tonight, she didn't want to again.

"Tomorrow morning, if you're available, we can fly to Houston and return in the afternoon."

"That's fine," she replied as the waiter removed their dishes and brought green salads. Tomorrow she would spend the day with him. Her appetite had fled and she sipped her water.

"In your bedroom," she said, "the painting should be something pleasing and relaxing, something you really like. What do you enjoy?"

"I don't think you're going to want to paint that on my wall," he drawled, and she had to laugh in spite of her irritation. She didn't want his charm. Keep the barriers, she reminded herself.

"What are some of your favorite things?" she asked. "It used to be bikes, tinkering with cars and baseball, but, of course, I don't know what you like now."

"I haven't changed that much. My fascination with bikes has changed to cars. I enjoy baseball. Now I can enjoy things I couldn't then. I like fishing, skiing, golf, mountain climbing and snow boarding. As far as a subject for a mural for my bedroom—I'll have to think about that," he replied.

"I'll come up with possibilities for the subjects, too. That's my job."

As they talked about business and about the murals, she noticed he didn't have a big appetite, either. They kept the conversation off anything personal and she repeatedly thought about her job and changes she could make because of the money that would pour into her business, yet her train of thought wandered constantly back to Cade. Why hadn't he married? Why wasn't there a woman in his life now?

She shoved her questions aside. She wanted to keep everything as impersonal and professional as possible between them. He was now her client and she had to try to keep the past out of mind as long as she worked for him. Do the job and avoid thinking about their history—how many times would she have to remind herself? Had he ever loved her or had it all been a lie?

She took a deep breath and drank her water, trying to cool down and stop recalling the past, but she could only let go of memories a few minutes at a time and then soon, they were back in her thoughts again. She tried to pay attention to what he was saying as they talked in generalities and he inquired about different jobs she'd had, but her mind wandered. When her attention went to his mouth, she remembered his hot possessive kisses.

"You're not eating," he observed, drawing her abruptly back to the present. She felt her cheeks flush and hated that she couldn't control her blush.

"You haven't eaten very much yourself," she replied. "I'm tense anyway when I start a new job and maybe even more edgy tonight," she said.

"Relax," he said, reaching across the table to take her hand. "I'm no ogre to work for and I know you're an artist."

He held her hand, his thumb running back and forth lightly over her hand and then her wrist and she knew he probably felt her racing pulse. His dark eyes bore into her and their surroundings ceased to exist for her, leaving only Cade.

"Katherine," he said coaxingly, and for an instant, she wanted to lean closer to him until she realized how she was responding.

"Stop, it. I suppose it's from not seeing anyone for a long time, but I'm more susceptible than I want to be. You show some restraint or this isn't going to work."

"Sure, it'll work," he said softly.

They each left a large portion of their dinners untouched. The evening was a strain, and she was ready for it to end before she lost her composure with him again.

"Want to dance?" he asked, gazing at her with a level, flat stare that made her wonder what he felt and what was going through his mind.

"No, I don't, Cade. Let's keep anything between us strictly business."

"You know I paid royally for this evening with you," he said easily. "I haven't danced in a while. It seems to me, the night should include at least a dance," he said, standing and coming around the table. He pulled out her chair and she stood, trying to bite back her comments.

"You're definitely accustomed to getting your way," she said, standing, her pulse racing at the thought of dancing with him. Everything involving him was two-sided. Attraction caused her nerves to sizzle while anger kept her in a knot as she struggled to avoid another outburst with him.

He led her to the dance floor and the moment she walked into his embrace, her pulse jumped. Why did this seem so right? He held her close against him, and she felt the soft wool of his tux. She could detect the scent of his aftershave, feel the brush of his thighs against hers.

She danced with him as if time had vanished and it was nine years earlier. Every step was familiar, every move was seduction. Her heart pounded and heat burned inside her. They danced together in perfect coordination as if they had been dancing together every night for the whole nine years.

"This is good, Katherine, to hold you," he whispered, and his breath was warm against her ear. Her arm curled across his shoulder and she was careful to keep her hand on his coat and to avoid touching his neck. He swung her down in a dip and she instinctively clung to him as she looked into his dark eyes. She wanted him and there was no stopping what she felt.

In silence, she danced with him, closing her eyes only to be carried back in time again, remembering seductive moments in his arms when she had been wildly in love.

His arm tightened around her waist, pulling her closer. It was pure torment because they fit too well, moved together in perfect rhythm and every step stirred up damnable memories of dances in the past…seduction…Cade kissing her.

The instant the dance ended, she turned to walk back to the table. She tingled all over from being in his arms. Dancing together had stirred too many memories and sent desire to scalding levels.

Physically, she wanted to kiss and love him. She almost groaned out loud, caught herself and coughed, hoping she could cover the sound she had made.

She picked up her purse and faced him. "I know you paid a fortune for the evening, but as soon as possible, I'd like to end it. After all, you accomplished what you intended when I agreed to work for you."

"That's true," he said, taking her arm. "We'll go."

In the limousine he sat beside her again, closer this time, turning to face her. "I gave your address to the driver. I thought you'd live at the ranch."

"No, I moved out nine years ago and got an apartment. Now I own my own house and live in town. I have a house at the ranch. All of us do and Dad has given all of us land. We get together about twice a month, if possible."

"Nick told me he sees you fairly often."

Startled, she looked at Cade. "You sound as if you know Nick."

He shrugged. "Because of business dealings, we've crossed paths a few times."

She was startled to learn Nick had never mentioned Cade to her and wondered why he hadn't, deciding Nick probably thought it would be painful for her.

"I'm surprised he's civil to you," she said. "When you left, my brothers weren't living here at the time. If you remember, they were both in college. When they found out what you'd done, they went after you, but you and your family had left the state and they couldn't find you, which was a relief."

"That's not surprising."

Trying to avoid the past, she thought about her new job. "Actually I can be free right away to start thinking about your murals."

"Do you have someone you can really trust to run things if you're gone a long time?"

"Yes. I've been away for jobs a lot. Also, Houston to Fort Worth isn't so far that I can't get back if I have to."

"That's fine," he said easily, gazing intently at her. He wasn't touching her, but he still could set her aflame with his sexy brown eyes and his supercharged presence.

"Are you an early riser? I can pick you up and we'll go in my plane to Houston tomorrow. Is seven too early?"

"Seven works."

"Fine. That's a good time to go."

"Tomorrow I'll get your address and location," she said. "I'll find a motel nearby where I can set up my office and I can stay."

"No, that won't be necessary at all," he answered easily.

"Why not? I'm not commuting every day."

"Of course not. You don't need to commute. You'll live at my place," he replied.

Three

"No! I can't live with you," she snapped, twisting in the seat to face him, angry that he even suggested it.

"Of course you can stay at my place instead of a hotel," he replied smoothly. "You won't be 'living with me,' you'll be residing at my house," he said, unfastening his coat and pushing it open. "There's a world of rooms. Thirty rooms, as a matter of fact. You'll be right where you're working. If you don't want to bring your car, I can put one at your disposal. There's no reason not to stay there."

There were a dozen good reasons to avoid staying at his house, not the least of which was that the man was larger than life to her. Whether she liked it or not, she could never view him as she did other men. His touch was fiery and his look could hold her immobile. Her pulse was faster right now, just riding in the limo beside him. She was too susceptible to him, far too vulnerable.

Each minute with him compounded the attraction that tugged at her senses.

"Stop worrying, Katherine," he said quietly. "I'm no ogre. I'll be at work. The place is huge."

"I didn't expect to ever see you again. Now the idea of working for you, living under the same roof, spending time together, is unsettling. Give me as much space and solitude as possible. Your murals will turn out better, I'm sure."

"Is that a roundabout threat to leave you alone?"

"Not at all. I'm simply telling you that I'll work more efficiently under those conditions," she said, wanting to keep as much distance as possible between them.

He leaned close and drew his finger along her hand, making her tingle. "Let's not argue every step of the way. I'm paying you a fortune. In return, I want cooperation."

"Do you ever hear 'no'?"

"Occasionally, and if there's a logical reason, I pay attention. Can you give me a sensible cause for not staying at my place to do your painting?"

She gazed into his dark eyes. "You're giving me one good reason right now. You're too close. You're touching me constantly."

"Why is all that bad?" he asked.

"I'm susceptible to you, dammit, and I don't want to be. Does that make you feel better? Give me room."

He leaned away, his gaze intent. "I'll give you room, and you move into my house. It's large enough, Katherine. You'll see tomorrow."

Knowing she couldn't refuse to cooperate with him when he was being reasonable, she shrugged. "All right, Cade. I'll have to get measurements. I would prefer to look at all the rooms and then to focus on one at a time. I'll get a proposal put together for you and we can meet at my office to go over it."

"Sounds fine," he said. They turned into her gated area,

passed through the graceful white metal gates with Cade's driver using the combination she had given Cade on her card. They slowed and stopped in front of her one-story redbrick house that was set back in a landscaped yard with oak trees.

"Beautiful trees and house, Katherine," Cade said as he walked her to her door.

On the porch she faced him. "Thank you for your bid, for dinner and for your job offer. You've helped a lot of children tonight and you've given me a wonderful job opportunity."

"I'll get my money's worth," he said softly.

She frowned. "I hope there's no innuendo in your statement. You'll get six murals, nothing else. My body isn't included."

"I didn't expect it to be," he said, standing too close, gazing at her too intently.

For a few seconds they stared at each other. Her pulse raced and she could remember too many times he had kissed her good-night. Hastily, she removed her key and turned to open her door. Stepping inside, she switched off her alarm and turned back to find him standing in the open doorway. She had no intention of inviting him inside.

"Good night, Katherine. I'm looking forward to your work," he said, holding out his hand.

Reluctantly, she reached out to shake hands with him and had that electric sizzle that spun to her toes the instant his hand closed around hers. She wanted to yank her hand away, but instead, she merely withdrew it gently after a second. She didn't want this intense, fiery reaction to him, but there was no stopping it or keeping it from happening.

She watched him stride back to the waiting limousine. She closed the front door and leaned back against it, rubbing her forehead. Was he going to break her heart a second time?

She was going to live in his house and he would be there, watching what she was doing. All evening the question had plagued her of how she could resist him. Could she cope with being around him and not succumb to seduction?

Why was she so certain he would try to seduce her?

She could be wrong, but he hadn't done too well at keeping his hands off her tonight. She was equally uncertain whether she could continually hold her fury in check. He stirred opposing emotions in her constantly. One minute she was attracted, afraid she would fall in love again, the next minute she was fighting to control her temper.

She thought about when she had lost her temper with him tonight. At least the outburst had been brief. When she moved into his house, she hoped she could remain coolly professional with him and avoid him when she wasn't working.

She was drained and exhilarated all at once. Cade was here! She wished she could shake him right out of mind, but it was impossible. Everything inside her screamed a reminder that he had returned. After nine long years, Cade was back!

And then she thought about the murals and the payment she would get.

Her eyes flew open. Ten million dollars! She spun around in a circle, flinging out her arms and letting her purse fly, not caring when it hit the door and fell on the polished oak floor. She could open more offices—one at a time so she could get them started and running well before she moved on to another one. It had been her dream and now she would be able to do all she had planned.

Certain sleep was impossible, she kicked off her shoes and hurried to the office she had in her house. Switching on lights, she entered a room that was lined with shelves filled with books, drawings and awards. Two computers sat on her desk and another on a table.

She got down some books to look at pictures that might inspire her or trigger an idea.

As she poured over the pictures, her thoughts kept slipping

back to Cade and the time she had just spent with him, remembering dancing with him, being held in his arms again, something she had never expected to have happen.

Where had he made his fortune? Why was he angry with her? Why had he been so insistent that she take the job instead of another painter? She knew there were others who were as good as she was and he could have hired someone for far less. Why was he still single when he was so handsome and successful? Questions besieged her and she recalled that first moment she looked into his brown eyes and recognized him—everything inside her had clamored for her to throw herself in his arms. She was going to live in his house with him. The thought alone set her pulse racing. The house would be a palace, but if it were five times the size of a hotel, it wouldn't be large enough to keep fireworks from exploding between them.

Sooner or later, the past would rise up and all the money in the world couldn't keep it from happening. Shutting her eyes, she remembered how they had met. Clearly, she could recall hot, mid-afternoon July sunshine. She was home from college after her sophomore year, twenty years old. With the radio blaring, she was driving a battered pickup, the oldest on the Ransome ranch. Racing ten miles over the speed limit on the usually deserted county road, she sang as she headed home.

A truck passed driven by a cowboy, who honked and waved. It wasn't anyone she recognized, but she waved in return because most people who traveled the road lived somewhere in the general area.

Next she heard a bike and saw a guy on a Harley behind her. His shaggy, black hair was blowing behind him. He wore a red headband, a ragged T-shirt and frayed jeans. He pulled alongside her and honked.

She glanced at him, saw he was good-looking, so she smiled and then turned back to driving. He honked again and she flashed him a look.

Since she had been twelve years old, she had been receiving attention from males, so she was accustomed to honks, whistles, smiles, waves and guys hitting on her.

The biker wasn't anyone she knew. He persisted and then when he didn't get much reaction from her, he pulled ahead of her and slowed, causing her to slow or else she would hit him. When she signaled to pass him, he waved one arm frantically and as she tried to pass, he pulled over so she couldn't.

Annoyed, she started to pull to the right to try to pass him, but he swung over to the right and kept waving his arm, only now he was pointing and jabbing the air to his right with his index finger. If he wanted her to stop, he was crazy.

She wasn't afraid because she knew most people in her county and the surrounding area. She had her cell phone ready if she needed help.

He slowed, blocking her path.

She leaned on her horn and got within an inch of the back of his bike as they still drove down the highway, only now going below the speed limit. He shook his head, peeled out of her way and she pushed the accelerator, racing past him, sticking her tongue out at him as she roared past.

She glanced in her rearview mirror, saw him pull off to the side of the road and point to the right with a repeated jabbing sign. She was far enough past him, that if he was up to no good, she could get away, so she slowed, pulled off the deserted road to the shoulder. The pickup rolled to a stop and she climbed out, walking to the back. She glanced at the bed of the pickup and swore.

She heard the bike and turned to see him riding toward her. She knew now he'd been trying to help so her concern about him evaporated as she peered beyond him down the road.

He pulled up and stopped, cut his motor and swung his leg over his bike to climb off and walk up to her.

With midnight brown eyes, thick black hair, a firm jaw and

prominent cheekbones, he was the best-looking guy she'd ever seen and she couldn't keep from staring at him. She became conscious of her low-cut, faded and torn cutoffs, her T-shirt that ended inches above her small waist. His gaze raked over her in a blatant male assessment that made her tingle all over. Fire streaked in her and she became totally aware of him. Her gaze roamed down to his mouth, to his full sensual underlip. His shoulders were broad and he bulged with muscles and his powerful chest tapered down to a flat stomach, narrow hips and long legs.

She realized how she was looking him over and jerked her gaze up to see a heated look in his eyes and a faint, mocking smile lifting one corner of his mouth.

Her heart pounded as he strolled closer and stopped only inches in front of her. "I'm Cade Logan. You're—"

He waited, and she drew her breath. "Katherine Ransome," she said breathlessly, wondering what was happening. She never had such a volatile response to any guy. She felt weak-kneed, fluttery inside, and she tried to stop staring at him.

"Are you Matt Ransome's sister, Katherine?" he asked.

"Yes. You know Matt?"

He shrugged, a lazy lift of his shoulder that was as sensual as everything else about him. "We went to school together at Rincon High. I was a year ahead of Matt. I'm twenty-four now, and you're—?"

"Old enough to know what I like to do," she answered with a grin, suddenly wanting to flirt with him. His chest expanded as he drew a deep breath.

He gazed at her with hot speculation in his eyes. "I think I'm going to have to find out exactly what you like," he drawled in a husky voice that curled her toes. "But we'll have to postpone that discovery a bit. You've got bales—"

"The hay!" she exclaimed, remembering that her pickup now held only half the bales of hay it had held when she left town.

One dark eyebrow arched wickedly. "Made you forget your hay, didn't I," he drawled, and her gaze snapped back to him.

She slanted him a look, flirting with him again. "Might have, as a matter of fact. Hay isn't the most fascinating thing there is," she said in a languid drawl that caused a flicker in the depths of his eyes. "There are other things much more exciting to me."

"So what excites you, Katherine?" he asked, his innuendo unmistakable and her pulse drummed. As the question hovered between them, she looked at his mouth.

"Lots of things, but I don't do them with strangers. Or discuss them."

"So someone has to get to know you—I'll agree with that."

She smiled, and one corner of his mouth quirked in a crooked grin as he reached out to touch her cheek. "I didn't know why you were honking and waving," she said.

His mouth curled up in a knowing grin and he gave her another swift appraisal. "You're probably so used to guys honking at you that you barely notice."

She drew a deep breath, making her breasts strain against her T-shirt and seeing him lower his gaze. "You look like the type to honk and wave at a woman."

"Yeah," he said in a voice that had lowered a notch. "I like beautiful women, that's for sure. We can pursue this conversation later. Right now, you better get those bales off the road before someone has a wreck."

"Oh, my!" she said, realizing he was right and she'd forgotten the hay again. "Thanks," she called over her shoulder as she dashed toward the door of her pickup.

"I'll help you," he said and climbed on his bike.

She shrugged, climbed into the truck and made a U-turn to head back the way she came. She switched off the radio that had helped distract her from the falling bales of hay. Soon she spotted the first bale and a few others were scattered along the road just yards beyond.

She pulled off on the shoulder and he slowed to a stop behind her, coming around her truck. Before she could step out on the road, he took her arm to hold her back. "You drive on the shoulder and I'll pick 'em up and put them in your truck."

"This is the oldest, worst truck on the ranch and we don't usually drive it to town, but I was late and my car's in the shop, so I took it. I knew it was full of hay, but I didn't think the bales would bounce out."

"You should get the tailgate closed good."

"It's broken," she said. "Maybe now Dad will get rid of this clunker, but it's all right for ranch driving."

"This road's bumpy and filled with potholes so that added to your problem. Going over eighty didn't help, either. You're a fast woman, Katherine Ransome."

His sexy remark slithered across her nerves and made her tingle. She tilted up her chin.

"Only when I want to be," she answered, and he grinned.

"So what does it take to make you want to be? I may have to explore that one later. Right now, I'll get those bales."

Cade ran out into the road and picked up a bale to toss it into the back of her pickup. She climbed inside and drove slowly beside the road while he picked up more bales. His muscles flexed, pulling his T-shirt taut, and she drew a deep breath. He was strong, fit and appealing.

When there were no more bales in sight, he came around to her window.

"I think you have more back down the road. You've lost a bunch. Every time you'd hit a bump one would go out. I'll hide my bike off the road in the bushes and go with you to help you."

"Your bike will be stolen if you do."

"I'll take a chance," he said.

"Besides, I can lift a bale of hay when they're this size."

"I can lift them easier. You wait right here for me," he said and was gone to move his bike. She was tempted to drive off, but she was more tempted to wait and spend the time with him.

When he slid into the seat beside her, she drove back onto the road. Aware he sat and watched her, she tingled. "Sure of yourself, aren't you?"

He shrugged. "Sometimes."

"There are some more," she said, seeing bales ahead in the road. "I don't know how many were back there. Thank goodness there's so little traffic. We passed one car and he must have swerved around all of these."

"Where'd you drive from today?" Cade asked.

"Rincon," she replied.

"So did I. If you've just driven from Rincon, these are the first bales you lost because I didn't see any before this bridge."

She slowed, pulled onto the shoulder and climbed out. "I can help you," she said.

Before she picked up a bale, she yanked a bandana from her pocket. Catching her blond hair in her hand, she reached up to tie her hair behind her head with the bandana. As she did, he watched her intently, his gaze lowering to her breasts when her T-shirt pulled tautly against them.

She yanked the handkerchief into a knot. "There! I'm ready."

"So am I now," he said in a husky tone that gave a double entendre to his statement and she drew a deep breath. He was handsome and sexy, a lethal combination to a female heart. She wondered who he was and where he lived. Cade Logan meant nothing to her.

When the pickup was loaded, Cade climbed into the back and pushed the bales against the cab. "Now if you'll slow down, watch the bumps and potholes and keep your eye on these, you should get home with everything intact. I can follow you and see that you do," he said, jumping down beside her.

He dropped lightly to his feet like a cat and she was aware of how fit he was.

"Thanks for helping me," she said.

"Sure. Want to meet me for a burger tomorrow at lunch?" he asked, his brown eyes focusing intently on her.

She had a split second debate with herself because there was a raw sexuality to him that made her suspect if she had lunch with him, it would lead to more.

His eyes narrowed. "Are you scared to?"

She looked into his dancing dark eyes that were filled with speculation. "No, I'm not scared," she replied with a toss of her head. "I'll meet you at noon at Judd's."

"See you then, Katie," he said and drew his finger along her arm. He turned, climbed on his bike, revved the motor and was gone.

Remembering, she was astounded again how far he had come from where he had been back then. When she had met him, he lived with his family of four boys and no father in a dilapidated two-bedroom house that was in the poorest part of Rincon.

He was four years older than she was, and in high school she hadn't known him. Earning his living as a mechanic and buying and selling old cars on the side, he had dropped out of school his senior year, but he had known both of her brothers. From the day she had met Cade, she'd always thought he was the most exciting person she had ever met.

She vowed with every ounce of willpower she had that she would not fall in love with him a second time around and open herself to hurt like she had years ago.

Staring into space, she replayed over and over the past hours' events. She wanted to call her brothers to tell them the latest developments, but she would do that tomorrow before she left for Houston. Both of them were early risers and she could call after six.

She worked far into the night before she went to bed and fell asleep only to dream about Cade, dreams of kisses and

lovemaking that left her in a bigger turmoil when she awoke
the next morning.

She showered and dressed, wearing a navy suit and pumps
because she was determined to look professional to try to keep
a wall between them. With care she looped and pinned her
blond hair on her head.

About fifteen minutes before Cade was to pick her up, she
called her brother and after two rings heard his deep voice.
"Nick. It's Katherine. I'm leaving town and wanted to talk to
you first."

"How'd the auction go?"

"It was very good. They made a lot of money."

"Great! Glad to hear it and Julia will be, too. Who bid for
you?" he asked with amusement in his voice. "I'll bet Hank
Monroe did. I wonder if he'll still be trying to go out with you
when you're sixty years old," Nick remarked and laughed at
his own statement.

"Several men bid," she replied casually. "Cade Logan is
back. He won the bid and the evening with me. We went to
dinner last night."

She held the phone away from her ear while her brother
swore. "Why'd you go out with Cade Logan?"

"Because he was the highest bidder, Nick," she said patiently.

"You sound damned happy about it," Nick snapped. "It's
not back on between the two of you, is it?"

"No! I'm going to work for Cade. He made me the proverbial offer I couldn't refuse," she said, her pulse jumping at the
thought of announcing her client's offer to her brothers.

"It must have been damn high," Nick said, sounding
grumpy over the phone. "I'd like to beat him to a pulp,
Katherine."

"Well, don't. You'd go to jail, and I'd lose a lucrative
contract that will set me up in my business in a way I never
dreamed possible."

"Okay, how much?" Nick asked, and she wished she could see his face.

"Cade has a new home in Houston and he wants me to paint six murals in it."

"And— C'mon. He must be paying you a fortune for you to take the job and sound cheerful today."

"How's ten million for the six murals?"

She held the phone away from her ear again as Nick swore and whistled loudly and yelled to Julia to come let Katherine tell her something. Next, she had to tell her sister-in-law, Julia, about the deal she had made with Cade. Then Nick was back on the phone.

"You've made a bargain with the devil," Nick snapped. "But for that sum, I don't blame you. I knew he was doing well, but I didn't know it was that good. How in sweet hell has he made that kind of money?"

"Look who's asking," she said, momentarily amused because Nick had made a huge fortune in only a few years.

"I had backing to start. I had Dad and his finances and a bit on my own and an education, et cetera, et cetera. Cade had nothing. Worse than nothing. He had a bad background."

"Don't build him up," she said dryly.

"Dammit, he's going to break your heart again. Is he married?"

"No, he won't break my heart and no, he's not married. This is the deal of a lifetime. I'll be careful."

"Yeah, right. And we'll try to pick up the pieces later."

"Ridiculous! I'm over him," she announced, but her words were hollow and conjured up her racing pulse and pounding heart and breathlessness too many times the night before. "This morning he's flying me to Houston to see his house. You can get me on my cell phone if you need to."

"For ten million, he wants you a hell of a lot. I know you're good at what you do, but Katherine, he's coming after you."

"No, he's not. He just thinks I'm good at murals."

"I know you're damned good, but you don't command prices like that."

"I might now," she said with glee, always feeling a competitive edge with her brothers even though she loved them dearly.

"I hope the job is worth what you get."

"It's going to be, Nick. I have plans."

"You be careful and if you want me, call anytime."

"You sound as if I'm walking into danger."

"I just remember what you went through before."

She glanced at her watch. "Gotta run. Thanks, Nick, for being the brother you are. I'd like to tell Matt and Dad about my deal."

"I don't blame you except give me time to drive out to Dad's place. I'll leave in thirty minutes. He'll be in such shock that he might have a heart attack."

"No, he won't. You don't have to go there. I'll break the news easily," she said, smiling. "Better run." She closed off the conversation and called Matt to tell him and listened to his ire change to shock over the fee she would receive. She let Matt talk her into allowing both brothers to break the news to their dad. She knew her father despised Cade and she decided Matt probably knew best, so she told him to go ahead and she would call their father later.

Chimes rang and she hurried to the door. In a short-sleeved black knit shirt and charcoal slacks, Cade was as handsome as ever, only now, the knit shirt revealed powerful shoulders and bulging biceps that ignited a flame.

Heightening her reaction, his gaze drifted slowly and appreciatively over her.

"Good morning," he said and his voice was husky, causing an unwanted sizzle. "Sleep all right?" he asked.

"I slept great," she replied emphatically with a twinge of conscience over the uncustomary lie, but she had no intention of informing him that he had destroyed her sleep and her peace.

"You look beautiful this morning, but you could have dressed casually, and you could have left your hair down," he added, touching locks of her hair.

"Thank you. You're a client now, and this is a business trip, so I selected clothes accordingly," she replied. "I have to close the door to activate my alarm and then I'm ready to go," she said.

He draped one hand over her head on the doorjamb and leaned closer, and her pulse had another rush. "I'm causing you to activate your alarm?" he drawled in a voice that made her forget her house alarm totally.

"Don't flirt, Cade," she said breathlessly, wanting to flirt back with him, annoyed that he would tease her. "We're not going there again."

"With you it's difficult to avoid," he said, his voice changing as he dropped his arm and turned his back.

She glared at his back, realizing he had the same mixture of anger and attraction that she experienced.

When the alarm was set, she emerged, and closed and locked the door. He took her arm to walk to the limo. Another touch on her arm—the constant physical contacts with him had commenced again and fueled fires that had started yesterday in her. As she sat down and crossed her legs, she looked up to catch him watching her.

"So why are you building a house in Houston?" she asked him while they drove away from her house.

"I bought an oil company that has its headquarters there. Houston has a lot of possibilities for me."

"From what I've read about you, you buy and sell companies. Do you always move where you invest?"

"No, I don't." He rubbed the back of his neck as if he were battling some inner turmoil, and she let it drop and rode in silence. "This is my home state, and I wanted to come back and see what things are like after nine years," he explained.

"I'll have to admit that I couldn't resist letting hometown folks see that I've done all right."

"With the astronomical donation you made last night to the children's charity, I'm sure you'll impress all the hometown folks. The auction is written up in the morning paper and you've shown everybody how successful you've been."

"That wasn't the point of my high bid," he said dryly. "It was to get you out with me again so I could make my offer."

"You succeeded in not only getting me out with you, but in talking me into taking you as a client."

"Not many people would have turned down my offer," he remarked. "If the auction is in the paper, someone may get curious about my bid for you and our past history and we may become interesting to the media."

"I hope not," she said with a shudder. "I don't want the past dredged up again. The bachelorette auction had a small article in the society section this morning, because they cover fancy charity events. There are a few pictures, but not ours, thank heaven!"

"That may not be the end of news about us if any reporter with a memory gets hold of the story."

She tilted her head and stared at him. "So you came back to show everyone how well you've done."

"I came because of business. I'll admit, I hope some of the people I grew up with in Rincon know about my new house. Foolish as it is, there's a part of me that has to prove something. I had some rough times," he replied.

"I know you did," Katherine said quietly as she tried to ignore memories of his struggles and his family's poverty while hers had wealth. She didn't want him to stir her sympathy, but she knew too well that he'd had tough years when he was growing up.

"So you built in Houston to impress the home folks," she repeated.

"I guess it's ego, Katherine. Otherwise, I probably would have just purchased a condo. A condo would have been sufficient for business. If you recall, everybody thought I'd turn out badly."

"I never did think you would," she declared, and he looked into her eyes in a fiery gaze that startled her with its smoldering anger.

"You said you didn't," he stated with so much cynicism, her surprise grew.

"And you think in truth, that I did?" she asked. "Do you think I intended to marry someone I thought was bad? Why on earth would I do that?"

"Rebellion," he replied quietly.

"That's absurd, Cade. Rebelling against what?" she asked, astounded by his reply.

"Your father. I remember how you fought him."

"If I'd married you to get back at him, it would just spite myself."

"You wouldn't be the first. You told me how all of you clashed constantly with him. You said Nick and Matt fought him when they were growing up and that's why Nick left as soon as he could."

"I argued with my dad over dating you," she said, gazing into Cade's angry dark eyes. "But I didn't go out with you because of anger at my dad. Not ever."

"Do you remember what you felt when you were twenty?" Cade asked, and his voice dripped with sarcasm.

"I remember precisely," she snapped.

The limo stopped, interrupting their conversation that had done nothing to mollify her anger with him. She dismissed Cade's answer to her about rebellion because that had never been a reason for her to see him.

At the Fort Worth business airport Cade exited the limo and turned to help her. Yards away, a sleek, white Learjet waited.

Ignoring Cade's outstretched hand, Katherine emerged
into warm sunshine. She wanted to do everything for herself,
to stop the physical contacts that were pure fire. She hated that
she still found him appealing and despised the instant bone-
deep response to him when they touched each other. Every
look, each touch was electrifying and unwanted to her and
now she was going to his house to live. A big mural could take
almost two weeks. She was facing possibly more than two
months with him. She inhaled, lecturing herself on resistance.

To avoid his taking her arm, she strode ahead of him and
climbed the stairs into the jet. The moment he stepped inside
the luxurious plane, Cade dropped his hand on her shoulder.

"Sit where you want. I'll speak to our pilot and then join you."

Drawing a deep breath, she watched him go through the
plane. There was no stopping her racing pulse. Was getting
involved with Cade again going to be worth all the money she
was making?

With another deep breath she pulled her gaze from his purposeful stride and selected a cushioned chair that gave her a
window view. In minutes he returned to sit facing her, stretching his long legs out in front of him, almost touching hers.

"This will be a little over an hour and a half flight, so you
can relax."

She wondered if she could ever relax around him, but she
wouldn't tell him. His cell phone rang and she turned to look
out the window again while snatches of his conversation indicated he had a business call.

Glancing at Cade while he talked, she was surprised to find
him watching her. She turned back to the window.

She wanted to demand that he tell her why he had walked
out on her, but at the same time, she wanted him to explain
without her having to ask. Why had she foolishly expected an
explanation and an apology? She had thought she was over
him and had forgotten him, until last night when she looked

up into his eyes and time fell away and she knew then, in some ways the years didn't matter. The hurt and the attraction remained. Forgetting and indifference were impossible. Something had stirred his anger at her, as well, and she couldn't imagine what.

The pilot announced they had been cleared for takeoff. Katherine and Cade were buckled in and she looked out the window as they gained speed, then they were airborne.

Chatting politely with Cade, she couldn't concentrate on what was being said. Her thoughts jumped to business possibilities while her physical awareness of Cade ignited memories. As their small talk barely registered, she watched Cade, his long legs and well-shaped hands. Trying to focus on the task ahead, she attempted to sound him out on what kind of art work he preferred, realizing he had eclectic tastes.

"You've done amazingly well in nine years," she observed, wondering about him. "You left here with nothing."

His dark eyes flashed in an expression that puzzled her, and she suspected she had said something that angered him, but she didn't know why.

"How did you get where you are today?" she asked.

Four

"When I left here we went to California. About as far as we could get in this country."

"Who's 'we'?" she asked even though she was certain of his answer, but now that they were into the past, she couldn't keep from inquiring. "Your whole family?"

"Yes. We all left here together," he replied and her curiosity increased. For nine years she had speculated why he might have walked out like he did, but she could never come up with a reason for him to have left without telling her.

"We drifted across the country and went to L.A. For a few months I held odd jobs, but then I was fortunate to land employment with Edwin Talcott, a multimillionaire entrepreneur and financier. I became his chauffeur, as well as sort of a handyman and mechanic for his cars. Occasionally, I helped his gardener."

"You've come a long way from chauffeur and gardener," Katherine remarked, wondering what had happened in the intervening years. She glanced again at his hands, that weren't the hands of a gardener.

"Edwin decided I had some sense and he started helping me, teaching me things and sending me to college. I was a walk-on that first year and then I got a scholarship to play football and when it wasn't football season, I worked for him doing office work. I picked up what he was teaching me and with his help, I made some investments. When those grew, I made more. I didn't finish college because I was doing well with the investments and I worked for him."

"That's a leap to the point where you are today," she said, suspecting he was leaving events out of his story.

"Not really," Cade answered easily. "I went on my own and did even better. I've been lucky. Edwin didn't have any family and he left his fortune to me. I inherited it three years ago and since that time I've doubled the amount. Money generates money."

"Then it was better for you to leave here, wasn't it?" She gazed into his unfathomable brown eyes, and she couldn't guess what he was thinking, but she was surprised when she didn't receive an affirmative answer from him immediately.

"I suppose it depends on where you place your values," he replied finally, and her pulse jumped. Had he meant that he would have been better off staying here? She wondered. Did Cade have regrets? She shrugged away the notion because he could have come back in the intervening years.

"So where do you place your values?" she asked, surprised by his answer.

"Family is more important than income," he said and she stared in disbelief.

"All that you did since you left here has made you enormously wealthy while you're still young, plus given you some education," she said, not mentioning that the rough edges about him had disappeared. "If you'd stayed, you would have married. That you can do anyway, and I'm surprised you haven't already. Why haven't you married?" she asked. "Or is that getting too personal?"

"I never found anyone that I wanted to marry," he replied in a husky voice and gave her a piercing look that sizzled along her nerves and made her feel that in some manner, his statement was aimed directly her. "Why haven't you married?" he asked.

"I'm wed to my work," she replied. "That's where my time and attention goes."

To her surprise, he leaned forward to draw his fingers down her cheek and then he slipped his hand across her nape, sliding his fingers around to rest his hand on her throat. "Work doesn't take all your attention. Right now, your pulse is racing, Katherine. You're passionate and responsive. You're a gorgeous woman, and I know men have been in your life. There's a lot more to life than your work."

"And you're offering to reenter my life and show me what I've been missing? No, thank you," she replied, trying to hang on to her poise and hating that he could feel her racing pulse.

"No, I've no intention of getting us back together. We've got too many hurtful moments between us. I'm just surprised you're not married and curious why you're not," he said.

He was too close to her, and his dark gaze bore into her. She was aware of his fingers lightly pressing against her throat. She couldn't keep from looking at his mouth and then she jerked her gaze back to meet his. "If you're pushing for me to say I've been waiting for you to come back, give it up."

"Of course not. I'm amazed to find you single and no particular man in your life. You're too beautiful to sit home alone nights."

"Thank you for the compliment, but when I do get a chance to sit home alone, it's a relief to not have to do anything. There's no one, Cade, and I'm fine with that. You said there's no one in your life, either, so why tell me I need someone?" While she talked, his gaze drifted slowly over her features, making her tingle. He ran his index finger lightly across her lower lip.

"Don't get personal, Cade," she remarked and he leaned away, smiling at her.

"I didn't intend to disturb you."

"You don't disturb me!" she snapped. His eyebrow arched wickedly, and he gave her an amused look.

"I don't?" he asked, leaning close again to trail his hand along her arm. "That doesn't cause a jump in your pulse? I'll admit it," he said, with his voice becoming husky, "it makes mine race." He placed his hand on her throat. "Let me see if you're wrong, and I do disturb you—"

"All right, you know damned well you do!" she said, scooting back and getting a mocking grin from him. "Don't make much of it. I'm a woman and you're an attractive male."

"And you're getting angry over it. Enjoy the attraction."

"No, thanks. I don't want a relationship. I don't want a friendship. Either would be absolutely impossible."

He gazed at her solemnly and nodded. "You're beautiful and I—" He broke off abruptly. "There are moments when I forget all our past, but you're right." He clamped his jaw closed and turned away and she wondered what he had been about to say.

At Houston Hobby Airport they came down through clouds and rolled to a smooth stop. When the door opened, Cade took her arm lightly as wind buffeted them and thunder rumbled in the distance.

Instead of another waiting limousine, a chauffeur stepped out of a black sedan and handed the keys to Cade, who led her around to the passenger side to open the door for her.

As soon as she was seated, Cade circled the car and slid behind the wheel to drive. She buckled her seat belt and shifted slightly to watch him. He threaded through traffic winding through town and then into a residential area of increasingly larger homes.

She rode in silence, prickly, too aware of him, tingling from his touch. While she thought about what he'd just told her, she watched him drive.

Finally, they went through tall, black iron gates that had an attendant who waved at Cade. They followed a winding, tree-lined street with an occasional mansion set back on well-tended lawns. More gates swung open to Cade's private drive and as he wound along it, they passed an immaculate, emerald lawn shaded by tall oaks draped with feathery Spanish moss and magnolia trees. When they rounded a curve, a mansion spread before her in a setting of tall pines.

Stunned, she stared at a structure that awed her with its beauty and size that had been inadequately represented in the simple line drawings of his blueprints. Once again, he surprised her.

"It's a palace!" she exclaimed, looking at a three-story stone structure with slate roofs, mullion windows and huge wings spreading away to the east and west. Trucks of various types and sizes were parked near the west wing, and scaffolding and ladders were against the walls as workmen scrambled over the incomplete wing.

After the first shock at the size of the place and the elegant fountain in front and formal gardens, her second thought was that she and Cade would never see each other because the place was so huge, causing relief to swamp over her.

"How can you stay here all by yourself?" Instantly, she realized she shouldn't have inquired. "Sorry. I was out of place to ask you. It's none of my business. And you haven't lived here long, have you?"

"I don't mind your questions. No, I haven't stayed in the house a lot. The builders have finished, all except one wing and the guest house, and the decorator has finished part of the house so I have furniture, and the place is livable. As far as residing alone, I'm comfortable with a big place. Remember, I grew up with three brothers and two bedrooms."

"I know," she remarked, not adding that she recalled everything about him.

"All my houses are large and I guess it's because of my past. Plus, it's an investment. Perhaps the big houses are part security blanket, part a balm for my ego. You're the only person I've ever admitted that to," he said. "I'm not looking for sympathy because you know my past, but I don't ever want to be hungry or crowded again."

She inhaled, hating that she had gotten them on a personal basis because it did prompt her sympathy, which she didn't want to feel.

"Since it's your first visit, I'll take you in the front door," he said when he stopped the car.

"Trying to impress me?" she asked.

"Of course," he replied with a grin, and she couldn't resist smiling in return, while he climbed out and went around the car in long strides.

"Keep the conversation impersonal," she whispered to herself as she watched him. "Don't tell only me your inner feelings and motives," she added, knowing he couldn't hear her. When he opened her door, she stepped out of the car.

The mammoth porch and stately Corinthian columns were magnificent. He was building a showplace. Taking a deep breath, she walked along beside him as they crossed the porch and he touched a button beside a plate with an intercom.

"You don't carry a key?" she asked.

"Not to the front of any of my houses. If I carried all my keys, I'd jingle like a sleigh."

When the door swung open, a uniformed maid greeted Cade with a big smile.

"Good morning, Mr. Logan."

"Morning. Mrs. Wilkson, this is Miss Ransome, who'll be moving in soon to paint murals for me." He turned to Katherine. "This is Mrs. Wilkson, Katherine."

"I'm glad to meet you," Katherine said, stepping into the enormous, elegant entrance hall with marble floors and a soaring vaulted ceiling.

"Pleased to meet you, too, ma'am," Mrs. Wilson said as she closed the front door. Katherine was relieved to discover there would be other people in the mansion, but she should have guessed in such a large place, Cade would have help. She received more surprises when Cade took her arm and they walked along the hall.

"I'll introduce you to my staff," Cade said. "If you ever need to find one of them, their schedules are posted in the pantry," he added. While she wondered how big a staff he had, she was even more relieved that there would be several people present in the house and she wouldn't be alone with him.

"Where do they stay?" she asked, guessing they had quarters in the huge mansion, probably on the third floor.

"They have their own small houses," he answered, and she glanced up at him.

"I'm surprised. This place is huge. You could have had them stay here and they'd never be in your way. When I was growing up we had a live-in nanny and a live-in cook and a live-in maid. Their quarters were all on the top floor. Of course, the ranch was too far away for anyone to drive back and forth daily."

"I could've done that, too, but that isn't what I want," he answered evenly. "I intend for people who work for me to have their own places and their privacy. I want my staff to like their work. I treat them as I would want to be treated if I had their jobs."

She nodded. "That's because of your past," she observed.

"Damn straight, it is. I've been poor and done menial work

and know what it is to be treated like you're insignificant. I'm not knowingly doing that to anybody."

"So you don't adhere to the old adage, 'Familiarity breeds contempt.'"

"Not that kind of familiarity. I believe respect creates a better relationship."

"I can't argue that one," she said, remembering the small rooms that their help had when she was young.

Mouthwatering smells of baking bread and barbeque floated in the air, reminding her that she had eaten only a few bites of her breakfast.

They stepped into a state-of-the art kitchen with polished oak cabinets and granite countertops. Large windows let sunlight spill into the spacious room that opened into a living area with a stone fireplace, a sofa, chairs and a long, polished wooden table that would seat ten people. Near an oven, a short, barrel-chested man with a shiny bald head and toothy smile faced her.

"Katherine, this is Creighton, who's been with me several years and is one of the best chefs in the world. Creighton, meet Miss Ransome."

They talked politely for a moment and then Cade took her arm to steer her into the hall again. "Let's find your room and then you can have a tour of the finished part of my house."

"How many work for you here?"

He shrugged. "My gardener and his crew. One of them is a chauffeur when I need one. I have two cleaning people—one is Mrs. Wilkson. I have Creighton and I have a handyman."

She was astounded, but more reassured than ever that she wouldn't be alone with Cade often.

Her good feelings about avoiding him vanished when he showed her a suite that was to the left of the sweeping main staircase to the second floor.

As she entered the sitting room, he said, "This is where I

thought you might like to stay. The rooms across the hall can be used for your office and studio."

"Fine," she said, barely seeing the room because Cade stood close by her side. "And you stay where?" she asked, expecting him to be in the opposite end of their wing.

"My suite is next to this one."

She turned to stare at him. "In this enormous mansion, you're putting me next to you?"

"Don't worry, Katherine. I'll leave you alone," Cade answered, and this time the steel was clearly present and fire flashed in his dark eyes. "The west wing is under construction, so I can't stay in it. In this wing, these are the only two bedroom suites. If you don't want to stay in here, there are other smaller bedrooms down the hall."

"This is fine," she said, knowing there would be no avoiding him some of the time. "So we'll see each other and we'll be together," she said.

"Is contact between us a problem?" he asked, placing his hands on his hips and studying her. He moved closer and her pulse jumped. "Why is it a problem?"

"Cade, you've hired me to do a job for you, and I intend to do it. In the meantime, I'm trying to keep the lid on my anger with you. I'm not certain I'll be able to if we are constantly together."

"That was nine years ago," he reminded her, increasing her fury.

"You expect me to *forget?*" She flung the words at him, hurt boiling in her. "You simply left without a word—" She clamped her mouth closed, not wanting to go into the past, knowing if she started flinging accusations, she would say things she'd regret. She thought about the job he had hired her to do and knew she had to focus on it totally and forget everything else.

"Dammit, Katherine! You sound as if you think you were the only one hurt!" he snapped and a muscle worked in his jaw.

"You did just what you wanted to do, and you didn't tell me. There's nothing that would justify the way you walked out!" she cried, clenching her fists and shaking. "You hurt me in the worst possible way!"

"And were you in love with me, or just using me to get back at your father?"

"In the plane today I told you that was never any part of why I became engaged and intended to marry you. And I never expected you to turn out badly. I never saw you as bad."

"Oh, come on! At first you didn't let any of your family know you were seeing me. You sure as hell didn't let your brothers know."

"All right, I'll admit I didn't at first because you were wild and you had dropped out of school, which they wouldn't have liked. But it wasn't a big thing."

"The hell it wasn't."

She drew a deep breath. "I knew you were wild, but that's all. And I never once went out with you to get back at my dad. You're giving me a doubting look," she added with her anger increasing.

He shrugged one shoulder. "Maybe we should have had this conversation nine years ago, but my temper ruled my judgment and your father made a good case. I was—"

"My father!" she exclaimed. "What did my father have to do with making a 'good case' to you?"

"Plenty," he replied. "I was a boy then, defensive about my life. Your father told me that your interest in me was out of rebellion—that there wasn't any love," Cade snapped.

"You never told me that he talked to you," she said, astounded.

"Oh, he talked all right," Cade said, fury burning in his dark eyes.

"And without asking me, you believed him?"

"Damn straight I did. Why wouldn't I? I heard it from others. He said your brothers would say the same thing if I asked them. They weren't in town to ask. I didn't know them well and they were both away. But I knew how you fought with your father."

"You knew my father would do all sorts of things to get what he wanted—"

"And so would his daughter—"

Rage exploded in her and she reached out again to slap him. Just as deftly as before, Cade caught her wrist and yanked her up against him, holding her arm behind him. She was pressed tightly against his hard length, both of them breathing hard. "You always did have a temper, Katherine."

"Let go of me."

"Tell me you didn't want to marry me to get back at your father. You fought with him over everything that year."

"No! Damn you for believing him, and him for telling you such a thing!" With her free hand she pushed against Cade's shoulder, and it was like shoving a rock. Only she wasn't pressing against a rock, but warm, solid muscles. He shifted, releasing her wrist and wrapping her in his arms to hold her so tightly she could barely breathe.

"I was in love with you!" she cried.

"Then, dammit, after I left here, why didn't you take my calls or answer my letters?" he snapped.

"Why would I since you walked out without a word? I never wanted to see you again!" She looked up into his dark eyes that flashed with fire. She was held tightly against him while his scalding gaze devoured her. Anger burned away, and the moment transformed.

"No!" she whispered, but her protest was breathless, almost inaudible as she strained with her arms to get free of his grasp.

"Stand still, Katherine," he commanded as he looked intently at her.

His gaze lowered to her mouth and her heart slammed

against her ribs. "I remember absolutely what it was like to kiss you," he said.

Her heart thudded and heat flooded her, demolishing her anger because she, too, could remember exactly how it had been to kiss him. She looked at his mouth and then into his dark gaze and she was lost.

He leaned down, placing his mouth on hers and she went up in flames. Years and anger didn't exist. His kiss was seduction, sending jolts of electricity that fanned the flames already low inside her.

His hand went into her hair, and he released his other arm that circled her waist. When he did, she slipped her arms around his neck. Yielding to desire, she wanted to devour him and she felt as if that was what he was doing to her. He leaned over her, molding her against him while his kiss deepened and possessed, his tongue stroking her with fervor.

Craving pounded in her and she thrust her hips against him. She wanted him with a pent-up desperation of nine long years, a yearning that dimly shocked her, but had instantly spun out of control the moment his lips touched hers.

His kiss inflamed her. While her pulse roared, lights exploded behind her closed eyes. Aching for all of him, tremors shook her. Her world rocked and spun topsy-turvy. Wisdom was ashes and need was overwhelming.

Her hair tumbled down, but she was only dimly aware of it falling. His hand slid slowly down her back, a stroke that she could barely detect through her suit coat, but then she felt his hand roam over her bottom. He shifted her slightly, his hand drifting to her front, easing up over her hip and ribs.

Through her navy silk blouse, his fingers caressed her breast and rubbed her nipple, heightening her ecstasy and torment.

Powerful, relentless and seductive, his kiss awakened desires in her that she had thought were gone forever.

She knew that she had to slow him or they would be at the

point of no return and she would be mired in a legion of complications with him. Reason was vague, a faint nagging that she wanted to ignore. She ran her hands across Cade's broad shoulders and a sob tore from her throat, but was taken in his kiss—a kiss that she had dreamed about, longed for, tried to forget for so many years. His kiss burned her like a brand now and caused her hips to shift. She wanted him more than ever before.

His hands were beneath her blouse, cupping her breasts and then pushing away her bra, his fingers circling her nipples with fiery caresses that finally broke through the blanket of longing that enveloped her.

Moaning, she clutched his wrists, leaning back to look up at him. "You have to stop now!" she gasped.

Desire blazed in his dark eyes and took her breath. There was no question that he wanted her.

Was this what he had intended from the start—seduction? Was he coming back into her life only to break her heart all over again?

Was she going to let him?

She gasped for breath and noticed his breathing was as ragged as hers. His lips were red from their kiss, and his hungry gaze looked as if he wanted to consume her totally. He played with a lock of her hair.

"You burn me to cinders," he whispered, and her heart pounded. "That was the kiss of a lifetime," he added, shaking her even more. While she agreed with him, she wouldn't admit it. Aching to pull his head down and continue kissing, she clenched her fists. At the same time, her fury simmered, and now it was fueled by anger at herself for succumbing to him.

"We're not going there, Cade. Never again!"

"Shhh!" He placed his finger on her lips, and her heartbeat quickened.

"No, we're not," she said, snapping at him and jerking her head away. "If that's what you expected—"

"Just don't say 'never' about something as exciting as when we kiss." While he studied her features, he combed his fingers through her hair. "Your hair is soft," he whispered as the last pins fell around her feet.

She caught his wrist in her hand. "You know I can't turn down a fee worth millions, but I don't want this. I don't want your kisses—"

"You didn't act that way a minute ago," he drawled, one dark eyebrow arching.

"So I respond to you physically!" she snapped. "It's lust. I don't go out often with men. I'm vulnerable about some things, but I don't want to kiss," she said, tucking her silk blouse back into her skirt. "Look at me! I look—"

"Like you've been kissed," he said in a velvet tone that heated her. "You're more beautiful now than you used to be," he said.

"Thank you," she replied in clipped words, trying to ignore her racing pulse or the rush of pleasure over his compliment. "I don't want intimacy or to get close or to trust you that way again. You killed my trust and if you thought I didn't love you, you were wrong. If you thought my only reason for marrying you was because I was rebelling against my father and trying to get back at him, you should have told me. Leave me alone." She started to walk away, but he jerked her around to face him, holding her squarely by the shoulders.

"Dammit, Katherine, you don't even know what lengths your father went to, or why I left, and you never did care or even want to find out when I wrote and called."

"You keep talking about my father—so he talked to you and you believed him without even asking my side."

"He did a hell of a lot more than talk."

Surprised, she wondered if she were hearing the truth. In the past Cade had always been honest with her and there was no reason to deceive her now. He had already gotten what he really wanted from her—the agreement to paint his murals.

"What else? What else could my dad have done to make you walk out on our wedding?"

Five

"If he'd threatened you physically or beaten you up, that would have just made you all the more determined," she persisted.

"You're right and I'm sure he knew that."

"Then what was it?" she asked, unable to imagine her father doing anything to sway Cade, who had a stubborn streak.

"Time and again he offered to pay me off to get me to walk out."

"I don't believe you," she said, stunned at first, stepping back and staring at Cade who placed his hands on his hips. "My dad will go to great lengths to get what he wants, but he's never hurt any of us deeply in order to get his way. He wouldn't hurt me that way."

"Well, he did hurt you—or contribute to me hurting you. The first few times he offered to pay me off if I'd get out of your life, I turned him down."

"Why didn't you tell me?"

"I didn't see any reason to cause you more anger toward your dad."

"I don't believe you." She started to walk past Cade to leave the room and get away from him.

"The first time he offered me two hundred and fifty thousand dollars to leave the state."

She stopped with her back to him, wanting to throw her hands over her ears and rush out of the room to avoid hearing what she thought were lies, but she couldn't move.

"Then he offered four hundred thousand. He wanted me out of your life badly. One of the conditions, of course, was that you would never know. I'm breaking that condition right now."

She spun around. "You took the money?" she asked, barely able to get out the words because it meant Cade was telling the truth. She was stunned to know her father would hurt her like that. "I can't believe that the payment was worth more than our love. That's the deepest hurt of all, Cade. And I don't believe that my dad would hurt me so badly," she said without being aware she was saying the words aloud.

"He probably thought he was doing what was best for you and your future happiness. He damn well told me enough times that I was bad for you, I had nothing to offer you, no hope for the future. I would drag you down."

"You knew I didn't feel that way."

"Your father pointed out I had a brother in trouble with the law, no father in our family, no means to do anything for you, no future hope. I'd been in trouble at school for cutting classes. I was wild, poorly educated—he made it very clear that if I loved you, I'd get the hell out of your life."

Stunned, she chilled as she stared at Cade and knew he was telling her the truth. "I loved you and I wanted to marry you."

"You know your dad was partially right and at the time, I thought he was dead right about all of it. I didn't expect to go into the world and make a fortune—there's nothing in my background or anyone else in my family that indicated such a thing."

"You should have told me."

"You would have argued with me and said his accusations didn't matter—if you loved me. If you were rebelling as he said you were, you would have quarreled with me and said it didn't matter, too. Either way, your reaction would have been the same. At the time I did love you, Katherine, and I hurt because I thought you were marrying out of rebellion. It was easy to believe your dad. Except for actually telling me you wanted to marry me for that reason, you gave every indication of rebellion. You argued with your dad. We went out without you telling him who you were with. You complained to me how dictatorial he was. You did things he told you not to—taking the car when you weren't supposed to, calling me long distance when you weren't supposed to. You wore clothes that you knew he wouldn't approve of—do I need to continue? You know you were rebellious."

"So that's why you walked," she said, staring at him and wondering what would have happened if they had confronted each other with their accusations at the time. "You took four hundred thousand dollars in exchange to walk out on me." She knew Cade would have believed it when her dad told him he was nothing and would hurt her future because Cade had worried about that himself. And with the poverty of Cade's family, she could see where the money looked like a lifetime fortune to him, but she wouldn't have taken any amount to walk out on him. "I wouldn't have walked on you for any amount," she said.

"Oh, it wasn't the money," Cade said in a bitter tone. "I turned him down on that, so he came back with an offer I couldn't reject."

"What?" she asked, hurting all over with old wounds and fresh new ones.

"Leave it to your dad to figure out how to get to me. I was inexperienced in so many ways, Katherine. We both were."

"What else?" she asked, puzzled and reeling from Cade's revelations.

"Your dad raised the amount of money he offered, but that wasn't what got me. He offered to save my brother."

"How?" she asked.

"My oldest brother, Luke, was in jail, facing trial for robbery and assault because he got into a fight with a night watchman when he and two other guys were trying to break into a store and steal some bikes. Luke had been in trouble once before so he was facing prison. With all of his influence and contacts, your father saw to it that he could get the charges against my brother dropped by the people involved."

"No!" she cried. "My dad would never do that. He was enraged with you disappearing like you did."

"That was a damned act, Katherine. What would you expect him to do—admit what he'd done?"

"I don't believe you," she said stiffly, unable to accept that her father would do something so underhanded to one of his children.

"It's the truth," Cade insisted. "I made a promise I was never to tell you, but I'm breaking it right now. If I walked out on you without a word and left the state with my family, all charges against my brother would be dropped."

"Then you couldn't refuse him," she observed, dazed and hurting.

"In addition to helping us get along, your father agreed to give me half a million dollars. I wasn't going through with a marriage that would only hurt you in the future and at the same time see my brother go to prison when I could have kept him out. On top of all that were the nagging doubts about whether you even loved me or if you were marrying out of rebellion. How long would that last?"

He crossed the room in two quick strides and held her upper arms tightly. "Put all that together and what would you have done?" he demanded. "And then when I couldn't stand to be away from you and couldn't bear to think how I'd hurt you, and I called you—you wouldn't take my calls. Or answer my letters."

"I just don't believe my father would hurt me that way," she said, staring at Cade, wondering what had really happened.

"I don't know whether he would admit the truth if you asked him. I doubt if he would."

"I called Nick and Matt this morning to tell them you've hired me to paint your murals," she said, thinking about her father. "Matt's going to tell Dad. My dad couldn't have done anything that cruel to me, Cade," she repeated.

"Ask him, Katherine. You know your own father."

"I will ask him."

"If he denies it, he's lying. Why would I make all this up now?"

She wondered the same thing. "I'm ready to get back to Fort Worth."

He nodded. "All right, but before we leave here, let's step across the hall and you look at the rooms I have for a studio and office for you here. You can tell me what else you would like to have in them."

With stormy emotions, she followed him across the hall and entered a room that had a glass-and-iron desk, oak cabinets, a computer center with a copier, a fax machine and other electronic gadgetry. Sunshine spilled into the room from the floor-to-ceiling windows and from broad skylights in the ceiling.

"Your studio is here," he said, walking through a doorway into the next room. She entered a room that held a drawing board, easels, supplies of all types, a worktable and file cabinets. There was a large sink for her use with paints and an adjoining bathroom.

"It's great," she said, barely seeing any of it, seething over all he had disclosed and doubting him more by the minute. She expected her father to deny everything and if he did, she would believe him.

She couldn't imagine why Cade would lie to her about the past or that he expected her to accept what he said without confronting her father, but it was impossible to think her father had destroyed her future marriage.

Cade stood in the center of the room and looked around. "You can talk to my architect, tell him what you want and it'll be top priority."

"Thanks," she said stiffly.

"Ready to go? No tour of my house?"

"Let's tour another day. I want to get back and talk to Dad."

"If you're going to see him, Katherine, I'd like to be present," Cade said as they walked along the wide upstairs hallway and descended the stairs.

"Why do you want to be there?"

"I want to hear what he says and I broke a promise to him. I want to give him his money back. I don't want one damn dime from your dad."

"If he denies your accusations, Cade, and it's your word against his, I'll believe him," she said, but was uncertain if she really would, because her father would go to all sorts of lengths to get what he wanted sometimes. Except she had never thought he would with his children. They all clashed with him, particularly the years they were growing up, but he had never done anything as cruel and terrible as Cade accused him of doing. At least, nothing she had known about.

Shaken and worried, she was silent until they reached the first-floor hallway. "Our mother walked out when we were young. She fell in love with someone else."

"Maybe you ought to check that out," Cade stated solemnly.

"No. I'm sure Dad told us the truth there. He raised us

alone and sometimes he was harsh and did things we didn't like and meddled in our lives when we were older. The only one who didn't clash with him often was my brother Jeff."

"He died mountain climbing, didn't he? I read about him."

"Yes. He was wild and spoiled and Dad let him have and do most anything he wanted. They didn't go head-to-head like Dad did with Matt. Matt is more like my father, and they had some terrible battles, but Dad never did anything to hurt any of us badly, except…" she said and her voice trailed away. "I just can't believe it," she said, more to herself than to Cade.

"Except what?" Cade asked.

"He tried to buy off Olivia so she wouldn't marry Matt," Katherine replied, hurting and beginning to accept Cade's story more. "I have to hear him say that he did that to me," she said.

Cade shrugged. "Frankly, I expect him to deny it. If he does, then it comes down to his word against mine and my family. Plus the half-million-dollar deposit that I put into accounts in California banks when we went out there. Where else would we have gotten that amount?"

She stiffened, thinking things through again. "You're telling me the truth," she declared. She knew Cade's family was poor and his mother went from one menial job to another. "My father caused you to go," she said, remembering how kind her father had been to her and how furious he had been toward Cade. "He's always been strong-willed and wanted his way, but I just can't believe he would hurt me like that."

"Katherine, don't you understand—he thought he was saving you. He told me how I would ruin your life and your promising future. He was trying to protect you."

"That was my choice, and I wanted to marry you."

"That doesn't answer why you wouldn't even take my calls."

"I was so furious with you. I didn't want to talk to you again."

"You should have known that I was calling to give you my side."

"At the time after walking out on me, I didn't really care. There was nothing you could have said that would have smoothed things over. If you'd told me all you just did and every word was true—or worse—I wouldn't have wanted to get back together. Some hurts are too deep, Cade. But now, I want to hear him admit what he did."

"We'll go back." When they reached the front door, Cade held it open and as she passed him, she saw the muscle working in his jaw.

She rubbed her forehead. "How will we ever work together?"

He placed his hand lightly on her shoulder. "Easily. We've gotten through this and we're still speaking. My house is big, and we'll have a professional, working arrangement. We'll do all right. Maybe I'll fly back to California and stay away and you'll have the place to yourself."

When they climbed into the car, thunder boomed, and Cade pulled his cell phone from his pocket. "I'll call my pilot about the weather. He told me when we landed we might have a storm this afternoon, but then it should clear off in time for us to get back to Fort Worth I didn't expect to return this soon, so I didn't give the weather much thought."

Katherine was silent, her thoughts going back to her father, while Cade talked on the phone about the weather. When he finished, he turned to her. "There's a storm blowing in and it's not the best time to leave. We haven't had lunch anyway, so I'll take you to lunch and then we'll see if we can get out. How's that?"

"Fine," she replied, not really hungry, her emotions churning after Cade's revelations and her nerves raw from his kiss that she knew she would never forget.

He switched on the engine to drive away. Before they made the turn, she glanced over her shoulder and was amazed to think that in a few more days she would be living in his mansion. And her life may have changed there this morning because if what Cade said were true, she had a feeling that things would never be the same between her and her father.

Cade drove her to a small Italian restaurant and by the time he turned into the lot, a driving rain changed to hail. Cade pulled beneath an overhang. "Wait a minute," he said, switching off the car engine. "When this lets up a little, I'll take you to the door."

Unbuckling her seat belt, she turned to face him, while he did the same, facing her and stretching one long arm across the car seat. The pounding hail changed to a downpour and she felt closed into a tiny world with only Cade.

He played with a lock of her hair and the faint tugs pulled against her scalp. "I like your hair down."

"I can imagine what it looks like," she remarked dryly.

He moved his hand to draw circles on her knee with his index finger. "So what do you want out of life?" he asked her.

"To be a success," she answered instantly.

"You're already that," Cade said.

"Not like I want. I'll have to admit, Dad always fostered competitiveness in us—not in Jeff, but between Matt and Nick. I was the little sister, so I always tried to keep up, too. I think we all feel like we're competing with Dad."

"Damn. Your father—"

"Taught us how to achieve goals. There's some good in that."

"So how do you define success for you?"

"I want to open branch offices in five more cities, and with your murals, I'll have the finances. I want to get better at what I do and gain a bigger clientele for my murals. Frankly, I want a bigger income than Matt or Nick. Or at least as big."

"So do you know how much you're aiming to earn? Do you even know what they make?" he asked with amusement, and she smiled as she shook her head.

"No, I don't, but I'll know when they begin to take me seriously."

"I'd think your ten-million-dollar fee would make both of them take you seriously. Your dad, too."

"Maybe it has. My brothers sounded impressed."

"Money is cold comfort, Katherine. It can buy only so much."

"That's a peculiar thing to hear you say after the way you grew up and the money you've earned," she said. "You know what it means to be without it and you know what it means to have it."

"Money and success are fabulous, but they don't take the place of family."

"I'm surprised you feel that way," she said, staring at him and wondering how he could say such a thing with the background he'd had. "I'm amazed your income isn't your top priority in life."

"I'm astonished you don't place family first. You're close to yours."

"I love my family," she said, "but success is the most important thing in my life."

"So what are you afraid of in life, Katherine? I mean the big things, not thunderstorms and mice. What scares you? You can't even imagine being poor, so it isn't that."

She thought a moment. "Failure. I hate failing at something I try. I'm not afraid of being poor because I don't even relate to that. I guess that's what drives you and what you fear."

"No. I've lived with poverty and beaten it. Of course, it's influenced my life and it's why I like big houses and fancy cars and luxury and a pantry stocked with food."

"How many cars do you own?"

He grinned. "I have cars everywhere I go. I have a warehouse of antique and special cars. About fifty."

"You're afraid of poverty or you wouldn't collect all those cars," she said. "What else? Is there anything else in the world you fear?"

"Being alone all my life," he answered solemnly and quickly. "That would be the worst."

Startled by his answer, she gazed up at him. "Then I'm surprised you aren't married with a batch of kids. That would be insurance against being alone the rest of your life."

"I haven't found the right woman and while I want a family, I want a woman I love and like. Not just someone to fill a void. So what about you? What's the real reason why you aren't married?" he asked, watching her intently.

"I got hurt too badly when you left," she admitted. "I'll never go through that again. I won't trust anyone enough to fall in love and let someone break my heart a second time. I want my career and I want success more, anyway."

He leaned closer and tilted her head up, holding her chin in his fingers. Rain pounded on the car and they were enclosed in their own steamy space. She was aware of the closeness, of his dark eyes and his tempting mouth.

"What a waste, Katherine," he said softly. "You're beautiful, loving and passionate. You were meant for living life fully and giving to others and having children, not for boardrooms and long hours of work and balance sheets. It's an incredible waste," he said.

"It's what I want," she answered, taking a deep breath and drawing herself up as she jerked her head out of his hand. "What do you want, Cade?"

"A family," he replied instantly.

"What a thing for you to say you want when you ran away from the chance to have children."

"I never expected to earn a fortune until after I had worked for Edwin Talcott. Those first years in California, I put making money as my main goal, but I could stop work now and never lift a hand again and be wealthy. What's the point in driving to make more now?"

"I can't imagine that I'll ever feel that way, but I want the acknowledgments that come with success. I want my father's respect and my brothers' respect."

"I think you have always had that and their love."

She looked away, knowing she wanted to dazzle them with her business success. "I think you and I are poles apart—more than when we were young. It doesn't matter now. Our priorities are vastly different," she said.

"When you've finished this job, we'll go our own ways so it doesn't matter."

"If you want a family, that should be the easiest thing in the world for you to acquire. You're handsome, wealthy, sexy, charming," she admitted to him.

"Thank you. I feel that you're keeping the other half of your opinion to yourself. There's a 'but' in there somewhere."

"There should be droves of women willing to become Mrs. Cade Logan," she said, ignoring his last remark, "and equally willing to give you children," she added.

"Marriage hasn't come close to happening. When I went to California, I was busy surviving, learning, taking care of my brothers and helping Mom. Then I was occupied with business, scrambling to make a fortune and learning how to deal with it. Also, I've never found anyone I loved except you."

"Well, that was long ago and over for both of us," she declared, ignoring a flutter stirred by his statement. "There are too many bad moments and hurts between us. What's left between us is lust and I'm not interested."

"Do you ever just let down and have a good time?" he asked.

"Yes, but no thanks if that's an offer to sleep with you."

"Please give me credit for being slightly more subtle than that."

She rubbed a window and peered out. "I think the rain has let up a lot."

"Then we'll go inside," he said, sliding back behind the wheel. He drove her to the door and reached across her to open her door to let her out. She could see midnight glints in his black hair and his clean-shaven jaw. His arm brushed against her middle, and his head was only inches in front of her. He looked into her eyes.

Her heart skipped a beat as she was held, unable to move or look away. He was so close, his mouth only inches from hers. "Cade, leave me alone," she whispered without realizing it until his eyes narrowed.

"I'm not even touching you," he said in a rasp.

"You don't have to and you know it. I'm susceptible, dammit. Don't push me."

"Katherine, there's no way I'm 'pushing' you now. And I don't know how you can be very susceptible when you're brimming with wrath."

"Move out of my way," she said, her words breathless and her pulse racing. He released the open door and leaned away. The minute he moved, she slid out of the car and hurried into the restaurant without looking back. She heard the door slam and the engine roar as he pulled away to park.

When she stepped inside the restaurant to wait for him, she was breathing hard. She walked around the entrance, looking at pictures of Naples on the walls without really seeing them as she tried to regain her composure. Then Cade came through the door and her pulse escalated again.

They sat in a corner booth at a wooden table covered with a red-and-white-checkered tablecloth, then they both ordered penne and bread sticks.

"Now, shall we try a truce?" he asked as he ate.

"Of course, Cade," she replied with far more poise than she felt.

"To get on safer ground, let's discuss your office. What would you like in it?"

"I think you've covered everything in the way of furniture and lighting and electronic equipment. I'll have my laptop and I'll move one of my computers there. I want my own computers that already have the software I need."

He nodded and became silent and they ate in a quiet tension that set her nerves on edge even more. All that Cade had revealed spun in her thoughts repeatedly and each time she considered whether her father had bought off Cade or not, she had a sinking feeling that he had done exactly that.

She had little appetite and soon she glanced over her shoulder at the front windows. "I think it stopped raining completely. Call and see if we can fly out now."

"I don't have to call. I know we can if the storm has passed. I'll call my pilot and tell him we're on our way."

In less than an hour they were airborne, flying back to Fort Worth. She called and told her father that she wanted to come see him and he agreed with a cheerful tone of voice. Next she told him that she had Cade with her.

When she put away her cell phone, she glanced up to find Cade watching her. "I couldn't keep from hearing you," he said. "He doesn't want to see me, does he?"

"No, but he will. I'll take you with me unless you'd rather not go."

"I'll go. I told you that I want to give him back his money. I have it ready here on the plane."

"You're carrying that kind of cash?"

"I have a check. I intended to see him and get it back to him sometime this weekend. I don't expect him to welcome me. Far from it."

"His health hasn't been good in the last couple of years. Whatever he's done, he's still my father and I don't want to upset him," she said.

"I don't intend to disturb him," Cade replied. "I'm just going to give him a check for half a million dollars—exactly what he gave me that night."

"Where was I?"

"At home. He had me meet him at the Millington in a private room."

"You know seeing him will be troublesome," she said tightly.

"Sorry, but I want to pay the money back myself."

She shook her head, wishing the whole encounter could be avoided, yet she had to ask her father. "I'm in denial about what you told me, but if you're paying him back half a million, then it has to be true. I just can't completely accept it."

"Sorry. My intention wasn't ever to hurt you. But until you knew the truth, you'd never forgive me."

She stared at him, wondering if they could get past how they had hurt each other years ago.

They rode quietly, yet Cade sat across from her, his legs stretched out with only a breath of space between their legs, enough room to avoid touching, yet too close to forget how easily she could touch him.

"Tell me about your family, Katherine. I see Nick occasionally."

"He's married now and busier than ever and business is growing. He thrives on it just as I do. Matt is the one who stayed on the ranch and took over for Dad. Matt has his own house there and he's married. Last January they had a little boy they named Jeff."

"For your brother. That's great, Katherine. So you're an aunt."

"Yes," she said. "I've kept Jeff occasionally and, naturally, I think he's adorable. I even have his picture," she said, fishing it out of her purse to see Cade giving her a sardonic look.

"What?" she asked.

"You—whose main goal in life is success—are carrying your baby nephew's picture."

"I love my family. I never said I didn't. I just don't expect to marry and have a family of my own."

"Uh-huh," he said doubtfully as he took the picture of little Jeff. "Cute baby," he said and handed back the photo.

"What about your family?" she asked, mostly to keep from thinking about seeing her father, a moment she dreaded.

"I have a house near L.A., and so do all of us. We live in our own compound so we see each other often. I built a house there for Mom. I have a condo In L.A., as well."

Katherine remembered his mother as a plain woman who looked older than her years. The boys must have inherited their looks from their father, not their mother, Katherine thought.

"Mom's having the time of her life and I'm glad. All of us take care of her and she's found hobbies she likes and she runs on the beach every morning." He fished out his billfold and he leaned forward, his knees touching Katherine's and she drew a deep breath.

He pulled a picture out of his billfold and placed it in front of her. "Here we all are," he said. "Here's Luke, the oldest, then Micah's next and Quinn's the youngest."

She looked at four handsome men, all of them except Cade with pretty women at their sides. The only single man in the picture was Cade. He pulled out another picture. "Here's Mom."

"This is your mother?" Katherine asked in surprise. She studied a picture of a woman she didn't recognize. "She's changed completely," she said, amazed by the transformation. "She looks younger and she's very attractive," Katherine said.

"Thanks," he said, putting away his pictures. "She's had her hair styled and got contact lenses and had her teeth fixed. Little things that make a difference. She works out every day. She did the best she could for us."

Katherine marveled again at the changes in Cade and his family. "What do your brothers do?"

"They work for me. I sent them to college and two majored in finance, Micah majored in marketing and now he has a two-year-old boy."

"So you're an uncle now."

"Yes, I am. We all get together on holidays and as much as we can."

"Good, Cade. I'm glad things worked out for you and your

family," she said. "My family gets together twice a month if we possibly can." She was quiet for a long time and then looked around to see him watching her.

"You're worried, aren't you?" he asked.

"Yes. I hate to upset Dad now that his health isn't good."

"Then let it drop."

She shook her head. "No. I have a right to know if he did what you say."

"He did it, Katherine, and all the denials in the world won't change the truth."

She clamped her lips closed and turned to look out the window. Her trepidation increased with every passing hour and by the time she was finally in her father's house she was tense, dreading seeing him. Too aware of Cade by her side with a check in his pocket, she strode down the wide hall. The door stood open to the family room where she knew her father would be waiting.

"Last chance to escape," she said to Cade outside the door, and he shook his head.

"No. I want this meeting. I've waited nine years for it, Katherine."

Six

As she entered the room, Katherine called hello. Standing, Duke Ransome smiled until his gaze went past her. His face flushed and he scowled.

"Katherine, I recall telling you to come alone."

"I wanted to see you, Mr. Ransome," Cade replied easily before she could answer. He passed her to face her father. Neither man offered to shake hands.

"Katherine, you should leave," Duke snapped while watching Cade.

"I want to stay," she said and received a deeper scowl.

Duke turned to Cade. "I thought I had an agreement with you that we wouldn't ever see you again. Since you're here, I take it that you've broken your promise and you've told everything to Katherine."

Her insides knotted because in that moment, she knew absolutely that Cade had told her the truth. Her father had caused Cade to walk out on her and then misled her about it.

Hurting, she wanted to scream at her father, but it was over and nothing would ever undo the past, so she clamped her mouth shut. She was chilled, lightheaded, even though she wasn't given to fainting. Her own father had caused her heartbreak. She hurt all over because she felt betrayed, first by Cade and now by her father.

Cade withdrew his check. "I'm paying you back, Mr. Ransome," Cade said. "Here's a check to you for five hundred thousand dollars. Paid in full," Cade said grimly. "I used it well and through the investments you allowed me to make, I'm where I am today. Actually, I owe you a debt of gratitude for enabling me to achieve financial success." Cade tossed the check on a chair.

"How can you stand there and be so polite!" Katherine cried, finally unable to hold her emotions in check. She clenched her fists and shook. "Dad, how could you have hurt and deceived me the way you did?" Before he could answer, she turned to Cade. "And how can you so politely pay him back when he tore up our lives and our futures?"

Cade shrugged. "It's the truth, Katherine. I'm where I am today because of your father and his money. Absolutely and directly," he said emphatically to Duke, whose face was flushed and his fists were clenched.

"Damn you! You always were trouble—we had a deal," Duke said to Cade.

"Yes, sir, we did, but I'm breaking my promise to never return to Texas. In preventing me from marrying your daughter, you got what you wanted and now you have your money back. Don't mess with me, Mr. Ransome. I can buy out everything you own," Cade said quietly. "Katherine has agreed to paint some murals for me. You have a very talented, successful daughter and I guess Katherine owes some of her success to you, too." Cade turned to her. "Katherine, I'll wait out in the car. I'm through in here."

Cade left and closed the door behind him, and she faced her father. "How could you have done that to me?"

"I did it for your benefit," Duke answered. "If Cade had stayed here, he would never have been what he is now."

"Dad, I'll never understand how you could have hurt me like you did."

"Always remember I did it for you. Cade was trash. He wouldn't have amounted to anything if he had stayed right here. His brother was going to prison. None of us knew he would turn out like he did."

"He wasn't trash," she said stiffly.

"Don't go to work for him. You'll fall in love again and get hurt again because he's out for revenge."

"If he'd wanted revenge, would he have given you all the money back?"

"He probably enjoyed every moment of paying me the money," Duke snapped, his voice filled with disgust.

She didn't want to hear any more about it and she turned, hurrying out of the room, hearing her father calling her name, but she kept going. Not once nine years ago had it occurred to her that her father might have been the reason for Cade's disappearance. At the time she had known her father hadn't approved of him, but she'd thought he had accepted her pending marriage.

She stepped outside to see Cade leaning against the car, his feet crossed at his ankles while he waited. As he watched her approach, she forgot some of her anger and hurt.

"Let's go get some dinner," he said, draping his arm across her shoulders.

"I can't eat," she replied.

"Maybe you can by the time we get back to Fort Worth." He pulled out his cell phone, called a number and made dinner reservations.

"I'll take you to a quiet place, and we can have the evening out that I bid on."

"We had that last night," she said as he opened the door on the passenger side of the car, but he blocked her from sitting inside.

"We've gotten a lot of things out in the open since last night," he said. "We can do the evening over and this time maybe it'll be better."

"I thought it was good last night," she replied, and his chest expanded as he inhaled.

"It'll be better tonight, Katherine. You'll see," he said with his voice lowering a notch, getting that husky rasp that made her tingle.

"Cade, keep your distance. I'm still reeling from all I've learned."

"I know you are," he replied gently, "but there's no reason to sit home alone stewing over it. C'mon. One evening, that'll be better than last night," he reminded her. "That's easy."

He made it sound easy, but she knew there was a tangled history that would always be a cloud and there was the constant hot attraction that could explode into complications in their lives.

"Come on. One evening. You'll eat somewhere."

"Arm twister," she said with a sigh, knowing he was right. If she were alone, she would hurt more, let her anger ferment, and dwell on all that she'd learned today.

When she nodded, Cade stepped aside and she slid into the car.

"I know he thought he was doing it for me, but it hurts so badly," she whispered and Cade squeezed her shoulder lightly.

"Sorry."

When they drove back to Fort Worth, to her surprise, Cade stopped at his hotel. "Come up while I change. I'm taking you to a restaurant where I'll need to wear a coat and tie."

"Another visit to your hotel room," she teased.

"It'll be as harmless and uneventful as last time unless you want otherwise."

"Uh-uh. And what happens if you want otherwise?"

"Wait and see," he said with a gleam in his eye, and she smiled.

Inside the hotel lobby they took the elevator to the top floor. At Cade's suite, he held the door to let her go inside ahead of him. "I'll be right back," he said. "Make yourself comfortable."

She strolled to the balcony and pulled on the door, thinking she would go outside and enjoy the view. Turning the lock and pulling, she remembered opening the door last night.

"The door sticks," he called, striding out of the bedroom and crossing the room. He had yanked off his knit shirt and wore only his slacks as he pulled on a white dress shirt. His muscled chest was well-defined. When she looked at him, her mouth went dry and her pulse jumped. She couldn't keep her gaze from roaming all over him. She remembered caressing that chest, pouring kisses over him.

"I meant to call housekeeping and have them fix that door, but I forgot," he said.

She barely heard him, standing breathless as he jiggled the door and gave it a yank. It came open and he turned. "There you are—" He bit off his words and she looked up, realizing how she was staring at his chest.

"You remember," he whispered, catching both her hands and placing them on his chest. He was thicker, more filled out than when he was younger, and he was more muscled. He still had a washboard stomach. He was rock hard, his skin smooth, his body warm, too enticing.

She yanked her hands away as if he had placed them against burning coals. "No, Cade!"

"Why not?" he demanded. He tangled his hand in her hair and tilted her head back to give him access to her mouth. "You remember touching me," he said softly. "Why not now? Why do you want to avoid touching me? You have plenty of times in the past."

"I told you the things I want us to avoid," she whispered.

"I know what I don't want to avoid. I want your kisses and I want your hands on me now," he said. "When you look at me like that, you set me on fire. You may not know it, but your eyes are expressive and the look you're giving me ought to make me break out in flames. There's no way I can just walk away and ignore you. Put your hands on my chest."

"No!" she whispered. The word was as weak as a sigh. She looked into his dark eyes, which added to her pounding pulse. "Let me go, Cade. I told you—"

Her words were smothered by his kiss when he placed his mouth on hers. His tongue slid into her mouth, stroking, stirring fires and making her want him. Desire burst into a blaze and her hands flew to his chest to push, but then when she touched him, once again, she was hopelessly lost to passion.

Her hands drifted across his sculpted chest, feeling the flat male nipples, tracing over his powerful shoulders and then down to his strong, muscled stomach. Her hand strayed down his side, then along his thigh, before inching up to his chest again. She tore her mouth away from his. "No! Cade, we're not—"

"Yes, we are. You want me to," he whispered and kissed her, his mouth coming down hard and his tongue going deep, and all her protests ended. Her hands drifted over his chest and slid around his waist to his smooth, muscled back. She didn't notice when he pushed away her suit coat, but she felt his fingers on her blouse and then it fell on the floor beside her. Her lacy bra went next and she was pressed against his bare chest, memories taunting her, taking her back to hours of passion with him.

Trembling and torn between caution and need, she kissed him.

It was Cade in her arms, out of her dreams into her embrace and kissing her. Hunger for his caresses absorbed her. She wanted to touch and kiss him. Tangling her tongue with his, she moaned. When she thrust her hips against him, she felt his hard erection.

"No!" she gasped, pulling away. "Cade, we're different people now with different aims in life and we can't pick up where we left off," she exclaimed while her heart thudded. His heavy-lidded gaze was hot while he looked at her breasts and cupped them in his hands. When his thumbs circled her nipples, she cried out.

He leaned down, taking her breast in his mouth, his teeth nipping lightly at her nipple and then his tongue circled her taut bud.

Bombarded by sensations, she clung to his shoulders. Desire was ablaze and she moved her hips, wanting him inside her.

His hands tugged up her skirt and slid along her thighs and his fingers slipped inside her lacy thong to rub her.

Crying out, she wound her fingers in his hair as need heightened and she knew in another minute she would be over the brink. She pulled him up, her hand sliding over his thick rod, but then she pushed against his chest and leaned away. Holding his wrists, she gazed up at him. "We can't do this. No."

"We can, Katherine," he argued. "There's no reason not to when we both want to touch and kiss and love."

"There are a million reasons," she cried. "You've given me one heartbreak. Don't give me two!" She slithered into her blouse, wadded up her bra and stuffed it into her purse and then hurried to pick up her suit jacket.

When she turned, he was watching her. "What are you afraid of?"

"I just told you—heartbreak a second time. I wasn't sure I'd survive the first one. I know I don't want to have another one," she replied.

"This time we don't have to make any commitment."

"That isn't reassuring. If we make love, then I'm committed, Cade. My heart will be in it and I don't want that. We're not going back. There are too many hurts, too much has happened in the past."

"Dammit, the past is over."

"No, it's not. And the last hour brought it back to life. You're looking for a family. Look somewhere else," she snapped.

He looked at her so intently, her heart thudded and she wondered what he was thinking. Then he yanked up his shirt and spun away, but not before his glance had raked over her again.

The minute his door closed behind him, she let out her breath. How could she work for him?

Strolling to a mirror, she combed her hair with her fingers and peered at her image. Her mouth was red, her face was flushed and her hair was a tangle. She did what she could to straighten her clothing and comb her hair, letting it fall freely over her shoulders.

She ached with wanting him and kept reassuring herself that her desire was only lust.

Deciding that she could take a cab home now and have peace and quiet, she crossed the room and opened the door to the hall.

"Katherine, wait," Cade said.

When she turned around, her heart skipped a few beats. In his charcoal suit and white shirt and tie, he was incredibly handsome and it took strong willpower to keep from walking into his arms.

"Don't go without me. C'mon, we'll have a pleasant dinner," he said.

Unable to resist him, she paused. "You look handsome," she said, thinking what an understatement that was. He took her breath and dazzled her. And undressed, he did even more.

"Thank you," he said. "Ready to go?"

She nodded and they left, riding the elevator in silence.

Cade drove them to a supper club that was quiet, with soft lights, a piano bar and a small dance floor. The piano player sang as he played and Cade and Katherine were given a table that was in a secluded, cozy corner.

When she ordered a glass of red wine and the waiter disappeared, Cade's eyebrow arched. "So tonight you'll try the wine."

She shrugged. "It sounds more inviting. More than a cup of coffee or a glass of iced tea. Cade, when we finish eating, if you'd like, we can go by my office and I can show you the murals I've done. I never do the same thing twice, so at least you'll know what you can't have, but I can find out what sort of picture you prefer."

"Sure," he said. "After we dance. I paid five hundred thousand dollars for an evening with you—which you've made very clear that I had my dance last night. I think I might be entitled to at least five dances with you—that would be paying one hundred thousand dollars per dance. That's not unreasonable, is it?" he asked matter-of-factly, but his eyes twinkled, and she had to laugh and shake her head.

"Cade, I'll dance with you as much as you want. For what you're paying me, I'm willing to do a great deal to please you."

"Are you now? I recall not very long ago you emphatically refusing to please me."

"There's a limit. Dancing with you is on the 'will do' list."

"So what's on the 'will not do' list?"

"Making love."

"Let me get this straight," he said, leaning close and running his hand over hers and then taking her hand to hold it while he rubbed her knuckles with his thumb. "Dancing is 'will do'?"

"That's right."

"How about kissing?" he said, looking at her mouth and she realized she had walked into flirting and a sexy conversation with him that was already making her tingle.

"Kisses on the mouth are 'will do.' Anything beyond that, 'will not do.'"

"I think I'll stop asking and find out by trial and error."

"Right," she said, smiling at him. "You're doing something right now."

"Just holding your hand," he said in great innocence. "That's nothing. It's a great evening and I'm with a gorgeous blonde so why not hold hands and dance and kiss?"

"Remember, we're out in public."

"I can remedy that at any time. My hotel is only five minutes away."

"No. Stop flirting, Cade."

"I can't with you. You're irresistible. While we wait for our dinners, let's dance," he said, standing and tugging lightly on her hand.

She walked to the dance floor and as they began to dance, her heart drummed. How right it felt to be in his arms! She danced with him, their legs brushing, their thighs together, her hand in his.

"You used to laugh a lot," he said softly to her.

"Life isn't as easy as it was then," she answered. "And now, between us, there's very little reason for laughter."

"Relax, Katherine. There's plenty of reason for smiles between us. We're on better terms than we were this time last night. You know what happened in the past and I know why you wouldn't take my calls or answer my letters. We can move on." He smiled at her and her heart skipped. "For starters," he said, "tell me how you started in business."

"It's difficult to carry on a friendly, inconsequential conversation when I'm still in shock. The hurt and anger isn't far away."

"Give it your best shot," he said quietly, his breath warm on her temple. They moved in perfect unison and she knew there was no faulting their dancing.

"Come on. Tell me how you got started," he urged, tightening his arm around her waist and pulling her closely against him while they slow-danced and barely moved.

"I'm sure at some point I told you that I took art all through high school and I've painted murals since my junior year, but back then, it was mostly murals in my friends' bedrooms. Occasionally, someone's mother would hire me to paint a mural in a utility room or a nursery. Then in college I painted some murals on buildings and began to get more jobs. I was into computers and I put the two together. I worked in advertising and did internships. I went to work for an ad agency, but I moonlighted and before long, my moonlighting was earning more than my regular job so I quit and went on my own and the rest is history."

"And you said that there's been no one man in your life since nine years ago."

"No, there hasn't been," she said, slanting him a look. "Does that make you feel better?"

"Infinitely," he answered, and they both smiled.

"And no one seriously in your life in all that time," she said. "I don't believe it, so don't even say it."

"I was telling the truth. No commitments by either of us. Think that means anything?"

"It means we're busy and we're particular," she replied lightly. "Or—"

"There is no 'or.' Forget that."

"You've changed in the intervening years," he said. "You're more beautiful, you're more serious."

"Of course, I have. The world is different. You've certainly changed."

"How?" he asked, leaning back slightly to watch her as she answered him.

"You're self-assured now. You're sophisticated. You're better looking."

"Thank you," he said with a slight nod as he gazed intently

at her. Dancing in his arms and looking into his dark eyes sent her pulse galloping. Desire simmered constantly and it took only the slightest touch or look to heat her. They stayed in one place, their feet barely moving, while they looked at each other and she couldn't take her gaze away. He was all that she had said and more, still the most appealing man she had ever known. She hungered for his kisses that could turn her inside out and always stirred her more than any other man's kisses ever had.

Was she being foolish in guarding her heart and refusing to go back into a relationship with him?

He pulled her close and leaned his head down. "I want you," he whispered and her heart thudded.

She pulled away to look up at him. "That doesn't go with your payment. We've already settled the issue."

"Of course not. Not for one second did I think I was buying sleeping with you," he said bluntly. "This is different and what I would feel if you weren't going to work for me. It has nothing to do with your painting."

She looked up at him, for one fleeting moment wondering about letting down the barriers around her heart, trusting him again. "Old hurts would always be there between us and a chance to hurt each other again," she said.

He gazed down at her and she couldn't guess from his expression what his reaction was. "I think I can let go of the past more easily than you can. I can put it aside completely."

"Then you're fortunate," she said. The music ended and she walked back to their table with him and sat facing him. "At least my father won't meddle in my life now."

"He can't where I'm concerned, but your father is a meddler and he won't change."

Their crab and lobster dinners were left only half-eaten when they had cups of coffee poured. After a few more minutes Cade stood and took her hand. "How about my third dance?"

On the dance floor he held her close against him and they danced to a slow ballad. "This is good, Katherine. So damn good. I like having you in my arms."

"Cade, everything in you is aimed at seduction."

"No, Katherine. When I'm aimed at seduction," he said softly, "you'll know it. I'm just making a comment now."

"Right," she said, shaking her head at him. "Let's put getting personal on the 'will not do' list," she said lightly, hoping she could keep the evening light and impersonal.

"Let's not," he replied. "I like slow-dancing. I like getting personal with you. I like kissing you—"

"Cade," she said in exasperation, leaning back to look up at him, and he gazed down at her with a crooked smile.

"All right. Impersonal. What mural have you painted that you like the best?"

"Actually, the one I enjoyed the most was a mountain scene in a lodge in Colorado. I loved the place and I liked doing the mural. Speaking of murals, if we're going by my office, we should go soon."

"We can go now. I'll claim my remaining dances another time," he said easily, taking her hand as they left the dance floor.

Another time ran through her thoughts. How long could she resist him? How much would she see him in the future? She suspected a lot.

It took only a few minutes to get to Ransome Design on the tenth floor in the Renaissance Building. She switched on lights as she entered her corner office and turned to find him looking around.

"Nice, Katherine," he said and she glanced at her office that had an antique mahogany desk, an elegant mahogany table with chairs around it, comfortable upholstered chairs, bookshelves, oil paintings on the walls and tall potted plants.

"There's a bar," she said, motioning toward double doors. "I'll get the books with the murals," she said, reaching up to a high shelf. As she started to pull out books, Cade's arm stretched overhead and he grasped the books.

"Tell me which ones and I'll get them," he said, taking down books for her. He had shed his coat and as soon as they had the books, he shed his tie and unbuttoned the top button of his shirt. Turning away, she slipped out of her suit coat and glanced around to find him watching her. She drew a quick breath and met his gaze.

"You're not wearing anything under that silk blouse," he said in a husky voice.

"Cade—"

"Here are your books," he said, his voice still low. Her office was warm, slightly stuffy, and she didn't want to pull on her suit coat and it seemed ridiculous to, but she also didn't want to stir Cade's desire. Dismissing it, she sat down at the table and opened a book.

"Pull up a chair," she instructed, trying to sound all business. "What I'd like to do is get the presentation for the first mural, get your approval and start painting. Then there'll be times I can work up ideas for the second one. That way we can start sooner, and I can concentrate on one mural at a time."

"Sounds like a good plan to me," he agreed.

He sat beside her and they looked through books while he made comments. Taking notes, she was aware of brushing their hands together, more faint touches that fanned fires. Soon, she realized he was going to be easy to please because he liked most everything she showed him.

Losing track of time, she finally had enough ideas to make suggestions and sketches that she thought she might work up into a proposal for him.

To her surprise, he picked out what he liked. He leaned close as she sketched out a drawing of an outdoor scene from a balcony that would look like an extension of the room. Beyond the balcony, land stretched away with a European flair in the beds of flowers, trees and in the distance a stream with a bridge.

"I'll draw and paint this scene. Pick at least two more for me to paint and present to you so you have a choice."

"No need to. I like this and you know exactly what I like," he said, his tone changing, and she forgot the drawing to look at him.

"Are you going to flirt constantly?" she asked.

"Every time I can," he replied.

His shoulder and arm touched hers and he was close beside her. He ran his finger along her jaw. "You don't need to do this one up in a sketch for me. I can tell from the drawing you've done that that's what I'd like to start with in the dining room."

"Then I'll do it for myself so I can see how it'll look. You're easy, Cade," she said, breathlessly, thinking about him more than the mural.

"Too bad you're not easy," he whispered, drawing his index finger lightly around the curve of her ear and creating tingles.

"So we're set and I can move in and start drawing?" she asked.

"As soon as you can," he replied. All the time they talked, they gazed into each other's eyes.

She tried to think clearly, looked away and struggled to get her mind back on the matter at hand. "I guess I can move in by next Tuesday."

"Monday we'll go to your bank," he said.

"I'll have to wind up things here Monday, too."

"I'll get an appointment at the bank for us. Where do you bank?"

When she told him, he nodded. She pushed back her chair and stood. The room had closed in and was hot and she needed to get space between them before she did something foolish.

"Just leave the books here. I'll put them away later," she said.

As he smiled and gathered them up, she shrugged and picked up her suit jacket.

Instantly, he set the books down on the table and reached out to take her arm and draw him to her. "Before you put on that coat," he said, pulling her close. "Come here, Katherine," he said in a husky voice.

Desire flashed in his dark eyes and her pulse jumped.

"Cade—"

He slid his arms around her and leaned down to kiss her in the manner that always stopped her protests.

His mouth covered hers and her heart thudded as his tongue went deep into her mouth. She wound her arms around his neck. One kiss fluttered through her mind and then all thoughts were gone. She was lost in a magic world of his kiss that awakened every nerve and fanned the flames she already struggled to keep under control.

She wasn't aware of him tugging her blouse out of her skirt, but she was conscious of his hands sliding over her bare skin and caressing her breast, rubbing his palm over her nipple in a delicious friction that made her thrust her hips against him.

"Cade—" she repeated his name and his mouth covered hers, possessive and demanding and she moved against him, feeling his thick rod. He was hard and ready for her, wanting her.

Her skirt fell away and he held her hips, leaning back to look at her, making her tremble. She wore only her thigh-high hose and her thong and his hot gaze raked over her like a caress.

"You're so damn gorgeous…" he whispered and pulled her to him, leaning over her as he kissed her, bending down so she would mold against him and cling to him. She felt his crisp white shirt, warm because of his body, his soft wool trousers and belt buckle pressing against her.

His hands slid over her bare bottom and along the back of her thighs and then his hand went between her legs, slipping beneath her thong to stroke her. She held him, moving her hips, moaning with craving for more of him as her hand slid down to his trousers and she rubbed his hard shaft.

With a sob she pushed against him. He straightened and she stepped away.

"We're not going to make love!" she cried. "You're not going to seduce me!" With shaking hands she yanked up her clothes, feeling his hot gaze pouring over her as she grabbed her skirt and stepped into it, and yanked on her blouse.

Gasping for breath she turned to face him. "You're not getting my heart the second time. We'll hurt each other again," she cried. He stood in a wrinkled shirt with half the tail hanging out over his waist. His erection pressed against his wool trousers. Cade's face was flushed and he was gasping for breath as much as she and in spite of doing what she thought was the wise course of action, part of her wanted back in his arms to kiss and love him.

"I never ever wanted to hurt you," he said, grinding out the words in a husky voice. "Not then, not now."

"Don't even say that! Back then, when you left, you may have thought it was best for my future, but you knew you were hurting me and you did it to save your brother."

"So I should have stepped back and let him go to prison?" Cade snapped.

"No, of course not. I didn't mean that. You did what you had to do, but you knew you were hurting me. And we're poles apart now with different lives and lifestyles."

"We've been over this," he said and she clamped her mouth shut.

She pulled on her suit coat as if it were armor, tugging it closed over her breasts. Her blouse was only partially buttoned, the tail of it hanging out of her skirt, but she didn't care. "I'm ready to go."

He crossed the room and walked beside her without touching her. She switched off the lights, glancing at her worktable and wondering how long it would be before she could look at that table and not see Cade standing beside it, disheveled, aroused, wanting to make love.

They returned to the car and rode in silence while she tried to regain her composure. And beneath it all, desire was a scalding flame, hotter than ever.

At her house, he stood facing her. "You let me know when you'll be ready to move and I'll send movers to get your things."

"I won't have that much," she said, shaking her head. "I can get my things in my car."

"Pack enough to last. Six murals will take a while."

She nodded. "I'm glad you told me what happened," she said quietly, and he nodded.

"I know it's put a rift between you and your dad."

"I'd rather know. In a way it was the most important time in my life. Rift or not, the truth is best."

"I'm glad you think so," he said, looking intently at her. The moment drew out and she knew if she didn't move, she might be back in his embrace.

"Good night," she said and stepped inside, closing the door quickly behind her without looking back.

She let out a long sigh as she walked to her room. The events of the day ran through her mind, but the predominant images and memories were of standing in Cade's arms in her office while he kissed and caressed her.

She was moving to his house Tuesday. How would her heart survive the challenge of being with him?

Seven

As Cade strode down the hall to the dining room of his mansion, he slowed and walked more quietly. It was Thursday and over a week ago on Tuesday, Katherine had moved into his Houston home. Last Thursday morning he'd had to fly to California. It had been one week that seemed as if he had been away from her for a month. His eagerness to see her increased with every step he took.

Pausing in the open doorway, he looked inside. Scaffolding was along one wall. The furniture had been moved to one end of the room and draped with cloths as an extra precaution to keep paint off. Drop cloths were spread on the floor beneath the scaffolding and ladders. Katherine stood on a platform as she drew on the wall.

When his gaze flicked over her, his pulse jumped. She was in a T-shirt and cutoffs and had one thick braid that hung down her back. Taking his time, he looked down her long, shapely legs, and then up over her round bottom, mentally peeling away her cutoffs.

With his pulse racing, he leaned one shoulder against the doorjamb and continued to look at her. She had always set him on fire and she could now more than ever. She was more beautiful than she had been when she was twenty. He thought about her kisses when they had been in her office. Just memories aroused him.

He liked watching her work. It fascinated him how swiftly she drew and her certainty in what she was doing. He had come back to Texas with an opposing mix of emotions, wanting to see her, hoping to hire her, but still steaming over her refusal to answer his calls and letters. And then when he saw her at the auction, she had taken his breath away with her beauty and he wanted her more than he ever had. He'd had no intention of getting involved emotionally with her again because of their stormy history, but now that was fading and accusations were in the open and reasons clarified.

Cade watched her draw. With the past put behind them, the big barrier of her damnable drive and ambition and craving for success remained. He didn't want to fall in love with a woman who was bound heart and soul to her career. He didn't want that in his life. But he wanted Katherine in his bed. She made his blood boil, and he wasn't sleeping nights because of thinking about her and wanting her. Never had he known a woman he desired the way he did her. And he hadn't met any who could kiss or make love like Katie. She was beautiful, sexy and off-limits.

He remembered their kisses in her office and knew she wasn't totally off-limits. She couldn't resist passion, either. His gaze roamed over her with speculation. He wanted her in his bed. And soon.

Trying to get his mind back to other things and cool down, he thought about the evening. He had something to tell her and he debated whether he should or keep everything to himself. As always when he had such a decision to make, he viewed it from whether or not he would want to know if it were he who was in the dark. Good or bad, he'd want to hear it.

She glanced over her shoulder, saw him and paused. "I didn't hear you."

"I didn't intend to startle you."

"You didn't."

"I'm enjoying the view."

She wrinkled her nose at him. He wanted to go get her down off the platform and kiss her, but he knew she wouldn't want him to. Dropping his navy suit coat and navy tie on a chair, he strolled across the room. Halting near her, he put his hands on his hips and looked up at her drawing.

"How long have you been standing there?" she asked.

"Not long. It's fascinating. Absolutely gorgeous," he said, stepping closer to the foot of a ladder. His gaze drifted over her legs again. "Perfect," he said.

"You're not talking about my art work."

"No, I'm not," he said. "I'm standing here drooling over the view. Come down here."

"I don't think so," she said lightly. "If I did, that might be the end of my work today and I'm getting things done."

"We can get things done together," he responded and she smiled.

"Seduction? I can get more drawing finished. I'm not climbing down."

"If I didn't think we'd fall off the platform, I'd come get you, but ladders, I take seriously. Of course, getting to kiss you, I take rather earnestly, too."

"You keep your feet on the floor," she said. "Kisses aren't part of this deal as I have to continually remind you."

"As if you didn't enjoy them, too," he reminded her while she turned back to continue her sketching.

He watched her sure strokes. "It doesn't scare you to just start drawing on my wall?" he asked.

"No. I've done this a lot and drawing on your wall is exactly what you paid me to do," she said, going back to her drawing.

"Looks like you're making a lot of progress. You're fast, Katherine."

"Why do I feel you've been telling me that since we first met?"

He grinned. "Come down here and say that," he coaxed in a husky voice.

"Not on your life," she snapped.

"Want to take a break?"

She glanced at her watch. "I can't believe it's half past five. I thought it was about three. I didn't realize it was so late."

"Even though it's October, it's a warm, humid day. The pool will be great. Want to join me?"

She shook her head. "I'll keep drawing."

"Scared to swim with me?" he asked.

"Don't try to goad me into it. I'm going to continue drawing."

"I'm leaving again tomorrow afternoon to fly to back to California. I'll be gone until next week. Think you can get along without me?" he asked, and when she glanced over her shoulder at him, she smiled.

"I'll manage, Cade. When you're gone, it's very quiet and I can get a lot done."

"So I'm dismissed." He turned away, picking up his coat and tie. "I can take a hint," he said over his shoulder and left to go to his room and change for a swim.

Later he heated the grill and began to cook shrimp kabobs. They sizzled on the grill when he heard her approach. Turning to watch her, his pulse jumped.

She had combed her hair out, catching it behind her head with a blue ribbon, and she wore a pale blue cotton blouse, blue skirt and sandals and she looked beautiful.

Putting down the spatula he held, he gave her his full attention. He crossed the patio to place his hands on her shoulders. When her big blue eyes focused on him, he wanted to wrap his arms around her and kiss her.

"You look as gorgeous as ever," he said quietly instead. "And you smell delectable, too."

"Thank you. You don't look so bad yourself," she replied lightly.

"I'm almost ready to put everything on the table."

"So where is Creighton?" she asked.

"Gone. I gave all of them the night off. We have the house to ourselves and I'm cooking."

"I don't know whether that's good or bad—your cooking, that is. Having the house to ourselves is tempting fate."

He smiled. "So you'll admit that I'm temptation," he drawled.

"You know your answer. You've been temptation since you pulled alongside my pickup that afternoon. Now my dinner may burn, so you better see about it."

"Yeah, I'm hungry, too," he said.

The cool evening was pleasant and Cade enjoyed her company and relished even more just looking at her.

It wasn't until they finished eating that he stood and walked around to her side of the table, pulling up a chair to sit close, facing her. "I want to talk to you."

With a questioning arch of her eyebrows, she waited while he placed his elbows on his knees and leaned closer. For a second he forgot what he intended. He studied her, thinking he could look at her for hours. Her skin was smooth and flawless and her full red lips were enticing, while her big blue eyes and rosy cheeks added to her beauty. Longing to touch her, he kept his hands to himself.

"I have something to tell you," he said, trying to break the news as gently as possible and wondering again if he were doing the right thing or not, but he was committed now.

She frowned slightly. "I have the feeling that you're going to tell me something I don't want to hear and you're getting me braced for it. My family's all right, isn't it?"

"Of course. Sorry, I didn't mean to frighten you about them," he said, squeezing her shoulder lightly and then letting his hand linger, wanting to let it drift down to her soft, full breast. Instead, he gazed into her eyes and tried to focus on what he was telling her. "As far as I know you family is fine, and that isn't what's on my mind at all."

"I didn't really think it was because you would've told me about them immediately. What is it? Just tell me."

"Long ago you told me about your mother walking out on all of you."

As Katherine drew a sharp breath, her breasts thrust against the cotton blouse and he couldn't keep from looking. "I'm not certain I want to hear this," she said.

"That's up to you, but I thought I ought to give you the choice. I know what happened to her. If you don't want to know, I'll drop it now and never bring it up again. It'll hurt to hear," he warned her.

Rubbing Katie's shoulder lightly, he waited. He didn't want to hurt her, but he thought that she, as well as her brothers, had a right to know. Why one of them hadn't checked into it, he couldn't imagine, except they had probably grown up convinced of Duke Ransome's lies about their mother.

Katherine gazed at him and, in spite of the tense moment, longing for her rocked him again. He always thought of her as Katie, not Katherine, and it was an effort for him to remember to address her by her full name. He turned a lock of her hair around his index finger and could remember running his hands through her silky hair.

"Tell me," she said finally.

"Did you know she had an affair with another man?"

"That's what I heard when I was grown. Growing up, I didn't

know anything except that she left us and was never coming back. We were always told she didn't want to see any of us."

Cade moved closer and let his knee touch Katherine's lightly. "Your father found out about the other man and was so enraged that he sent her packing and told her to never come back."

"No! He said she didn't want to have anything to do with us or him."

"Maybe with him, but not with her children."

"No, no!" Katherine exclaimed. Closing her eyes, she put her head in her hands. "All those years—our mother—" She raised her head. "Did she marry the other man?"

"No. It was a short affair. You father threatened her if she ever tried to contact any of you in any way. She believed him and she's stayed out of your lives, but she's in Houston."

"Houston!" Katherine exclaimed. "All the years we were growing up she's been here in Texas?"

"Yes, but it's part way across the state," he said, avoiding telling her that her mother had kept up with all of them and gone to see them when she knew they would be out where she could observe them without them seeing her.

"Cade, I don't know my dad at all," Katherine said, looking stricken. "How could he do that to his own children?"

"She had an affair and your dad is an unforgiving man. He's a hard man. He's strong-willed. You know he gets angry when he doesn't get his way."

"To separate us from her all that time. We should have been able to see her occasionally!"

"I agree, Katherine, and I'm sorry. My father died when I was young and I was angry over losing him and hurt for years. In a way, what happened with your mother is worse because it could've been avoided."

"Olivia has asked me about her twice and she's talked to Julia. They urged us to look up our mother, but Matt, Nick and I didn't want to because Dad drummed it into us when we were little, that she left and didn't want any part of us ever. That's painful."

"I'm sure it is."

"It hurts to discover my Dad has such a dark side. I knew he did things to other people, but I didn't think he would be so cruel to his own family. All those years he deceived us."

"Let's get something straight here," Cade said firmly. "You brought it up about your mother. I felt like you had a right to know the truth if you wanted to hear it. I didn't tell you to be vindictive toward your father. I don't hate your father, Katherine," Cade said solemnly. "It wasn't what he intended, but he helped lift my family and me out of the gutter. He kept my brother out of prison. He gave us the money that I used to start investing. We were dirt poor and we knew how to live on nothing, so we took that money and made the best possible uses of it we could. At the time, I hated your dad, but after about four years, that hatred had diminished to dislike. I'll never like him, but I don't hate him and I don't feel any need for revenge. I meant what I said when I told him that I owed him gratitude for what he did for us."

"I'm glad you told me about our mother. I have to let the others know," she said. "I'm close to Nick and Matt. I told both of them what he did to us."

"Did they believe you?"

"Oh, yes. They've had more run-ins with our dad than I ever had. They weren't surprised. They were surprised you paid him back. Especially Nick. Nick has a vindictive streak, but I think it's mellowed since he met Julia."

"I don't want his money now."

"Cade, have you talked to my mother?"

"Yes. If you want to meet her, you can. All of you can," he said, sliding his hand to Katherine's nape, knowing she wasn't even aware of his touch. He couldn't resist touching her and, right now, when he looked at her full lips, he thought about how incredibly soft they were, how they burned him like fire.

"Yes, I'd like to meet her and I imagine Nick and Matt will, too. Especially after they learn the truth. How did you find out all this?"

"It wasn't hard. I guessed that none of you have ever tried to look her up."

"No, we haven't," Katherine said with a twinge of guilt. "Olivia thought we should try to find out and hear her side of the story. Olivia's not overly fond of Dad, but then he tried to buy her off, too."

"The bribe worked for me because of my brother. He must not have had anything else to hold over Olivia's head."

"No, he didn't, I'm sure. You said it was easy to find my mother. How come you even looked?"

Cade leaned forward to place his hands on his knees. "I was going to come back here to build this house and when I decided that I wanted you to do the murals, I hired a P.I. to check into things here. I wanted him to let me know about you and your family. It came up about your mother and I told him to check that out, too, because it pays to know as much as you can. When I found out about her and that she was in Houston, I was curious enough to go see her myself and I had a long, interesting visit with her."

"What's she like?" Katherine asked.

"She's a beautiful woman. She went back to school and got a law degree. She paints, too. She was friendly to me."

"Has any female ever been unfriendly to you?" Katherine asked, and he grinned. "I want to meet her," Katherine said. "How long have you known about her?" she asked, tilting her head to study him.

"I found out several months before I came to Houston to pick out a lot for my house. It was sometime last year."

"Last year! Why didn't you tell me that first night? It's my mother."

"That didn't seem to be the time. And later, you were shocked to learn what your father did to us. I didn't want to break it to you right then on top of everything else you had just learned about."

"So you just kept it all bottled up," she said. "What else have you kept quiet about concerning me?"

"No more family secrets. The only thing I've kept from you is telling you how much I want you in my bed," he said, unable to keep his voice from thickening. Her big, blue eyes widened as she focused on him and he looked at her full, sensuous mouth that was made for kisses. He leaned forward to pick her up and place her in his lap.

She struggled and his arm tightened around her waist while he kissed her neck behind her ear. "Be still. I've been gone since last week and all I could think about was you."

"Cade, don't turn on that seductive charm of yours," she said, wriggling to get off his lap.

He wanted her and he knew how to end her protests. He shifted slightly, tightened his arm and kissed her. The minute his mouth covered hers, he was aroused. He tucked her against his shoulder as he leaned over her to kiss her long and hard.

She struggled for a second, pushing against his chest while she wiggled, but then her arm slid around his neck and she turned against him, pressing against his chest while they kissed.

His pulse roared and he shook with a hunger that wasn't going to be satisfied until he made love to her for hours. She was ready for loving, coming apart now in his arms as she shook and moaned softly and kissed him back with enough passion to burn his mouth.

As if he could kiss away her damnable drive for success, he leaned over her and kissed her as passionately as he possibly could. His hand slid down her throat, caressing her lightly, slowly, and then going lower, down over her breast. His fingers twisted free buttons and in seconds his hand was beneath her blouse, unfastening her lacy bra. He cupped her breast in his hand. Soft and warm, she was irresistible.

He ached with wanting her, leaning over her and letting his hand slide down her length and then back up under her skirt. Her skin was smooth. She was all curves and softness and fire.

He framed her face with his hands. "I want you," he said, the words a rasp while his heart pounded and he looked into her blue eyes, that were heavy-lidded now with passion. Her red lips were swollen from his kisses and her hair fell over her shoulders, the ribbon lost. "I want you, Katherine, and you'll be mine. I want to make love to you for hours."

"No! Cade, we're not complicating our lives that way again," she protested, but she was breathless and he could feel her racing pulse and desire burned in her eyes in spite of her words.

"You want to love. You kiss like each time is your last," he whispered, kissing her throat and stroking her. He shook with desire, burning to peel her out of her clothes and kiss her all over. There had never been anyone who set him on fire like she did. He had never been able to get her out of his mind and now that he was with her again it was as if the years between never existed.

He raised his head to look into her eyes. "I'd swap all my millions to be that poor kid on my bike and have you making love to me and letting me make love to you again."

"We can't go back—"

"We don't have to go back when it comes to loving," he whispered, kissing her and stopping all her conversation. She had stiffened when she had protested, but now with his kiss, she lost her resistance and molded against him, her hand sliding down to caress him and he groaned with pleasure.

He raised his head. "I'm going to kiss you and love you until you forget all about that business you crave more than anything else. I can make you forget it," he declared, and his mouth covered whatever she had been about to reply. He held her tightly, and then turned her on his lap to straddle him, giving him access to her so he could slide his finger into her panties and fondle her while he kissed her.

She moaned and twisted and moved on him, driving him wild in turn. He ached to possess her, but he knew she wasn't going to let him yet.

He groaned again, her hands were on him and she was tugging away his belt. Her skirt was full and he shoved it out of his way and yanked off her blouse and bra as he kissed her.

He cupped her breasts, relishing her softness that filled his hand, so incredibly soft and curvy. Sliding down to her tiny waist his hands moved over her, and then one went back beneath her panties to stroke her while he slid his other hand over her bottom and back to her nipple.

He rubbed her, a friction that made her move her hips. When he pleasured her, she set him on fire with her responses. He was rock hard, feeling as if he would burst with need, aching and wanting her softness to envelope him.

"I want inside you, darlin'," he whispered. "I want to take you and make you mine and love you for hours," he said until her mouth covered his and she kissed away his words. He shifted and placed her on the chaise that was at hand and then moved between her legs, leaning down to put his tongue on her intimately where his hand had been. With her knees hooked over his shoulders, he watched her, wanting to drive her to a frenzy.

"No!" she cried emphatically, pushing against him, wriggling and scooting away to stand. Her skirt fell in place, but not before he got a view that burned him like a brand. Every inch of her was gorgeous. He gasped for breath and could hear her raspy breathing as she looked around and grabbed her blouse to yank it on.

"Cade, we're not doing this," she said.

He wondered if she had the remotest idea had badly he wanted her and how beautiful she looked to him right now. She was disheveled, her silky blond hair spilling over her shoulders. Her skirt was a mass of wrinkles and her blouse was open as she began to button it. Her lips were red from his kisses. In the throes of passion he had made declarations of desire and told her how he wanted her and he had meant everything he said, but he doubted if she heard or would remember any of it.

"We're not going to become lovers! That's not part of the deal," she snapped.

"I want you. And that isn't part of any deal. It's just a man telling a woman that he desires her."

"There's no future for us," she said fastening the last button and jamming her blouse beneath her skirt. "None. We're worlds apart. You want a family. I want my career unencumbered by a family. End of conversation." Her head came up. "End of lovemaking. That ought to be clear enough." Stepping off the chaise, he walked toward her. Her eyes widened and she edged away from him.

"Do you hear me?" she asked, taking another step back.

"I hear you perfectly clearly," he answered calmly. "I know what I want—I've always known. How long did it take me to settle on what I wanted for the first mural?"

She had backed up to the brick wall that circled one side of the patio. He put his hands out on either side of her to block her in.

"Move out of my way," she said breathlessly and sounding as if she didn't possibly mean it.

"I know what I want and I go after what I want and often I get what I want," he said quietly. "What a waste, Katherine, for you to give priority to an office over a home and family. You don't even want both like many women do."

Her big blue eyes gazed up at him and snapped with fire, but her lips were parted and he suspected she was only half-angry with him, while the other half of her wanted him.

"I'm not changing any more than you are."

"That doesn't mean we can't make love. You want to and I want to."

Something flickered in the depths of her eyes while she shook her head. "No. I can't be casual about loving or go into it knowing it's temporary and inconsequential. That's impossible. I don't want the entanglement."

He was hard, aroused, and he wanted her. But he didn't want to send her off and spend the evening alone. He wanted her company. He jerked his head.

"Sit down. I'll get us cold drinks and let's see if we can let the dust settle and calm down and just talk. C'mon, Katherine. Talking isn't anything."

"It is with you," she said in a small voice that made him draw a quick breath.

He fought the impulse to reach for her again because of her remark. Instead, he turned away. "Sit down. What would you like to drink? How about some pop?"

"Fine. I want to call my brothers and tell them about our mother. Cade, you know her. Would you call her tonight and tell her I'd like to meet her and talk to her."

"Sure. You'll find she's easy to talk to," he said. He pulled out his wallet and retrieved the slip of paper with her phone number and got out his cell phone to call.

When Laura Ransome answered, he talked softly, and in a minute turned to Katherine. "She said why don't you come see her tonight. We're in the same city."

"Now?" Katherine asked, her eyes going wide.

"Sure. I'll take you. You can go in and see her without me."

Katherine nodded and he made arrangements. When he

broke the connection, he glanced at her. "I told her we're leaving now."

"No, we're not! Let me change and comb my hair," she said, rushing inside. He watched her hurry away, knowing while all three younger Ransomes would probably be happy to find their mother, Duke Ransome would be an enemy forever after tonight. Cade didn't care. There wasn't anything Duke could do to him any longer.

He left to get ready himself to go and then returned to the patio to wait for Katherine, who appeared in minutes.

He glanced over her plain black dress that ended above her knees and hugged her hips. Her hair was swept to one side of her head and pinned, and she took his breath away.

"You clean up right nice, Miss Ransome," he said, and she smiled.

"Thank you. Cade," she said, grasping his arm. "I feel all fluttery and nervous," she said. He was aware of her clinging to him, so uncustomary for Katherine. He draped his arm across her shoulders and squeezed lightly.

"You'll be fine and you'll like her, Katherine, and then you can tell your brothers."

They hurried to his car and he drove to the residential area to a redbrick house nestled in tall pines.

"I can wait in the car so you two can be alone."

"Don't you do it," Katherine said. "You know her. You come with me. Please, Cade."

"Two words I never thought I'd hear," he said dryly as he got out to go around the car and open her door. He held her arm and waited beside her until the front door opened and they faced a tall, black-haired woman with huge blue eyes and still beautiful skin, and Cade knew where Katherine got her looks.

Eight

Katherine couldn't get her breath as she gazed into blue
eyes that matched her own. Cade held her arm lightly.

"Mrs. Ransome, here's your daughter, Katherine."

Laura Ransome reached to take her daughter's hands, and
Katherine grabbed and held tightly. Then Laura hugged her and
Katherine wrapped her arms around the slender woman in return.

"I used to dream about you and imagine this moment,"
Katherine said.

"This is so wonderful," Laura said, releasing her. "Come
inside. There's no need to stand out here."

"Katherine, if you two—"

"Come on, Cade. If it weren't for you, this wouldn't be
happening." Katherine wiped away tears as she caught his
hand and tugged lightly. He followed her and closed the door.

"We'll go to the back living area. That's where I spend all
my time," Laura said. Katherine looked at the warm house that
was beautifully furnished with oil paintings on the walls and

polished wood floors and green plants in pots and vases. They entered a room that had a brick fireplace, sofas and chairs in bright upholstery, a piano in the corner and bookshelves. There were baby pictures on the shelves, along with pictures taken later, and Katherine recognized herself and her brothers. She crossed the room to a picture and picked it up, looking around in wonder at her mother. "This is my high school graduation."

"I hope you don't mind that I took your picture without you knowing about it," Laura said.

"Why didn't I see you?" Katherine wondered, staring at her mother.

"You wouldn't have known me if you'd looked right at me," Laura said gently.

Katherine replaced the picture on the shelf and saw more of herself and her brothers and she realized her mother had been in her life in a small way all through the years.

"I wish I'd known."

"We can't undo the past. Come sit and tell me about yourself." She glanced at Cade. "Probably Cade has filled you in on a lot." Katherine sat on the sofa beside her mother and talked about her life. All the time they talked, she took in her surroundings and the woman she faced and she was equally aware of Cade sitting quietly in the wing back chair near her, his foot propped on his knee.

Laura Ransome had smooth clear skin and large luminous blue eyes that were thickly lashed. Her black hair had only a few strands of gray, and when she smiled or laughed she had a dimple in one cheek and even, white teeth.

Katherine liked her instantly and tried to avoid thinking about the lost years. All she could do was pick up and go on from here and be profoundly thankful that Cade had searched for her mother and then had told her about Laura.

Once she glanced around at Cade. "Bored with all this talk

about the Ransomes' early years?" she asked him, and he shook his head, smiling at her.

"Of course not. Go ahead and talk. I like hearing about the Ransomes," he said easily.

"I can imagine," Katherine said, smiling at him and turning back to Laura.

Katherine tilted her head to one side. "What do I call you?"

"Whatever you like. It's Mom, Katherine. Mother is fine. Ma—that's okay, too. If you're more comfortable with Laura, I can understand."

Katherine laughed. "Mom. I can't believe it, Mom. My mother, Mom." The two looked at each other and both reached out at the same time to hug.

When the hour grew later, Laura got them mugs of hot chocolate and they sat around the kitchen table, sipping the chocolate while Katherine told her more about herself and her brothers and fished pictures from her purse to show Laura.

When it was nearly midnight, Cade took Katherine's arm. "It's late, Katherine. We should go. You two can see each other again soon."

"I didn't realize," Katherine exclaimed, standing. "I'm sorry to have kept you so late."

"I loved every minute and I stay up until after midnight anyway," Laura said, standing and walking to the door with them.

"We'll all get together. I'll call Matt and Nick tomorrow and you'll probably hear from them, too." At the door she turned to face her mother. "My mother. I can't believe it after dreaming about this moment all the years I was growing up."

"Oh, Katherine," Laura exclaimed and wrapped her arms around Katherine. Katherine held Laura, joy filling her to finally find her mother.

They separated and said goodbyes and then Cade slipped his arm around Katherine as they walked to his car.

Laura stood on the porch, waving and watching them drive away. As soon as they rounded the corner out of sight, Katherine threw her arms around Cade's neck and hugged him tightly.

"Hey!" he said, pulling to the curb and stopping instantly. "You'll make us have a wreck," he said, laughing.

"Thank you, Cade," she said, on her knees with her arms around his neck. "Thank you for finding her, for telling me and for going with me tonight. Thank you, thank you!"

"Katherine, can you save all this gratitude and show me when we get home?"

She laughed and kissed his cheek and he caught her around the waist and hauled her onto his lap, cramming her between the steering wheel and him while he kissed her hard. Startled for an instant, she was immobile and then desire flashed white-hot with his kiss and she wrapped her arms around his neck to kiss him until his hands fumbled for her zipper. She sat up abruptly and moved away.

"We're out in public in your car!" she exclaimed, scooting back on the passenger side.

"You started it," he said, breathing hard and looking at her intently.

She waved her hand at him. "Just drive us home. I'll calm down and I just wanted to thank you."

"Any chance of getting that thank-you from you again at home?"

"Absolutely none," she answered with amusement. "Well, maybe a little, but not the kind of gratitude you have in mind."

"Why am I not surprised?"

She laughed. "Cade, I'm so happy to find her and she's all I dreamed about."

"You don't know that. You've only been with her a few hours."

"It's the second time you've been with her and you liked her and don't rain on my parade."

"I wouldn't think of it. She does seem great," he said

solemnly. "I'm glad you're happy because I've worried about telling you. It was sort of damned if you do and damned if you don't."

"You've made an enemy forever of my dad," she said solemnly. "He's not a good person to cross, Cade."

"He can't hurt me, and I don't give a damn."

"I'm so glad you told me. So, so, so glad."

"You just hold that thought," he said.

She placed her hand on his knee and his head whipped around. She patted his knee and smiled at him. "Pay attention to your driving. I'm just about to explode with happiness."

"I wish I could make you that happy."

"You have tonight."

"No. For different reasons."

"You've made me even happier in the past and you know it," she said solemnly, removing her hand.

"Don't lose all that joy," he said. "I'm glad for you and for her, Katherine. She was thrilled and happy to meet you. She seems like a great person."

"Cade, she's beautiful. How could Dad have done that?"

"Just an angry man whose ego blinded him."

"I'm not worrying about what Dad has done. I can't undo any of it and at least now, I know about him and know what happened and I've found my mother. I'm calling Nick right now."

"It's after midnight."

"He won't mind." She got out the phone and glanced at Cade, who seemed to be concentrating on his driving and she put away her phone. After a few minutes, Cade looked around.

"I thought you were calling your brother."

"You've spent the evening listening to me talk about growing up and telling my mother about Matt and Nick and Jeff. Now you don't have to sit and listen to me telling Nick what I've been doing."

"Call him. I'd rather you call him right now. I might get another hug of gratitude when we get home."

When we get home. The words sizzled in her each time he said them. How right it seemed in so many ways, and he couldn't ever guess how grateful she was to him for what he had done in finding their mother.

She called Nick and told him and then had to tell Julia and answer questions. Finally she was off the phone. "It's too late tonight to call Matt. I'll call him in the morning. Nick said you did what he should have done a long time ago. Each time he and Matt talked about it, they decided to leave it alone. All of us were told that she never wanted to see us again and we just grew up believing Dad about it. Nick said he should have guessed it might not be the truth. He's surprised that Matt accepted it all these years."

"Well, you know now," Cade said, pulling into an open garage. As soon as they were in the house and he had locked the door he turned to face her.

"Now, Katherine, come here and thank me."

Katherine's pulse jumped as she faced him. Closing the distance between them, she wound her arms around his neck again.

"Thank you," she said, gazing into his dark eyes and smiling at him. "You're wonderful!"

He wrapped his arms around her waist tightly. "I want to make you this bubbly and happy and hear you say that to me for another reason."

"I can't," she replied solemnly. "There are too many things in the way. Face it, you want sleeping together without commitment and, ultimately, you want a wife and family, children. I can't do either."

"You mean you don't want to," he said, his dark eyes clouding and a muscle working in his jaw.

"I'm married already to my job. And I don't have time for

children. I don't have time for a husband. Now, that said, for tonight—thank you. I'm so grateful for what you did. It's the most wonderful thing you could possibly do!" She wrapped her arms tightly around his neck, pulled his head down and kissed him.

His arms tightened around her waist and he leaned over her and kissed her. Her heart thudded while she gave herself over to kissing him.

His kiss deepened, plundered her mouth. Again, he framed her face with his hands. "I want you and you'll be mine, Katherine. I want that joy for life and your exuberance."

"I can't give you what you want, Cade. This is lust and you want to make love and that'll satisfy you, but it won't me. I'm way too complicated to simplify it down to that. So, no, I can't meet those terms. But I am grateful beyond measure to you for tonight."

She walked away from him, her pulse racing from his kiss. She was aware he watched her with his dark eyes heated by desire.

"Maybe soon we can all get together. Come with me, Cade. I want you there," she urged, turning to face him across the kitchen.

"All right, I will. In the meantime, it's a warm night and you're too excited to sleep. Let's swim and then we can have a glass of wine."

"That sounds like a plan for seduction."

"Come on, Katherine. You're not going to sleep and you can always fend me off. All it takes is a no that you mean."

"If I say no, I mean no," she said, in a haughty tone, half teasing him because she was still thrilled and excited. "How about we cut the swim, have the glass of wine and just talk?"

"It's a deal. Anything to be with you," he said. He opened a bottle of red wine and poured them both glasses and got out a chunk of cheese and a box of crackers.

As she watched him, she kicked off her shoes and sat on the kitchen sofa, crossing her long legs at her ankles. He brought everything in to set it all on the fruitwood table in front of the sofa.

The minute he sat beside her, he reached out to wind her hair in his fingers. "I'm happy for you. I thought she was very nice, but I did worry and debate about telling you. I'm glad you're happy and you liked her."

"I love her, Cade. I thought it would be awkward and like a stranger, but it wasn't. And I'm glad you went with me."

A corner of his mouth quirked up. "Why? I didn't do anything."

She shrugged, looking into his dark eyes, aware of his hand playing with her hair that made slight tugs on her scalp. He was so close, sitting beside her, his hip pressed against hers.

"At first I was nervous, and it helped to have you with me."

"I'm surprised, but pleased." He handed her a glass of wine and held his up in a toast. "Here's to finding your mother."

"Oh, Cade, I'll drink to that," she said, touching his glass and watching him intently over the rim as he sipped.

He watched her, his dark eyes burning with desire that made her pulse race. She was excited, happy and she tingled beneath his steady gaze. Setting down his glass, he took hers from her. He picked her up to set her on his lap.

When he did, she wound her arms around his neck. "I thought we were going to sit and talk," she said breathlessly, promising herself just a few kisses with him and then she'd stop.

"You want me to kiss you," he whispered, showering kisses on her neck. "I can see it in your eyes." His kisses went up over her ear and then he leaned back to look at her. Her eyes were closed and her fingers played in his hair.

She opened her eyes to meet his mocking gaze before he lowered his head to kiss her.

As she clung to him to kiss him in return, her heart thudded.

His kiss spun her into a vortex of desire. From the moment she had looked up into his eyes at the auction, longing had torn at her with a hunger for his lovemaking that she had fought steadily. But need had built and Cade had fueled the flames with each encounter. She was in his arms, kissing him, and she wanted him. She had debated with herself, fought desire and finally yielded to searching her heart for what she truly wanted.

She knew her desire wasn't going to end. Now she was in his arms and no matter what the future held for them, she suspected only heartbreak again because they were on divergent paths in life, but she wanted him now.

Her pulse pounded as she wound her fingers in his hair, pressed her hips against him and kissed him, pouring all her heat and longing into the kiss. He twisted free her buttons and shoved off her blouse. Her lacy bra was gone in seconds and then he unfastened her skirt and pushed it around her hips.

As his hands roamed over her, he groaned deep in his throat, but she barely heard the sound for her roaring pulse.

"I want you!" she gasped, crying out the words as she slipped her hands over his powerful shoulders, relishing his sculpted muscles.

"You set me on fire, Katie," he whispered, and hearing him call her Katie sent another tingle spiraling in her. Time vanished and took with it painful memories and old hurts and anger. She was in Cade's arms again, loving him and she let go of everything from the past except her love for him.

Heartbreak might lie ahead, but at the moment it was a dim threat that she didn't care to acknowledge. Cade in her arms, his body hers again, hers to kiss and touch and love was all that mattered.

"You're so gorgeous, you take my breath," he whispered, his hands sliding to her waist to hold her away from him while he looked at her in a slow assessment that was hot enough to burn her to cinders. His hands followed his gaze, drifting over her shoulders and down to cup her breasts as he stroked them.

Mesmerized, she closed her eyes, tilted back her head and held his arms. He leaned forward slightly to take her nipple in his mouth and circle the taut bud slowly with his wet tongue.

"Cade," she whispered in ecstasy.

He slid his hands lower slowly, down over her ribs and she opened her eyes to find him watching her and then his gaze slipped down again as he slid his hands between her legs and rubbed her, holding her away from him to watch her when she reached for him.

"I'm going to drive you wild with desire," he whispered.

He toyed with her languidly while she gasped and cried out and squirmed to reach for him, but he held her where he could watch her.

"Come here!" she cried.

He scooped her into his arms and carried her into a downstairs bedroom to set her on her feet in front of a full-length mirror, turning her back to him as he slid his hot, hard rod between her legs. "Ride me, Katie," he ground out the command in a husky rasp. "Give me pleasure while I make you want me."

His legs pressed against hers, squeezing her against his gorged rod, that was thick and torrid between her legs. Wrapping his tanned arm around her pale waist, he held her close against his solid, naked body.

"Look at us, your beautiful body. Look how you excite me," he whispered, kissing her ear while he fondled her breasts.

He was heated, his shaft pressing against her intimately, a pressure that tantalized and drove her to new heights as she moved against him. "Cade!" she gasped, placing her head back against him and wanting to turn to kiss him, but he held her.

"Cade!" she gasped as the sizzling friction between her legs drove her. "Please—"

"Open your eyes and look at us together," he said, his voice a thick rasp. "Open them, Katie, love."

Love. The word sent tremors spilling in her.

"Look at us now," he ordered again. "Open your eyes and see what we do to each other."

Her eyes flew wide. She saw her pale body against him, his broad shoulders dark behind her, his long legs covered in short, black hairs. Their images barely registered because feelings consumed her, heightening her need for release as she moved her hips frantically.

"You're wickedly sinful, Cade," she whispered.

"Not as wickedly sinful as I intend to be before I take you and make you mine totally. I want to love you right out of your mind."

"You already are," she whispered, closing her eyes and moving her hips, holding his narrow hips while sensation escalated. She ached for him and ran her hands over his hips, trying to reach him as she twisted and writhed against him. "Cade!"

"I want to call you Katie again. I want to seduce you, make you mine in every way possible. I could devour you, I want you so badly," he whispered. His hand circled her nipple, increasing her need. "I've dreamed of you—"

A sob escaped her. He was driving her wild physically while his words were propelling her emotions to as great a need as her body. Desire was a raging fire, roaring in her veins.

With a cry she pulled away from him, turning to press his thick rod against her while she wound her arms around his neck and pulled his head down to kiss him again.

His hands slid down her back, easing over her bottom and stroking the back of her thighs while he kissed her. Their tongues tangled, stroking and going deep.

She trailed kisses along his throat and then down to his chest, her tongue circling his nipple while her hand teased his other nipple. He played with her breasts, in turn stroking her.

She knelt in front of him, her tongue flicking over his thighs, around his throbbing shaft, while he groaned and tangled his fingers in her hair and finally thrust his manhood against her mouth.

She opened her mouth to take him, sliding her lips so slowly over him, trying to build the fires in him that he had in her. Seduction went two ways and was a delight and a torment and she wanted him to feel all that she did.

"You're mine, Cade," she whispered, not expecting him to hear her. "You're mine in a way you'll never be anyone else's." Then words were gone as she drew her tongue along his shaft, licking him while her hand slid between his legs and she stroked him lightly, cupping him and touching him.

Finally she took him fully in her mouth, her tongue circling his velvet tip. Then she slid her tongue up and down the length of him, stroking and licking him slowly.

With a groan his hands slipped beneath her arms and he lifted her to her feet so he could wrap her in his arms to kiss her.

He lowered her to the floor and rolled her on her stomach, moving between her legs while he showered kisses on her nape and she curled her hands against the floor, wondering how much she could stand before she had to turn over and kiss him.

Lost in streaks of fire, she clenched her fists and tried to roll over, but he gently held her.

"Let me love and kiss you and look at you. You're beautiful, Katie," he whispered. He traced kisses down her back, over the curve of her bottom and then his warm breath was between her legs and she sobbed and bucked and tried to turn to kiss him.

"Wait, darlin'," he urged. "Let me love you long and slow until you're ready for me."

"I'm ready for you," she tried to cry out, but it came out a breathy rasp. "Cade, I want you."

"Not half as much as I want you," he replied, skimming

kisses down the back of her thigh and then his tongue was behind her knee while his hands dallied over her and one hand slid between her legs.

"Cade, now! Let me turn over."

He shifted and she rolled over while he knelt between her legs and pushed her shoulders as she started to sit up.

"Let me look at you all I want," he whispered. "And see what I can do to make you want more. Do you like me to touch you here?" he asked, his hand stroking her breasts and she closed her eyes and caught her lower lip between her teeth as she moved her hips slightly. She stroked his thick rod.

"Yes, I like it and you already know it," she gasped. Her eyes flew open.

"Cade, there hasn't been anyone else. I couldn't. Not ever," she confessed. "I wanted to because I was so hurt and angry and I went out intending to wipe out memories of you and get back at you, but I couldn't. You're the only man."

"Lord help us, Katie," he said, blinking and staring at her and then he pulled her into his embrace to kiss her with such passion that she shook in his arms and forgot what she had admitted.

"I'm going to love you all night," he said when he released her slightly. Dazed, she barely heard him as she pulled his head to her to kiss him again.

After a moment he raised his head only a fraction. "Are you protected?" he asked.

"No. I'm not," she answered. His mouth covered hers again.

She didn't know how long they caressed and kissed each other, but then he scooped her into his arms to carry her to the bed. He left, retrieving his trousers, striding back to her as he retrieved a packet.

"Hurry, Cade!" she gasped, reaching for him.

As he knelt between her legs, she watched him pull on the condom. His shaft was dark, thick and ready. And she was eager for him, locking her legs around him to tug him toward her while her hands stroked his thighs.

"Hurry. Come here and make love to me," she gasped, watching him intently.

He lowered himself to kiss her. His eyes were midnight black now with pinpoints of desire heating their darkness. His gaze raked over her before he wrapped her in his embrace and kissed her.

Her heart pounded and she arched to meet him. She felt the hot tip press against her and then ease so slowly inside her. Her cry was bitten off with his kiss.

Ecstasy enveloped her at the same time. And the knowledge that Cade was in her arms, added to her eagerness. "I've waited nine years!" she gasped, the words whispered and she suspected they were lost on him.

"I've wanted you like this. Make love to me," she cried and then kissed him again.

"Katie, love!" he gasped as he eased slowly into her until he filled her. He withdrew and plunged again, taking his time to increase her need.

Her heart thudded from his words and from his lovemaking. She thrashed wildly beneath him and her hands raked over him, clutching his firm butt to pull him closer. He moved slowly, tantalizingly, easing in and out of her in an exquisite torment that drove her to desperate need.

She moaned and cried out while her hips thrust against him. Her long legs were locked around him, holding him.

Sweat dotted his forehead now and she knew he was holding back to pleasure her.

"Let go, Cade. Lose your control!" she cried. Desire raged with a dizzying urgency.

"Want me the way I want you," he said. He ground out the words in a tight, husky voice that she barely heard.

"I do!" she cried in return.

"Katie, give me all of you, everything, your passion, your body, your heart. Put me first again in your life and allow us both another chance."

She could barely hear his raspy whisper, but she did hear the words. They meant little at the moment. Now she saw blinding lights exploding behind her closed eyelids, heard nothing except his whisper and her roaring pulse.

Her craving for him intensified. She gasped for breath and raked her hands over him, clutching him, relishing every inch of his powerful body.

"Now!" she cried, feeling a climax building toward an explosion of relief. Then release came, sending tremors that shook her.

He thrust, moving his hips even faster as he plunged deep into her softness and finally he groaned.

"Katie, Katie, love!" he cried, holding her tightly with one arm beneath her as he pumped into her and finally sagged on her and held her.

Their galloping heartbeats and ragged breathing gradually slowed to normal. He rolled on his side, keeping her with him. He combed damp strands of hair from her face with his fingers and he gazed into her eyes.

"Katie, I've dreamed of that too many nights to count. How I wanted you! I missed you, wanted to see you, fantasized about you."

She gazed at him solemnly. "I have, too, Cade."

"I should have let you know sooner. In fairness, I tried and you didn't want to know. Then I was angry and tried to let it all go, but I never could," he said, and her pulse drummed.

She ran her hands up and down his smooth back, which was damp with sweat. "That's past. Let it go and I will, too."

"I'm happy to forget it," he said showering kisses on her temple as he stroked her hair away from her face.

"Cade, we just complicated our lives horribly."

"No, we didn't," he argued, propping his head on his hand to look down at her. "Move in with me."

"Slow down. Just go slower. You want it all at once," she urged, running her hands across his powerful shoulders, and then threading her fingers in his hair.

"Damn straight, I do. If I could," he said, nuzzling her neck and then tracing the curve of her ear with his tongue, "I'd keep you naked in my arms for the next week."

She laughed and wound her fingers in his hair, looking into his dark eyes. "That's not such a bad idea—"

"Darlin', you're giving me hope!"

They gazed into each other's eyes. Satisfaction brimmed in his brown eyes and she felt it mirrored her own feelings. She wasn't thinking one minute beyond where they were and she had replied flippantly to his remark, knowing he hadn't been in earnest, either.

"This is paradise," he said, pulling her tightly in his embrace to hold her close against him. "I've dreamed of this so many nights that I couldn't possibly count them."

"So have I," she whispered, running her free hand down his back and over his bottom. She slid her fingers back up along his hip, relishing touching him even though she was satiated.

"You've filled my thoughts constantly," he said. "I don't like leaving here to go to California to work or anywhere else. I want to be here with you. I would like you all to myself, un-interrupted, nothing else going on."

"That's impossible and you know it," she said. She placed her fingers on his lips. "We're not going to argue on this night. No discussions of the past or future. Just now, Cade. We have this night and I want to enjoy it to my heart's content because I have dreamed about having it a thousand times over."

His eyes darkened and he gazed deep into hers before he kissed her again, a deep, consuming kiss that was a confirmation of intimacy and closeness. They had forged a new bond tonight and, fleetingly, she hoped that bond didn't turn into golden chains tugging at her.

He shifted away and combed her long hair from her face. "Beautiful, beautiful," he whispered, kissing her lightly.

She caressed and kissed him languidly, wrapped in his arms and in euphoria over the lovemaking that she had desired for years.

"Come shower with me," he said later. He stood, picking her up to carry her upstairs to his bathroom to his shower.

"Cade, this is the biggest shower I've ever seen, short of something for a gym," she said, looking at his huge glass-and-marble shower.

"I hope it doesn't look like a gym shower," he said without taking his gaze from her as he became aroused again. He turned on the water, running his hands over her, sliding his warm palms over her wet nipples.

She gasped with pleasure, closing her eyes and caressing him, turning to rub her bottom against his hard shaft. She was giggly, playful, happy over loving him and ignoring every caution and worry and reason to resist.

They played together beneath a warm spray of water while he seemed to enjoy her as much as she did him. Finally, after getting a condom, he lifted her, braced himself against the wall, spread his legs and slowly let her slide down onto his ready shaft. His dark eyes bore into her and then she gasped with pleasure and closed her eyes.

Her legs were locked around him while she held him and moved with him and he thrust his hips, filling her and withdrawing as hot need rekindled and blazed.

They climaxed together, his cry of her name dim over her roaring pulse. Not until her breathing and heartbeat had returned to normal did he lower her to her feet.

"I don't think I can stand alone," she said, smiling at him while she stroked his cheek.

He turned his head to kiss her hand. "You can better than I can," he said. "Let's rinse off and get back to bed."

"That means another round of lovemaking," she said and received a probing scrutiny.

"Is that bad?"

"Not for me," she replied and he flashed her a smile that almost buckled her knees.

"Don't give me one of your million-watt smiles. My knees will go," she told him as they washed and he turned off the water.

Taking the towel from her, he dried her, sliding the rough cloth over her slowly in tantalizing strokes that stirred desire again.

She dried him at the same time. "If you don't stop that, we'll be back in the shower and we'll never get out of here."

"Fine with me," he said, sliding the towel between her legs and drawing it back and forth while he watched her.

She drew a swift breath, making her chest expand and her nipples thrust toward him. He raised the towel to rub circles on her nipples and she closed her eyes as ecstasy streaked again, tingles mixing with heat inside her to increase her yearning for him.

Her hips moved and she grabbed his wrist to tug at him. "Stop," she whispered. "You're tormenting me."

"You don't like this?" he asked, kneeling down to draw the towel slowly between her legs.

"Yes," she gasped, winding her fingers in his hair as she moved her hips faster. He dropped the towel and kissed her, pulling her into his tight embrace and leaning over her and they forgot everything except passion.

It was almost dawn when he fell asleep in her arms in his big bed. She gazed around his room. A low light burned and she looked at Cade's mammoth television screen, his desk with a laptop opened on it, shelves of books that made her wonder when he had become such a reader. She looked at him, holding her close against his side with his tanned arm around her waist.

His dark lashes were black shadows on his cheeks and his jaw had a faint stubble.

As she looked at him, her heart thudded. She had always loved him and he was the only man she'd ever loved. There was no future for them, though, and she was certain he felt the same way about tomorrow that she did.

She had meant what she'd told him. She wanted her career. She was equally certain that he had been sincere when he had said that he wanted marriage and a family. It surprised her that he did, but he'd have to find them somewhere besides with her. She had no place in her life for either of those things.

She dozed and drifted into a fitful sleep with dreams of Cade.

Hours later, she stirred and opened her eyes in bright sunlight. She turned her head to see Cade's dark gaze on her.

"You know what I want?" he asked in a deep voice.

"I can well imagine," she said, running her hands over his chest as she turned on her side to face him.

"Any chance you want the same thing?" he asked, caressing her breast.

With the first feathery stroke of his fingers over her nipple, she closed her eyes. Desire burst inside her and she wanted all of him again as if they'd never spent hours making love the night before.

"Cade," she whispered, opening her eyes to look into his briefly before she cupped the back of his head, leaned closer and kissed him.

He rolled her over beneath him, keeping his weight only partially on her as he supported himself slightly and kissed her. Her pulse drummed and she wanted him with a desperation that startled her. Her hands slid over his back, his buttocks, his thighs. She couldn't get enough of his muscular, strong male body.

Kneeling between her legs, he moved lower, taking her nipple in his mouth and licking so slowly in a hot, wet torment while his hand stroked between her legs.

Desire rocked her, building with each caress and kiss.

Pushing him down, she climbed over him, slathering kisses on him and then taking his rod into her mouth until he growled. He sat up to swing her into his arms, cradling her head against his shoulder while he kissed her senseless. In minutes he moved her over him to straddle him, settling her on his stiff manhood.

She gasped with pleasure as he eased into her, filling her, driving her wild. She thrashed, going faster and faster until her climax burst and she sprawled over him while he climaxed and held her.

They settled again and finally she could breathe normally once more.

"Katie, you're amazing. And you've melted my bones. When I can stand, we'll shower—"

"No. There's no 'we'," she said, rolling over to face him. "I have work today and you do, too. I'll use my own shower and you can have yours all to yourself."

"Can I come watch?"

"No. Not this morning. If you look, we'll make love again."

"And that's bad?" he asked, looking amused, but he was watching her intently.

"That's not in today's order of events."

"Oh, damn. A plan for the day. How about kisses between your legs for the top priority instead?" he asked in a husky voice that added to seduction. He leaned closer to kiss her neck. "How about half an hour of kisses like that or my hands here," he said, circling her nipple with his thumb. "Or my hand here?" he asked, caressing her bottom.

She slid out of bed and hurried away, certain he watched her. She grabbed a towel from the floor and wrapped it around herself before looking back at him. He stood by the bed. He was naked, aroused and male perfection. One look at him and her blood heated.

"Katie, will you move in here with me?" he asked.

Nine

He stood waiting, wanting her right now with a hunger that had grown instead of diminishing.

"That's not fair, Cade, and we've discussed this," she said.

"We discussed a lot of things, but not you moving into my room. I want you in here at night. I can love you, hold you all night, and that's what I'd like. And I hope what you'd prefer," he said quietly, wanting her there more than he could remember wanting anything in a long time. She was in his blood and he didn't think he could ever get enough of her.

"Think about it," he urged, buying time because by tonight, she would be more susceptible to his touch and his caresses.

When she nodded, his pulse jumped. He watched her turn and leave the room. He wanted to go after her, but he knew he should leave her alone.

The big barrier between them was her craving for success. He didn't want to fall in love with a woman who was totally wed to her career. And he reminded himself that he damn well better remember that before he was in love with her for the second time and setting himself up for another disaster.

He swore, but then he looked back at the bed and remembered her there in his arms, and he was in flames again with wanting her.

He showered and dressed in jeans and a T-shirt. He didn't have to fly out until the afternoon, so he was staying home this morning to enjoy her company. He realized, wryly, that she might boot him out anyway. He found her in the kitchen with Creighton serving her breakfast. Two smiling faces turned toward him.

Cade spoke to both of them, barely aware of Creighton.

"Morning, Mr. Logan," Creighton said. "I'll have your breakfast right away."

Cade sat down across from her. In one swift look, he took in her cutoffs, her T-shirt and her bare legs with her feet in sneakers.

"Fine. No hurry," he said, looking into her wide blue eyes while she smiled at him and made his heartbeat quicken.

"What's your schedule?" he asked her.

"To spend the day drawing," she said. "Soon I can start painting."

He nodded. "You'll stop and take time to have lunch with me before I leave, won't you?"

"Yes," she said. He wanted to take her hand and pull her into his lap. He resisted the urge and they talked about inconsequential things, but he was aware that he wasn't alone with her. By the time they finished toast, orange juice and omelets, he couldn't remember anything they had talked about and he ached to pull her into his arms and kiss her.

After breakfast he strolled with her to the dining room. As soon as they entered the room, he closed the double doors. She turned to give him a quizzical look.

"What are you doing? Your staff might come in to clean or for some other reason."

"I feel like I haven't kissed you for a month," he said, his pulse pounding.

"Cade, I'm getting ready to work."

"I'm going to kiss you. That's a helluva lot more important," he said, sliding his arms around her waist. "You have to learn to prioritize, Katie."

"You're back to calling me Katie. I think Katie is long gone—"

He pulled her to him and kissed her, silencing her conversation. She was Katie to him always and he wanted to call her by the nickname. He leaned over her, kissing her hard, getting another rush of pleasure when her slender arms wrapped out his neck and she kissed him.

He was on fire with wanting her. Still kissing her, he saw a long table with blueprints spread on it. Cade's fingers twisted free the buttons of her cutoffs and pushed them away. He slipped his hand beneath her shirt to cup her breasts, caressing her nipple, leaning down to push away her shirt and bra and take the taut bud in his mouth. His tongue drew lazy circles around her nipple while she moaned, wound her fingers in his hair and moved her hips.

"I want you. You'll be mine, Katie," he said and then he leaned back and pulled off her T-shirt and tossed it aside, unsnapping her bra and letting it fall while he cupped both breasts and leaned down to circle her nipple with his tongue.

Her shaking hands were at his belt buckle, unfastening his belt and jeans to push them off his hips.

"Katie, love…" he said showering kisses on her. He wound his hands in her hair and tilted her face up. Her eyes opened slowly and focused on him.

"You're mine," he said, grinding out the words and then he leaned down to kiss away any protest.

As he kissed her, she peeled away his shorts and he yanked off her lacy panties. With a swoop of his arm, he sent the blueprints flying from the table.

He picked her up and placed her on the table, spreading her legs and grasping her bottom to pull her to him.

"Cade," she whispered, her hips moving, her blond hair fanned behind her head. She was beautiful and naked and open to him.

"We're not alone—" she whispered.

"Yeah, we are," he answered, leaning over her to kiss her and lifting her hips with his hands as she wrapped her legs around him. He thrust into her softness and then they were moving frantically as she cried out with pleasure.

He thrust fast, pounding in her, driving her to a swift climax, and then she took him to release. They were gasping for breath. He pulled her into his arms and she wrapped herself around him while he carried her to a chair and sat to hold her close.

"Cade, you're scandalous—"

"No, I'm not. I'm a man who desires a beautiful, sexy woman. You're temptation and fire and rapture," he whispered, brushing her hair away from her face with his fingers.

She kissed his throat. "Suppose someone knocks on the door?"

"I'll tell them to go away," he said, barely thinking about it. "Every time I make love to you, I want you more than before."

"I know," she answered solemnly, raising her head to look into his eyes. Her mouth was red and swollen from his kisses and she was naked in his lap. He let his hand drift lightly across the tips of her breasts.

She inhaled and closed her eyes for an instant. Then she looked at him. "We're like a runaway train on a track headed to disaster."

"No, we're not. You're irresistible."

"I'm getting my clothes," she said, climbing off his lap.

He knew he should, as well, and he put them on while watching her.

"I'm going up to shower again," she said, turning to him. "I may lock you out of this room."

He held up his hands as if in an act of surrender. "I have some work to do before I leave again for California."

When she nodded and hurried away, he went to his room to freshen up. Glancing at her closed door, he wondered if they were headed for disaster. Could he walk away from her again and not have his heart torn out a second time?

It was hours later as he flew over the Arizona desert and tried to concentrate on the papers spread in front of him that his thoughts went back to Katie. He didn't want to give her up. He suspected no one would ever talk her out of her drive for her career. He recalled her statements to him: *"I want my career, unencumbered by a family. End of conversation"* and *"I'm married already to my job. And I don't have time for children. I don't have time for a husband"* and *"I want my career and I want success."* Repeatedly, she had given every indication that she'd meant what she said to him—no kids or marriage for her. Her career was all-important and he might as well accept that fact.

At least for now, he wanted her in his bed every night he was in Houston, and he expected to succeed into talking her into that.

He clenched his fists and wished he were back in Texas with her. Was he falling in love with her again? Had he ever really stopped loving her? He faced the question squarely. Was he in love with her still—once and always in love. He closed his eyes and thought about life without her. He'd hated the last trip when he'd had to leave her behind.

Was what he felt really love or lust and hunger for what he'd lost in the past? They were two different people now, so did he love her?

In the nine years between leaving Texas and returning, he'd tried to forget her, he'd gone out with other women, but no one ever captured his heart except Katie. He clamped his jaw so tightly closed that it hurt. She was stubborn, determined and she'd spent a lifetime competing with her brothers and father. Cade knew she meant what she said when she declared her career came first.

Cade stared out the window and saw her big blue eyes. He loved her and he might as well decide what he was going to do about it this time. Before he had walked out on her. Was he going to have to again? Or declare his love and let her reject him? Had his exorbitant fee for her murals pushed her solidly into a life choice of her career? Or was there some way to win her love?

He opened his clenched fists. She had loved him enough in the past to plan to marry him. Could he win her love again to that extent? It was too late to run from falling in love with her. He was already deeply in love with her if he faced his feelings honestly. Now what was he going to do about it? Was there any way for them to have a future together?

Katherine drew, concentrating on her work and refusing to think about the morning or last night or kissing Cade goodbye this afternoon when he left for another short trip to California.

Cade wanted her to move into his bedroom, be in his bed every night when he was here in Houston. Was that a wise course of action for her to pursue?

She drew a line and leaned back to look at the fountain she was drawing. She studied it, climbed down and walked back to look from a distance. Satisfied, she climbed back and continued drawing, concentrating until she remembered Cade's kisses.

With a long sigh, she focused on her drawing. She wasn't going to let her heart rule her life and right now she was consumed by Cade's lovemaking. She had managed her life without him before. She could do it again, she reassured herself, but it was hollow. She already missed him. When he was gone, the mansion was big and empty. Cade's presence filled it and added excitement and vitality. She wanted him here now.

She remembered their lovemaking, his hands caressing her and his hot kisses until she was breathing hard, wanting him and aching.

She gazed out the window, but only she saw Cade's dark eyes, heard his whispers. *Katie, love.* She could hear him saying the endearment, but she reminded herself that it was in the throes of passion. She knew he wanted her, but she didn't know if he would let himself go and love her and if he did, she couldn't return his love the way he'd want her to with marriage.

She ran her hand across her forehead. She wasn't the same person as that twenty-year-old girl he'd fallen in love with long ago. She had changed and her aims in life were different now. Katie Ransome was now Katherine, so dissimilar.

Her gaze ran over the empty dining room. She knew the staff had gone to their homes and she had the mansion to herself. It was empty, lonely and no wonder Cade didn't want to spend his life alone in the mansions he must own!

She loved him. It was that simple if she were honest with herself. She loved him, always had, probably always would. There had never been another man for her that she truly loved. "I love you," she whispered in the big, empty room and looked at the dining table covered in a drop cloth. What woman would be the hostess at that table? What children would he have?

Katherine hurt. She loved him, but it didn't change one thing. She didn't want to give up her career for a husband and family. Not now, especially when she was on the brink of getting to do all she had ever dreamed about in her business. She had always planned that the next office she would open would be Houston, to be followed by Kansas City, but with Cade living in Houston, she decided to open Kansas City first and get time and space between them.

Focusing on drawing, she managed to go another half hour before her thoughts returned to Cade. He wanted her to move in with him. That would just make it more difficult later. By the time she lived with him and finished his murals, she would be so wildly in love it would be devastating to leave. At the same time, if she stayed and worked, there was no way she could resist him and stay out of his arms and out of his bed.

She bit her lip and frowned as she drew and then stepped back and looked at her lines. She erased her light pencil lines furiously and concentrated with all her effort to keep Cade out of her thoughts.

"Cade," she whispered, knowing she loved him and this job would be unavoidable heartbreak because she wasn't going to marry him.

The phone rang and she hurried to answer, wondering if Cade were calling. Her pulse jumped at the sound of his voice and she sat down on a chair by the phone. It was an hour later when he told her goodbye, promising to call her later.

Humming, she switched on lights and went back to work, working until late and pleased with how much she was getting done.

It wasn't until late that night when she lay in bed alone that she let her thoughts go back to replay every minute of the night before with Cade and she ached to be with him right now.

Last night had been rapture to make love and touch and kiss all night. To talk and laugh together. Even to just sleep together wrapped in each other's arms

Was he going to interfere in her work? Probably to a small extent. Was he going to break her heart again? She couldn't answer her own question, but she suspected he would. They had different goals in life and she couldn't see Cade changing. Nor did she care to change. His princely sum for her art had cemented her ambition.

A pang of longing tore at her when she thought of kissing

him goodbye. He'd looked into her eyes while tension pulsed between them. When he had turned and walked out, she had watched him and it had hurt to see him leave.

What would she do when he walked out for good? Or when she finished the job and told him goodbye?

Saturday morning while she was drawing, Mrs. Wilkson appeared with a phone in hand. "Ma'am, this call is for you. It's someone from the Chavin Corporation."

Katherine climbed down and took the call, crossing to a work-table to get a pen and piece of paper. A deep male voice introduced himself as Gary Tarlington with the Chavin Corporation and he wanted to meet with her to discuss murals for his business.

Friday afternoon of the following week, Cade climbed out of his car near a back entrance to his Houston home. As he strode toward the door, he thought about his decision. Katie had told him she didn't want a relationship without commitment. He knew she had declared that she didn't want any obligation because it would interfere with her career. She didn't want children, and he did. They were at an impasse, but he didn't know how strongly she really felt about it. He intended to find out because he wanted her in his life permanently. He had never forgotten her, never gotten over her, and if that wasn't love, he couldn't imagine what was.

They needed to get it all in the open and find out where they were going. He wanted her and at the same time, he wanted a family and children. He loved her, but he wasn't going to settle for a future with a wife who put her career first and who wouldn't give him children.

On edge, yet with his pulse racing over being with her, he unlocked the back door and strode into the hall. When he passed the kitchen, he stopped to say hello to Creighton, who was nowhere to be seen.

The table was set for two with crystal, candles and flowers, and he smiled, turning to stride toward the dining room, expecting to find her on the scaffolding painting the mural. He peeled off his charcoal suit coat and shed his tie, tossing them on a chair in the hall. His heels clicked on the marble floor as he strode toward the dining room.

"Cade."

He looked up the sweeping stairs. Dressed in a short, indigo dress and high-heeled sandals, Katie stood at the top of the stairs. His heart slammed against his ribs.

The moment he saw her, she smiled and started down the steps.

His heart thudded because she was beautiful. Her hair was pinned high on either side of her head and in back it fell loosely across her shoulders. Her slender hand was on the banister and she kept her gaze on his as she descended the steps.

"You look fantastic!" he said.

"Thank you. You look quite nice yourself," she said, stopping inches in front of him on the second step and wrapping her arms around his neck to kiss him.

His arms circled her waist instantly, holding her close. She was incredibly soft and sweet-smelling, and her curves crushed against him. She held him tightly while she kissed him. Aroused, his blood heated with a hunger that had built each minute he had been away from her. He wrapped his arms tightly around her, wanting to hold her and never let go. He leaned over her and kissed her in return as he reached behind her to tug down her zipper.

Her hands flew over him, caressing him, unbuttoning and unfastening and pushing away his clothing as swiftly as he peeled her out of her wisp of a dress.

"We're here alone, aren't we?" he asked.

"Yes," she said, pulling him close to kiss again until he leaned down to take her breast and stroke her nipple with his tongue.

She gasped with pleasure, caressing his thick shaft until he groaned and picked her up.

As he kissed her, she wrapped her legs around him. He spread his feet to brace himself while he lowered her on his thick manhood. Her softness and warmth enveloped him. Hot and wet, she was ready, and he moved his hips, thrusting with all the driving need that had grown in him while he had been away.

"Katie, love!" he gasped, grinding out her name before his mouth covered hers again.

Clinging tightly to him, she moved and moaned. Her hips pressed against him and his heart thudded while his pulse roared. Fire raged in him as he plunged wildly until his climax burst in a release that sent shudders through him.

She cried out, clutching him and moving frantically until she sagged against him.

He stroked her back with one hand and showered kisses on her face and throat. "Katie, my love," he whispered. "I've missed you beyond belief. I couldn't think, couldn't work efficiently, couldn't sleep."

He leaned back to look at her. Perspiration dotted her forehead and her hair was a silky, disheveled tangle around her face. Her full lips were swollen and red and looked delectable to him and she had a half-lidded lethargic gaze that heated him in spite of his release.

"I've missed you," she said solemnly. "I'm glad you're home."

He leaned close to kiss her briefly and then pulled back. "I saw the table," he said. "Dare I hope we're celebrating my return?"

"Yes, plus a little bit more. Put me down and let me get on some clothes."

"You won't eat like you are now?"

"I certainly won't. Put me down."

"I'll put you down in the shower with me," he said, setting her on her feet and then scooping her back into his arms to carry her to a downstairs bathroom, where they showered together. She stepped out, grabbed a towel to dry swiftly, waving her hand at him. "Dry yourself," she said, throwing him a towel. "I want to go eat dinner."

Watching her, he thought he could look at her naked body forever. She was feminine perfection in his eyes, all curves and soft and long legs and blond hair.

He placed his hands on his hips to focus totally on her and she paused, blushing.

"Get dry and stop staring at me."

"Look what you do to me so easily," he said. He was aroused, hard and wanting her again in spite of just making love.

"I'll get out of here and you step under cold water and cool down so we can eat. I have things to tell you."

He barely heard her, but he watched her wrap a towel around herself and rush out of the room. Even though he wanted to reach for her, he let her go. There would be later, after dinner. His stomach growled with hunger, but that wasn't the consuming hunger he ached to appease. He desired her again. He wanted to make love to her by the hour.

He stepped into the shower to take a brief, cold shower and see if it would cool him.

After drying, he wrapped a towel around his middle to go get his clothes. She met him in the doorway with his clothing in her hand.

"Looking for these?" she asked, holding them out.

"Thanks," he replied, trailing his fingers along her arm and hand before taking his clothes. "I'll be right there," he said. She nodded and left and he watched the slight sway of her hips as she walked away and he knew the cold shower had been useless.

Katherine went to the kitchen to put finishing touches on their dinner and to wait for him. She paused, thinking the moment was perfect because right now her career was skyrocketing and Cade was back in her life. It was all she could possibly want.

She knew it wouldn't last—not the part with Cade and that hurt and she decided to refuse to think about it as long as they were together. She couldn't wait to tell him her news and share her happiness with him.

"Here I am," he said, striding into the room in tan slacks and a dark brown shirt that heightened his tan. "What's got you so excited?"

"You, of course," she said smiling at him while he crossed the kitchen to open white wine she had chilled. "Plus a surprise that I wanted to tell you in person."

"There's something besides me that's making you glow? Could it be cold, hard cash?" he asked and she laughed.

"Don't be cynical! I have a surprise that I'll share with you," she said, kissing the corner of his mouth and wishing he would smile.

"Tell me now," he said with a dark premonition of disaster. "You're too excited. This is something big, isn't it?"

"Yes! It's big and it's partially because of you and I'm thrilled and gloriously happy."

He held her away from him to look at her. "You look radiant. I'm waiting, Katie," he declared solemnly, his foreboding increasing. "What's your big news?"

"Have you ever heard of the Chavin Corporation?" Katherine asked.

"Sure, old international manufacturing firm that has diversified in the last ten years and now is into various types of business. They own a chain of retail stores, hotels. They've moved some of their manufacturing overseas."

Cade crossed the room. "Let me pour glasses of wine, and then before we have dinner while we drink our wine, you can tell me," he said. "I'm sure they've made you an offer of some sort."

"You're right," she said, watching him open the bottle of white wine and pour two glasses. Carrying them as they walked to the sofa, he handed her a glass.

"Now tell me."

"You're right," she said, excitement bubbling in her. "They knew you'd hired me to paint these murals for you."

"How the hell did they know that?" he asked.

"They called my office and wanted to talk to me and the person they spoke to told them. I think it made a difference, Cade, because the first time they called, they were just making inquiries about my company."

"They called again?"

"Yes. Their vice president called me and I have an appointment to fly to their headquarters in Pennsylvania to talk to them about painting murals for their hotel chain. They indicated a large number of murals."

"Congratulations," he said quietly. "That's fantastic and evidently, just what you want."

"It won't interfere with the job I'm doing for you. I've already discussed that with them on a conference call. It would be after I finish this job." She grinned and took his wine from him to give him a hug.

"Thank you! If I hadn't done this work for you, I'm not sure they'd be as eager to hire me as they are. Between this job and that—if I get it—my future will be set!" she exclaimed, looking up at him as he swung her down to hold her in the crook of his arm. His dark gaze bore into her and she realized his expression was stormy, as a muscle worked in his jaw.

"What's wrong? You look angry, Cade," she said solemnly.

"We've gotten back together and twice now, I've had to return to California. I don't like it when I'm away from you, but it's bearable because I know I'll be here with you again. When I'm gone, I miss you, Katie."

She ran her fingers along his jaw, feeling the faint stubble of his beard. "I've missed you when you've been gone. Couldn't you tell?" she asked with a smile.

He didn't smile in return and she drew a sharp breath. She sat up and scooted off his lap to face him.

"I'd think you'd be happy. We've gotten together again—"

"Up to a certain point. Where are we going in our relationship?" He took her hands in his. His dark eyes blackened to midnight and the stormy expression deepened.

"I figured we were taking a day at a time," she answered solemnly.

"I love you," he said quietly, drawing his fingers along her cheek. Her heart pounded and a mixture of emotions rocked her. Magic words! Words that complicated her life! Words that she had yearned to hear. Words that were coming at the wrong time now.

"I love you, Cade," she replied solemnly. "I always have."

"I love you and I've always loved you," he repeated. "I want you to be my wife. Marry me, Katie."

Ten

Stunned, she couldn't breathe or move. "You've said you want family, a wife and children."

"Yes, I do," he answered evenly.

"I don't, Cade. I've made it clear to you that I don't. Or I thought I'd clarified my feelings. I'm on the brink of having an enormous expansion in my business and with your fee, I've already made more money than I ever dreamed about. Now, I'm set to put me on top in my business. I'll be able to take the jobs I want, command the pay I want—"

"I love you," he said, interrupting her and grinding out the words in a husky voice. He hauled her into his embrace, lifting her onto his lap again as he leaned over her to kiss her.

His tongue thrust deep into her mouth, and her protests vanished instantly. She moaned, winding her arms around his neck as he caressed her with one hand while he held her with the other arm and kissed her. Momentarily forgetting his anger, proposal or anything else, she clung to him, moving her hips with fires building again.

Abruptly, he stopped and looked at her. "Marry me. Love is a lot more important than career and money. Cash is damn cold comfort."

"Success is wonderful comfort!" she snapped. "That's so easy for you to say when you've done all this and you've made a fortune and you're a success beyond anyone's wildest dreams. You have it all! I want it! It's my turn, Cade!"

"I have the successful career and money, but I'd toss it if it meant I could have you."

"No!" she said. "You didn't toss it over nine years ago when you could have had me!"

"I left to protect my brother. I'd repeatedly turned down your father's offers of money until that time," he said. His eyes blazed and he kissed her again, silencing her protests, leaning over her and plunging his tongue into her mouth until she forgot their conversation and held him tightly. Her hips moved and she moaned.

As suddenly as before, he stopped. "You like being kissed, Katie. You like it a lot. You were meant for life and love and family and children."

"Don't tell me again what I'm meant for! I know what I want! I want my career, not marriage."

"You say one thing and then you do another. You respond to every touch, every kiss. You make love like it's the only time in your life you'll get to."

"Cade, I've gone into a relationship with you when I said I wouldn't. We're living here together, sleeping together. Why do you have to have marriage right now?"

"I want you forever," he said and her heart lurched.

"I can't do that."

"I want children with you. I want you to be the mother of my children because I think you'd be wonderful. I want my wife with me, though. I want a full-time wife who isn't sharing home life with a career."

"I don't want to do that," she said, rubbing her forehead.

"You're throwing a full life away with both hands," he said.

"If I say no to your proposal, does it mean you'll withdraw your offer about the murals?" she asked bluntly.

"No, you don't have to marry me to keep the damn mural job and get your millions!" he snapped while his face flushed.

"I just wanted to know where I stand with you," she said, getting up and breathing hard. His words hurt as much as a slap and anger shook her.

He stood and wrapped his arms around her waist. "I love you," he declared again. "I guess I've always loved you. After settling in California, I tried to forget you and thought I'd succeeded. When I returned to Texas, it was for the reasons I told you—to build my ego with the hometown folks, to hire the best mural painter, to have a connection to businesses in Houston and Texas. I wouldn't even let myself think about you except where business was concerned."

"So what happened that you do now?" she asked, looking up at him while her pulse drummed.

"You. When I saw you walk into the spotlight in that auction, I wanted you with a longing that I can't ever describe. I would have paid anything for the evening with you. And then when we were together, time and anger and hurt just fell away. The minute I kissed you, in some ways, we were back where we were nine years ago."

Drawing herself up and closing her eyes briefly, she placed her hands over her ears.

"Don't tell me those things! We're not back where we were nine years ago!" she cried, her eyes flying wide. She shook with hurt and anger. "I love you, Cade. I always have and I always will, but I love other things, too. I want a life you've achieved. You've been there and done that. I want my moment in the sun. I want success and my business to grow and the attention I'll get and the money I'll make. I want to flaunt it with my dad. Now, more than ever. Too many times he's made me feel small and incompetent."

"Dammit, grow up, Katie, and forget your dad. You don't have to prove a damn thing to him. He's still running your life if you do."

"Again, that's easy for you to say," she replied stiffly, angry with him and knowing they had an impossible chasm between them.

While they stared at each other, anger seethed and she could feel the clash of wills.

"I love you," he repeated quietly.

"I love you, too, Cade. But I know what I want and it isn't marriage, at least not on your terms." She walked away from him to look out the window without really seeing anything. She hurt and knew their relationship had changed again and the magic hours of lovemaking were over.

She heard his footsteps as he left the room and she turned to stare at the empty doorway.

She went back and sat on the sofa and picked up the wineglass to swirl the pale, amber liquid, watching it swish in the crystal glass. She hurt all over as if she had taken a bad fall. Everything ached and she knew he was angry and hurt, as well.

She swiped at tears. She wasn't going to cry over Cade again. She didn't want to marry and she had gone into a relationship with him when he'd sounded as if he would be satisfied to have that arrangement with her. Now he wanted marriage and with Cade it meant a full-time wife and it meant children.

She couldn't and she wished it didn't hurt so badly.

She heard his footsteps and looked up to see him with a briefcase in hand. "I'm leaving, Katie. You can have the place to yourself. When you want me to look at a mural, just let my office know and leave a message about what you want," he said.

Afraid if she answered him she might break into tears, she merely nodded.

He crossed the room to the door and then turned back to look at her. She gazed into his blazing dark eyes that burned with desire and suddenly he spun around.

Dropping the briefcase, he crossed the room in long strides to sweep her into his arms and kiss her, leaning over her. His mouth came down hard and his tongue thrust deeply into her mouth, stroking, plunging.

Unaware that salty tears spilled down her cheeks, she wrapped her arms around his neck and clung to him, kissing him back as wildly. Then she wanted him, wanting to kiss him and make love to him and give herself completely one more time.

Instead, he released her so abruptly she rocked on her heels and he was gone, striding away. He went through the door and slammed it shut behind him and in minutes she heard his car as he drove out of her life.

Hurting, she stood rooted to the spot for a few minutes until she put her head in her hands to cry.

Saturday morning she threw herself into work. The night had been sleepless and miserable, and today, the house was empty. She wanted to finish this job and get away from Houston.

Concentrating on her painting, she looked around when Mrs. Wilkson brought her the phone.

"You have a call," she said. Katherine's heart skipped a beat, as she hurriedly put down her brush and climbed down. To her disappointment, it was Matt, not Cade, and she listened to her brother.

"We want to get together with Laura—Mom. That seems weird to say when I haven't met her. Nick's in Europe, but I've talked to him and we thought we'd all fly to Houston next week to get together with you and her. We're aiming for Thursday night about seven and she'll have dinner catered. Bring Cade if you'd like. He's the reason this is happening."

"Sounds fine, Matt," she replied.

"You don't sound fine," he said.

"I'm fine. Really," she said.

"I can't believe it after all this time. We need to thank Cade. She sounds nice."

"She's wonderful," Katherine said.

"She can't wait to see Jeff. She's overjoyed to have a grandson that she's going to get to know."

"He's adorable and she'll love him," Katherine said and to her dismay, tears spilled over again.

"You're sure you're all right? You sound funny. Are you sick?"

"No. I'm fine. I'm working."

"Where's Cade?"

"He's gone back to California. He comes and he goes."

"All right. I'll let you know later what time we'll arrive. Katherine, I confronted Dad about it. It set him back and he's angry, but in time, I'm sure he'll adjust like he always does."

"Think he'll ever see her?"

"I can't predict that answer. It'll be good to see you, too, this week," he added.

"Sure. You're a great brother," she said impetuously.

"Thanks. You're a great sister," he replied, and she ran her fingers over the phone as she broke the connection. She thought about her brother Matt and his concern. They would all soon be together. Her mother and her brothers and her baby nephew. Family. What Cade valued so highly.

Returning to work, she painted automatically while she thought about her brothers that she had always been competitive with because her father threw them up against each other and goaded them about one being better than the other. Why was she competing with Matt and Nick? They didn't compete with her, but they had vied with their dad and with each other over the years. They teased and tormented her at times when they were kids, but she knew it had been a big brothers and little sister thing. Since they had been grown, Matt and Nick never hesitated to show their fondness for her.

And why was she striving to best their father? What difference did it make? He was older and in frail health. Did she still crave his approval that badly?

She thought about Cade's advice to grow up.

You don't have to prove a damn thing to him. He's still running your life if you do. Remembering Cade's remarks, she knew he had been right. Was what she really wanted money and fame? Or had that become her substitute when Cade walked out and a way to get over the hurt?

Was she tossing away happiness? She thought about Nick and Matt, who, since their marriages, seemed happier than they had ever been in their lives. Little Jeff was precious and when she kept him, she missed him when they took him home.

She went back to work, her mind on her future and what she really wanted. What if she gave up her career?

She couldn't imagine doing such a thing. For the past nine years it had been the driving force in her life and she loved her work. How much did she love it? She had to ask herself.

She endured a sleepless night, struggling with losing Cade and facing a future without him.

She constantly reflected on her future. She could feel happiness slipping away, yet at the same time, she couldn't imagine getting out of business just when she was on the brink of having everything she had dreamed of and more besides.

Sunday morning gave her a quiet hour in church where she didn't hear anything that was said, but simply pondered her life. Halfway through the afternoon, she climbed down to take a break, get a cold drink and sit down. She stared at the phone. Cade had moved on and she knew he would.

On the other hand, she hurt more with every passing hour. She put her head in her hands and rubbed her forehead. Give it all up and marry Cade. She thought about what it would be like and raised her head to look at the mural.

She wouldn't have to stop painting, just stop working. It was the same thing in her mind. Yet she wasn't getting happier with her decision.

She wanted him back. Could she give up her business and be Cade's wife?

She returned to painting, working carefully while her thoughts churned over her future. The more she weighed the possibilities, the better it seemed to accept Cade's proposal. If she didn't, her life now would be about as good as it would get and today wasn't that great.

She missed dinner without realizing it, but she was on the verge of calling Cade and telling him she had changed her mind.

She kept telling herself to give it time, to be sure, because she would be tossing away all she had worked for, but she felt stronger as time passed with her decision to call him.

Finally, she stopped painting, and stood and stared into space. She knew she wanted him and marriage and she'd give up her career for him, and she knew she didn't have to wait days to be sure about her decision.

She climbed down and picked up the phone to call his cell number. Her heart raced and she felt as if a burden had lifted from her heart.

Her heart thudded when she heard his deep hello.

Eleven

"Cade, it's Katherine."

"It's good to hear your voice," he said. "I've missed you, darlin'."

Her heart thudded and she gripped the phone tightly. "I want to see you. I thought I'd fly to L.A. if you're going to be there. I think the soonest I can make arrangements is the weekend because Matt and Nick are coming this week and we're all going to see Laura."

"I don't think I'll be in L.A. this weekend," he said and her heart plummeted because chances were, that meant that he didn't want to see her. She couldn't imagine that Cade wouldn't be able to switch his appointments around.

"Cade, I want to talk to you," she said.

"Good, Katie. That's really great to hear because I want to talk to you, too. Why don't we talk now?"

"I didn't want to over the phone. It's better in person."

"I agree with that—" he said and she heard his voice clearly and in person. She spun around to see him standing in the doorway with his cell phone in his hand.

"Cade!" she shrieked and dropped the phone. Ignoring the clatter of the phone, she dashed across the room without thinking.

He stepped inside, closed the dining room doors and caught her when she threw her arms around his neck.

"You're here!" she said, covering his mouth with hers before he could answer. He held her tightly against him. Her feet weren't touching the floor, but she didn't care while they kissed passionately, her heart thudding that he was here in her arms, holding her, kissing her.

"I missed you," she cried and then kissed him again.

"Hey," he said, leaning back to look at her. "Don't cry," he said gently, wiping her eyes with his thumb. "Why're you crying, darlin'?"

He picked her up and carried her to a chair covered by a drop cloth where he sat and placed her on his lap. "Don't cry, Katie. There's no need for tears."

"I love you," she whispered, stroking his face. "I want to marry you, Cade."

His eyes darkened and he inhaled deeply. He bent his head to kiss her again, a kiss that scorched her and turned her toes and made her want him desperately. And convinced her she was making the right decision.

"Ah, Katie, you'll make me the happiest man on this earth." He framed her face with his hands. "Why the change of heart?" he asked, studying her.

"I was miserable without you," she said. "I thought about what you said about competing with Matt and Nick. That's foolish. They're not competing with me. Not that I'm any competition for them," she added.

"You are now, but your brothers love you and they're not

trying to keep you down or throw in your face that they make more money than you—which they may not any longer."

He gazed at her solemnly. "It was pure hell without you, Katie."

"Oh, Cade! My life is empty without you. And I thought about Matt and Olivia and Jeff—how happy they are. You're right."

"You think so? You're agreeing with me? You'll marry me?" he asked.

"Yes! Oh, yes!" she said, her pulse racing. She ran her hands over his shoulders and up to wind her fingers in his hair.

"What about a family, Katie? That's something that you have to want, not because I do, but because you do."

"I love my family and always have and we're together when we can be. You're right, Cade. That's all more important."

He pulled her to him to kiss her again hard, a kiss that reaffirmed their need and love. Her heart pounded with joy as she held him. Finally, he leaned away to look down at her.

"I've been thinking about us and the future, too."

"Is that why you came back here?" she asked, and he nodded.

"I'm glad you did—"

"Katie, I told you I didn't want my wife to work. I wanted my wife with me. I've thought about that and I guess I was unreasonable. You have a right to your life and your painting—that would be a crime when you're so talented if you gave up your painting. I can deal with it if you just don't have to have an international business or accept jobs that take you away from me for long periods of time. Can we compromise on that?"

She laughed. "I can compromise on anything! I let go of that drive, Cade. Dad's the one that shoved me into it. I don't need to work like I'm starving or have to own the biggest ad company or the most famous or anything."

He let out his breath. "That's the best news I've heard in

years," he said. "You're sure?" he asked, gazing at her solemnly with his probing, dark gaze.

"I'm very sure."

"I don't want you to wake up one morning and accuse me of taking your life away from you."

"No danger of that happening," she purred. "Not as long as you make love to me constantly and give me babies—"

"This is a big turnaround for you. Have you thought this through—?"

"Yes," she said, sobering. "I have. When you left, I hurt badly. Both times. I don't want to go through the rest of my life without you. The nine years have been dreadful enough. My work filled that void, but it was an emptiness in my life and in my heart."

"Oh, Katie, love!" he said, kissing her again, another long, hot kiss that set her pulse drumming.

When he paused, he said, "Wait a minute—" He tried to get to his trouser pocket beneath her bottom.

She wriggled. "What're you doing?" she drawled, rolling her eyes at him.

"Lean over," he said.

"Oh, my!" she gasped playfully and he grinned. He pulled a velvet box out of his pocket.

"Come back here," he said and handed her the box.

Surprised, she looked at the box and at him. She opened it to see a dazzling diamond. "Cade, it's beautiful!"

"Will you marry me?" he asked again.

"Oh, yes! Yes, yes!" she exclaimed, gloriously happy as he slipped the ring on her finger and then drew her back into his embrace to kiss her.

Two hours later in his big bed she waved her hand in front of them as she lay in the crook of his arm. "We're all getting together with Laura—Mom—Thursday night. We can announce our engagement then."

"Will it detract from your brothers meeting her for the first time?" Cade asked.

"I don't think so. We'll wait until later in the evening when things have settled."

"Sounds good to me."

"They want you to come anyway. I think Matt and Nick both want to thank you for looking her up."

"I'm glad I did. I told you that I debated about it and about telling you." He turned on his side and raised up, propping his head on his hand to look at her. "How soon can we marry?"

She thought about it. "We could just run away and do this and not have all that aggravation we went through before."

"It's whatever you want," he said drawing his finger lightly over the curve of her breasts just above the sheet that she had tucked beneath her arms. "You were sort of left standing at the altar, so to speak, last time. If it makes you feel better, we can have the biggest, showiest wedding ever. My family will all want to come."

She laughed. "All right. My family will want to be there— I don't know about Dad. He's going to be angry that you and I are marrying."

"We can carry on without him if we have to."

She thought about it. "Big wedding it is."

"I have the money so you can do whatever you want."

"So do I," she said, grinning at him.

"Then between us, pay people and get it done as soon as possible."

"Let's get a calendar," she said, sitting up. He stepped out of bed and crossed the room and her gaze raked over his muscled, naked body. "You are one good-looking man," she drawled when he returned and he grinned.

"You keep that up and you'll get me up."

"It's just talk," she said. "You're the best kisser, the sexiest man on earth—"

He rolled her over, moved on top of her to kiss her and the calendar fell to the floor until an hour later when they returned from the shower and she snatched it up to study it. She sat cross-legged and naked on the bed with the sheet tucked around her and beneath her arms. Cade lay beside her and drew his fingers over her back.

"This is almost the end of October. If you want it soon— how about a Christmas wedding?"

"Entirely too far in the future. We can have it sooner than that."

She studied the calendar. "Thanksgiving weekend? That's really soon."

"Too far away," he repeated. "Give me at least the week before Thanksgiving."

"Impossible!" she argued, remembering how quickly Nick and Julia planned their wedding. "Thanksgiving weekend is the soonest we possibly can."

He grinned. "You win since you're the bride and the main part of the wedding."

"I believe you have an equal part."

"Not at all. People won't even know I'm there."

"All the women will," she said, wrinkling her nose at him.

He pulled her down in his arms. "Thanksgiving it is."

Epilogue

With a fanfare of trumpets Katherine started up the aisle while her gaze was on Cade, who was breathtakingly handsome in his black tux. Her arm was linked through her father's. Olivia, Julia and five of Katherine's friends were bridesmaids, all smiling at her. She barely glanced at them because she couldn't look away from Cade.

Her father placed her hand in Cade's and together she and Cade turned to the minister. Her heart pounded with joy and she looked into Cade's dark eyes as they repeated vows.

Losing all sense of time and forgetting the guests, she saw only Cade, thrilling as he declared his vows in his familiar deep voice.

Finally, they were pronounced man and wife and introduced to the guests. Cade linked her arm in his, and with trumpets and organ and violins playing, she walked back down the aisle as Mrs. Cade Logan.

In a blur they posed for pictures, Olivia and Julia helping straighten her white satin cathedral train.

"You're gorgeous," Cade said, leaning down to whisper to her before the photographer had them pose for the first picture.

"Let's have all the Ransomes together please. Husbands, wives, babies. Let's have a family picture," the slender photographer said.

"Well, here's the test for your dad," Cade said. "He almost didn't walk you up the aisle because of Laura. Now, will he get in the family picture if she does?"

"I don't know, but we all wanted her to join us, and she promised us she would pose with us," Katherine said, holding Cade's hand. She didn't want to stop touching him, longing to be alone with him, but she knew they had hours to go yet.

Laura, in a pale blue silk dress, stepped to one side of Nick's wife, Julia. Katherine saw her father standing off to one side of the room. "Dad?" Katherine called.

He clamped his lips together and went to stand beside her, crowding in between Katherine and Matt, who stepped aside to make room.

They posed and she wondered if he had even spoken to Laura, or Laura to him, but Katherine couldn't worry about her father on her wedding day. The minute the family pictures were over, the older Ransomes disappeared from the group.

After the pictures Katherine and Cade rode in his limousine to the country club for the reception that was already in full swing with tables laden with food, flowers lining the walls and the musicians playing.

When Cade claimed her for the first dance, she had already unfastened the long train and she stepped into his arms in the slim, white satin dress that had a straight skirt.

"I want you all to myself," he said, his warm brown eyes devouring her.

Feeling giddy, she smiled up at him. "My sentiments exactly."

"So how soon can we get out of here?" he asked.

"Hours from now," she replied as they danced together in unison. "We cut the cake, we talk to everyone, we mingle—"

He glanced beyond her. "Do you really think anyone would miss us?"

She laughed. "Yes! And I'm not doing that on my big day. Finally, Mr. Logan, you're hooked! It took me ten long years counting from the time we started seeing each other. You're mine now and I want the world to know it!"

He grinned. "And you're mine," he said, his voice dropping as he leaned close to her ear. "And I want you to know it in bed tonight. I want to kiss every delectable inch of you."

She slanted him a heated look. "Whatever you get to do, I get to do it, too."

He groaned. "Now you're tormenting me. I'm going to set the clocks faster."

"It won't work, so forget it."

"Here comes your brother for a dance with you." The music ended as Matt stepped up to claim her for the next dance.

He smiled down at her and she gazed at her oldest brother fondly. "I thanked Cade again for going to see Laura. He's a smart guy, Katherine."

"I think so."

Matt smiled at her. "I hope you both have as much happiness as Olivia and I've found."

"Thanks," she said.

"I'm glad, too, you married and you're cutting back to working part-time. You've got people who can run the agency for you."

"I know I do. I'll see how it goes. I may cut back more later."

"Dad's in the corner in a grump."

"Will he ever speak to Laura?"

Matt shrugged. "I don't know. I'd say he hurt himself all

those years, too. She seems great. I don't like to think how he deprived us."

"No, don't because we can't undo the past. Our dad isn't the easiest person."

"Amen to that one," Matt said. "Here comes brother Nick to dance with you. I'm glad for you and Cade."

"Thanks, Matt," she said, turning to her other brother to dance with him.

"You look radiant today, my very beautiful little sister. Don't you let Cade whisk you off to California."

She smiled. "He won't all the time. Maybe some, but you two can come see us."

"His family is nice. They're friendly people. I remember one of his brothers from when they lived here before. I didn't know the others."

"Dad is giving them a wide berth, but they don't care and neither does Cade."

Nick smiled at her. "I hope you're very happy with Cade. Marriage can be paradise."

"I'm glad, Nick. You and Matt are happily married and you both deserve it."

"I don't know about deserving it, but we're happy and it's great. Here comes your new hubby. I guess he couldn't stay away through two whole dances." Nick released her hand and placed it in Cade's. "Here's my sister. Take care of her."

"I intend to," Cade said easily, looking at her and taking her into his arms. "Tell me again how long before we can go?"

"About ten minutes shorter than the last time I told you," she said. "Are you going to pester me with that all afternoon?"

"Probably until I get my way. If we have to mingle, let's begin," he said, taking her hand to go talk to guests.

Within a few minutes they were separated. Later, she was with him to cut the cake and then people clustered to talk to them and she was separated from Cade again until shadows grew longer across the club lawn.

Cade appeared at her side. "Now?" he asked, tapping his watch.

"What a pest!" They both laughed, and she nodded. "Now."

"C'mon. Just go change and no goodbyes. Instead, you can say hello when we get back," he said, taking her hand and leaving with her to climb into the limousine and drive to the business airport, where he had his private jet waiting.

Within hours they were in a villa on an island in the Caribbean where their bedroom opened to the beach. She stepped outside and inhaled. "It's gorgeous and it smells wonderful!"

"I agree absolutely," he said in a husky voice, coming to stand behind her. "We have this island to ourselves for the next two weeks. This place is stocked with food. On Saturday, a crew comes to clean and restock, and we can swim and laze on the beach and stay out of their way. Otherwise, it's just us."

She turned to wind her arms around his neck. "This is wonderful, Cade."

"It is. See, I told you I'd get my money's worth that night I bid for an evening with you."

She wrinkled her nose at him. "I'm glad you bid and got the evening with me. I'm glad you came back."

"Your father didn't speak to me today. All he did was glare at me."

"I suspect it's more for bringing Laura into our lives than for marrying me. Either way, he'll start speaking to you when you give him a grandchild. That's the way he was with Olivia and now you saw how he dotes on her."

"Well, for the time being I want you all to myself before we start on this presenting him with a grandchild business."

"I'm not getting younger. My biological clock is ticking."

"You've got a little time left, old girl. Give me a few months before we start on a baby."

"A few months of spoiling you and loving you and giving you all my attention," she said, showering him with kisses between each word while her hands moved over him, pushing away his tux coat that fell in a heap. He stepped out of his shoes while he kissed her and his hands went behind her to unzip the pale blue silk dress that he pushed off her shoulders.

Her dress fell around her ankles while she unfastened the studs on his shirt and pushed open his shirt. His arms slid around her and he pulled her tight against him.

"I love you, Katie. I've always loved you."

"You're the only man in my life, Cade," she answered solemnly. "You're the only one I've truly loved ever," she said. "I've waited to be Mrs. Cade Logan a long time and we have nine years of loving to make up for."

"And we're starting now," he replied. He kissed her, his mouth coming down hard on hers.

She wound her arms around his neck and stood on tiptoe, kissing him in return, moving closer against him while she held him. "Cade," she whispered, raising her head. "I love you."

"I feel like I've waited forever to marry you," he said. "You're mine, now, Katie. Now and forever."

She closed her eyes and kissed him again. Happiness filled her and she knew he was the only man for her for all time.

* * * * *

MILLS & BOON®

Sparkling Christmas sensations!

This fantastic Christmas collection is fit to burst with billionaire businessmen, Regency rakes, festive families and smouldering encounters.

Set your pulse racing with this festive bundle of 24 stories, plus get a fantastic 40% OFF!

Visit the Mills & Boon website today to take advantage of this spectacular offer!

www.millsandboon.co.uk/Xmasbundle

1114_INSHIP

MILLS & BOON®

'Tis the season to be daring...

The perfect books for all your glamorous Christmas needs come complete with gorgeous billionaire bad-boy heroes and are overflowing with champagne!

These fantastic 3-in-1s are must-have reads for all Modern™, Desire™ and Modern Tempted™ fans.

**Get your copies today at
www.millsandboon.co.uk/Xmasmod**

MILLS & BOON®

Want to get more from Mills & Boon?

Here's what's available to you if you join the exclusive **Mills & Boon eBook Club** today:

- ✦ *Convenience – choose your books each month*
- ✦ *Exclusive – receive your books a month before anywhere else*
- ✦ *Flexibility – change your subscription at any time*
- ✦ *Variety – gain access to eBook-only series*
- ✦ *Value – subscriptions from just £1.99 a month*

So visit **www.millsandboon.co.uk/esubs** today to be a part of this exclusive eBook Club!

EBOOK_SUBS_2014

MILLS & BOON®

Sparkling Christmas Regencies!

A seasonal delight for Regency fans everywhere!

Warm up those cold winter nights with this charming seasonal duo of two full-length Regency romances. A fantastic festive delight from much-loved Historical authors. Treat yourself to the perfect gift this Christmas.

Get your copy today at www.millsandboon.co.uk/Xmasreg

Also available on eBook

_ST_4